Collected Stories and Sketches: 2
Living with Ghosts

Etching by William Strang, 1898

R.B. Cunninghame Graham

Collected Stories and Sketches

Volume 2

Living With Ghosts

Edited by Alan MacGillivray and John C. McIntyre

Kennedy & Boyd
an imprint of
Zeticula
57 St Vincent Crescent
Glasgow
G3 8NQ
Scotland
http://www.kennedyandboyd.co.uk
admin@kennedyandboyd.co.uk

Thirteen Stories originally published in 1900
Success originally published in 1902
Progress, and Other Sketches originally published in 1905
This edition copyright © Zeticula 2011
Frontispiece from *Etchings of William Strang* by Frank Newbolt, Newnes, 1907.

Contributors:
R. B. Cunninghame Graham: The Life and The Writings
© Alan MacGillivray 2011
Introduction to *Thirteen Stories* © Alan MacGillivray 2011
Introduction to *Success* © Ronald W. Renton 2011
Introduction to *Progress, and Other Sketches* © Ronald W. Renton 2011
Cunninghame Graham's Use of the Scots Language, ©Alan MacGillivray2011

Cover photograph *"Palmares de Rocha" in Rocha,Uruguay* © Piero Gallego
Battagliese 2011
Cover design by Felicity Wild
Book design by Catherine E. Smith

ISBN 978-1-84921-101-7

"I, writing as a man who has not only seen, but lived with ghosts, may perhaps find pardon for this preface, for who would run in heavily and dance a hornpipe on the turf below which sleep the dead?"

(*Thirteen Stories*, Preface)

Contents

Preface to the Collection

Robert Bontine Cunninghame Graham first came to public attention as a Radical Liberal Member of Parliament in the 1880s, when he was in his thirties. The apparent contradiction between his Scottish aristocratic family background and his vigorous attachment to the causes of Socialism, the Labour movement, anti-Imperialism and Scottish Home Rule ensured that he remained a controversial figure for many years right up to his death in the 1930s. Through his father's family of Cunninghame Graham, descended from King Robert II of Scotland and the Earls of Menteith, he had a strong territorial connection with the West of Scotland. On his mother's side, he had significant Hispanic ties through his Spanish grandmother and a naval grandfather who took part in the South American Wars of Liberation. His own world-wide travels, particularly in the Americas, Spain and North Africa, and his amazingly wide circle of friends and acquaintances in many countries and different walks of life gave him a cosmopolitan breadth of experience and a depth of insight into human nature and behaviour that would be the envy of any writer.

And it is as a writer that we now have primarily to remember Graham. His lasting political monuments are the Labour Party and the Scottish National Party, both of which he was deeply involved in founding. Yet he has to share that credit with others. His literary works are his alone. He wrote books of history, travel and biography which were extensively researched but very personal in tone, so that, although highly readable, they might not easily withstand the objective scrutiny of modern scholarship. Rather it is in his favoured literary forms of the short story, sketch and meditative essay, forms often tending to merge into one another, that Graham excels. Over forty years, between 1896 and 1936, he published fourteen collections of such short pieces, ranging over many subjects and lands. With such a wealth of life experience behind him, Graham did not have to dig deep for inspiration. Probably no other Scottish writer of any age brings such a knowledge and awareness of life's diversity to the endeavour of literary creation. However, the quality of his achievement has not as yet been fully assessed. One reason is not hard to find. There has never yet been a proper bringing together of Graham's separate collections into a manageable edition to provide the essential tools for critical study. Consequently literary attention has never been really focused on him, something for which the climate of twentieth-century Scottish, and British, critical fashion is partly responsible. Neither the Modernist movement nor the Scottish Renaissance seems to be an appropriate pigeonhole for Graham to inhabit. He has instead had to suffer the consequences of being too readily stereotyped. Perhaps entranced by the glamour of his apparent flamboyant persona of 'Don Roberto', the Spanish hidalgo, the Argentine gaucho, the Scottish laird, the horseman — adventurer, a succession of editors have republished incomplete collections of stories and sketches selected more to reinforce an image of Graham as larger-than-life legend rather than as the serious literary man he worked hard to be.

The purpose of this series is to make Graham's literary corpus available in a convenient format to modern readers as he originally intended it. Each collection of stories is kept intact, and they appear in chronological order with Graham's own footnotes, and retaining his personal idiosyncrasies and eccentricities of language and style. It is not the intention of the editors to make magisterial judgements of quality or to present a fully annotated critical edition of the stories. These purposes would go far beyond the bounds of this series in space and time, and must remain as tasks for future scholars. We merely hope that a new generation of general readers will discover Graham's short stories and sketches to be interesting and stimulating for their own sake and in their own right, diverse and revealing of a strong and generally sympathetic personality, a richly-stocked original mind and an ironic, realistic yet sensitive observer of the amazing variety of life in a very wide world.

Alan MacGillivray
John C. McIntyre

Robert Bontine Cunninghame Graham

The Life

Robert Bontine Cunninghame Graham belonged to the old-established family of Cunninghame Graham, which had its ancestral territory in the District of Menteith lying between Stirling and Loch Lomond. The family had at one time held the earldom of Menteith and could trace its ancestry back to King Robert II of Scotland in the fourteenth century. The title had been dormant since the seventeenth century, and the Cunninghame Grahams showed no real interest in reviving it. In fact, Graham passed his childhood officially bearing the surname of Bontine, because, during his youth, owing to a strange legal quirk relating to the entailing of estates and conditions of inheritance, the name 'Graham' could only be borne by Robert's grandfather who held the main Graham estate of Gartmore. Robert's father, William, an army officer, had to take another family surname, Bontine, until he inherited Gartmore in 1863. As a young man thereafter, Robert does not seem to have bothered which name he used, and when he in his turn inherited Gartmore, he kept Bontine as a middle name.

Graham was born in London in 1852. His half-Spanish mother preferred the social life of London, while his father had his responsibilities as a Scottish landowner. Accordingly, Graham's boyhood years were spent moving between the south of England and the family's Scottish houses at Gartmore in Menteith, Ardoch in Dunbartonshire and Finlaystone in Renfrewshire. Before going to preparatory school, he spent a lot of time with his Spanish grandmother, Doña Catalina, at her home in the Isle of Wight and accompanied her to Spain on a number of visits. This was his introduction to the Spanish way of life and the Spanish language, in which he became proficient. At the age of eleven he went to a prep school in Warwickshire, before going to Harrow public school for two years. He apparently disliked Harrow intensely and in 1866 was taken from it and sent to a Brussels private school which was much more to his taste. It was during his year there that he learned French and had instruction in fencing. After a year in Brussels, Graham's formal education ended and he spent the next two years until he was seventeen between his homes in Britain and his grandmother's family in Spain, developing along the way his passion for horses and his considerable riding skills.

Graham's adult life began when in 1870, with the support and financial encouragement of his parents, he took ship from Liverpool by way of Corunna and Lisbon for Argentina. The primary motivation was to make money by learning the business of ranching and going into partnership on a Scottish-owned estancia, or ranch. This was seen as a necessity, given that the Graham family had fallen into serious financial difficulties. Graham's father, Major William Bontine, had sunk into madness, the final consequence of a severe head injury in a riding accident, and had engaged in wild speculation with the family assets. Consequently, the estates were encumbered with debts and the Major's affairs had been placed under the supervision of an agent of the Court of Session. As the eldest of three sons, Robert had to find his own fortune and eventually pay off his father's debts. Much of his travelling in the following decades, both alone and later with his wife, Gabriela, had the search for profitable business openings at its heart.

Between 1870 and 1877, Graham undertook three ventures in South America. The ranching on the first visit came to nothing, although, being already an accomplished horseman and speaker of Spanish, he very quickly adapted to the life of the gauchos, or cowboys. He also observed at first hand some of the violence and anarchy of the early 1870s in Argentina and Uruguay; he contracted and recovered from typhus; and finally he undertook an overland horse-droving venture before returning to Britain in 1872. The following year he returned to South America, this time to Paraguay with a view to obtaining concessions for cultivating and selling the yerba mate plant, the source of the widely drunk mate infusion. In his search for possible plantation sites, Graham rode deep into the interior and came across the surviving traces of the original seventeenth and eighteenth century Jesuit settlements, the subject, many years later, for one of his best books. He had little success in his efforts and returned to Britain in 1874. After a couple of years travelling, mainly in Europe, but also to Iceland and down the coast of West Africa, Graham set out again, this time with a business partner, bound for Uruguay, where he contemplated ranching but actually set up in the horse trading business, buying horses in Uruguay with a view to driving them into Brazil to be sold to the Brazilian army. This (again) unsuccessful adventure was later described in the novella, "Cruz Alta"

(1900). Graham again returned to Britain and took up residence at his mother's house in London, becoming a familiar man about town and a frequenter of Mrs Bontine's literary and artistic salon, where he began to develop his wide circle of friends and acquaintances in the literary and cultural fields. It was his experiences in South America in the 1870s that formed his passion for the continent and directed so much of his later literary work. Out of this came the appellation of 'Don Roberto', which is now inescapably part of his personal and literary image.

Paris was another of Graham's favourite places, and it was there in 1878 that he met the woman whom he very rapidly made his wife, much to the apparent hostile concern of his family, particularly his mother. The mystery and (probably deliberate) uncertainty surrounding the circumstances of his marriage cry out for proper research among surviving family documents. One can only sketch in the few known facts and legends. Graham met a young woman who was known as Gabriela de la Balmondière. By one account she had been born in Chile with a father of French descent and a Spanish mother. She had been orphaned and brought up in Paris by an aunt, who may or may not have had her educated in a convent. By another account, she was making a living in Paris as an actress.

After a brief acquaintanceship, she and Graham lived together before coming to London and being married in a registry office in October, 1878, without family approval. In time everybody came to accept her as an exotic new member of the family, although there seems to have been some mutual hostility for several years between her and Graham's mother. It was not until the 1980s that the discovery of Gabriela's birth certificate showed that she was in fact English, the daughter of a Yorkshire doctor, and her real name was Caroline, or Carrie, Horsfall. Why Graham, and indeed the whole Graham family, should have gone on through the whole of his and her lives, and beyond, sustaining this myth of Gabriela's origins invites speculations of several kinds that may never be resolved.

After a few months of marriage, Robert and Gabriela set out for the New World, first to New Orleans, and then to Texas with the intention of going into the mule-breeding business. Over the next two years they earned a precarious living by various means both in Texas and Mexico, until the final disaster when a Texas ranch newly acquired by Graham and a business partner was raided and destroyed by Apaches. The Grahams finally returned to Britain in 1881 with substantial debts, and lived quietly in Spain and Hampshire. The death of Graham's father in 1883, however, meant that Robert finally inherited the main family estate of Gartmore with all its debts and problems, and had to live the life of a Scottish laird with all its local and social responsibilities.

The restrictions placed upon Graham by his new role could not confine such a restless spirit for long, and in 1885 he stood unsuccessfully for Parliament as a Liberal. The following year he was elected the MP for North-West Lanark, the beginning of an active and highly-coloured political career that continued in one form or another for the rest of his life. He spent only six years actually in Parliament, a period in which he soon revealed himself as more a Socialist than a Liberal, espousing a number of Radical causes and becoming deeply involved and influential in the early years of the Labour movement, being, along with Keir Hardie, one of the co-founders of the Labour Party. The high point of his time in Parliament was when he was arrested and committed to prison, accused of assaulting a policeman during the 'Bloody Sunday' demonstration in Trafalgar Square on 13th November, 1887. From his maiden speech onwards, he wrote and spoke out forcefully on behalf of Labour causes and finally in 1892 stood unsuccessfully for Parliament directly as a Labour candidate. Even out of Parliament Graham continued to be active politically. Although he gradually ceased to be a leading figure in the new Labour Party, his new-found talent as a polemical journalist, in great demand in the serious papers and journals of the day, enabled him to remain in the public eye with his concern about social conditions and his unfashionable anti-Imperial attitudes. He was opposed to the Boer Wars, as he was also to the new imperialism of the USA, shown during the Spanish-American War of 1898, which affronted his strong attachment to Spain and Latin America. His commitment to Scottish Home Rule led him in his later years to find a new role as a founder of the Scottish National Party.

After leaving Parliament in 1892, Graham and his wife were free to travel more frequently, sometimes together but more often pursuing their diverging interests apart, and always on the look-out for possibilities of improving their finances. Spain and Morocco were the main areas of their travel. Graham also began to diversify in his new-found interest in writing into the prolific production of travel books and collections of short stories and sketches. Yet nothing could stave off for ever the inevitable consequences of his father's irresponsibility. The debt-ridden estate of Gartmore had eventually to be sold, and the Grahams settled for financial security on the smaller family estate of Ardoch on the northern side of the Firth of Clyde. Even so, a worse blow was to befall Graham. Gabriela had never been physically strong and was prone to pleurisy (not helped by her chain-smoking habit). She died in 1906 on the way back from one of her many visits to the drier warmth of Spain. Her marriage with Robert of more than a quarter of a century had been childless, but they were a close couple and Robert missed her greatly.

As his life advanced into late middle age and old age through the new century, Graham developed his writing with more collections of short stories and works of biography centred on Mexican and South American history. His astonishingly wide circle of friends in all fields of society and his continuing political activities kept him close to the centre of society and often in the public gaze. At the outbreak of the First World War, though he had been critical of the warmongering attitudes that had marked the years from 1910 to 1914, Graham, at the age of 62, volunteered for service and was charged with two missions to South America, one in 1914-15 to Uruguay to buy horses for the Army, and the second to Colombia in 1916-17 to obtain beef supplies. The first mission enabled him to recapture some of the excitement of his early years on horseback in South America, although it made him desperately sad as a horse-lover to think of the dreadful fate awaiting the animals he bought. The second mission turned out to be unsuccessful, owing to a lack of shipping.

After the war, Graham continued to travel, now more for relaxation and for the sake of his health. He had a new close companion and friend, a wealthy widow, Mrs Elizabeth ('Toppie') Dummett, whose artistic salon in London he frequented and who travelled with him on most of his journeys. Back in Scotland, Graham continued to spend summers at Ardoch, and was well known round the Glasgow and Scottish literary scene, as well as being involved in Scottish political controversy. Among his literary friends were the poet Hugh MacDiarmid (C.M.Grieve) and the novelist and journalist, Neil Munro. Graham made a point of attending the dedication of a memorial to Munro in the summer of 1935. Graham was then eighty-three years old. A few months later, Graham set out on what he probably knew would be his last journey, back to Argentina, the scene of his first youthful adventures. In Buenos Aires, he contracted bronchitis and then pneumonia, and after a few days he died. His funeral in Buenos Aires was a large public occasion attended by the Argentine President, with two horses belonging to Graham's friend,

Aimé Tschiffely, the horseman-adventurer, accompanying the coffin as symbols of Don Roberto's attachment to the gaucho culture that had been such an influence on his life and philosophy.

Robert Bontine Cunninghame Graham is buried near his wife Gabriela in the family burial place at the Augustinian Priory on the little island of Inchmahome in the Lake of Menteith. A memorial to him is now placed near the former family mansion of Gartmore.

The Writings

It may not be too much of an exaggeration to say that the greatest blessing bestowed upon Robert Bontine Cunninghame Graham in his boyhood years was an incomplete formal education. Two years at prep school, two years at Harrow and one 'finishing' year in Brussels gave him little of the classical education deemed essential for the well-born Victorian gentleman. Instead he reached the age of eighteen with considerable fluency in Spanish and French, and an undoubted acquired love of reading gained from the books in the libraries of his family's Scottish houses and his mother's house in London. His extensive (if difficult to decipher) letters home to his mother from abroad make this latter fact clear. The proficiency in Spanish and French gave him immediate entry into two major literatures of the modern world in addition to English, a more bankable asset for the modern writer-to-be than any familiarity with the classical writings of Greece and Rome.

It is conventional to ascribe the beginnings of Graham's writing career to the period after he left Parliament and was settled back in Gartmore, in the last decade of the century. However, the habit of writing had undoubtedly been acquired by him over many years preceding, when he was writing long letters home about his experiences in the Americas, and, later on, writing speeches and articles as part of his work as a strongly involved and committed Radical Liberal Member of Parliament.

Nevertheless, we can only begin to speak of Graham as a true writer when in the years after 1890 he began to publish both fiction and non-fiction on a regular basis. Probably beginning with an essay, "The Horses of the Pampas", contributed to the monthly magazine, *Time*, in 1890, Graham went on to write extensively for the *Saturday Review* and other periodicals. There were essays, sketches and short stories, and, later, books of travel and history. Graham's confidence in himself as a writer can be seen to grow during this period, especially when he acquired the literary and critical friendship of the publisher, Edward Garnett.

What makes Graham very different in his writing from any other late Victorian upper-class traveller and man of action is his conscious awareness and absorption of the realistic spirit and literary techniques of contemporary European writers. His main subjects initially are his beloved South America and Spain, as filtered through his personal experiences as a younger man, and aspects of life in Britain, perhaps especially Scotland. Yet he describes these with, in the main, a detached unsentimental insight gained from his reading of the short stories and sketches of Guy de Maupassant and Ivan Turgenev. Equally, after reading *La Pampa*, a set of vignettes of gaucho life written in French by Alfred Ébélot, on the recommendation of his close friend, W.H. Hudson, he came to see how his memories of life among the gauchos could be structured into short tales blending close detailed observation and brief narrative. Yet it would not be true to think of Graham as always being a totally controlled and dispassionate writer. There is both fire and anger in those of his pieces that set out to confront rampant and racist imperialism, social injustice and cruelty directed against helpless human or animal targets.

There is perhaps a tentative quality about Graham's first two books. *Notes on the District of Menteith* (1895) is a highly personal short guidebook to the part of Scotland he knew at first hand surrounding the ancestral home. It almost seems to be a practice for the real thing, before going out into the territory of the big book. Similarly, *Father Archangel of Scotland, and Other Essays* (1896) is an initial attempt at the short story collection, in which Graham shares the contents with his wife, Gabriela.

Graham's first true full-length book conceived as a single narrative is his account of personal experiences in Morocco, *Mogreb-El-Acksa* (1898). The book, whose title translates as 'Morocco the Most Holy', deals in the main with Graham's time there in the later months of 1897. Paradoxically, for a man who travelled so extensively throughout his long life, it is one of the only two real travel books that Graham ever wrote. The other is *Cartagena and the Banks of the Sinú* (1920), which arose out of Graham's mission to Colombia in 1916-17. It is clear that he came to see his experiences in the wider world primarily as a fertile and energising source for fiction.

Between 1899 and 1936, Graham published thirteen collections of sketches and short stories. Generally, his approach for these collections was to bring together stories and short pieces of a rather heterogeneous nature, with settings ranging from his favourite locales of South America and Spain, and increasingly North Africa, to Scotland, London, Paris and more distant parts of the globe. Some of the stories are crafted narratives; others may be little more than detailed descriptions of life and manners with a minimum of narrative, or even personal essays on a range of diverse topics. Although his tone is mostly detached and often ironic, the persona of the writer is never far away and at times Graham's partialities emerge clearly through the text.

The first two collections, *The Ipané* (1899) and *Thirteen Stories* (1900), give the impression of being the most diverse, partly because of the throwaway nature of their titles. 'Ipané' is merely the name of an old river boat that appears in the title story of the first collection. The book has a random quality about it with no sense of a central thread behind the choices.

Thirteen Stories, as a title, suggests an equal randomness. Indeed the main story in the collection is in fact a novella, "Cruz Alta", which takes up fully a third of the length of the book on its own, the other stories being very diverse in their settings and themes. However, the collections that follow in the years before and during the First World War have titles that seem to show a more directed thinking by Graham about their central thrust or themes. *Success* (1902) and *Progress, and Other Sketches* (1905) imply an inspirational quality. *His People* follows in 1906, and *Faith* (1909), *Hope* (1910) and *Charity* (1912) seem to be linked as a group within Graham's mind. *A Hatchment* (1913) and *Brought Forward* (1916) bring to an end the first cycle of Graham's fictional output. Thereafter, there is a gap of eleven years before the final late collections, *Redeemed, and Other Sketches* (1927), *Writ in Sand* (1932) and *Mirages* (1936), the titles of which seem to suggest a disengagement from the serious business of life. And yet perhaps too much weight can be attached to the titles of these works. In all of them, the stories are equally varied and exotic in their sources, and Graham never lets himself be pinned down by a reader's or critic's desire to pigeonhole him as a fiction writer on a particular subject or theme.

It is in his historical writing that Graham does reveal himself as having a specific interest and purpose. Beginning in 1901, he published a sequence of works, mostly biographical, dealing with aspects of South American history from the time of the sixteenth-century Conquistadors right down to his own lifetime. For the writing of these books, he undertook extensive research into the original source documents, a labour in which his knowledge of Spanish proved to be invaluable. The largest group of historical biographies deals with prominent figures in the conquest of

South America by the Spaniards. *Hernando de Soto* (1903), *Bernal Diaz del Castillo* (1915), *The Conquest of New Granada* (1922), *The Conquest of the River Plate* (1924), and *Pedro de Valdivia* (1926) show his interest in most areas of Latin America, not merely his own beloved Argentina. Indeed, his travel book, *Cartagena and the Banks of the Sinú* (1920), includes a sketch of the history of Colombia from the Conquest onwards. In that same year Graham also published his biography of the Brazilian religious revolutionary leader of the 1890s, Antonio Conselheiro, under the title, *A Brazilian Mystic.* Two biographies of later figures in South American history are *Jose Antonio Paez* (1929), dealing with one of the heroes of the liberation of Venezuela from Spain in the 1820s, and *Portrait of a Dictator: Francisco Solano Lopez* (1933), about the leader of Paraguay through the disastrous Triple Alliance War of the 1860s. How popular these books about a continent and culture little-known in Britain could ever be is questionable. In writing them, Graham was undoubtedly trying to counteract the contemporary craze for writings about the British Empire, an institution about which he held distinctly unfashionable views. Probably the most enduring of his historical works has turned out to be *A Vanished Arcadia; Being Some Account of the Jesuits in Paraguay, 1607 to 1767* (1901), for reasons more to do with its later cinematic connections than any historical appeal. A historical biography of more personal significance to Graham was *Doughty Deeds* (1925), an account of the life of Graham's own direct eighteenth-century ancestor and namesake, Robert Graham of Gartmore.

Graham's wife, Gabriela, had literary aspirations of her own and published a number of works, frequently infused by the deep religious feeling that developed as she grew older. Her main work was a two-volume biography of Saint Teresa, to which she devoted years of travel and research. Graham clearly played a major role in encouraging her in her writing, and helped in its publication. He had collaborated with her in *Father Archangel of Scotland, and Other Essays* (1896). After her death in 1906, he arranged for the posthumous publication of a new edition of *Santa Teresa* (1907), her poems in 1908, and a new collection of her shorter writings, *The Christ of Toro and Other Stories* (1908).

This survey has touched on all the books that Graham published in his lifetime. Selections have been made by some of his many admirers from his considerable output of short stories and sketches, usually focusing on specific subject areas of his work, such as South America, Scotland or his passion for horses. One unfortunate effect of this may have been to stereotype Graham as a particular kind of writer, an exotic breed who sits uncomfortably in a literary climate dominated by the Modernists of the earlier twentieth century. The extravagant larger-than-life image that has built up about him has perhaps skewed our perceptions of his writing, which is more European in its sensibility than British Edwardian or Georgian. Paradoxically, despite his class origins and cosmopolitan experience, Graham can also often seem to be closer in tone and outlook to twentieth-century Scottish writers like George Douglas Brown, Hugh MacDiarmid or Lewis Grassic Gibbon, writers whose work he almost certainly knew well. There is a great deal of scholarly work waiting to be done on Graham as a Scottish writer, not least the unquantifiable task of bringing into print the large body of his articles, journalism and letters that have never been properly investigated. The full canon of his work has still to be established. Until that is done, it is not possible to make any true assessment of the literary significance of Robert Bontine Cunninghame Graham.

Alan MacGillivray

Note to Volume 2

The three story collections reprinted here were published between 1900 and 1905, when Graham was moving into middle age (he turned fifty in 1902). After years of struggle with the problems of managing a large estate, and oppressed by constant financial insecurity, he had been forced to sell the ancestral home of Gartmore in 1900. Despite the pain associated with this decision, Graham seemed to experience a sense of release and his literary career began to take off. In consequence, he published eight collections of stories and sketches in the years preceding the outbreak of the First World War in 1914. *Thirteen Stories* (1900), *Success* (1902) and *Progress* (1905) set the pattern for this period. They contain a mix of narrative, descriptive and reflective writings on widely diverse topics, but focusing particularly on Graham's three main areas of interest and experience: the Hispanic world of Spain and Latin America, North Africa (mainly Morocco) and Scotland.

Alan MacGillivray
John C. McIntyre

Thirteen Stories

R. B. Cunninghame Graham

To

George Morton Mansel

I Dedicate [sic] these sketches, stories, studies, or what do you call them. We have galloped together over many leagues of Pampa, by day and night, and therefore I hope he will find the tales (or what do you call them) as near square by the lifts and braces, as is to be expected from a mere landsman.

Introduction

Thirteen Stories was the second collection of short stories and sketches that Graham published that were entirely his own. It followed *The Ipané* (1899) by only a few months, suggesting that Graham had already built up a store of short pieces which he felt, probably with the strong encouragement of Edward Garnett, were ready for placing before a wider reading public. The title of the collection seems not to have had much thought devoted to it. There are indeed thirteen stories, but the first of them is in fact what we could describe as a novella, "Cruz Alta", set in South America, which occupies a full third of the total length. The other twelve stories are all short, with locales ranging from Spain and North Africa to Mexico, and Paris and London to New Zealand and the South Pacific. In his Preface to the collection, Graham justifies the need for an introduction to his stories on the grounds that they deal with events and people in countries now changed for ever by progress and belonging to a past now existing only as memories, particularly his own memories. This is not strictly true. Three or four of the stories derive their power from the contemporary immediacy of their setting and atmosphere. They are stories not coming from Graham's youthful experience but from the world in which he is currently writing.

"Cruz Alta" is a first-person narrative of an attempt to buy horses in Uruguay, drive them to Rio de Janeiro in Brazil and sell them to the Brazilian army. The narrator and his unnamed companion get as far as the town of Cruz Alta in the Rio Grande province of Brazil before realising that the venture is doomed to failure. After spending two months in Cruz Alta, they manage to sell off their herd and return to Uruguay by a roundabout route involving a ride through Paraguay to the capital Asunción and a trip down river by mail-boat to the mouth of the River Plate. The events and feelings described in a clear and colourful, and highly personal, style are closely modelled on Graham's own experiences in the years 1876-77, when he set out with his friend, George Morton Mansel, to whom the collection is dedicated, to make money from ranching and horse-dealing. Yet Graham never claims the story as his own, as autobiography. For him it is story, a story of action and the constant struggle to surmount hardships, a story set in a faraway place and a vivid past when human and animal lives were cheap. Above all, as Graham makes clear early on in the novella, it is a story that has failure at its heart. Loss and disappointment stalk beside the narrator throughout. Mere success would not have fixed that venture in his mind for life. "Failure alone is interesting."

Long journeys that end in failure, or worse, are a recurring theme in the *Thirteen Stories* collection. "The Gold Fish" and "A Hegira", in their different locales and with very different characters, each involve a lengthy trek through harsh landscapes with death waiting at the end. "The Gold Fish" is set in Morocco and recounts the attempt by a faithful messenger to deliver a fine glass bowl containing beautiful goldfish imported from the Far East that are a gift from the Khalifa to the Sultan. The messenger surmounts many hardships but is at length lost in a sandstorm and dies of thirst along with the fish. "A Hegira" is set in Mexico and deals with a real event which Graham knew of and partly witnessed when he was living with his new wife in Texas and Mexico in the early 1880s. A group of Mescalero Apaches escape from custody in Mexico City and try to return to their own territories. They are hunted down over hundreds of miles and are all eventually killed. Their flight, as observed and reported by the narrator, is striking as a moral lesson in "tenacity of purpose, the futility of life and the inexorable fate that mocks mankind". Each story, however, ends on a positive note: the fine glass bowl remains intact and the Apaches' little dog is faithful unto death, mourning over his owners' graves. A more desperately affecting journey to death is described in terms of anger and disgust by Graham in "Calvary". Here his love of horses and rage at their cruel treatment come together in the account of a fine Argentinian colt, living in freedom on the pampas and then sold to horse-dealers, who ship him under cruel conditions to Britain and a new life of slavery pulling cabs on the streets of London. As he grows older and less fit, he slides down the social scale of such labour and eventually dies between the shafts of a fish-hawker's cart, brutally beaten by his owner and left as a corpse amid the London traffic. Here there is nothing positive; only Graham's bleak vision of the cruelty of so-called civilisation.

Another type of journey, this time the journey through life, is the theme of several other stories. "Sidi Bu Zibbala" describes the life of a

Christian Arab from the Lebanon who travels widely, following many different jobs and business ventures, knowing both East and West, sampling both Christianity and Islam, marriage and solitude, until he finds eventual satisfaction as a hermit, Sidi Bu Zibbala, the lord of the dunghill, owning nothing and living in peace. "Higginson's Dream" expresses a similar dissatisfaction with civilisation. The self-made successful Higginson, who has made a fortune opening up the Pacific territory of New Caledonia to colonial progress and development, comes to realise what has been lost, the innocence of the unspoiled life he had enjoyed there as a boy with his Polynesian friends.

In these latter two stories, Graham is probably writng at a slight distance from his material, articulating some *fin-de-siècle* doubts about the supposed benefits of colonialism and the Westernisation of natural societies. Similar doubts, more centred on the activities of his fellow Scots, surface in "In a German Tramp" and "A Pakeha". The first of these stories vividly describes the difficulties encountered by an old tramp steamer in clearing a North African harbour during heavy weather and sympathetically evokes the character of its North German captain, Rindelhaus. However, the sharper edge of the story comes in Graham's unsympathetic portrayal of a group of Scottish Presbyterian missionaries at work in that part of North Africa. His distaste for them and their activities comes through strongly, to the point where his physical descriptions of individuals lapse into caricature. In "A Pakeha", Graham is more sympathetic in his treatment of old Mr Campbell, a neighbour he meets on a wet day in Menteith, who reminisces about his days in New Zealand many years before, working as a surveyor and shepherd and brick-maker. He of course was not a colonial exploiter, but a practical man doing honest jobs, and Graham clearly approves of him and his secret wish that he had stayed on in New Zealand to live the free life of a squatter with a beautiful Maori woman to be his companion.

"A Pakeha" is one of several stories in which Graham places the burden of the narrative upon another voice than his own. Campbell is the first-person narrator of most of the story, with his hearer, the "laird", merely introducing him and occasionally responding briefly. The technique works very well, principally because Graham shows that he can handle the writing of the Scots idiom of Mr Campbell quite skilfully. In "La Clemenza de Tito", a very slight tale where the title, derived from a

Mozart opera, seems to carry more cultural weight than the story merits, his main narrator is a well-read English ship's engineer who describes a brief encounter with an African prostitute, inconclusive because he has moral scruples on discovering that she is at least nominally Christian. Graham makes his character convincing, yet the story remains slight and, to our sensibilities, rather distasteful, probably Graham's intention. Where Graham seems to fail in his evocation of character through a distinctive national voice is in the two stories, "In a German Tramp" and "Rothenberger's Wedding". His use of a supposedly Germanic fractured English for the characters of Rindelhaus and Rothenberger just does not convince the reader. This way of creating German speakers of English, coming as it does from an age before two world wars and the growth of a European consciousness, simply smacks of the patronising "comic foreigner" approach that is unacceptable now. Rindelhaus's character is saved because he is so clearly a good man; Rothenberger, a successful man in his fashionable faddish medical field, is held up to ridicule in his aspiration to make a good English marriage, mainly through his faulty command of the language of his adopted country. Graham's patronising attitude is intensified by the ungrammatical speech he gives to Rothenberger. He would never have done this to a Spanish- or French-speaking character.

The three remaining stories in *Thirteen Stories* show Graham as more assured and successful as a writer, principally because the subjects are really close to his own experience and attitudes. "La Pulperia" comes directly out of his youthful experiences in Argentina. The little bar and trading-post in the great expanse of the pampas is brilliantly evoked, with its goods for sale, the drinking and quarrelling, and fighting, the dancing and singing, the "china girls", or prostitutes, and their gaucho clients, the echoes of Argentina's violent history – all burst straight out of the vivid memory that Graham said in his Preface was the well-spring of his stories. "Sohail", by contrast, is a meditation on the Moorish influence upon Spain, especially in Andalusia, an area which Graham knew from many visits from childhood onwards. Finally, "Victory" is a bitter observation and encapsulation of the two sides in the Spanish-American War of 1898, a story written in the heat of Graham's unfashionably pro-Spanish partisanship. The contrast between the Americans in the Paris hotel, vulgarly gloating over the news of their victory, and the impeccable Castilian caballero with his daughter, hearing with stoicism of the Spanish naval defeat, is brilliantly captured by Graham in one of his most powerful sketches.

Thirteen Stories, despite its weak elements, is a significant collection and marks Graham's true entry upon the literary scene as an original writer of imaginative and quasi-autobiographical fiction.

A.MacG.

Thirteen Stories

Contents

Preface

To-day in warfare all the niceties of old-world tactics are fallen into contempt. No word of outworks, ravelins, of mamelons, of counter-scarps, of glacis, fascines; none of the terms by means of which Vauban obscured his art, are even mentioned. Armies fall to and blow such brains as they may have out of each other's heads without so much as a salute. And so of literature, your "few first words," your "avant-propos," your nice approaches to the reader, giving him beforehand some taste of what is to follow, have also fallen into disuse. The man of genius (and in no age has self-dubbed genius called out so loud in every street, and been accepted at its own appraisement) stuffs you his epoch-making book full of the technicalities of some obscure or half-forgotten trade, and rattles on at once, sans introduction, twenty knots an hour, like a torpedo boat. No preface, dedication, not even an apology *pro existentiâ ejus* intervening betwixt the bewildered public and the full power of his wit. A graceless way of doing things, and not comparable to the slow approach by "prefatory words," "censura," "dedication," by means of which the writers of the past had half disarmed the critic ere he had read a line. I like to fancy to myself the progress of a fight in days gone by, with marching, countermarching, manoeuvring, so to speak, for the weather-gauge, and then the general engagement all by the book of arithmetic, and squadrons going down like men upon a chess-board after nice calculation, and like gentlemen.

Who, hidden in a wood, watching a nymph about to bathe, would care to see her strip off her "duds" like an umbrella-case, and bounce into the river like a water-rat? — a lawn upon the grass, a scarf hung on a bush, a petticoat rocked by the wind upon the sward, then the shy trying of the water with the naked feet, and lastly something flashing in the sun which you could hardly swear you had seen, so rapidly it passed into the stream, would most enchant the gaze of the rapt watcher hidden behind his tree. And so of literature, wheedle me by degrees, your reader to your book, as did the giants of the past in graceful preface, dedication, or what do you call it, that got the readers, so to speak, into the book before they were aware. It seems to me, a world all void of grace must needs be cruel, for cruelty and grace go not together, and perhaps the hearts of the pig-tailed, pipe-clayed generals of the past were not more hard than are the hearts of their tweed-clad descendants who now-a-days blow you a thousand savages to paradise, and then sit down to lunch.

Let there be no mistake; the writer and the reader are sworn foes. The writer labouring for bread, or hopes of fame, from idleness, from too much energy, or from that uncontrollable dance of St. Vitus in the muscles of the wrist which prompts so many men to write (the Lord knows why), works, blots, corrects, rewrites, revises, and improves; then publishes, and for the most part is incontinently damned. Then comes the reader cavalierly, as the train shunts at Didcot, or puffs and snorts into Carlisle, and gingerly examining the book says it is rubbish, and that he wonders how people who should have something else to do, find time to spend their lives in writing trash.

I take it that there is a modesty of mind as deep implanted in the soul of man as is the supergrafted post-Edenian modesty of the body; which latter, by the way, so soon is lost, restraints of custom or convention laid aside.

Who that would strip his clothes off, and walk down Piccadilly, even if the day were warm (the police all drunk or absent), without some hesitation, and an announcement of his purpose, say, in the columns of the *Morning Post*?

Therefore, why strip the soul stark naked to the public gaze without some hesitation and due interval, by means of which to make folk understand that which you write is what you think you feel; part of yourself, a part, moreover, which once given out can never be recalled?

So of the sketches in this book, most of them treat of scenes seen in that magic period, youth, when things impress themselves on the imagination more sharply than in after years; and the scenes too have vanished; that is, the countries where they passed have all been changed, and now-a-days are full of barbed-wire fences, advertisements, and desolation, the desolation born of imperfect progress. The people, too, I treat of, for the most part have disappeared; being born unfit for progress, it has passed over them, and their place is occupied by worthy men who cheat to better purpose, and more scientifically. Therefore, I, writing as a man who has not only seen but lived with ghosts, may perhaps find pardon for this preface, for who would run in heavily and dance a hornpipe on the turf below which sleep the dead? And if I am not pardoned for my hesitation, dislike, or call it what you will, to give these little sketches to the world without preamble, after my fashion, I care not overmuch.

In the phantasmagoria we call the world, most things and men are ghosts, or at the best but ghosts of ghosts, so vaporous and unsubstantial that they scarcely cast a shadow on the grass. That which is most abiding with us is the recollection of the past, and . . . hence this preface.

R. B. Cunninghame Graham.

Thirteen Stories

Cruz Alta

Pasted into an old scrap-book, chiefly filled with newspaper cuttings from Texan and Mexican newspapers containing accounts of Indian fights, the prowess of different horses (notably of a celebrated "claybank," which carried the mail-rider from E1 Paso to Oakville, Arizona), and interspersed with advertisements of strayed animals, pictures of Gauchos, Indians, Chilians, Brazilians, and Gambusinos, is an old coffee-coloured business card. On it is set forth, that Francisco Cardozo de Carvallo is the possessor of a "Grande Armazem de Fazendas, ferragems, drojas, chapeos, miudezas, e objectos de fantasia e de modas."

All the above, "Com grande reduccao nos preços." Then occurs the significant advertença, "Mas A Dinheiro," and the address Rua do Commercio, No. 77. — CRUZ ALTA.

Often on winter nights when all the air is filled with whirling leaves dashing against the panes, when through the house sweep gusts of wind making the passages unbearable with cold, the rooms disconsolate, and the whole place feel eerie and ghostlike as the trees creak, groan and labour, like a ship at sea, I take the scrap-book down.

In it are many things more interesting by far to me at certain times than books or papers, or than the conversation of my valued friends; almost as great a consolation as is tobacco to a bruised mind; and then I turn the pages over with delight tinged with that melancholy which is the best part of remembrance.

So amongst tags of poetry as Joaquim Miller's lines "For those who fail," the advertisement for my fox-terrier Jack, the "condemndest little buffler" the Texans called him, couched in the choicest of Castilian, and setting forth his attributes, colour and name, and offering five dollars to any one who would apprehend and take him to the Callejon del Espiritu Santo, Mexico, curious and striking outsides of match-boxes, one entire series illustrating the "Promessi Sposi"; of scraps, detailing news of Indian caciques long since dead, a lottery-ticket of the State of Louisiana, passes on "busted" railways, and the like, is this same coffee-coloured card.

I cannot remember that I was a great dealer at the emporium, the glories of which the card sets forth, except for cigarettes and "Rapadura"; that is, raw sugar in a little cake done up in maize-leaves, matches, and an occasional glass of white Brazilian rum.

Still during two long months the place stood to me in lieu of club, and in it I used to meet occasional German "Fazenderos," merchants from Surucaba, and officers on the march from San Paulo to Rio Grande; and there I used to lounge, waiting for customers to buy a "Caballada" of some hundred horses, which a friend and I had brought with infinite labour from the plains of Uruguay. Thinking upon the strange and curious types I used to meet, clad for the most part in loose black Turkish trousers, broad-brimmed felt hats kept in their place by a tasselled string beneath the chin, in real or sham vicuña ponchos, high patent-leather boots, sewn in patterns with red thread; upon the horses with silver saddles and reins, securely tied to posts outside the door, and on the ceaseless rattle of spurs upon the bare brick floors which made a sort of obligato accompaniment to the monotonous music of the guitar, full twenty years fall back.

Yet still the flat-roofed town, capital of the district in Rio Grande known as Encima de la Sierra, the stopping-place for the great droves of mules which from the Banda Oriental and Entre Rios are driven to the annual fair at Surucaba; the stodgy Brazilian countrymen so different from the Gauchos of the River Plate; the negroes at that time slaves; the curious vegetation, and the feeling of being cut off from all the world, are fresh as yesterday.

Had but the venture turned out well, no doubt I had forgotten it, but to have worked for four long months driving the horses all the day through country quite unknown to me, sitting the most part of each night upon my horse on guard, or riding slowly round and round the herd, eating jerked beef, and sleeping, often wet, upon the ground, to lose my money, has fixed the whole adventure on my memory for life.

Failure alone is interesting.

Successful generals with their hands scarce dry from the blood of half-armed foes; financiers, politicians; those who rise, authors whose works run to a dozen editions in a year: the men who go to colonies with or without the indispensable half-crown and come back rich, to these we give our greetings in the market-place; we make them knights, marking their children with the father's bourgeois brand: we marvel at their fortune for a brief space, and make them doctors of civil law, exposing them during the process to be insulted by our undergraduates, then they drop out of recollection and become uninteresting, as nature formed their race.

But those who fail after a glorious fashion, Raleigh, Cervantes, Chatterton, Camoens, Blake, Claverhouse, Lovelace, Alcibiades, Parnell, and the last unknown deck-hand who, diving overboard after a comrade, sinks without saving him: these interest us, at least they interest those who, cursed with imagination, are thereby doomed themselves to the same failure as their heroes were. The world is to the unimaginative, for them are honours, titles, rank and ample waistbands; foolish phylacteries broad as trade union banners; their own esteem and death to sound of Bible leaves fluttered by sorrowing friends, with the sure hope of waking up immortal in a new world on the same pattern as the world that they have left.

After a wretched passage down the coast, we touched at Rio, and in the Rua Direita, no doubt now called Rio *[sic = Rua]* Primero de Mayo or some other revolutionary date, we saw a Rio Grandense soldier on a fine black horse. As we were going to the River Plate to make our fortunes, my companion asked me what such a horse was worth, and where the Brazilian Government got their remounts. I knew no horses of the kind were bred nearer than Rio Grande, or in Uruguay, and that a horse such as the trooper rode, might in the latter country be worth an ounce. We learned in Rio that his price was eighty dollars, and immediately a golden future rose before our eyes. What could be easier than in Uruguay, which I knew well and where I had many friends (now almost to a man dead in the revolutions or killed by rum), to buy the horses and drive them overland to the Brazilian capital?

We were so confident of the soundness of our scheme that I believe we counted every hour till the boat put to sea.

Not all the glories of the Tijuca with its view across the bay straight into fairyland, the red-roofed town, the myriad islets, the tall palm-tree avenue of Botafogo, the tropic trees and butterflies, and the whole wondrous panorama spread at our feet, contented us.

During the voyage to the River Plate we planned the thing well out, and talked it over with our friends. They, being mostly of our age, found it well reasoned, and envied us, they being due at banks and counting-houses, and other places where no chance like ours of making money, could be found. Arrived in Buenos Ayres, a cursed chance called us to Bahia Blanca upon business, but though we had a journey of about a thousand miles to make through territory just wasted by the Indians and in which at almost every house a man or two lay dead, we counted it as nothing, for we well knew on our return our fortunes were assured.

And so the autumn days upon the Arroyo de los Huesos seemed more glorious than autumn days in general, even in that climate perhaps the most exhilarating of the world. Horses went better, "maté" was hotter in the mouth, the pulperia caña seemed more tolerable, and the "China" girls looked more desirable than usual, even to philosophers who had their fortunes almost as good as made.

Our business in the province of Buenos Ayres done, and by this time I have forgotten what it was, we sold our horses, some of the best I ever saw in South America, for whatever they would fetch, and in a week found ourselves in Durazno, a little town in Uruguay, where in the camps surrounding, horses and mules were cheap.

About a league outside the town, and in a wooded elbow of the river Yi, lived our friend Don Guillermo. I myself years before had helped to build his house; and in and out of season, no matter if I arrived upon a "pingo" shining with silver gear, or on a "mancaron" with an old saddle topped by a ragged sheepskin, I was a welcome guest.

Ah! Don Guillermo, you and your brother Don Tomas rise also through the mist of twenty years.

Catholics, Scotchmen, and gentlemen, kindly and hospitable, bold riders and yet so religious that, though it must have been a purgatory to them as horsemen, they used to trudge on foot to mass on Sunday, swimming the Yi when it was flooded, with their clothes and missals on their heads, may God have pardoned you.

Not that the sins of either of them could have been great, or of the kind but that the briefest sojourn in purgatory should not have wiped them out.

To those rare Catholic families in Scotland an old-world flavour clings. When Knox and that "lewid monk," the Regent Murray, all agog for progress and so-called purer worship, pestered and bothered Scotland into a change of faith, those few who clung to Catholicism seemed to become repositories of the traditions of an older world.

Heaven and hell, no resting-place for the weaker souls between, have rendered Scotland a hard place for the ordinary man who wants his purgatory, even if by another name. Surely our Scottish theologians had done well, although they heated up our hell like a glass furnace, to leave us purgatory; that is if "Glesca" be not purgatory enough even for those who, like North Britons, have no doubt on any subject either in heaven above, or in the earth below. So to the house of Don Guillermo — even the name has now escaped me, though I see it, mud-built and thatched with "paja," standing on a little sandy hill, surrounded on two sides by wood, on the others looking straight out upon the open "camp" — hot foot we came. Riding upon two strayed horses known as "ajenos," bought for a dollar each in Durazno, we arrived, carrying our scanty property in saddle-bags, rode to the door, called out "Hail, Mary!" after the fashion of the country and in deference to the religion of our hosts, which was itself of so sincere a caste that every one attempted to conform to it, as far as possible, whilst in their house; received the answer "Without sin conceived"; got off, and straightway launched into a discussion of our plan.

Assembled in the house were Wycherley, Harrington and Trevelyan, and other commentators, whose names have slipped my mind. Some were "estancieros," that is cattle or sheep farmers; others again were loafers, all mostly men of education, with the exception of Newfoundland Jack, a sailor, who had left the navy in a hurry, after some peccadillo, but who, once in the camp, took a high place amongst men, by his knowledge of splicing, making turks' heads, and generally applying all his acquired sea-lore to saddlery, and from a trick he had of forcing home his arguments with a short knife, the handle fixed on with a raw cow's tail, and which in using he threw from hand to hand, and generally succeeded in burying deeply in his opponent's chest. Our friends all liked the scheme, pronounced it practical and businesslike, and, to show goodwill, despatched a boy to town to bring a demijohn of caña back at full speed, instructing him to put it down to our account, not to delay upon the way, and to be careful no one stole it at the crossing of the Yi.

Long we sat talking, waiting for the advent of the boy, till at last, seeing he would not come that night, and a thick mist rising up from the river having warned us that the night was wearing on, we spread our saddles on the floor, and went to sleep. At daybreak, cold and miserable, the boy appeared, bringing the caña in a demijohn, and to our questions said he had passed the river, hit the "rincon," and heard the dogs bark in the mist; but after trying for an hour could never find the house. Then, thinking that his horse might know the way, laid down the reins, and the horse took him straight to the other horses, who, being startled at the sudden apparition of their friend saddled and mounted in the dead of night, vanished like spectres into the thickest of the fog. Then tired of riding, after an hour or two, took off his saddle, and had passed the night, as it appeared at daybreak, not a quarter of a mile away.

Between the town and Don Guillermo's house there ran a river called the Yi; just at the pass a "balsa" plied, drawn over by stout ropes. On either side the "pass" stood pulperias, that is camp-stores, where gin and sardines, Vino Carlon, Yerba, and all the necessaries of frontier life could be procured. Horses and cattle, mules and troops of sheep passed all the day, and gamblers plied their trade, whilst in some huts girls, known as "Chinas," watched the passers-by, loitering in deshabille before their mare's hide doors, singing "cielitos," or the "gato," to the accompaniment of a guitar, or merely shouting to the stranger, "Che, si quieres cosa buena vente por acá." A half-Arcadian, half-Corinthian place the crossing was; fights there were frequent, and a "Guapeton," that is, a pretty handler of his knife, once kept things lively for a month or two, challenging all the passers-by to fight, till luckily a Brazilian, going to the town, put things in order with an iron-handled whip.

The owner of the "balsa," one Eduardo Peña, cherished a half-romantic, half-antagonistic friendship for Don Guillermo, speaking of him as "muy Catolico," admiring his fine seat upon a horse, and yet not understanding in the least the qualities which made him a man of mark in all the "pagos" from the Porongos to the Arazati. "Catolico," with Peña, was but a matter of pure faith, and going to mass a work of supererogation; and conduct such as the eschewal of the China ladies at the pass, with abstinence from all excess in square-faced gin, dislike to monté, even with "Sota en la puerta," and the adversary with all his money staked upon another card, seemed to him bigotry; for bigotry is after all not so much mere excess of faith or want of tolerance, but a neglect to fall into the vices of our friends. So, mounted on our two "agenos," one a jibber, the other a kicker at the stirrup, and extremely hard to mount, we scoured the land. Gauchos, Brazilians, negroes, troperos, cattle-farmers, each man in the whole "pago" had at least a horse to sell. Singly, driven, led, pulled unwillingly along in raw-hide ropes, and sitting back like lapdogs walking in the park, the horses came. We bought them all after much bargaining, and then began to hunt about at farms, estancias, and potreros, and to inquire on every side where horses could be got. All the "dead beats," "sancochos," buck-jumpers, wall-eyed and broken-backed, we passed in a review. An English sailor rode up to the place, dressed as a Gaucho, speaking but little English, with a west-country twang. He, too, had horses, which we bought, and the deal over, launched into the story of his life.

It seemed that he had left a man-of-war some fifteen years ago, married a native girl and settled down, and for ten years had never met an Englishman. In English, still a sailor, but in Spanish, a gentleman, courteous and civil, and fit to take his place with any one; full of fine compliments, and yet a horse-coper; selling us three good horses, and one, that the first time I mounted him kicked like a zebra, although our friend had warranted him quite free from vice, well bitted, and the one horse he had which he reserved in general for the saddle of his wife.

In a few days we had collected sixty or seventy, and to make all complete, a man arrived, saying that specially on our account, thirteen wild horses, or horses that had run wild, had been enclosed. He offered them on special terms, and we, saddling at once, rode twelve or thirteen leagues to see them; and after crossing a river, wading through a swamp, and winding in and out through a thick wood for several miles, we reached his house. There, in a strong corral, the horses were, wild-eyed and furious, tails sweeping to the ground, manes to their knees, sweating with fear, and trembling if any one came near. One was a piebald dun, about eight years of age, curly all over like a poodle; one Pampa, that is, black with a head as if it had been painted white to the ears; behind them, coal-black down to his feet, which, curiously enough, were all four white. A third, Overo Azulejo, slate-coloured and white; he was of special interest, for he had twisted in his mane a large iron spur, and underneath a lump as large as an apple, where the spur had bumped upon his neck for years during his gallop through the woods and plains. Each horse had some peculiarity, most had been tame at one time, and were therefore more to be dreaded than if they had been never mounted in their lives.

As it was late when we arrived we tied our horses up and found a ball in progress at the house. Braulio Islas was the owner's name, a man of some position in the land, young and unmarried, and having passed some years of his life in Monte Video, where, as is usual, he had become a doctor either of law or medicine; but the life had not allured him, and he had drifted back to the country, where he lived, half as a Gaucho, half as a "Dotorcito," riding a wild horse as he were part of him, and yet having a few old books, quoting dog Latin, and in the interim studying international law, after the fashion of the semi-educated in the River Plate. Fastening our horses to long twisted green-hide ropes, we passed into the house. "Carne con cuero" (meat cooked with the hide) was roasting near the front-door on a great fire of bones. Around it men sat drinking maté, smoking and talking, whilst tame ostriches peered into the fire and snapped up anything within their reach; dogs without hair, looking like pigs, ran to and fro, horses were tied to every post, fire-flies darted about the trees; and, above all, the notes, sung in a high falsetto voice of a most lamentable Paraguayan "triste," quavered in the night air and set the dogs a-barking, when all the company at stated intervals took up the refrain, and chanted hoarsely or shrilly of the hardships passed by Lopez in his great camp at Pirayú.

Under the straw-thatched sheds whole cows and sheep were hung up; and every one, when he felt hungry, cut a collop off and cooked it in the embers, for in those days meat had no price, and if you came up hungry to a house a man would say: "There is a lazo, and the cattle are feeding in a hollow half a league away."

A harp, two cracked guitars, the strings repaired with strips of hide, and an accordion, comprised the band. The girls sat in a row, upon rush-seated chairs, and on the walls were ranged either great bowls of grease in which wicks floated, or home-made candles fixed on to nails, which left them free to gutter on the dancers' heads. The men lounged at the door, booted and spurred, and now and then one walked up to the girls, selected one, and silently began to dance a Spanish valse, slowly and scarcely moving from the place, the hands stretched out in front, and the girl with her head upon his shoulder, eyes fast closed and looking like a person in a trance. And as they danced the musicians broke into a harsh, wild song, the dancers' spurs rattled and jingled on the floor, and through the unglazed and open windows a shrill fierce neigh floated into the room from the wild horses shut in the corral. "Dulces," that is, those sweetmeats made from the yolk of eggs, from almonds, and from nuts, and flavoured with cinnamon and caraways brought by the Moors to Spain, and taken by the Spaniards to the Indies, with sticky cakes, and vino seco circulated amongst the female guests. The men drank gin, ate bread (a delicacy in the far-off "camp"), or sipped their maté, which, in its little gourds and silver tube, gave them the appearance of smoking some strange kind of pipe.

"Que bailen los Ingleses," and we had to acquit ourselves as best we could, dancing a "pericon," as we imagined it, waving our handkerchiefs about to the delight of all the lookers-on. Fashion decreed that, the dance over, the "cavalier" presented his andkerchief to the girl with whom he danced. I having a bad cold saw with regret my new silk handkerchief pass to the hand of a mulatto girl, and having asked her for her own as a remembrance of her beauty and herself, received a home-made cotton cloth, stiff as a piece of leather, and with meshes like a sack.

Leaving the dance, as Braulio Islas said, as more "conformable" to Gauchos than to serious men, we started bargaining. After much talking we agreed to take the horses for three dollars each, upon condition that in the morning Islas and all his men should help us drive a league or two upon the road. This settled, and the money duly paid, we went to bed, that is, lay down upon our saddles under the "galpon." To early morning the guitars went on, and rising just about day-break we found the revellers saddling their horses to depart in peace. We learned with pleasure there had been no fight, and then after a maté walked down to the corral. Knowing it was impossible to drive the horses singly, after much labour we coupled them in twos. I mounted one of them, and to my surprise, he did not buck, but after three or four plunges went quietly, and we let the others out. The bars were scarcely down when they all scattered, and made off into the woods. Luckily all the drivers were at hand, and after three or four hours' hard galloping we got them back, all except one who never reappeared; and late in the evening reached Don Guillermo's house and let our horses into a paddock fenced with strong posts of ñandubay or Tala and bound together with pieces of raw hide.

So for a week or two we passed our lives, collecting horses of every shade and hue, wild, tame and bagualon, that is, neither quite wild nor tame, and then, before starting, had to go to "La Justicia " to get a passport with their attributes and marks.

I found the Alcalde, one Quintin Perez, sitting at his door, softening a piece of hide by beating on it with a heavy mallet of ñandubay. He could not read, but was so far advanced towards culture as to be able to sign his name and rubricate. His rubric was most elaborate, and he informed me that a signature was good, but that he thought a rubric more authentic. Though he could not decipher the document I brought for signature, he scrutinized the horses' marks, all neatly painted in the margin, discussed each one of them, and found out instantly some were from distant "pagos," and on this account, before the signature or rubric was appended, in addition to the usual fee, I was obliged to "speak a little English to him," which in the River Plate is used to signify the taking and receiving of that conscience money which causes the affairs of justice to move pleasantly for all concerned. Meanwhile my partner had gone to town (Durazno) to arrange about the revision of the passport with the chief authorities. Nothing moved quickly at that time in Uruguay; so after waiting one or two days in town, without a word, he quietly let loose his horse in a by-street at night to save his keep, and casting about where he should leave his saddle, thought that the cloak-room of the railway-station might be safe, because the station-master was an Englishman. The saddle, having silver stirrups and good saddle-cloths and silver-mounted reins and bit, was worth more than the horse, which, being a stray, he had bought for a couple of dollars, and was not anxious to retain.

After a day or two of talk, and "speaking English," he wanted his saddle, and going to the station found it gone. Not being up at that time in the ways of the Republic, he informed the police, waited a day, then two days, and found nothing done. Luckily, just at that time, I came to town and asked him if he had offered a reward. Hearing he had not, we went down to see the Commissary of Police, and found him sitting in his office training two cocks to fight. A rustle and the slamming of a door just marked the hurried exit of a lady, who must have been assisting at the main. Compliments duly passed, cigarettes lighted and maté circulating, "served" by a negro soldier in a ragged uniform with iron spurs upon his naked feet who stood *[to]* attention every time he passed the gourd in which the maté is contained to either of us, we plunged into our talk.

"Ten dollars, Comissario."

"No, señor, fifteen, and a slight gratification to the man who brings the saddle back."

We settled at thirteen, and then the Commissary winked slowly, and saying, "This is not Europe," asked for a little something for himself, received it, and calling to the negro, said —

"Tio Gancho, get at once to horse, take with you one or two men, and scour the 'pago' till you bring this saddle back. See that you find it, or I will have your thumbs both broken as your toes are, by San Edovige and by the Mother of our Lord."

A look at Tio Gancho showed both his big toes had been broken when a slave in Brazil, either to stop him walking, or, as the Commissary thought, to help him to catch the stirrup, for he was a noted rider of a redomon.[1]

Duly next day the saddle was brought (so said the Commissary) into the light of justice, and it then appeared one of the silver stirrups had been lost. The Commissary was much annoyed, reproached his men, being, as he said he was: "Un hombre muy honrado." After thinking the case well out, he returned me two and a half dollars out of the thirteen I had agreed to pay. Honour no doubt was satisfied upon both sides, and a new silver stirrup cost ten dollars at the least; but as the saddle was well worth sixty, we parted friends. That is, we should have parted so had not the "Hombre muy honrado" had another card to play.

"How long do you want the thief detained?" he asked. And we, thinking to be magnanimous and to impress him with our liberal ideas, said loftily —

"A month will do."

"All right," he answered, "then I must trouble you for thirty dollars more for the man's maintenance, and for the gaoler's fee." This was a stopper over all, and I said instantly —

"Being ignorant of your laws, perhaps we have looked at the man's offence too hardly, a week will do." So after paying five dollars down, we invited the Commissary to drink, and left him well knowing that we should not be out of sight before the man would be released, and the five dollars be applied strictly towards the up-keep of "justice" in the Partido of the Yi. Months afterwards I heard the culprit worked two days cutting down weeds with a machete in the public square; then, tired of it, being "un hombre de á caballo," had volunteered to join the army, was received into the ranks, and in a few weeks' time rose to be sergeant, for he could sign his name.

All being ready, and some men (one a young Frenchman born in the place) being found with difficulty, the usual revolution having drained off the able-bodied men, we made all ready for the start. We bid good-bye to Don Guillermo, and to Don Tomas, giving them as an addition to their library (which consisted of some lives of saints and an odd volume of "el culto al Falo," which was in much request), our only book

---

1 A redomon is a half-tamed horse.

the "Feathered Arrow," either by Aimard or by Gerstaeker, and mounting early in the morning after some trouble with the wilder of our beasts, we took the road.

For the first few leagues Don Guillermo rode with us, and then, after a smoke, bade us goodbye and rode away; his tall, lithe figure dressed in loose black merino trousers tucked into his boots, hat tied beneath his chin, and Pampa poncho, fading out of sight, and by degrees the motion of his right arm touching his horse up, Gaucho fashion, at every step, grew slower, then stood still, and lastly vanished with the swaying figure of the rider, out of sight. Upon what Pampa he now gallops is to me unknown, or whether, where he is, horses accompany him; but I would fain believe it, for a heaven on foot would not be heaven to him; but I still see him as he disappeared that day swaying to every motion of his horse as they had been one flesh. "Adios, Don Guillermo," or perhaps "hasta luego," you and your brother Don Tomas, your hospitable shanty, and your three large cats, "Yanish" and "Yanquetruz," with one whose name I cannot now recall, are with me often as I think on times gone by; and still to-day (if it yet stands), upon the darkest night I could take horse outside Durazno, cross the Yi, not by the "balsa," but at the ford below, and ride without a word to any one straight to your house.

Days followed one another, and nights still caught us upon horseback, driving or rounding up our horses, and nothing interested us but that "el Pangare" was lame; "el Gargantillo" looked a little thin, or that "el Zaino de la hacinda" [sic = hacienda] was missing in the morning from the troop. Rivers we passed, the Paso de los Toros, where the horses grouped together on a little beach of stones refused to face the stream. Then sending out a yoke of oxen to swim first, we pressed on them, and made them plunge, and kept dead silence, whilst a naked man upon the other bank called to them and whistled in a minor key; for horses swimming, so the Gauchos say, see nothing, and head straight for a voice if it calls soothingly. And whilst they swam, men in canoes lay down the stream to stop them drifting, and others swimming by their side splashed water in their faces if they tried to turn. The sun beat on the waste calling out the scent of flowers; kingfishers fluttered on the water's edge, herons stood motionless, great vultures circled overhead, and all went well till, at the middle of the stream, a favourite grey roan mare put up her head and snorted, beat the water with her feet, and then sank slowly, standing quite upright as she disappeared.

Mountains and plains we passed, and rivers fringed with thick, hard thorny woods; we sweltered in the sun, sat shivering on our horses during the watches of the night, slept fitfully by turns at the camp fire, ate "charqui" and drank maté, and by degrees passing the Paso de los Novillos, San Fructuoso, and the foot-hills of Haedo and the Cuchilla de Peralta with its twin pulperias, we emerged on to the plain, which, broken here and there by rivers, slopes toward the southern frontier of Brazil. But as we had been short-handed from the first, our "caballada" had got into bad ways. A nothing startled them, and the malign example of the group of wildlings brought from Braulio Islas, led them astray, and once or twice they separated and gave us hours of work to bring them back. Now as a "caballada" which has once bolted is in the future easily disposed to run, we gave strict orders no one was to get off, though for a moment, without hobbling his horse.

Camped one cold morning on a river, not far from Brazil, and huddled round a fire, cooking some sausages, flavoured with Chile pepper, over a fire of leaves, one of our men who had been on horseback watching all the night, drew near the fire, and getting off, fastened his reins to a heavy-handled whip, and squatted on them, as he tried to warm his hands. My horse, unsaddled, was fastened by a lasso to a heavy stone, and luckily my partner and the rest all had their horses well secured, for a "coati" dived with a splash after a fish into the river. In a moment the horses all took fright, and separating, dashed to the open country with heads and tails erect, snorting and kicking, and left us looking in despair, whilst the horse with the whip fastened to the reins joined them, and mine, tied to the stone, plunged furiously, but gave me time to catch him, and mounting barebacked, for full five hours we rode, and about nightfall brought the "caballada" back to the camp, and driving them into an elbow of the river, lighted great fires across the mouth of it, and went to sleep, taking it conscientiously in turns to curse the man who let his horse escape.

Five leagues or so upon the road the frontier lay, and here the Brazilian Government had guards, but we being business men smuggled our horses over in the night, led by a noted smuggler, who took us by devious paths, through a thick wood, to a ford known to him, only just practicable, and this we passed swimming and wading, and struggling through the mud. The river wound about through beds of reeds, trees known as "sarandis" grew thickly on the banks, and as we passed "carpinchos" [1] snorted; great

1 Carpinchos: Hydrochoerus capybara

fish leaped into the air and fell with a resounding crash into the stream, and in the trees was heard the scream of vultures, as frightened by our passage they rose and weltered heavily through the thick wood. By morning we were safe into Brazil, passing a league or more through a thick cane-brake, where we left several of our best horses, as to pursue them when they straggled was impossible without running the risk of losing all the rest. The crossing of the river had brought us to another world. As at Carlisle and Gretna in the old days, or as at Tuy and Valenza even to-day, the river had set a barrier between the peoples as it had been ten miles instead of a few hundred yards in width. Certainly, on the Banda Oriental, especially in the department of Tacuarembò, many Brazilians had emigrated and settled there, but living amongst the Gaucho population, in a measure they had been forced to conform to the customs of the land. That is, they practised hospitality after the Gaucho fashion, taking no money from the wayfaring man for a piece of beef; they lent a horse, usually the worst they had, if one came to their house with one's horse tired; their women showed themselves occasionally; and not being able to hold slaves, they were obliged to adopt a different tone to men in general than that they practised in the Empire of Brazil. But in the time of which I write, in their own country they still carried swords, slaves trotted after the rich "fazendero's" horse, the women of the family never sat down to table with the men, and if a stranger chanced to call on business at their house, they were as jealously kept from his eyes as they had all been Turks.

The "Fazenda" houses had great iron-studded doors, often a moat, and not infrequently a rusty cannon, though generally dismounted, and a relic of bygone time. The traveller fared, as a general rule, much worse than in the Banda Oriental, for save at the large cattle-farms it was impossible to buy a piece of meat. Admitted to the house, one rarely passed beyond the guest-chamber, a room with four bare white-washed walls; having for furniture a narrow hard-wood table with wrought-iron supports between its legs; chairs cut apparently out of the solid block, and a tin bucket or a large gourd in the corner, with drinking-water; so that one's sojourn at the place was generally brief, and one's departure a relief to all concerned. Still on the frontier the Gaucho influence made itself a little felt, and people were not so inhospitable as they were further in the interior of the land. Two or three leagues beyond the pass there was a little town called "Don Pedrito," towards which we made; but a

"Pampero," whistling from the south, forced us to camp upon a stream known as the "Poncho Verde," where, in the forties, Garibaldi was reported to have fought.

Wet to the skin and without food, we saw a fazenda not a mile away, rode up to it, and for a wonder were asked inside, had dinner in the guest-chamber, the owner sitting but not eating with us; the black Brazilian beans and bacon carried in pompously by three or four stalwart slaves, who puffed and sweated, trod on each other's naked toes, and generally behaved as they had been carrying sacks of corn aboard a ship, only that in this instance no one stood in the gangway with a whip. Much did the conversation run on politics; upon "A Guerra dos Farapos," which it appeared had riven the country in twain what time our host was young. Farapo means a rag, and the Republicans of fifty years ago in Rio Grande had adopted the device after the fashion of "Les gueux." Long did they fight, and our host said: "Praise to God, infructuously," for how could men who wore moustaches and full beards be compared to those who, like our host himself, wore whiskers carefully trimmed in the style of those which at the same epoch in our country were the trade-mark of the Iron Duke? Elective kings, for so the old "conservador" termed presidents, did not find favour in his eyes; and in religion too the "farapos" were seriously astray. They held the doctrine that all creeds should be allowed; which I once held myself, but now incline to the belief that a religion and a name should be bestowed at baptism, and that it should be constituted heresy of the worst kind, and punishable by a fine, to change or palter with either the name or the religion which our fathers have bestowed.

Politics over, we fell a-talking upon other lands; on Europe and England, Portugal, and as to whether "Rondon" was larger than Pelotas, or matters of that sort. Then our host inquired if in "Rondon" we did not use "la bosa," and I not taking the thing up, he rose and stretching out his hands, set them revolving like a saw, and I then saw our supposed national pastime was what he meant; and told him that it was practised, held in repute, and marked us out as a people set apart; and that our greatness was largely founded on the exercise he had endeavoured to depict. We bade farewell, not having seen a woman, even a negress, about the place; but as we left, a rustling at the door showed that the snuff-and-butter-coloured sex had been observing us after the fashion practised in Morocco and in houses in the East. The hospitable "conservador" sent down a slave with a great basket full of oranges; and seated at the camp we ate at least three dozen, whilst the man waited patiently to take the basket back.

Night caught us in the open "camp," a south wind blowing, and the drops congealing as they fell. Three of us muffled in ponchos rode round the horses, whilst the others crouched at the fire, and midnight come, the riders rode to the fire, and stretched on the wet mud slept fitfully, whilst the others took their place. Day came at last; and miserable we looked, wet, cold, and hungry, the fire black out, matches all damp, and nothing else to do but march till the sun rose and made life tolerable. Arrived at a small rancho we got off, and found the owner was a Spaniard from Navarre, married to a Brazilian woman. In mongrel Portuguese he bade us welcome; said he was no Brazilian, and that his house was ours, and hearing Spanish brightened up, and said in broken Spanish, mixed with Portuguese, that he could never learn that language, though he had passed a lifetime in the place. The country pleased him, and though he had an orange garden of some three acres in extent, though palms, mameyes and bananas grew around his door, he mourned for chestnuts, which he remembered in his youth, and said he recollected eating them whilst in Navarre, and that they were better than all the fruit of all Brazil; thinking, like Naaman, that Abana and Pharpar were better than all the waters of Israel, or rivers of Damascus; or perhaps moved in some mysterious way by the remembrance of the chestnut forests, the old grey stone-roofed houses, and the wind whistling through the pine woods of some wild valley of Navarre. At the old Spaniard's house a difficulty cropped up with our men. I having told a man to catch a horse which looked a little wild, he answered he was not a horse-breaker, and I might ride the beast myself. I promptly did so, and asked him if he knew what a wild horse was, and if it was not true that horses which could be saddled without tying their hind legs were tame, and the rest laughing at him, he drew his knife, and running at me, found himself looking down the barrel of a pistol which my partner with some forethought had produced. This brought things to a crisis, and they all left us, with a hundred horses on our hands. Several Brazilians having volunteered, we took them, bought a tame horse accustomed to carry packs, procured a bullock, had it killed, and the meat "jerked"; and making bags out of the hide, filled them with food, for, as the Spaniard said, "in the country you intend to cross you might as well be amongst Moors, for even money will not serve to get a piece of beef." A kindly soul the Spaniard, his name has long escaped me, still he was interesting as but the truly ignorant can ever be. The world to him was a great mystery, as it is even to those who know much more than he; but all the little landmarks of the narrow boundaries of his life he had by heart; and they sufficed him, as the great world itself cannot suffice those who, by living in its current, see its muddiness.

So one day told another, and each night found us on horseback riding round the drove. Through forest, over baking plain, up mountain paths, through marshes, splashing to the saddle-flaps, by lone "fazendas," and again through herds of cattle dotting the plain for miles, we took our way. Little straw huts, each with a horse tied day and night before them, were our fairway marks. Day followed night without adventure but when a horse suddenly threw its rider and a Brazilian peon uncoiled his lasso, and with a jangling of spurs against the stirrups, sprang into life, and in a moment the long snaky rope flew through the air and settled round the runaway just underneath his ears. Once in a clearing, as we plodded on, climbing the last barrier of the mountain range, to emerge upon the district called "Encima de la Sierra," a deer appeared jumping into the air, and coming down again on the same spot repeatedly, the Brazilians said that it was fighting with a snake, for "God has given such instinct to those beasts that they attack and kill all snakes, knowing that they are enemies of man." [1] A scheme of the creation which, if held in its entirety, shows curious lacunæ in the Creator's mind, only to be bridged over by that faith which in itself makes all men equal, that is, of course, when they experience it and recognize its charm. So on a day we crossed the hills, rode through a wood, and came out on a plain at the far end of which a little town appeared.

For about ten leagues in circumference the plain stretched out, walled in with woods, which here and there jutted out into it, forming islands and peninsulas. The flat-roofed town straggled along three flat and sandy streets; the little plaza, planted with mameyes and paraiso trees, served as a lounging-place by day, by night a caravanserai for negroes; in time of rain the streets were turned to streams, and poured their water into the plaza, which became a lake. At the west corner of the square was situated Cardozo's store, the chief emporium, mart, and meeting-place (after the barber's and the chemist's) of the whole town. Two languid and yellow, hermaphroditic young Brazilians dressed in alpaca coats, white trousers, and patent leather boots dispensed the wares, whilst negroes ran about rolling in casks of flour, hogsheads of sugar, and bales of black tobacco

1 The Gauchos often lay a deer-skin on their saddles, and wear boots made of deer-

skin, alleging that serpents are afraid to touch them.

from Bahia, or from Maranhão. Such exterior graces did the little town of the High Cross exhibit to us, wearied with the baking days and freezing nights of the last month's campaign. Whether some Jesuit in the days gone by, when missionaries stood up before their catechumens unsustained by Gatling guns, sheltered but by a rude cross in their hands and their meek lives, had named the place, in commemoration of some saving act of grace done by Jehovah in the conversion of the heathen, none can tell. It may be that the Rood set up on high was but a landmark, or again to mark a frontier line against the heathen to the north, or yet it may have been the grave of some Paulista, who in his foray against the Jesuits in Paraguay died here on his return, whilst driving on before him a herd of converts to become slaves in far San Paulo, to the greater glory of the Lord. All these things may have been, or none of them; but the quiet sleepy place, the forests with their parrots and macaws, their herds of peccaries, their bands of screaming monkeys, the bright-striped tiger-cats, the armadillos, coatis, capibarás, and gorgeous flaming "seibos," all intertwined by ropes of living cordage of lianas, and the supreme content of all the dwellers in the district, with God, themselves, their country, and their lives, still after twenty years is fresh, and stirs me, as the memory of the Pacific stirs a reclaimed "beach-comber" over his grog, and makes him say, "I never should have left them islands, for a man was happy in 'em, living on the beach."

To this commercial centre (centro do commercio) we were advised to go, and there I rode, leaving my partner with the peons riding round the caballada upon the plains. Dressed as I was in the clothes worn by the Gauchos of the Banda Oriental, a hat tied underneath the chin with a black cord, a vicuña poncho, and armed with large resounding silver spurs, I made a blot of colour in Cardozo's shop amongst the quietly dressed Brazilians, who, though they were some of the smartest men in South America upon a horse, were always clad in sober-coloured raiment, wore ordinary store-cut trousers, and had their feet endued with all the graces of a five-dollar elastic-sided boot.

Half-an-hour's talk with the chief partner shattered all our plans. It then appeared that to take horses on to Rio was impossible, the country, after San Paulo, being one dense forest, and even if the horses stood the change of climate, the trip would take a year, thus running off with any profit which we might expect. Moreover, it appeared that mules were in demand throughout Brazil, but horses, till past San Paulo, five hundred miles ahead, but little valued, and almost as cheap, though much inferior in breed to those bred on the plains of Uruguay. He further told us to lose not a day in teaching all the horses to eat salt, for without that they would not live a month, as once the range of mountains passed between Cruz Alta and the plains, no horse or mule could live without its three months' ration of rock-salt; there being in the pasture some malign quality which salt alone could cure. Naturally he had the cheapest salt in the whole town, and as our horses were by this time so thin that it was quite impossible to take them further without rest, they having been a month upon the road, we set about to find an enclosed pasture where we could let them feed.

Xavier Fernandez, a retired slave- and mule-dealer, was the man on whom by accident we fell. Riding about the plain disconsolately, like Arabs changing their pastures, and with our horses feeding near a little pond, we met him. An old straw hat, bed-ticking trousers, and with his naked feet shoved into slippers of carpindo *[sic = carpincho?]* leather, and an iron spur attached to one of them and hanging down at least an inch below his heel, mounted upon a mule saddled with the iron-framed Brazilian saddle, with the addition of a crupper, a thing strange to our eyes, accustomed to the wild horses of the plains, he did not look the type of "landed gentleman," but such he was, owner of flocks and herds, and, in particular, of a well-fenced pasture, enclosing about two leagues of land.

After much talk of things in general, of politics, and of the revolution in progress in the republic we had left, upon our folly in bringing horses, which could go no further into the interior, and of the money we should have made had we brought "bestas," that is, mules, we agreed to pay him so much a month for the use of his fenced pasture, and for our maintenance during the time we stayed. Leaving the horses feeding, watched by the men, we rode to see the place. Upon the way Xavier imparted much of history, a good deal of his lore, and curious local information about Cruz Alta, duly distorted, as befits a reputable man, through the perspective of his predilections, politics, faith, opinions, and general view of life.

We learned that once Cruz Alta was a most important place, that six-and-thirty thousand mules used to be wintered there, and then in spring moved on to the great fair at Surucuba in the Sertão, that is the forest district of San Paulo, and then sold to the merchants from the upper districts of Brazil. But of late years the number had been much reduced, and then stood at about twelve thousand. This he set down to the accursed steam-boats which took them up the coast, to the continual fighting in the state of Uruguay, and generally to the degeneration which he thought he saw in man. In the heyday of the prosperity of the place "gold flowed from every hand," so much so, that even "as mulheres da vida" kept their accounts in ounces; but now money was scarce, and business done in general by barter, coin being hardly even seen except for mules, for which it was imperative, as no one parted with "bestas" except for money down. Passing a little wood we saw a row of stakes driven into the ground, and he informed us that they were evidently left by some Birivas, that is people from San Paulo, after having used them to secure their mules whilst saddling. The Paulistas, we then learned, used the "sirigote," that is, the old-fashioned high-peaked saddle brought from Portugal in times gone by, and not the "recado," the saddle of the Gauchos, which is flat, and suited better for galloping upon a plain than for long marches over mountain passes and through woods. All the points, qualities, with the shortcomings and the failings of a mule, he did rehearse. It then appeared a mule should be mouse-coloured, for the red-coloured mule is of no use, the grey soft-footed, and the black bad-tempered, the piebald fit "for a German," which kind of folk he held in abhorrence mixed with contempt, saying they whined in speaking as it had been the whining of an armadillo or a sloth. The perfect mule should be large-headed, not with a little-hammer head like to a horse, but long and thin, with ears erect, round feet, and upon no account when spurred ought it to whisk its tail, for that was most unseemly, fit but for Germans, Negroes, Indians, and generally for all those he counted senseless people — "gente sem razão"; saying "of course all men are of one flesh, but some are dog's flesh, and let them ride mules who whisk about their tails like cattle in a marsh." Beguiled by these, and other stories, we soon reached the gate of the enclosure, and he, dismounting, drew a key from one of the pockets of his belt and let us in. A short half-hour brought us up to his house, passing through ground all overgrown with miamia and other shrubs which did not promise to afford much pasturage; but he informed us that we must not expect the grasses of the plains up at Cruz Alta, and thus conversing we arrived before his house.

Surrounded by a fence enclosing about an acre, the house stood just on the edge of a thick wood. On one side were the corrals for horses and for cattle, and on the other the quarters of the slaves. In shape the houses resembled a flattish haystack thatched with reeds, and with a verandah rising round it, supported on strong posts. At either end a kind of baldachino, one used as a stable and the other as a kitchen, and in the latter a fire continually alight, and squatted by it night and day a negress, either baking flat, thin girdle-cakes made of maize, shaking the flour out of her hand upon an iron plate, or else filling a gourd of maté with hot water, and running to and fro into the house to give it to her mistress, never apparently thinking it worth while to take the kettle with her into the house.

The family, not quite so white as Xavier himself, consisted of a mother always in slippers, dressed in a skirt and shift, which latter garment always seemed about to fall down to her waist, and two thin, large-eyed, yellowish girls arrayed in vestments like a pillow-case, with a string fastening them at the narrowest place. Slave girls of several hues did nothing and chattered volubly, and their mistress had to stand over them, a slipper in her hand, when maize was pounded in a rough mortar hewn from a solid log, in which the slaves hammered with pestles, one down, the other up, after the fashion of blacksmiths making a horse-shoe, but with groans, and making believe to be extenuated after three minutes' work, and stopping instantly the moment that their mistress went into the house to light her cigarette.

An official in Cruz Alta, known as the Capitão do Matto, holding a status between a gamekeeper and a parish clerk, kept by the virtue of his office a whipping-house, to which recalcitrant or idle slaves were theoretically sent; but in the house of Xavier at least no one took interest enough in anything, except Xavier himself, to take the trouble; and the slaves ruled the female part of the establishment, if not exactly with a rod of iron, still to their perfect satisfaction, cooking and sewing now and then; sweeping, but fitfully; and washing when they wanted to look smart and figure at a dance. The Capitão do Matto was supposed to bring back runaways and keep a leash of bloodhounds, but in the memory of man no one had seen him sally forth, and for the blood-hounds, they were long dead, although he drew regular rations for their maintenance. In the interior of Brazil his office was no sinecure, but in Cruz Alta horses were plentiful, the country relatively easy, and slaves who ran away, which happened seldom, timed their escape so as to put a good day's journey between them and any possible pursuit, and on the evening of the fifth day, if all went well, they got across the frontier into Uruguay.

Terms once arranged, we let our horses loose, laid out rock-salt in lumps, first catching several of the tamest horses, and forcing pieces into their mouths; they taught the others, and we had nothing more to do. We paid our peons off, got our clothes washed, rested, and then found time at first hang heavy on our hands. Hearing an Englishman lived about ten leagues off, we saddled up and rode to visit him. After losing ourselves in a thick forest of some kind of pine, we reached his house, but the *soi-disant* Briton was from Amsterdam, could speak no English, was a little drunk, but asked us to get off and dine with him. During the dinner, which we had all alone, his wife and daughter standing looking at us (he too drunk to eat), pigs ran into the room, a half-grown tapir lay in a corner, and two new-caught macaws screamed horribly, so that, the banquet over, we did not stay, but thanked him in Portuguese, which he spoke badly, and rode off home, determining to sleep at the first wood, rather than face a night in such a place.

The evening caught us near to a forest, the trail, sandy and white, running close to a sort of cove formed in the trees, and here we camped, taking our saddles off, lighting a fire, and lying down to sleep just in the opening of the cove, our horses tied inside. All through the night people appeared to pass along the road. I lay awake half-dozing now and then, and watched the bats, looked at the fire-flies flitting about the trees, heard the harsh howling of the monkeys, the tapirs stamp, the splash made by the lobos and carpinchos as they dashed into the stream, and then slept soundly, and awoke to find one of the horses gone. The moon shone brightly, and, waking up my friend, I told him of our loss. We knew the horse must have a rope attached to him, and that he probably would try to get back to Cruz Alta, along the road we came. My horse was difficult to bit, but by the aid of tying up one foot, and covering his eyes up with a handkerchief, we bitted him, then mounted both of us upon his back, hiding the other saddle behind some grass, and started on the road. The sandy trail was full of horses' tracks, so that we could do nothing but ride on, hoping to catch him feeding by the way. About a league we rode, and then, not seeing him, turned slowly back to get the other saddle, make some coffee, and start home when it was light. To our astonishment, upon arriving at the cove, the other horse was there, and neighing wildly, straining on his rope, and it appeared that he had never gone, but being tied close to the wood had wandered in, and we, thinking he must have gone, being half-dazed with sleep, had never thought of looking at his rope.

Defrauded, so to speak, out of our Englishman, and finding that the horses, after the long journey and the change of water and of grass, daily grew thinner, making it quite impossible to move them, forwards or back, and after having vainly tried to sell them, change them for mules, or sugar, quite without success, no one except some "fazendero" here and there caring for horses in a land where every one rode mules, we settled down to loaf. Once certain we had lost our money and our pains, nothing remained but to wait patiently until the horses got into sufficient state to sell, for all assured us that every day we went further into the interior, they would lose flesh, that we should have them bitten by snakes in the forests, and arrive at Rio, if we ever got there, either on foot, or with but the horses which we rode.

For a short time we had almost determined to push on, even if we arrived at Rio with but a horse apiece. Then came reflection, that reflection which has dressed the world in drab, made cowards of so many heroes, lost so many generous impulses, spoiled so many poems, and which mankind has therefore made a god of, and we decided to remain. Then did Cruz Alta put on a new look. We saw the wondrous vegetation of the woods, felt the full charm of the old-world quiet life, watched the strange multi-coloured insects, lay by the streams to mark the birds, listened for the howlings of the monkeys when night fell; picked the strange flowers, admired the butterflies floating like little blue and yellow albatrosses, their wings opened and poised in the still air, or wondered when a topaz-coloured humming-bird, a red macaw, an orange-and-black toucan, or a red-crested cardinal flitted across our path. Inside the wood behind the house were clearings, made partly by the axe and partly by fire, amongst the tall morosimos, coronillos, and palo santos, and in the clearings known as "roças" grew beans and maize, with mandioca and occasionally barley, and round them ran a prickly hedge either of cactuses or thorny bush, cut down to keep out tapirs and deer, and usually in a straw hut a negro lay, armed with a flint-lock gun to fire at parrots, scare off monkeys, and generally to act as guardian of the place. Orange and lemon trees, with citrons and sweet limes, grew plentifully, and had run wild amongst the woods; bananas were planted in the roça; but what we liked the best was a wild fruit called Guavirami, which grew in patches on the open camp, yellow and round, about the size of a small plum, low-growing, having three or four small stones, cold as an icicle to taste upon the hottest day. A little river ran through the middle of the wood, and in a stream a curious machine was placed for pounding maize, driven by water-power, and unlike any contrivance of a similar nature I had ever seen before. An upright block of wood, burned from the centre of a tree, stood in the stream, hollowed out in the centre to contain the maize; water ran up a little channel, and released a pestle, which fell with a heavy thud upon the corn, with the result that if one left a basket full in the great mortar over-night, by morning it was pounded, saving that labour which God Himself seems to have thought not so ennobling after all, as He first instituted it to carry out a curse.

So one day told, and may, for all I know, have certified another, but we recked little of them, riding into Cruz Alta now and then and eating cakes at the confectioner's, drinking innumerable glasses of sweet Malaga, laying in stores of cigarettes, frequenting all the dances far and near, joining in cattle-markings, races, and anything in short which happened in the place.

Perhaps our greatest friend was one Luis, a slave, born in Angola, brought over quite "Bozal" (or muzzled, as the Brazilians say of negroes who can speak no Portuguese), then by degrees became "ladino," was baptized, bought by our host Xavier, and had remained with him all the remainder of his life. Black, and not comely in the least, bow-legged from constant riding, nose flat, and ears like flappers, a row of teeth almost as strong as a young shark's, flat feet, and crisp Angola wool which grew so thickly on his head that had you thrown a pin on it, it could not have reached the skin, he yet was honest and faithful to the verge of folly; but then, if heaven there be, it can be but inhabited by fools, for wise men, prudent folk, and those who thrive, have their reward like . singers, quickly, and can look for nothing more. He spoke about himself half-pityingly under the style of "Luis o Captivo," was pious, fervent in sacred song, instant in prayer (especially if work was to be done), not idle either, superstitious and affectionate with all the virtues of the most excellent Saint Bernard or Newfoundland dog, and with but little of the imperfections of a man except the power of speech. Often he had been with his master into Uruguay to purchase cattle, or to buy mules for the Brazilian market, and when I asked him if he did not know that he was free the instant that he stepped in Uruguay, said: "Yes, but here I was brought up when I first came from Africa; they have been kind to me, it is to me as the querencia[1] is to a horse, and were it not for that, small fear I should return, to remain here 'feito captivo'; but then I love the place, and, as you know, 'the mangy calf lived all the winter, and then died in the spring.' " He held the Christian faith in its entirety, doubting no dogma, being pleased with every saint, but yet still hankered after fetish,

1 Accustomed pasture.

which he remembered as a child, and seemed to think not incompatible with Christianity, as rendering it more animistic and familiar, smoothing away its angularities, blotting whatever share of reason it may have away, and, above all, giving more scope, if possible, to faith, and thereby opening a larger field of possibilities to the believer's mind.

So Luis with others of his kind, as Jango, Jico, and Manduco, became our friends, looking upon us with that respect mixed with contempt which is the attitude of those who see that you possess the mysterious arts of reading and of writing, but can not see a horse's footprint on hard ground; or if you lose yourself, have to avail yourself of what Luis referred to as "the one-handed watch the sailors use, which points the way to go."

Much did Xavier talk of the Indians of the woods, the "Bugres," as the Brazilians call them; about the "Botocudos," who wear a plug stuck in their lower lip, and shape their ears with heavy weights in youth, so that they hang upon their shoulders; and much about those "Infidel" who through a blowpipe direct a little arrow at the travelling "Christians" in the woods, whose smallest touch is death. It then appeared his father (fica agora na gloria) was a patriot, that is, 'twas he who extirpated the last of all the "Infidel" from the forests where they lived. Most graphically did he tell how the last Indians were hunted down with dogs, and in a pantomime he showed how they jumped up and fell when they received the shot, and putting out his tongue and writhing hideously, he imitated how they wriggled on the ground, explaining that they were worse to kill than is a tapir, and put his father and the other patriots to much unnecessary pain. And as he talked, the woods, the fields, the river and the plain bathed in the sun, which unlike that of Africa does not seem weary of its task, but shines unwearied, looking as it does on a new world and life, shimmered and blazed, great lizards drank its rays flattening themselves upon the stones in ecstasy, humming-birds quivered at the heart of every flower; above the stream the dragon-flies hung poised; only some "Infidel" whom the patriots had destroyed seemed wanting, and the landscape looked incomplete without a knot of them in their high feather crowns stealthily stealing round a corner of the woods.

In the uncomprehended future, incomprehensible and strange, and harder far to guess at than the remotest semi-comprehended past, surely the Spanish travellers and their writings will have a value quite apart from that of any other books. For then the world will hold no "Bugres"; not a "Botocodo" will be left, and those few Indian and Negro tribes who yet persist will be but mere travesties of the whites: their customs lost, their lore, such as it was, despised; and we have proved ourselves wiser than the Creator, who wasted so much time creating beings whom we judged unfit to live, and then, in mercy to ourselves and Him, destroyed, so that no evidence of His miscalculated plan should last to shame Him when He thought of His mistake. So to this end (unknowingly) the missionary works, and all the Jesuits, those who from Paraguay through the Chiquitos, and across the Uruguay, in the dark Moxos, and in the forests of the Andes, gave their lives to bring as they thought life everlasting to the Indians — all were fools. Better by far instead of Bibles, lives of saints, water of baptism, crucifixes, and all the tackle of their trade, that they had brought swords, lances, and a good cross-bow each, and gone to work in the true scientific way, and recognized that the right way with savages is to preach heaven to them and then despatch them to it, for it is barbarous to keep them standing waiting as it were, just at the portals of eternal bliss.

And as we lingered at Cruz Alta, Christmas drew near, and all the people began to make "pesebres," with ox and ass, the three wise men, the star of Bethlehem, the Redeemer (not of the Botocodos and the Bugres) swaddled and laid in straw. Herdsmen and negroes dismounted at the door, fastened their half-wild mules or horses carefully to posts, removed their hats, drawing them down over their faces furtively, and then walked in on tiptoe, their heavy iron spurs clanking upon the ground, to see the Wondrous Child. They lounged about the room, speaking in whispers as he might awake, and then departed silently, murmuring that it was "fermosisimo," and getting on their horses noiselessly were gone, and in a minute disappeared upon the plain. Then came the Novena with prayer and carols, the prayers read by Xavier himself out of a tattered book, all the assembled family joining with unction in the responses, and beating on their breasts. Luis and all the slaves joined in the carols lustily, especially in one sung in a minor key long-drawn-out as a sailor's shanty, or a forebitter sung in a calm whilst waiting for a breeze. After each verse there was a kind of chorus calling upon the sinner to repent, bidding him have no fear but still hold on, and thus exhorting him —

> "Chegai, Chegai, pecador, ao pe da cruz
> Fica nosso Senhor."

Christmas Day found us all at mass in the little church, horses and mules being tied outside the door to the trees in the plaza, and some left hobbled, and all waiting as if St. Hubert was about to issue forth and bless them.

Painfully and long, the preacher dwelt upon the glorious day, the country people listening as it were new to them, and as if all the events had happened on the plain hard by. In the evening rockets announced the joyful news, and the stars shone out over the woods and plains as on the evening when the bright particular star guided the three sheikhs to some such place as was the rancho of our host.

Christmas rejoicings over, a month sped past and found us still, so to speak, wind-bound in the little town. No one would buy our horses, some of which died bitten by snakes. It was impossible to think of going on, and to return equally difficult, so that there seemed a probability of being obliged to pass a lifetime in the place. People began to look at us half in a kindly, half contemptuous way, as people look in general upon those who fail, especially when they themselves have never tried to do anything at all but live, and having done it with considerable success look upon failure as a sort of minor crime, to be atoned for by humility, and to be reprobated after the fashion of adultery, with a half-deprecating laugh. Sometimes we borrowed ancient flint-lock guns and lay in wait for tapirs, but never saw them, as in the thick woods they move as silently as moles in sand, and leave as little trace. Luis told of how, mounted on a half-wild horse, he had long ago lassoed a tapir, and found himself and horse dragged slowly and invincibly towards a stream, the horse resisting terrified, the "gran besta" [1] apparently quite cool, so that at last he had to cut his lasso and escape from what he called the greatest peril of his life; he thought he was preserved partly by the interposition of the saints and partly by a "fetiço" which, in defiance of religion, he luckily had hanging round his neck.

Just when all hope was gone, and we thought seriously of leaving the horses to their fate, and pushing on with some of the best of them towards Rio, a man appeared upon the scene, and offered to buy them, half for money and half "a troco," that is barter, for it appeared he was a pawnbroker and had a house full of silver horse-gear, which had never been redeemed. After much bargaining we closed for three hundred

1 The Brazilians call the tapir "O gran besta." The Guarani word is Mborebi.)

41

dollars and a lot of silver bridles, spurs, whips, and other stuff, after reserving four of the best horses for ourselves to make our journey back. At the head of so much capital our spirits rose, and we determined to push on to Paraguay, crossing the Uruguay and Parana, ride through the Misiones, and at Asuncion, where I had friends, take ship; *aguas abajo*, for the River Plate. We paid our debts and bid good-bye to Xavier, his wife and sallow daughters, and to all the slaves; gave Luis a silver-mounted whip, bought some provisions, put on our silver spurs, bridles, and as much as possible of the silver gear we had become possessed of, and at daybreak, mounted upon a cream-and-white piebald, the "Bayo Overo," and a red bay known as the "Pateador," leading a horse apiece, we passed out of Xavier's "potrero," [1] and started on the road.

During the last few days at Xavier's we had taught the horses we intended to take to Paraguay to eat Indian corn, fastening them up without any other food all day, and putting salt into their mouths. The art once learnt, we had to stand beside them whilst they ate, to keep off chickens and pigs who drove them from their food, the horses being too stupid to help themselves. If I remember rightly, their ration was eight cobs, which we husked for them in our hands, blistering our fingers in the process as they had been burned. But now the trouble of the process was repaid, the horses going strongly all day long. We passed out of the little plain, skirted a pine-wood, rode up a little hill, and saw the country, stretching towards the Uruguay, a park-like prairie interspersed with trees. Cruz Alta, a white patch shining against the green-grey plain encircled with its woods, was just in sight, the church-tower standing like a needle in the clear air against the sky. Half a league more and it dropped out of view, closing the door upon a sort of half Boeotian Arcady, but remaining still a memory after twenty years, with all the little incidents of the three months' sojourn in the place fresh, and yet seeming as they had happened not to myself, but to a person I had met, and who had told the tale.

By easy stages we journeyed on, descending gradually towards the Uruguay, passing through country almost unpopulated, so large were the "fazendas," and so little stocked. In the last century the Jesuits had here collected many tribes of Indians, and their history, is it not told in the pages of Montoya Lozano, Padre Guevara, and the other chroniclers of the doings of the "Company," and to be read in the Archivo de Simancas,

---

1 Potrero is a fenced pasture, from "potro," a colt.

in that of Seville, and the uncatalogued "legajos" of the national library at Madrid? Throughout the country that we passed through, the fierce Paulistas had raided in times gone by, carrying off the Christian Indians to be slaves. The Portuguese and Spaniards had often fought — witness the names "O matto[1] Portogues, O matto Castelhano," and the like, showing where armies had manoeuvred, whilst the poor Indians waited like sheep, rejoicing when the butchers turned the knife at one another's throats. To-day all trace of Jesuits and Missions have long disappeared, save for a ruined church or two, and here and there a grassy mound called in the language of the country a "tapera," [2] showing where a settlement had stood.

We camped at lonely ranchos inhabited, in general, by free negroes, or by the side of woods, choosing, if possible, some little cove in the wood, in which we tied the horses, building a fire in the mouth, laid down and slept, after concocting a vile beverage bought in Cruz Alta under the name of tea, but made I think of birch-leaves, and moistening pieces of the hard jerked beef in orange-juice to make it palatable.

So after five or six days of steady travelling, meeting, if I remember rightly, not a living soul upon the way, except a Gaucho from the Banda Oriental, who one night came to our fire, and seeing the horrible brew of tea in a tin-pot asked for a little of the "black water," not knowing what it was, we reached the Uruguay. The river, nearly half-a-mile in breadth, flowed sluggishly between primeval woods, great alligators basked with their backs awash, flamingoes fished among the shallow pools, herons and cranes sat on dead stumps, vultures innumerable perched on trees, and in the purple bunches of the "seibos" humming- birds seemed to nestle, so rapid was their flight, and over all a darkish vapour hung, blending the trees and water into one, and making the "balsa," as it laboured over after repeated calls, look like the barque of Styx. Upon the other side lay Corrientes, once a vast mission territory, but today, in the narrow upper portion that we traversed, almost a desert, that is a desert of tall grass with islands of timber dotted here and there, and an occasional band of ostriches scudding across the plain.

Camped by a wood about a quarter of a league from a lonely rancho, we were astonished, just at even-fall, by the arrival of the owner of the

1 "Matto" is a wood in Portuguese, and at these two Mattos, tradition says, the rival armies had encamped.

2 Except for the Gaelic "larach," I know no word in any language which exactly corresponds to "tapera," as indicating the foundations of a house grassed over.

house mounted upon a half-wild horse, a spear in his hand, escorted by his two ragged sons mounted on half-wild ponies, and holding in their hands long canes to which a broken sheep-shear had been fixed. The object of his visit, as he said, was to inquire if we had seen a tiger which had killed some sheep, but his suspicious glance made me think he thought we had designs upon his cattle, and he had come to reconnoitre us; but our offer of some of the Cruz Alta tea soon made us friends, and after drinking almost a quart of it, he said "Muy rico," and rode back to his house.

The third day's riding brought us to the little town of Candelaria, built on a high bank over the Parana. Founded on Candlemas Day in 1665, it was the chief town of the Jesuit missions. Here, usually, the "Provincial" [1] resided, and here the political business of their enormous territory was done. Stretching almost from Cruz Alta to within fifty leagues of Asuncion del Paraguay, and from Yapeyú upon the Uruguay almost to the "Salto de Guayra" upon the Parana, the territory embraced an area larger than many a kingdom, and was administered without an army, solely by about two hundred priests. The best proof of the success of their administration is that in these days the Indians, now to be numbered by a few thousand, were estimated at about two hundred thousand, and peopled all the country now left desolate, or which at least was desolate at the time of which I write. Even Azara,[2] a bitter opponent of their system, writes of the Jesuit rule — "Although the Fathers had supreme command, they used their power with a gentleness and moderation which one cannot but admire." [3]

I leave to the economists, with all the reverend rabble rout of politicians, statistic-mongers and philanthropists, whether or not two hundred thousand living Indians were an asset in the world's property; and to the pious I put this question. If, as I suppose, these men had souls just as immortal as our own, might it not have been better to preserve their bodies, those earthly envelopes without which no soul can live, rather than by exposing them to all those influences which the Jesuits dreaded, to kill them off, and leave their country without population for a hundred years?

1 Provincial: called *Superior de las misiones.* .
2 Feliz de Azara, *Descripcion y Historia del Paraguay.*
3 Es menester convenir, en que aunque los padres mandaban alli en todo, usaron de
   su autoridad con una suavidad y moderacion que no puede menos de admirarse.
   - Azara, *Historia del Paraguay*, Tom. I, p.282: Madrid 1847.

But at the time of which I write neither my partner nor I cared much for speculations of that kind, but were more occupied with the condition of our horses, for, by that time, the "Bayo Overo" and the "Pateador" were become part and parcel of ourselves, and we thought more about their welfare than that of all the Indians upon earth.

La Candelaria, at the time when we passed through, was fallen from its proud estate, and had become a little Gaucho country town with sandy streets and horses tied at every door — a barren sun-burnt plaza, with a few Japanese ash-trees and Paraisos; the "Commandancia" with the Argentine blue-and-white barred flag, and trade-mark rising sun, hanging down listlessly against the post, and for all remnants of the Jesuit sway, the college turned into a town-hall, and the fine church, which seemed to mourn over the godless, careless, semi-Gaucho population in the streets. Here we disposed of our spare horses, bidding them good-bye, as they had been old friends, and got the "Bayo Overo" and the "Pateador" shod for the first time in their lives, an operation which took the united strength of half-a-dozen men to achieve, but was imperative, as their feet, accustomed to the stone-less plains of Paraguay, had suffered greatly in the mountain paths. In Candelaria, for the first time for many months, we sat down to a regular meal, in a building called "El Hotel Internacional"; drank wine of a suspicious kind, and seemed to have arrived in Paris, so great the change to the wild camps beside the forests, or the nights passed in the lone ranchos of the hilly district of Brazil.

A balsa drawn by a tug-boat took us across the Parana, here more than a mile broad, to Ytapua, and upon landing we found ourselves in quite another world. The little Paraguayan town of Ytapua, called by the Jesuits Encarnacion, lay, with its little port below it (where my friend Enrico Clerici had his store), upon a plateau hanging above the stream. The houses, built of canes and thatched with straw, differed extremely from the white "azotea" houses of the Candelaria on the other side. The people, dress, the vegetation, and the mode of life, differed still more in every aspect. The Paraguayan, with his shirt hanging outside his white duck trousers, bare feet, and cloak made of red cloth or baize, his broad straw hat and quiet manner, was the complete antithesis of the high-booted, loose-trousered, poncho-wearing Correntino, with his long knife and swaggering Gaucho air. The one a horseman of the plains, the other a footman of the forests; the Correntino brave even to rashness when taken man for man, but so incapable of discipline as to be practically useless as a soldier. The other as quiet as a sheep, and individually patient even to suffering blows, but once gathered together and instructed in the use of arms, as good a soldier, when well led, as it is possible to find; active and temperate, brave, and, if rather unintelligent, eager to risk his life at any time at the command of any of his chiefs. Such was the material from which Lopez, coward and grossly incompetent as he was, formed the battalions which for four years kept both Buenos Ayres and Brazil at bay, and only yielded when he himself was killed, mounted, as tradition has it, on the last horse of native breed left in the land.

But if the people and their dwellings were dissimilar, the countries in themselves were to the full at least as different All through the upper part of Corrientes the soil is black, and the country open, park-like prairie dotted with trees; in Ytapua and the surrounding district, the earth bright red, and the primeval forest stretches close to the water's edge. In Corrientes still the trees of the Pampas are occasionally seen, Talas and ñandubay with Coronillo and Lapacho; whereas in Paraguay, as by a bound, you pass to Curupay,[1] Tatané,[2] the Tarumá,[3] the Ñandipá[4] the Jacaranda, and the Paratodo with its bright yellow flowers; whilst upon every tree lianas cling with orchidaceæ, known to the natives as "flowers of the air" and through them all flit great butterflies, humming-birds dart, and underneath the damp vegetation of the sub-tropics, emphorbiaceæ, solanaceæ, myrtaceæ, and flowers and plants to drive a thousand botanists to madness, blossom and die unnamed. Here, too, the language changed, and Guarani became the dominant tongue, which, though spoken in Corrientes, is there used but occasionally, but among Paraguayans is their native speech, only the Alcaldes, officers, and upper classes as a general rule (at that time) speaking Spanish, and even then with a strange accent and much mixed with Guarani.

Two days we passed in Ytapua resting our horses, and I renewed my friendship with Enrico Clerici, an Italian, who had served with Garibaldi, and who, three years ago, I had met in the same place and given him a silver ring which he reported galvanized, and was accustomed to lend as a great favour for a specific against rheumatism. He kept a pulperia, and being a born fighter, his delight was, when a row occurred (which he

1 Piptadenia communis.
2 Acacia maleolens.
3 Vitex Taruma.
4 Genipa Americana.

styled "una barulla de Jesu Cristo"), to clear the place by flinging empty bottles from the bar. A handsome, gentlemanlike man, and terrible with a bottle in his hand, whether as weapon of offence or for the purposes of drink; withal well educated, and no doubt by this time long dead, slain by his favourite weapon, and his place filled by some fat, double-entry Basque or grasping Catalan, or by some portly emigrant from Germany.

Not wishing to be confined within a house, a prey to the mosquitoes, we camped in the chief square, and strolling round about the town, I came on an old friend.

Not far outside the village a Correntino butcher had his shop, a little straw-thatched hut, with strings of fresh jerked beef festooning all the place; the owner stood outside dressed in the costume of a Gaucho of the southern plains. I did not know him, and we began to talk, when I perceived, tied underneath a shed, a fine, dark chestnut horse, saddled and bitted in the most approved of Gaucho style. He somehow seemed familiar, and the Correntino, seeing me looking at his horse, asked if I knew the brand, but looking at it I failed to recognize it, when on a sudden my memory was lighted up. Three years ago, in an "estero" [1] outside Caapucú, at night, journeying in company with a friend, one Hermann, whose only means of communication with me was a jargon of Spanish mixed with "Plaat Deutsch," we met a Correntino, and as our horses mutually drowned our approach by splashing with their feet, our meeting terrified us both. Frightened, he drew his knife, and I a pistol, and Hermann lugged out a rusty sword, which he wore stuck through his horse's girths. But explanations followed, and no blood was shed, and then we drew aside into a little hillock, called in the language of the place an "albardon," sat down and talked, and asking whence he came was told from Ytapua. Now Ytapua was three days' journey distant on an ordinary horse, and I looked carefully at the horse, and wondered why his owner had ridden him so hard. He, I now saw, was the horse I had seen that night, and the Correntino recognized me, and laughing said he had killed a man near Ytapua, and was (as he said) "retreating" when he met me in the marsh. The horse, no doubt, was one of the best for a long journey I have ever seen, and after quoting to his owner that

1 "Estero" is the word used in Paraguay for a marsh. These marshes are generally hard at the bottom, so that you splash through them for leagues without danger, though the water is often up to the horse's girths.

"a dark chestnut horse may die, but cannot tire," [1] we separated, and, no doubt, for years afterwards our meeting was the subject of his talk.

No doubt the citizens of Ytapua were scandalized at our not coming to the town, and the Alcalde came to interview us, but we assured him that in virtue of a vow we slept outside, and in a moment all his fears were gone.

Striking right through the then desolated Misiones, passing the river Aguapey, our horses almost swimming, skirting by forests where red macaws hovered like hawks and parrots chattered; passing through open plains grown over here and there with Yatais,[2] splashing for hours through wet esteros, missing the road occasionally, as I had travelled it but once, and then three years ago, and at the time I write of huts were few and far between, and population scanty, we came, upon the evening of the second day, near to a place called Ñacuti. This was the point for which I had been making, for near it was an estancia[3] called the "Potrero San Antonio," the property of Dr. Stewart, a well-known man in Paraguay. Nature had seemed to work to make the place impregnable. On three sides of the land, which measured eight or ten miles in length on every side, forks of a river ran, and at the fourth they came so close together that a short fence, not half-a-mile in length, closed up the circle, and cattle once inside were safe but for the tigers, which at that time abounded, and had grown so fierce by reason of the want of population that they sometimes killed horses or cows close to the door of the house. A short "picada," of about a quarter of a mile in length, cut through the wood, led to the gate. Through it in times gone by I often rode at night in terror, with a pistol in my hand, the heavy foliage of the trees brushing my hat, and thinking every instant that a tiger would jump out. One night when close up to the bamboo bars I heard a grunt, thought my last hour had come, fired, and brought something down; approached, and found it was a peccary; and then, tearing the bars down in a hurry, got to horse, and galloped nine miles to the house, thinking each moment that the herd of peccaries was close behind and panting for my blood.

On this occasion all was still; the passage through the orange trees was dark, their scent oppressive, as the leaves just stirred in the hot north

1 Alazan tostado antes muerto que cansado. The Arabs think highly of the dark
  chestnut. See the Emir Abdul Kader on Horsemanship.
2 The Yatai is a dwarf palm. It is the Cocos Yatais of botanists.
3 Cattle-farm.

wind, and fire-flies glistened to and fro amongst the flowers; great bats flew heavily, and the quarter of a mile seemed mortal, and as if it led to hell.

Nothing occurred, and coming to the bars we found them on the ground; putting them up we conscientiously cursed the fool who left them out of place, and riding out into the moonlight, after a little trouble found the sandy, deep-banked trail which led up to the house. All the nine miles we passed by islands of great woods, peninsulas and archipelagos jutting out into the still plain, and all their bases swathed in white mists like water: the Yatais looked ghostly standing starkly in the grass; from the lagoons came the shrill croak of frogs, great moths came fluttering across our path, and the whole woods seemed filled with noise, as if the dwellers in them, silent through the day, were keeping holiday at night. As for the past two days we had eaten nothing but a few oranges and pieces of jerked beef, moistening them in the muddy water of the streams, our talk was of the welcome we should get, the supper, and of the comfortable time we then should pass for a few days to give our horses rest.

We passed the tiger-trap, a structure built after the fashion of an enormous mouse-trap, of strong bamboos; skirted along a wood in which an ominous growling and rustling made our horses start, and then it struck me as curious that there were no cattle feeding in the plain, no horses, and that the whole potrero seemed strangely desolate; but the house just showing at the edge of a small grove of peach-trees drove all these speculations out of my head: thinking upon the welcome, and the dinner, for we had eaten nothing since daybreak, and were fasting, as the natives say, from everything but sin, we reached the door. The house was dark, no troop of dogs rushed out to bark and seize our horses' tails; we shouted, hammered with our whips, fired our revolvers, and nothing answered us.

Dismounting, we found everything bolted and barred, and going to the back, on the kitchen-hearth a few red embers, and thus knew that some one had been lately in the place. Nothing to eat, the woods evidently full of tigers, and our horses far too tired to start again, we were just about to unsaddle and lie down and sleep, when a white figure stole out from the peach-trees, and tried to gain the shelter of the corral some sixty yards away. Jumping on horseback we gave chase, and coming up with the fugitive found it to be a Paraguayan woman, who with her little daughter were the sole inhabitants, her husband having gone to the nearest village to buy provisions, and left her all alone, warning her earnestly before he left to keep the doors shut during the night on account of the tigers, and not to venture near the woods even in daylight till he should have come back. Finding herself confronted by two armed, mounted men, dressed in the clothes of Correntinos, who had an evil reputation in Paraguay, her terror was extreme. Her daughter, a little girl of eight or nine, crept out from behind a tree, and in a moment we were friends. Unluckily for us, she had no food of any kind, and but a little maté, which she prepared for us. She then remembered that the trees were covered with peaches, and went out and gathered some, but they were hard as stones; nevertheless we ate a quantity of them, and having tied our horses close to the house, not twenty paces from the door, in long lush grass, we lay down in the verandah, and did not wake till it was almost noon. When we awoke we found the woman had been up betimes and gone on foot five or six miles away to look for food. She brought some mandioca, and two or three dozen oranges, and a piece of almost putrefied jerked beef, all which we ate as heartily as if it had been the most delicious food on earth.

To my annoyance I found my horse weak and dejected, and several large clots of dried-up blood under the hair of his mane, and saw at once a vampire bat had fixed upon him, and no doubt sucked almost a quart of blood. We washed him in a pond close to the house, and he got better, and after eating some of the hard and unripe peaches we again lay down to sleep. By evening the woman's husband had returned, and proved to be a little lame and withered-looking man, mounted upon a lean and skinny horse. He undertook to guide us to Asuncion, remarking that it was twenty years since he had seen the capital, but that he knew the road as if he was accustomed to go there every day. With a slight lapsus this turned out to be the case, and just at daybreak we left the Potrero San Antonio, where once before I had passed a month roaming about the woods, waiting for tigers in a tree at night, and never thinking that, in three years' time, I should return and find it desolate. It seemed that Dr. Stewart, not finding the speculation pay, had sold his cattle, and his manager, one Oliver, a Californian "Forty-niner," and his Paraguayan wife, had removed to a place some twenty leagues away, upon the road towards Asuncion.

There we determined to go and rest our horses, and left the place, our guide Florencio's wife impressing on him to be sure and bring her back a little missal from the capital, and he, just like an Arab or an Indian leaving home, unmoved, merely observing that the folk in Asuncion were "muy ladino" (very cunning), and it behoved a Christian to take care.

A day's long march brought us near Santa Rosa, and our guide here fell into his first and only error on the road. Pursuing an interminable palm-wood, we came out upon a little plain, all broken here and there with stunted Yatais, then to our great disgust the road bifurcated, and our guide insisted on striking to the left, though I was almost certain it was wrong. After an hour of heavy ploughing through the sand, I suddenly saw two immense palm-trees about a league away upon the right, and luckily remembered that they stood one on each side of the old Jesuit church at Santa Rosa, and after an hour of scrambling through a stony wood arrived at the crossing of the little river just outside the place. Girls carrying water-jars upon their heads, and dressed in long white shifts, embroidered round the neck with coarse black lace, were going and coming in a long procession to the stream. A few old men and about thirty boys composed almost the entire male population of the town. Women entirely ruled the roast *[sic = roost]*, and managed everything, and, as far as I can now recall, did it not much more inefficiently than men. The curious wooden church, dark, and with overhanging eaves, and all the images of saints still left from Jesuit times in choir and nave, with columns hewn from the trunks of massive trees, stood in the centre of the village, which was built after the fashion of a miner's *[miners']* "row," or of a St. Simonian phalanstery, each dwelling at least a hundred feet in length, and all partitioned off in the inside for ten or fifteen families. The plaza was overgrown with grass, and on it donkeys played, chasing each other up and down, and sometimes running up the wooden steps of the great church, and stumbling down again. Those who had horses led them down to bathe, cut "pindo"[1] for them, rode them at evening time, and passed their time in dressing and in combing them to get them into condition for the Sunday's running at the ring, which sport introduced by the Jesuits has continued popular in all the villages of the Misiones up to the present time. The women flirted with the men, who by their rarity were at a premium, gave themselves airs, and went about surrounded by a perpetual and admiring band. The single little shop, which contained needles, gunpowder, and gin, was kept by an Italian, who, as he told me, liked the place, lent money, was a professing and quite unabashed polygamist, and I have no doubt long ere this time has made a fortune, and retired to live at Genoa in the self-same green velvet suit in which he left his home.

1 Cocos Australis.

In this Arcadia we remained some days, and hired several girls to bathe the horses, which they performed most conscientiously, splashing and shouting in the stream for hours at a time, and bringing back the horses clean, and garnished with flowers in their manes. I rode one day to see a village two or three leagues away, where report said some of the Jesuit books had been preserved; got lost, and passed the night in a small clearing, where a fat and well-cared-for-looking handsome roan horse was tied. On seeing me he broke his picket-rope, ran furiously four or five times round me in circles, and then advancing put his nostrils close to the nostrils of my horse, and seemed to talk to him. His owner, an old Paraguayan, lame from a wound received in jumping from a canoe on to the deck of a Brazilian ironclad, told me his horse had been with him far into the interior, and for a year had never seen another horse. But, he said, "Tata Dios has given every animal its speech after its kind, and he is glad to see your horse, and is no doubt asking him the news."

During the night, I cannot say exactly what the two horses talked about, but the old Paraguayan talked for hours of his adventures in the lately terminated war. It appeared that he, with seven companions, thinking to take a Brazilian ironclad anchored in the Paraguay, concealed themselves in a small canoe, behind some drift-wood, and floating plants called "camalotes," drifted down with the stream, and coming to the ship jumped with a yell aboard. The Brazilians, taken by surprise, all ran below, and the poor Paraguayans thinking the ship was theirs, sat quietly down upon the deck to plan what they should do. Seeing them off their guard, some of the crew turned a gun upon them, and at the first fire killed six, and wounded my host, who sprang into the stream, and gained the bank, but most unluckily not on the Paraguayan side. As at that time the Chaco Indians, who had profited by the war to make invasions upon every side, killed every Christian, as my host said "sin perdon," so he remained half starving for a night and day. On the third morning, wounded as he was, and seeing he must starve or else be killed if seen by Indians, he got a fallen tree, and with great difficulty, and marvellously escaping the fierce fish who come like wolves to the scent of blood, and unmolested by the alligators, he reached the other side. There he was found by some women, lying unconscious on the river-bank, was cured, and though scarred in a dozen places, and lame for life, escaped, as he informed me, by his devotion to San José, whom he described under the title of the "husband of the mother of our Lord."

In the morning he rode a league with me upon the way, and as we parted his horse neighed shrilly, reared once or twice, and plunged, and when we separated I looked back and saw the devotee of St. Joseph sitting as firmly as a centaur, as his horse loped along the sandy palm-tree-bordered trail. During our stay at Santa Rosa, which was an offshoot from the more important mission of Santa Maria de Fé, although they had no priest the people gathered in the church, the Angelus was rung at evening for the "oracion," and every one on hearing it took off his hat and murmured something that he thought apposite. Thus did ceremony, always much more important than mere faith, continue, and no doubt blessed the poor people to the full as much as if it had been duly sanctified by a tonsured priest, and consecrated by a rightly constituted offertory. We left the place with real regret, and to this day, when in our hurried life I dream of peace, my thoughts go back to the old Paraguayan Jesuit "capilla" lost in the woods of Morosimo, Curupay, and Yba-hai, and with its two tall feathery palm-trees rustling above the desecrated church; to the long strings of white-robed women carrying water-jars, and to the old-world life, perhaps by this time altered and swept away, or yet again not altered, and passing still in the same quiet fashion as when we were there.

Little by little we left the relatively open country of the Misiones behind, and passing Ibyra-pucú, San Roque, and Ximenes, came to the river Tebicuary. We passed it in canoes, the horses swimming, with their backs awash and heads emerging like water-monsters, whilst an impassive Indian paddled in the stern, and a young girl stood in the bows wielding a paddle like a water-sprite. The river passed, we got at once into the forests, and followed winding and narrow paths, worn by the footsteps of the mules of ages so deeply that our heavy Gaucho spurs almost trailed on the ground, whilst overhead lianas now and then quite formed a roof, and in the heavy air winged animals of every kind made life a burden. At last, leaving the little town of Quiquyó upon the right, we emerged on to a high and barren plain near Caapucú. On the evening of the second day from where we crossed the river, we came to Caballero Punta, just underneath a range of flattish hills, and riding to the door at a sharp gallop, pulled up short, and found ourselves greeted by the ex manager of the Potrero San Antonio, my friend the "Forty-niner," and for the first time for four months saw a familiar face. Gentle and kindly, though quick on the trigger, as befitted one who had crossed the plains in '48 on foot, and with his whole possessions packed on a bullock, passing the Rocky Mountains alone, and through the hostile tribes at that time powerful and savage, John Oliver was one of those strange men who, having passed their lives in perils and privations, somehow draw from them that very kindliness which those living in what appear more favourable surroundings so often lack. Born somewhere in the Yorkshire Dales (these he remembered well), and as he thought "back somewhere in the twenties," he had suffered all his life from the strange fever which impels some men to search for gold. Not on the Stock Exchange, or any of those places where it might reasonably be expected to be found, but in Australia, California, Mexico, in short wherever life was hard, death easy, and experience to be gathered, he sought with pick and shovel, rocker and pan and cradle, the "yellow iron," as the Apaches used to call it, which sought and found after the fashion of his kind, enriches some one else. From California he had drifted to Peru, from thence to Chile, but finding silver-mining too laborious or too lucrative for his conversing, and hearing of a fertile diggings opened in the Republic of Uruguay, had migrated there, and arrived somehow in Paraguay to find that the enchantment of his life was done, and settled down to live. Tall, and with long grey hair hanging in Western fashion down his back, a careful horseman after the style of the trappers of the West, his pale blue eyes looked out upon the world as with an air of doubt; yet he had served in San Francisco as a "vigilante," sojourned with Brigham Young in Salt Lake City, leaving as he confessed two or three wives among the saints, sat in Judge Lynch's court a dozen times, most probably had killed a man or two; still, to my fancy, if the meek are to inherit any portion of the earth, his share should not be small.

He made us welcome, and his wife waited upon us, never presuming to sit down and eat, but standing ready with a napkin fringed with lace, to wipe our hands, pressing the food upon us, and behaving generally as if she found herself in the presence of some strange beings of an unfamiliar race. He said he had no children and was glad of it, for he explained that "Juaneeter was a good woman, but 'uneddicated,' and he had never taken thoroughly to half-caste pups, though he remembered some born of a Pi-Ute woman, way back somewhere about the fifties, who he supposed by now were warriors, and had taken many scalps." His wife stood by, not understanding any English and but little Spanish, which he himself spoke badly, and their talk was held in a strange jargon mixed with Guarani, without a verb, without a particle, and yet sufficient for the two simple creatures whom a strange fate, or a discerning, ever-watchful Providence, had thus ordained to meet. No books were in the place, except a Bible, which he read little of late years, partly from failing sight, and partly, as he said, because he had detected what seemed to him "exaggerations," chiefly in figures and as to the number of the unbelievers whom the Chosen People slew. Two days or more, for time was taken no account of in his house, we waited with him, talking late every night of Salt Lake, Brigham Young, the Mountain-meadows Massacre, Kit Carson, Cochise and Mangas Coloradas, and matters of that kind which interested him, and which, when all is said, are just as interesting to those attuned to them, as is polemical theology, theories of art, systems of jurisprudence, the origin of the Atoll Islands, or any of the wise futilities with which men stock their minds. We parted on the third or fourth, or perhaps the fifth or sixth day, knowing that we should never meet again, and taking off my silver spurs I gave them to him, and he presented me with a light summer poncho woven by his wife. Much did he thank me for my visit, and made me swear never to pass the district without stopping at his house. This I agreed to do, and if I pass again either by Caballero Punta or by Caapucú, I will keep faith; but he, I fear, will have deceived me, and in the churchyard of the "capilla," under a palm-tree, with a rough cross above him, I shall find my simple friend.

Three or four days of jogging steadily, passing by Quindy, and through the short "estero" of Acaai, which we passed splashing for several hours up to the girths, brought us to Paraguari, which, with its saddle-shaped mountain overhanging it, stood out a mark for leagues upon the level plain. Seldom in any country have I seen a railway so fall into the landscape as did the line at the little terminus of this the only railway in all Paraguay. The war had left the country almost in ruins, business was at a standstill, food was scarce, and but for a bale or two of tobacco, and a hide-sack or two of yerba, the train went empty to and fro. But as the people always wanted to go to the capital in search of work, six or eight empty trucks were always sent with every train. On them the people (mostly women) swarmed, seated like flies, upon the top and sides, dangling their legs outside like people sitting on a wharf, talking incessantly, all dressed in white, and every one, down to the smallest children, smoking large cigars. Six hours the passage took, if all went well, the distance being under fifty miles. If aught went wrong, it took a day or more, and at the bridges the trucks were all unhooked and taken over separately, so rotten was the state of the whole line, and in addition every here and there bridges had been blown away during the war, and roughly rendered serviceable by shoring up with wood. To meet a train labouring and puffing through the woods, the people clustering like bees upon the trucks, the engineer seated in shirt-sleeves, whilst some women stoked the fire, was much the same as it is to meet a caravan meandering across the sands. If you desired to talk with any one the train incontinently stopped, the passengers got out, relit their cigarettes, the women begged, the time of day was passed, and curiosity thus satisfied you passed on upon the road, and the "Maquina-guazu,"[1] as it was called, pursued contentedly the jolting and uneven tenor of its way. We naturally despised it, though the conductor, scenting business, offered to take us and our horses at almost any price we chose.

By the Laguna Ypocarai we took our way; skirting along its eastern shores, then desolate, and the whole district almost depopulated, we passed by palm-groves and deserted mandioca patches, reed cottages in ruins, watched the flamingoes fishing in the lake, the alligators lying motionless, and saw an Indian all alone in a dug-out canoe, casting his line as placidly as he had lived before the coming of the Spaniards to the land. A red-blue haze hung on the waters of the lake, reflected from the bright red earth, peeping between the trees, and on the islands drifts of mist gave an effect as if the palms were parachutes dropped from balloons, or perhaps despatched from earth to find out whether in the skies there could be anything more lovely than this quiet inland sea. Close to the top end of the lake stands Aregua, once under the Mercenary friars of Asuncion, who, as Azara says, having made the people of the place work for them for near two hundred years, began to think they were indeed their slaves, till an official sent from Spain in 1783 gave them their liberty, and the Mercenaries (as he says) at once retreated in disgust. Here we fell in with a compatriot, who at our time of meeting him was drunk. He told us that he passed his time after the fashion of the patriarchs in the Old Testament, and on arriving at his house it seemed he was provided with several wives, but of the flocks and herds, and other trade-marks of his supposed estate, we saw no trace. Still he was hospitable, setting the women to cut down pindo for the horses, take them to water, bathe them, and finally to cook some dinner for ourselves. His chief complaint was that his wives were Catholics, and now and then trudged off to mass, and left him without any one to cook his food. I doubted personally if

1 Guazu is big, in Guarani.

if a change of creed would better things, but held my peace, seeing the man set store by the faith which he had learnt in youth and still said he practised, but, as far as I could see, only by cursing the religion of the people of the place. We left his house without regret, though he was hospitable and half drunk for nearly all the time that we were there, and started on our last day's march considerably refreshed by meeting one who in a foreign land, far from home ties and moral influences, yet still pursued the simple practice of the faith which he had learned at home.

Luque, upon its little hill, the Campo Grande, like a dry lake, surrounded by thick woods on every side, and then the Recoleta, we passed, and entering the red sandy road made at the conquest to move troops upon, we saw the churches of Asuncion only a league away. And yet we lingered, walking our horses slowly in the deep red sand, passing the strings of countrywomen with baskets on their heads, driving their donkeys packed with sugar-cane, and smoking as they went; we lingered, feeling that the trip was done; not that we minded that our fortunes were not made, but vaguely felt that for the last five months we had lived a time which in our lives we should not see again, and fearing rather than looking forward to all the approaching change. The horses too were fat, in good condition, had become old friends, knew us so well we never tied them, but all night in camp left them to feed, being certain that they would not stray; and thus to leave them at the end of a long trip seemed as unreasonable as to part from an old friend simply because death calls.

The road grew wider, passed through some scattered houses, buried in orange and guayaba trees, ran through some open patches where grew wild indigo and castor-oil plants, with a low palm-scrub, entered a rancheria just outside the town, and then turned to a sandy street which merged in a great market, where, as it seemed, innumerable myriads were assembled, all chattering at once, or so it struck us coming from the open solitary plains and the dark silent woods. The lowness of the river having stopped the Brazilian mail-boat from coming down from Corumba, we put up at the "Casa Horrocks," the resort of all the waifs and strays storm-bound in Paraguay. The town buried in vegetation, the sandy streets, all of them water-courses after a night's rain, the listless life, the donkeys straying to and fro, the white-robed women, with their hair hanging down their backs, and cut square on the forehead after the style so usual amongst Iceland ponies, the great unfinished palaces, the squares with grass five or six inches high, and over all the reddish haze blending the palm-trees, houses, sandy streets, the river and the distant Chaco into a copper-coloured whole at sunset, rise to my memory like the reflection of a dream. A dream seen in a convex mirror, opening away from me as years have passed, the actual things, men, actions, and occurrences of daily life seem swollen in it at the far end of some perspective, but the impression of the whole fresh and clear-cut in memory, standing out as boldly as the last day when on the "Pateador" I had a farewell gallop on the beach. Adios, "Pateador," or "till so long" — horses will be born as good, better, ten thousand times more valuable, and dogs will eat them, but for myself, and for the owner of the "Bayo Overo," not all the coursers of the sun could stir the reminiscences of youth, of lonely camping-grounds, long nights in drenching rain, struggles with wind, wild gallops in the dark; the hopes and fears of the five months when we went fortune-seeking, and by God's mercy failed in our search, as the mere mention of those names forgotten to all the world except ourselves.

Eight or ten days had passed away, and we grew quite familiar with the chief features of the place, having made acquaintance with the Brazilian officers of the army and the fleet, the German apothecary, with Dr. Stewart, the chief European of the place, when news came that the Brazilian mail-boat had at last arrived. We bade our friends good-bye, entrusted both our horses to the care of Horrocks, fed them ourselves for the last time, and went on board the ship; a coppery haze hung over everything, the heat raising a faint quivering in the air, the thick yellowish water of the stream lapping against the vessel's sides like oil, the boat shoved off, our friends perspiring in the sun raising a washed-out cheer. The vessel swung into the stream, her paddles turned, the great green flag with the orange crown imperial flapped at the jackstaff, and the town dropped rapidly astern.

A quarter of a league and the church towers, tall palm-trees, the unfinished palaces, and the great theatre began to fade into the haze. Then sheering a little to the left bank, the vessel passed a narrow tongue of land covered with grass, whereon two horses fed. As we drew nearer I saw they were our own, and jumping on the taffrail shouted "Adios," at which they raised their heads, or perhaps raised them but at the snorting steamer, and as they looked we passed racing down stream, and by degrees they became dimmer, smaller, less distinct, and at the last melted and vanished into the reddish haze.

In a German Tramp

The tall, flaxen-haired stewardess Matilda had finished cutting Schwartzbrod and had gone to bed. The Danish boarhound slept heavily under the lee of the chicken-coops, the six or seven cats were upon the cabin sofa, and with the wind from the south-west, raising a terrific sea, and sending showers of spray flying over the tops of the black rocks which fringed the town, the S.S. *Oldenburg* got under way and staggered out into the gut.

The old white city girt on the seaward side by its breakwater of tall black rocks, the houses dazzlingly white, the crenelated *[sic USA = crenellated]* walls, the long stretch of sand, extending to the belt of grey-green scrub and backed in the distance by the sombre forest, lay in the moonlight as distinct and clear as it had been mid-day. Clearer perhaps, for the sun in a sandy landscape seems to blur the outlines which the moon reveals; so that throughout North Africa night is the time to see a town in all its beauty of effect The wind lifting the sand, drifted it whistling through the standing rigging of the tramp, coating the scarce dried paint, and making paint, rigging, and everything on board feel like a piece of shark-skin to the touch. The vessel groaned and laboured in the surface sea, and on the port quarter rose the rocks of the low island which forms the harbour, leaving an entrance of about half-a-mile between its shores and the rocks which guard the town.

West-south-west a little westerly, the wind ever increased; the sea lashed on the vessel's quarter, and in spite of the dense volumes of black smoke and showers of sparks flying out from the salt-coated smoke-stack, the tramp seemed to stand still. Upon the bridge the skipper screamed hoarsely in Platt-Deutsch down his connection-tube to the chief engineer; men came and went in dirty blue check cotton clothes and wooden shoes; occasionally a perspiring fireman poked his head above the hatch, and looking seaward for a moment, scooped off the sweat from his forefinger, muttered, "Gott freduma," and went below; even the Arab deck-hands, roused into activity, essayed to set a staysail, and the whole ship, shaken between the storm and the exertions of the crew, trembled and shivered in the yeasty sea. Nearer the rocks appeared, and the white town grew clearer, more intensely white, the sea frothed round the vessel, and the skipper advancing to a missionary seated silently gazing across the water with a pallid sea-green face, slapped him upon the back, and with an oath said, "Mister, will you have one glass of beer?" The Levite *in partibus*, clad in his black alpaca Norfolk jacket, grey greasy flannel shirt and paper collar, with the whole man surmounted by the inevitable pith soup-tureen-shaped hat, the trade-mark of his confraternity, merely pressed both his hands harder upon his diaphragm and groaned. "One leetel glass beer, I have it from Olten, fifty dozen of it. Perhaps all to be wasted; have a glass beer, it will do your shtomag good." The persecuted United Presbyterian ambulant broke silence with one of those pious ejaculations which do duty (in the congregations) for an oath, and taking up his parable, fixing the pith tureen upon his head with due precaution, said, "Captain, ye see I am a total abstainer, joined in the Whifflet, and in addeetion I feel my stomach sort o' discomposed." And to him again, good Captain Rindelhaus rejoined, "Well, Mister Missionary, do you see dat rocks?" The Reverend Mr. McKerrochar, squinting to leeward with an agonizing stare, admitted that he did, but qualified by saying, "there was sic a halgh, he was na sure that they were rocks at all." "Not rocks! Kreuz-Sacrament, dose rocks you see are sharp as razors, and the back-wash off them give you no jance; I dell you, sheep's-head preacher, dat point de way like signboard and not follow it oop himself, you better take glass beer in time, for if the schip not gather headway in about five minutes you perhaps not get another jance." After this dictum, he stood looking into the night, his glass gripped in his left hand, and in his right a half-smoked-out cigar, which he put to his mouth mechanically now and then, but drew no smoke from it. The missionary too looked at the rocks with increased interest, and the Arab pilot staggering up the ladder to the bridge stolidly pointed to the surf, and gave us his opinion, that "he, the captain and the faqui would soon be past the help of prayer," piously adding, "that it seemed Allah's will; although he thought the Kaffirs, sons of burnt Kaffirs, in the stoke-hole were not firing up."

With groans and heavings, with long shivers which came over her as the sea struck her on the beam, the vessel fought for her life, belching great clouds of smoke out into the clear night air. Captain and missionary, pilot and crew, stood gazing at the sea; the captain now and then yelling some unintelligible Platt-Deutsch order down the tube; the missionary fumbling with a Bible lettered "Polyglot," covered in black oil-cloth; and the pilot passing his beads between the fingers of his right hand, his eyes apparently not seeing anything; and it seemed as if another twenty minutes must have seen them all upon the rocks.

But Allah perhaps was on the watch; and the wind falling for an instant, or the burnt Kaffirs in the stoke-hole having struck a better vein of coal, the rusty iron sea-coffin slowly gathered headway, staggered as the engines driven to the highest pressure seemed to tear out her ribs, and forged ahead. Then lurching in the sea, the screw occasionally racing with a roar, and the black decks dripping and under water, the scuppers being choked with the filth of years, she sidled out to sea, and rose and fell in the long rollers outside the harbour, which came in from the west. Rindelhaus set her on her course, telling the Arab helmsman in the pigeon-English *[sic=pidgin English]* which served them as a means of interchanging their few ideas, "to keep her head north and by west a little northerly, and let him know when they were abreast of Jibel Hadid"; adding a condemnation of the Arab race in general and the particular sailor, whom he characterized as a "tamned heaven dog, not worth his kraut." The sailor, dressed in loose Arab trousers and a blue jersey, the whole surmounted by a greasy fez, replied: "Yes, him know Jibel Hadid, captain, him keep her head north and by west all right," and probably also consigned the captain and the whole Germanic race to the hottest corner of Jehannum, and so both men were pleased. The boarhound gambolled on the deck, Matilda peeped up the companion, her dripping wooden shoes looking like waterlogged canoes, and the Scotch missionary began to walk about, holding his monstrous hat on with one hand and hugging the oilskin-covered "Polyglot" under his left arm. Crossing the skipper in his walk, in a more cheerful humour he ventured to remark: "Eh! captain, maybe I could mak' a shape at yon glass of beer the now." But things had changed, and Rindelhaus looked at him with the usual uncondescending bearing of the seaman to the mere passenger, and said: "Nein, you loose your obbordunity for dat glass beer, my friend, and now I have to navigate my ship."

The *Oldenburg* pursued the devious tenor of her way, touching at ports which all were either open roadsteads or had bars on which the surf boiled with a noise like thunder; receiving cargo in driblets, a sack or two of marjoram, a bale of goatskins or of hides, two or three bags of wool, and sometimes waiting for a day or two unable to communicate until the surf went down. The captain spent his time in harbour fishing uninterestedly, catching great bearded spiky-finned sea-monsters which he left to die upon the deck. Not that he was hard-hearted, but merely unimaginative, after the way of those who, loving sport for the pleasure it affords themselves, hotly deny that it is cruel, or that it can occasion inconvenience to any participator in a business which they themselves enjoy. So the poor innocent sea-monsters floundered in slimy agony upon the deck; the boarhound and the cats taking a share in martyring them, tearing and biting at them as they gasped their lives away; condemned to agony for some strange reason, or perhaps because, as every living thing is born to suffer, they were enduring but their fair proportion, as they happened to be fish. Pathetic but unwept, the tragedy of all the animals, and we but links in the same chain with them, look at it all as unconcerned as gods. But as the bearded spiky fish gasped on the deck the missionary tried to abridge their agony with a belaying-pin; covering himself with blood and slime, and setting up the back of Captain Rindelhaus, who vowed his deck should not be hammered "like a skidel alley, all for the sake of half-a-dozen fish, which would be dead in half-an-hour and eaten by the cats."

The marvels of our commerce, in the shape of Waterbury watches, scissors and looking-glasses, beads, Swiss clocks, and musical-boxes, all duly dumped, and the off-scouring of the trade left by the larger ships duly received on board, the *Oldenburg* stumbled out to sea if the wind was not too strong, and squirmed along the coast. Occasionally upon arrival at a port the sound of psalmody was heard, and a missionary boat put off to pass the time of God with their brother on the ship. Then came the greetings, as the whole party sat on the fiddlee gratings jammed up against the funnel; the latest news from the Cowcaddens and the gossip from along the coast was duly interchanged. Gaunt-featured girls, removed by physical conditions from all temptation, sat and talked with scraggy, freckled, and pith-hatted men. It was all conscience, and relatively tender heart, and as the moon lit up the dirty decks, they paraded up and down, happy once more to be secure even for a brief space from insult, and to feel themselves at home. Dressed in white blouses, innocent of stays, with skirts which no belt known to milliners could ever join to the body or the blouse; with smaller-sized pith hats, sand-shoes and spectacles; their hands in Berlin gloves, and freckles reaching far down upon their necks, they formed a crushing argument in their own persons against polygamy. Still, in the main, all kindly souls, and some with a twinkle in their white-eyelashed steel-grey eyes, as of a Congregationalist bull-terrier, which showed you that they would gladly suffer martyrdom without due cause, or push themselves into great danger, out of sheer ignorance and want of knowledge of mankind. Life's misfits, most of them; their hands early inured to typewriting machines, their souls, as they would say, "sair hodden doon in prayer;" carefully educated to be ashamed of any scrap of womanhood they might possess. Still they were sympathetic, for sympathy is near akin to tears, and looking at them one divined they must have shed tears plentifully, enough to wash away any small sins they had committed in their lives.

The men, sunburnt yet sallow, seemed nourished on tinned meats and mineral table-waters; their necks scraggy and red protruded from their collars like those of vultures; they carried umbrellas in their hands from early habit of a wet climate, and seemed as if they had been chosen after much cogitation by some unskilled commission, for their unfitness for their task.

They too, dogged and narrow-minded as they were, were yet pathetic, when one thought upon their lives. No hope of converts, or of advancement in the least degree, stuck down upon the coast, far off from Dorcas meetings, school-feasts, or anything which in more favoured countries whiles away the Scripture-reader's time; they hammered at their self-appointed business day by day and preached unceasingly, apparently indifferent to anything that passed, so that they got off their due quantity of words a day. In course of time, and after tea and bread-and-butter had been consumed, they got into their boat, struck up the tune of "Sidna Aissa Hobcum," and from the taffrail McKerrochar saw them depart, joining in the chorus lustily and waving a dirty handkerchief until they faded out of sight. Mr. McKerrochar, one of those Scottish professional religionists, whom early training or their own "damnable iteration" has convinced of all the doctrine that they preach, formed a last relic of a disappearing type. The antiquated out-and-out doctrine of Hellfire and of Paradise, the jealous Scottish God, and the Mosaic Dispensation which he accepted whole, tinged slightly with the current theology of Airdrie or Coatbridge, made him a formidable adversary to the trembling infidel, in religious strife. In person he was tall and loosely built, his trousers bagging at the knees as if a horse's hock had been inside the cloth. Wrong-headed as befits his calling, he yet saw clearly enough in business matters, and might have marked a flock of heathen sheep had he applied his business aptitude to his religious work, or on the other hand he might have made a fortune had he chanced to be a rogue. He led a joyless stirring life, striving towards ideals which have made the world a quagmire; yet worked towards them with that simple faith which makes a man ten thousand times more dangerous, in his muddle-headed course. Abstractions which he called duty, morality, and self-sacrifice, ruled all his life; forcing him ever onward to occupy himself with things which really he had no concern with; and making him neglect himself and the more human qualities of courtesy and love. And so he stood, waving his pocket-handkerchief long after the strains of "Sidna Aissa Hobcum" had melted into the night air; his arms still waving as the sails of windmills move round once or twice, but haltingly, after the wind has dropped. Perhaps that class of man seldom or never chews the cud either of sweet or bitter recollection; and if, as in McKerrochar's case, he is deprived of whisky in which to drown his cares, the last impression gone, his mind hammers away, like the keys of a loose typewriter under a weary operator's hands, half aimlessly, till circumstances place new copy under its roller, and it starts off again to work.

He might have gone on waving right through the dog-watch had not the captain with a rough ejaculation stopped his arm. "Himmel, what for a semaphore, Herr missionary, is dat; and you gry too, when you look at dat going-way boat . . . Well, have a glass of beer. I tell you it is not good to look at boats and gry for noddings, for men that have an ugly yellow beard like yours and mine."

"I was na greetin', captain," said the missionary, furtively wiping his face; "it was just ane of thae clinkers, I think thae ca' the things, has got into my eye."

"Glinkers, mein friend, do not get into people's eyes when der ship is anchored," Rindelhaus replied; "still I know as you feel, but not for missionary boats. You not know Oldenburg eh? Pretta place; not far from Bremerhaven. Oldenburg is one of the prettaest places in the world. I live dere. Hour and half by drain, oot from de port. I just can see the vessels' masts and the funnel smoke as they pass oop and down the stream. I think I should not care too much to live where man can see no ships. Yes, yes, ah, here come Matilda mit de beer. Mein herz, you put him down here on dis bale of marjoram, and you goes off to bed. I speak here mit de Herr missionary, who gry for noddings when he look at missionary boat go off into de night.

"Ah, Oldenburg, ja, yes, I live there. Meine wife she live there, and meine littel Gretchen, she about den or twelve, I don't remember which. Prosit, Herr missionary, you have no wife; no littel Gretchen, eh? So, so, dat is perhaps better for a missionary."

The two sat looking at nothing, thinking in the painful ruminant way of semi-educated men, the captain's burly North-German figure stretched on a cane deck-chair. About a captain's age he was, that is, his beard had just begun to grizzle, and his nose was growing red, the bunions on his feet knotted his boots into protuberances, after the style of those who pass their lives about a deck. In height above six feet, broad-shouldered and red-faced, his voice of the kind with which a huntsman rates a dog, his clothes bought at a Bremerhaven slop-shop, his boots apparently made by a portmanteau-maker, and in his pocket was a huge silver keyless watch which he said was a "gronometer," and keep de Bremen time. Instant in prayer and cursing; pious yet blasphemous; kindly but brutal in the Teutonic way; he kicked his crew about as they had all been dogs, and yet looked after the tall stewardess Matilda as she had been his child; guarding her virtue from the assaults of passengers, and though alone with her in the small compass of a ship, respecting it himself.

After an interval he broke into his subject, just as a phonograph takes up its interrupted tale, as if against its will.

"So ja, yes, Oldenburg, pretta place; I not see it often though. In all eight years I never stay more to my house than from de morning Saturday to Monday noon, and dat after a four months' trip.

"Meine wife, she getting little sdout, and not mind much, for she is immer washing; washing de linen, de house, de steps; she wash de whole ship oop only I never let her come to see. The Gretchen she immer say, 'Father, why you not stop to home?' You got no littel Gretchen, eh? . . . Well, perhaps better so. Last Christmas I was at Oldenburg. Christmas eve [*sic*] I buy one tree, and then I remember I have to go to sea next morning about eleven o'clock. So I say nodings all the day, and about four o'clock the agent come and tell me that the company not wish me leave Oldenburg upon de Christmas day. Then I was so much glad I think I wait to eat meine Christmas dinner with meine wife, and talk with Gretchen in the evening while I smoke my pipe. The stove was burning, and the table stand ready mit sausage and mit bread and cheese, beer of course, and lax, dat lax they bring from Norway, and I think I have good time. Then I think on de company, what they say if I take favour from them and go not out to sea; they throw it in my teeth for ever, and tell me, 'Rindelhaus, you remember we was so good to you upon that Christmas day.' I tell the agent thank you, but say I go to sea. Meine wife she gry and I say nodings, nodings to Gretchen, and sit down to take my tea. Morning, I tell my littel girl, then she gry bitterly and say, 'What for you go to sea?' I kiss meine wife and walk down to the quay; it just begin to snow; I curse the schelm sailors, de pilot come aboard, and we begin to warp into the stream. Just then I hear a running on the quay, like as a Friesland pony come clattering on the stones. I look up and see Gretchen mit her little wooden shoes. She run down to the ship, and say, 'Why you go sea, father, upon Christmas day?' and I not able to say nodings but just to wave my hand. We warp out into the stream, and she stand grying till she faded out of sight. Sometimes I feel a liddel sorry about dat Christmas day . . . But have another glass beer, Herr missionary, it always do me good." Wiping the froth from his moustache with his rough hand he went below, leaving the missionary alone upon the deck.

The night descended, and the ship shrouded in mist grew ghostly and unnatural, whilst great drops of moisture hung on the backstays and the shrouds.

The Arab crew lay sleeping, huddled round the windlass, looking mere masses of white dirty rags; the seaman keeping the anchor-watch loomed like a giant, and from the shore occasionally the voices of the guards at the town prison came through the mist, making the boarhound turn in his sleep and growl. The missionary paced to and fro a little, settling his pith tureen-shaped hat upon his head, and fastening a woollen comforter about his neck.

Then going to the rail, he looked into the night where the boat bearing off his brethren had disappeared; his soul perhaps wandering towards some Limbo as he gazed, and his elastic-sided boots fast glued to the dirty decks by the half-dried-up blood of the discarded fish.

The Gold Fish

Outside the little straw-thatched *café* in a small courtyard trellised with vines, before a miniature table painted in red and blue, and upon which stood a dome-shaped pewter teapot and a painted glass half filled with mint, sat Amarabat, resting and smoking hemp. He was of those whom Allah in his mercy (or because man in the Blad-Allah has made no railways) has ordained to run. Set upon the road, his shoes pulled up, his waistband tightened, in his hand a staff, a palm-leaf wallet at his back, and in it bread, some hemp, a match or two (known to him as el spiritus), and a letter to take anywhere, crossing the plains, fording the streams, struggling along the mountain-paths, sleeping but fitfully, a burning rope steeped in saltpetre fastened to his foot, he trotted day and night — untiring as a camel, faithful as a dog. In Rabat as he sat dozing, watching the greenish smoke curl upwards from his hemp pipe, word came to him from the Khalifa of the town. So Amarabat rose, paid for his tea with half a handful of defaced and greasy copper coins, and took his way towards the white palace with the crenelated *[sic USA = crenellated]* walls, which on the cliff, hanging above the roaring tide-rip, just inside the bar of the great river, looks at Salee. Around the horseshoe archway of the gate stood soldiers, wild, fierce-eyed, armed to the teeth, descendants, most of them, of the famed warriors whom Sultan Muley Ismail (may God have pardoned him!) bred for his service, after the fashion of the Carlylean hero Frederic; and Amarabat walked through them, not aggressively, but with the staring eyes of a confirmed hemp-smoker, with the long stride of one who knows that he is born to run, and the assurance of a man who waits upon his lord. Some time he waited whilst the Khalifa dispensed what he thought justice, chaffered with Jewish pedlars for cheap European goods, gossiped with friends, looked at the antics of a dwarf, or priced a Georgian or Circassian girl brought with more care than glass by some rich merchant from the East. At last Amarabat stood in the presence, and the Khalifa, sitting upon a pile of cushions playing with a Waterbury watch, a pistol and a Koran by his side, addressed him thus: —

"Amarabat, son of Bjorma, my purpose is to send thee to Tafilet, where our liege lord the Sultan lies with his camp. Look upon this glass bowl made by the Kaffir, but clear as is the crystal of the rock; see how the light falls on the water, and the shifting colours that it makes, as when the Bride of the Rain stands in the heavens, after a shower in spring. Inside are seven gold fish, each scale as bright as letters in an Indian book. The Christian from whom I bought them said originally they came from the Far East where the Djin-descended Jawi live, the little yellow people of the faith. That may be, but such as they are, they are a gift for kings. Therefore, take thou the bowl. Take it with care, and bear it as it were thy life. Stay not, but in an hour start from the town. Delay not on the road, be careful of the fish, change not their water at the muddy pool where tortoises bask in the sunshine, but at running brooks; talk not to friends, look not upon the face of woman by the way, although she were as a gazelle, or as the maiden who when she walked through the fields the sheep stopped feeding to admire. Stop not, but run through day and night, pass through the Atlas at the Glaui; beware of frost, cover the bowl with thine own haik; upon the other side shield me the bowl from the Saharan sun, and drink not of the water if thou pass a day athirst when toiling through the sand. Break not the bowl, and see the fish arrive in Tafilet, and then present them, with this letter, to our lord. Allah be with you, and his Prophet; go, and above all things see thou breakest not the bowl." And Amarabat, after the manner of his kind, taking the bowl of gold fish, placed one hand upon his heart and said: "Inshallah, it shall be as thou hast said. God gives the feet and lungs. He also gives the luck upon the road."

So he passed out under the horseshoe arch, holding the bowl almost at arm's length so as not to touch his legs, and with the palmetto string by which he carried it, bound round with rags. The soldiers looked at him, but spoke not, and their eyes seemed to see far away, and to pass over all in the middle distance, though no doubt they marked the smallest detail of his gait and dress. He passed between the horses of the guard all standing nodding under the fierce sun, the reins tied to the cantles of their high red saddles, a boy in charge of every two or three: he passed beside the camels resting by the well, the donkeys standing dejected by the firewood they had brought: passed women, veiled white figures going to the baths; and passing underneath the lofty gateway of the town, exchanged a greeting with the half-mad, half-religious beggar just outside the walls, and then emerged upon the sandy road, between the aloe hedges, which skirts along the sea. So as he walked, little by little he fell into his stride; then got his second wind, and smoking now and then a pipe of hemp, began, as Arabs say, to eat the miles, his eyes fixed on the horizon, his stick stuck down between his shirt and back, the knob protruding over the left shoulder like the hilt of a two-handed sword. And still he held the precious bowl from Franquestan in which the golden fish swam to and fro, diving and circling in the sunlight, or flapped their tails to steady themselves as the water danced with the motion of his steps. Never before in his experience had he been charged with such a mission, never before been sent to stand before Allah's vicegerent upon earth. But still the strangeness of his business was what preoccupied him most. The fish like molten gold, the water to be changed only at running streams, the fish to be preserved from frost and sun; and then the bowl: had not the Khalifa said at the last, "Beware, break not the bowl"? So it appeared to him that most undoubtedly a charm was in the fish and in the bowl, for who sends common fish on such a journey through the land? Then he resolved at any hazard to bring them safe and keep the bowl intact, and trotting onward, smoked his hemp, and wondered why he of all men should have had the luck to bear the precious gift. He knew he kept his law, at least as far as a poor man can keep it, prayed when he thought of prayer, or was assailed by terror in the night alone upon the plains; fasted in Ramadan, although most of his life was one continual fast; drank of the shameful but seldom, and on the sly, so as to give offence to no believer, and seldom looked upon the face of the strange women, Daughters of the Illegitimate, whom Sidna Mohammed himself has said, avoid. But all these things he knew were done by many of the faithful, and so he did not set himself up as of exceeding virtue, but rather left the praise to God, who helped his slave with strength to keep his law. Then left off thinking, judging the matter was ordained, and trotted, trotted over the burning plains, the gold fish dancing in the water as the miles melted and passed away.

Duar and Kasbah, castles of the Caids, Arabs' black tents, suddra zaribas, camels grazing — antediluvian in appearance — on the little hills, the muddy streams edged all along the banks with oleanders, the solitary horsemen holding their long and brass-hooped guns like spears, the white-robed noiseless-footed travellers on the roads, the chattering storks upon the village mosques, the cow-birds sitting on the cattle in the fields — he saw, but marked not, as he trotted on. Day faded into night, no twilight intervening, and the stars shone out, Soheil and Rigel with Betelgeuse and Aldebaran, and the three bright lamps which the cursed Christians know as the Three Maries — called, he supposed, after the mother of their Prophet; and still he trotted on. Then by the side of a lone palm-tree springing up from a cleft in a tall rock, an island on the plain, he stopped to pray; and sleeping, slept but fitfully, the strangeness of the business making him wonder; and he who cavils over matters in the night can never rest, for thus the jackal and the hyena pass their nights talking and reasoning about the thoughts which fill their minds when men lie with their faces covered in their haiks, and after prayer sleep. Rising after an hour or two and going to the nearest stream, he changed the water of his fish, leaving a little in the bottom of the bowl, and dipping with his brass drinking-cup into the stream for fear of accidents. He passed the Kasbah of el Daudi, passed the land of the Rahamna, accursed folk always in "siba," saw the great snowy wall of Atlas rise, skirted Marakesh, the Kutubieh, rising first from the plain and sinking last from sight as he approached the mountains and left the great white city sleeping in the plain.

Little by little the country altered as he ran: cool streams for muddy rivers, groves of almond-trees, ashes and elms, with grape-vines binding them together as the liana binds the canela and the urunday in the dark forests of Brazil and Paraguay. At mid-day, when the sun was at its height, when locusts, whirring through the air, sank in the dust as flying-fish sink in the waves, when palm-trees seem to nod their heads, and lizards are abroad drinking the heat and basking in the rays, when the dry air shimmers, and sparks appear to dance before the traveller's eye, and a thin, reddish dust lies on the leaves, on clothes of men, and upon every hair of horses' coats, he reached a spring. A river springing from a rock, or issuing after running underground, had formed a little pond. Around the edge grew bulrushes, great catmace, water-soldiers, tall arums and metallic-looking sedge-grass, which gave an air as of an outpost of the tropics lost in the desert sand. Fish played beneath the rock where the stream issued, flitting to and fro, or hanging suspended for an instant in the clear stream, darted into the dark recesses of the sides; and in the middle of the pond enormous tortoises, horrid and antediluvian-looking, basked with their backs awash or raised their heads to snap at flies, and all about them hung a dark and fetid slime.

A troop of thin brown Arab girls filled their tall amphoræ whilst washing in the pond. Placing his bowl of fish upon a jutting rock, the messenger drew near. "Gazelles," he said, "will one of you give me fresh water for the Sultan's golden fish?" Laughing and giggling, the girls drew near, looked at the bowl, had never seen such fish. "Allah is great; why do you not let them go in the pond and play a little with their brothers?" And Amarabat with a shiver answered, "Play, let them play! and if they come not back my life will answer for it." Fear fell upon the girls, and one advancing, holding the skirt of her long shift between her teeth to veil her face, poured water from her amphora upon the fish.

Then Amarabat, setting down his precious bowl, drew from his wallet a pomegranate and began to eat, and for a farthing buying a piece of bread from the women, was satisfied, and after smoking, slept, and dreamed he was approaching Tafilet; he saw the palm-trees rising from the sand; the gardens; all the oasis stretching beyond his sight; at the edge the Sultan's camp, a town of canvas, with the horses, camels, and the mules picketed, all in rows, and in the midst of the great "duar" the Sultan's tent, like a great palace all of canvas, shining in the sun. All this he saw, and saw himself entering the camp, delivering up his fish, perhaps admitted to the sacred tent, or at least paid by a vizier, as one who has performed his duty well. The slow match blistering his foot, he woke to find himself alone, the "gazelles" departed, and the sun shining on the bowl, making the fish appear more magical, more wondrous, brighter, and more golden than before.

And so he took his way along the winding Atlas paths, and slept at Demnats, then, entering the mountains, met long trains of travellers going to the south. Passing through groves of chestnuts, walnut-trees, and hedges thick with blackberries and travellers' joy, he climbed through vineyards rich with black Atlas grapes, and passed the flat mud-built Berber villages nestling against the rocks. Eagles flew by and moufflons gazed at him from the peaks, and from the thickets of lentiscus and dwarf arbutus wild boars appeared, grunted, and slowly walked across the path, and still he climbed, the icy wind from off the snow chilling him in his cotton shirt, for his warm Tadla haik was long ago wrapped round the bowl to shield the precious fish. Crossing the Wad Ghadat, the current to his chin, his bowl of fish held in one hand, he struggled on. The Berber tribesmen at Tetsula and Zarkten, hard-featured, shaved but for a chin-tuft, and robed in their "achnifs" with the curious eye woven in the skirt, saw he was a "rekass," or thought the fish not worth their notice, so gave him a free road. Night caught him at the stone-built, antediluvian-looking Kasbah of the Glaui, perched in the eye of the pass, with the small plain of Teluet two thousand feet below. Off the high snow-peaks came a whistling wind, water froze solid in all the pots and pans, earthenware jars and bottles throughout the castle, save in the bowl which Amarabat, shivering and miserable, wrapped in his haik and held close to the embers, hearing the muezzin at each call to prayers; praying himself to keep awake so that his fish might live. Dawn saw him on the trail, the bowl wrapped in a woollen rag, and the fish fed with bread-crumbs, but himself hungry and his head swimming with want of sleep, with smoking "kief," and with the bitter wind which from El Tisi N'Glaui flagellates the road. Right through the valley of Teluet he still kept on, and day and night still trotting, trotting on, changing his bowl almost instinctively from hand to hand, a broad leaf floating on the top to keep the water still, he left Agurzga, with its twin castles, Ghresat and Dads, behind. Then rapidly descending, in a day reached an oasis between Todghra and Ferkla, and rested at a village for the night. Sheltered by palm-trees and hedged round with cactuses and aloes, either to keep out thieves or as a symbol of the thorniness of life, the village lay, looking back on the white Atlas gaunt and mysterious, and on the other side towards the brown Sahara, land of the palm-tree (Belad-el-Jerid), the refuge of the true Ishmaelite; for in the desert, learning, good faith, and hospitality can still be found — at least, so Arabs say.

Orange and azofaifa trees, with almonds, sweet limes and walnuts, stood up against the waning light, outlined in the clear atmosphere almost so sharply as to wound the eye. Around the well goats and sheep lay, whilst a girl led a camel round the Noria track; women sat here and there and gossiped, with their tall earthenware jars stuck by the point into the ground, and waited for their turn, just as they did in the old times, so far removed from us, but which in Arab life is but as yesterday, when Jacob cheated Esau, and the whole scheme of Arab life was photographed for us by the writers of the Pentateuch. In fact, the self-same scene which has been acted every evening for two thousand years throughout North Africa, since the adventurous ancestors of the tribesmen of to-day left Hadrumut or Yemen, and upon which Allah looks down approvingly, as recognizing that the traditions of his first recorded life have been well kept. Next day he trotted through the barren plain of Seddat, the Jibel Saghra making a black line on the horizon to the south. Here Berber tribes sweep in their razzias like hawks; but who would plunder a rekass carrying a bowl of fish? Crossing the dreary plain and dreaming of his entry into Tafilet, which now was almost in his reach not two days distant, the sun beating on his head, the water almost boiling in the bowl, hungry and footsore, and in the state betwixt waking and sleep into which those who smoke hemp on journeys often get, he branched away upon a trail leading towards the south. Between the oases of Todghra and Ferkla, nothing but stone and sand, black stones on yellow sand; sand, and yet more sand, and then again stretches of blackish rocks with a suddra bush or two, and here and there a colocynth, bitter and beautiful as love or life, smiling up at the traveller from amongst the stones. Towards midday the path led towards a sandy tract all overgrown with sandrac *[sic=sandarac]* bushes and crossed by trails of jackals and hyenas, then it quite disappeared, and Amarabat waking from his dream saw he was lost. Like a good shepherd, his first thought was for his fish; for he imagined the last few hours of sun had made them faint, and one of them looked heavy and swam sideways, and the rest kept rising to the surface in an uneasy way. Not for a moment was Amarabat frightened, but looked about for some known landmark, and finding none started to go back on his trail. But to his horror the wind which always sweeps across the Sahara had covered up his tracks, and on the stony paths which he had passed his feet had left no prints. Then Amarabat, the first moments of despair passed by, took a long look at the horizon, tightened his belt, pulled up his slipper heels, covered his precious bowl with a corner of his robe, and started doggedly back upon the road he thought he traversed on the deceitful path. How long he trotted, what he endured, whether the fish died first, or if he drank, or, faithful to the last, thirsting met death, no one can say. Most likely wandering in the waste of sandhills and of suddra bushes he stumbled on, smoking his hashish while it lasted, turning to Mecca at the time of prayer, and trotting on more feebly (for he was born to run), till he sat down beneath the sun-dried bushes where the Shinghiti on his Mehari found him dead beside the trail. Under a stunted sandarac tree, the head turned to the east, his body lay, swollen and distorted by the pangs of thirst, the tongue protruding rough as a parrot's, and beside him lay the seven golden fish, once bright and shining as the pure gold when the goldsmith pours it molten from his pot, but now turned black and bloated, stiff, dry, and dead. Life the mysterious, the mocking, the inscrutable, unseizable, the uncomprehended essence of nothing and of everything, had fled, both from the faithful messenger and from his fish. But the Khalifa's parting caution had been well obeyed, for by the tree, unbroken, the crystal bowl still glistened beautiful as gold, in the fierce rays of the Saharan sun.

A Hegira

The giant cypresses, tall even in the time of Montezuma, the castle of Chapultepec upon its rock (an island in the plain of Mexico), the panorama of the great city backed by the mountain range; the two volcanoes, the Popocatepetl and the Istacihuatl, and the lakes; the tigers in their cages, did not interest me so much as a small courtyard, in which, ironed and guarded, a band of Indians of the Apache tribe were kept confined. Six warriors, a woman and a boy, captured close to Chihuahua, and sent to Mexico, the Lord knows why; for generally an Apache captured was shot at once, following the frontier rule, which without difference of race was held on both sides of the Rio Grande, that a good Indian must needs be dead.

Silent and stoical the warriors sat, not speaking once in a whole day, communicating but by signs; naked except the breech-clout; their eyes apparently opaque, and looking at you without sight, but seeing everything; and their demeanour less reassuring than that of the tigers in the cage hard by. All could speak Spanish if they liked, some a word or two of English, but no one heard them say a word in either tongue. I asked the nearest if he was a Mescalero, and received the answer: "Mescalero-hay," and for a moment a gleam shone through their eyes, but vanished instantly, as when the light dies out of the wire in an electric lamp. The soldier at the gate said they were "brutes"; all sons of dogs, infidels, and that for his part he could not see why the "Gobierno" went to the expense of keeping them alive. He thought they had no sense; but in that showed his own folly, and acted after the manner of the half-educated man the whole world over, who knowing he can read and write thinks that the savage who cannot do so is but a fool; being unaware that, in the great book known as the world, the savage often is the better scholar of the two.

But five-and-twenty years ago the Apache nation, split into its chief divisions of Mescaleros, Jicarillas, Coyoteros, and Lipanes, kept a great belt of territory almost five hundred miles in length, and of about thirty miles in breadth, extending from the bend of the Rio Gila to El Paso, in a perpetual war. On both sides of the Rio Grande no man was safe; farms were deserted, cattle carried off, villages built by the Spaniards, and with substantial brick-built churches, mouldered into decay; mines were unworkable, and horses left untended for a moment were driven off in open day; so bold the thieves, that at one time they had a settled month for plundering, which they called openly the Moon of the Mexicans, though they did not on that account suspend their operations at other seasons of the year. Cochise and Mangas-Coloradas, Naked Horse, Cuchillo Negro, and others of their chiefs, were once far better known upon the frontiers than the chief senators of the congresses of either of the two republics; and in some instances these chiefs showed an intelligence, knowledge of men and things, which in another sphere would certainly have raised them high in the estimation of mankind.

The Shis-Inday (the people of the woods), their guttural language, with its curious monosyllable "hay" which they tacked on to everything, as "Oro-hay" and "plata-hay"; their strange democracy, each man being chief of himself, and owning no allegiance to any one upon the earth; all now have almost passed away, destroyed and swallowed up by the "Inday pindah lichoyi" (the men of the white eyes), as they used to call the Americans and all those northerners who ventured into their territory to look for "yellow iron." I saw no more of the Apaches, and except once, never again met any one of them; but as I left the place the thought came to my mind, if any of them succeed in getting out, I am certain that the six or seven hundred miles between them and their country will be as nothing to them, and that their journey thither will be marked with blood.

At Huehuetoca I joined the mule-train, doing the twenty miles which in those days was all the extent of railway in the country to the north, and lost my pistol in a crowd just as I stepped into the train, some "lepero" having abstracted it out of my belt when I was occupied in helping five strong men to get my horse into a cattle-truck. From Huehuetoca we marched to Tula, and there camped for the night, sleeping in a "meson" built like an Eastern fondak round a court, and with a well for watering the beasts in the centre of the yard. I strolled about the curious town, in times gone by the Aztec capital, looked at the churches, built like fortresses, and coming back to the "meson" before I entered the cell-like room without a window, and with a plaster bench on which to spread one's saddle and one's rugs, I stopped to talk with a knot of travellers feeding their animals on barley and chopped straw, grouped round a fire, and the whole scene lit up and rendered Rembrandtesque by the fierce glow of an "ocote" torch. So talking of the Alps and Apennines, or, more correctly, speaking of the Sierra Madre, and the mysterious region known as the Bolson de Mapimi, a district in those days as little known as is the Sus to-day, a traveller drew near. Checking his horse close by the fire, and getting off it gingerly, for it was almost wild, holding the hair "mecate" in his hand, he squatted down, the horse snorting and hanging back, and setting rifle and "machete" jingling upon the saddle, he began to talk.

"Ave Maria purisima, had we heard the news?" What! a new revolution? Had Lerdo de Tejada reappeared again? or had Cortinas made another raid on Brownsville? the Indios Bravos harried Chihuahua? or had the silver "conduct" coming from the mines been robbed? "Nothing of this, but a voice ran (corria una voz) that the Apache infidels confined in the courtyard of the castle of Chapultepec had broken loose. Eight of them, six warriors, a woman and a boy, had slipped their fetters, murdered two of the guard, and were supposed to be somewhere not far from Tula, and, as he thought, making for the Bolson de Mapimi, the deserts of the Rio Gila, or the recesses of the mountains of the Santa Rosa range."

Needless to say this put all in the meson almost beside themselves; for the terror that the Indians inspired was at that time so real, that had the eight forlorn and helpless infidels appeared I verily believe they would have killed us all. Not that we were not brave, well armed — in fact, all loaded down with arms, carrying rifles and pistols, swords stuck between our saddle-girths, and generally so fortified as to resemble walking arsenals. But valour is a thing of pure convention, and these men who would have fought like lions against marauders of their own race, scarce slept that night for thinking on the dangers which they ran by the reported presence of those six naked men. The night passed by without alarm, as was to be expected, seeing that the courtyard wall of the meson was at least ten feet high, and the gate solid "ahuehuete" clamped with iron, and padlocked like a jail. At the first dawn, or rather at the first false dawn, when the fallacious streaks of pink flash in the sky and fade again to night, all were afoot. Horsemen rode out, sitting erect in their peaked saddles, toes stuck out and thrust into their curiously stamped toe-leathers; their "chaparreras" giving to their legs a look of being cased in armour, their "poblano" hats, with bands of silver or of tinsel, balanced like halos on their heads.

Long trains of donkeys, driven by Indians dressed in leather, and bareheaded, after the fashion of their ancestors, crawled through the gate laden with "pulque," and now and then a single Indian followed by his wife set off on foot, carrying a crate of earthenware by a broad strap depending from his head. Our caravan, consisting of six two-wheeled mule-carts, drawn by a team of six or sometimes eight gaily-harnessed mules, and covered with a tilt made from the "istle," creaked through the gate. The great meson remained deserted, and by degrees, as a ship leaves the coast, we struck into the wild and stony desert country, which, covered with a whitish dust of alkali, makes Tula an oasis; then the great church sank low, and the tall palm-trees seemed to grow shorter; lastly church, palms and towers, and the green fields planted with aloes, blended together and sank out of sight, a faint white misty spot marking their whereabouts, till at last it too faded and melted into the level plain.

Travellers in a perpetual stream we met journeying to Mexico, and every now and then passed a straw-thatched "jacal," where women sat selling "atole," that is a kind of stirabout of pine-nut meal and milk, and dishes seasoned hot with red pepper, with "tortillas" made on the "metate" of the Aztecs, to serve as bread and spoons. The infidels, it seemed, had got ahead of us, and when we slept had been descried making towards the north; two of them armed with bows which they had roughly made with sticks, the string twisted out of "istle," and the rest with clubs, and what astonished me most was that behind them trotted a white dog. Outside San Juan del Rio, which we reached upon the second day, it seemed that in the night the homing Mescaleros had stolen a horse, and two of them mounting upon him had ridden off, leaving the rest of the forlorn and miserable band behind. How they had lived so far in the scorched alkali-covered plains, how they managed to conceal themselves by day, or how they steered by night, no one could tell; for the interior Mexican knows nothing of the desert craft, and has no idea that there is always food of some kind for an Apache, either by digging roots, snaring small animals, or at the last resort by catching locusts or any other insect he can find. Nothing so easy as to conceal themselves; for amongst grass eight or nine inches high, they drop, and in an instant, even as you look, are lost to sight, and if hard pressed sometimes escape attention by standing in a cactus grove, and stretching out their arms, look so exactly like the plant that you may pass close to them and be unaware, till their bow twangs, and an obsidian-headed arrow whistles through the air.

Our caravan rested a day outside San Juan del Rio to shoe the mules, repair the harness, and for the muleteers to go to mass or visit the "poblana" girls, who with flowers in their hair leaned out of every balcony of the half-Spanish, half-Oriental-looking town, according to their taste. Not that the halt lost time, for travellers all know that "to hear mass and to give barley to your beasts loses no tittle of the day."

San Juan, the river almost dry, and trickling thirstily under its red stone bridges; the fields of aloes, the poplars, and the stunted palms; its winding street in which the houses, overhanging, almost touch; its population, which seemed to pass their time lounging wrapped in striped blankets up against the walls, was left behind. The pulque-aloes and the sugar-canes grew scarcer, the road more desolate as we emerged into the "tierra fria" of the central plain, and all the time the Sierra Madre, jagged and menacing, towered in the west. In my mind's eye I saw the Mescaleros trotting like wolves all through the night along its base, sleeping by day in holes, killing a sheep or goat when chance occurred, and following one another silent and stoical in their tramp towards the north.

Days followed days as in a ship at sea; the waggons rolling on across the plains; and I jogging upon my horse, half sleeping in the sun, or stretched at night half dozing on a tilt, almost lost count of time. Somewhere between San Juan del Rio and San Luis Potosi we learned two of the Indians had been killed, but that the four remaining were still pushing onward, and in a little while we met a body of armed men carrying two ghastly heads tied by their scalp-locks to the saddle-bow. Much did the slayers vaunt their prowess; telling how in a wood at break of day they had fallen in with all the Indians seated round a fire, and that whilst the rest fled, two had sprung on them, as they said, "after the fashion of wild beasts, armed one with a stick, and the other with a stone, and by God's grace," and here the leader crossed himself, "their aim had been successful, and the two sons of dogs had fallen, but most unfortunately the rest during the fight had managed to escape."

San Luis Potosi, the rainless city, once world-renowned for wealth, and even now full of fine buildings, churches and palaces, and with a swarming population of white-clothed Indians squatting to sell their trumpery in the great market-square, loomed up amongst its fringe of gardens, irrigated lands, its groves of pepper-trees, its palms, its wealth of flowering shrubs; its great white domes, giving an air of Bagdad or of Fez, shone in the distance, then grew nearer, and at last swallowed us up, as wearily we passed through the outskirts of the town, and halted underneath the walls.

The city, then an oasis in the vast plateau of Anáhuac (now but a station on a railway-line), a city of enormous distances, of gurgling water led in stucco channels by the side of every street, of long expanses of "adobe" walls, of immense plazas, of churches and of bells, of countless convents; hedged in by mountains to the west, mouth of the "tierra caliente" to the east, and to the north the stopping-place for the long trains of waggons carrying cotton from the States; wrapped in a mist as of the Middle Ages, lay sleeping in the sun. On every side the plain lapped like an ocean, and the green vegetation round the town stopped so abruptly that you could step almost at once from fertile meadows into a waste of whitish alkali.

Above the town, in a foothill of the Sierra Madre about three leagues away, is situated the "Enchanted City," never yet fouled by the foot of man, but yet existent, and believed in by all those who follow that best part of history, the traditions which have come down to us from the times when men were wise, and when imagination governed judgment, as it should do to-day, being the noblest faculty of the human mind. Either want of time, or that belittling education from which few can escape, prevented me from visiting the place. Yet I still think if rightly sought the city will be found, and I feel sure the Mescaleros passed the night not far from it, and perhaps looking down upon San Luis Potosi cursed it, after the fashion that the animals may curse mankind for its injustice to them.

Tired of its squares, its long dark streets, its hum of people ; and possessed perhaps with that nostalgia of the desert which comes so soon to all who once have felt its charm when cooped in bricks, we set our faces northward about an hour before the day, passed through the gates and rolled into the plains. The mules well rested shook their bells, the leagues soon dropped behind, the muleteers singing "La Pasadita," or an interminable song about a "Gachupin" [1] who loved a nun.

The Mescaleros had escaped our thoughts — that is, the muleteers thought nothing of them; but I followed their every step, saw them crouched round their little fire, roasting the roots of wild "mescal"; marked them upon the march in single file, their eyes fixed on the plain, watchful and silent as they were phantoms gliding to the north.

---

1 It had a chorus reflecting upon convent discipline:
   "For though the convent rule was strict and tight,
   She had her exits and her entrances by night."

Crossing a sandy tract, the Capataz, who had long lived in the "Pimeria Alta," and amongst the Maricopas on the Gila, drew up his horse and pointing to the ground said, "Viva Mexico! — look at these footmarks in the sand. They are the infidels; see where the men have trod; here is the woman's print and this the boy's. Look how their toes are all turned in, unlike the tracks of Christians. This trail is a day old, and yet how fresh! See where the boy has stumbled — thanks to the Blessed Virgin they must all be tired, and praise to God will die upon the road, either by hunger or some Christian hand." All that he spoke of was no doubt visible to him, but through my want of faith, or perhaps lack of experience, I saw but a faint trace of naked footsteps in the sand. Such as they were, they seemed the shadow of a ghost, unstable and unreal, and struck me after the fashion that it strikes one when a man holds up a cane and tells you gravely, without a glimmering of the strangeness of the fact, that it came from Japan, actually grew there, and had leaves and roots, and was as little thought of as a mere ash-plant growing in a copse.

At an "hacienda" upon the road, just where the trail leads off upon one hand to Matehuala, and on the other to Rio Verde, and the hot countries of the coast, we stopped to pass the hottest hours in sleep. All was excitement; men came in, their horses flecked with foam; others were mounting, and all armed to the teeth, as if the Yankees had crossed the Rio Grande, and were marching on the place. "Los Indios! si, señor," they had been seen, only last night, but such the valour of the people of the place, they had passed on doing no further damage than to kill a lamb. No chance of sleep in such a turmoil of alarm; each man had his own plan, all talked at once, most of them were half drunk, and when our Capataz asked dryly if they had thought of following the trail, a silence fell on all. By this time, owing to the horsemen galloping about, the trail was cut on every side, and to have followed it would have tried the skill of an Apache tracker; but just then upon the plain a cloud of dust was seen. Nearer it came, and then out of the midst of it horses appeared, arms flashed, and when nearing the place five or six men galloped up to the walls, and stopped their horses with a jerk. "What news? have you seen anything of the Apaches?" and the chief rider of the gallant band, getting off slowly, and fastening up his horse, said, with an air of dignity, "At the 'encrucijada,' four leagues along the road, you will find one of them. We came upon him sitting on a stone, too tired to move, called on him to surrender, but Indians have no sense, so he came at us tired as he was, and we, being valiant, fired, and he fell dead.

Then, that the law should be made manifest to all, we hung his body by the feet to a huisaché tree." Then compliments broke out and "Viva los valientes!" "Viva Mexico!" "Mueran los Indios salvajes!" and much of the same sort, whilst the five valiant men modestly took a drink, saying but little, for true courage does not show itself in talk.

Leaving the noisy crew drinking confusion to their enemies, we rolled into the plain. Four dusty leagues, and the huisaché tree growing by four cross trails came into sight We neared it, and to a branch, naked except his breech-clout, covered with bullet-wounds, we saw the Indian hang. Half-starved he looked, and so reduced that from the bullet-holes but little blood had run; his feet were bloody, and his face hanging an inch or two above the ground distorted; flies buzzed about him, and in the sky a faint black line on the horizon showed that the vultures had already scented food.

We left the nameless warrior hanging on his tree, and took our way across the plain, well pleased both with the "valour" of his slayers and the position of affairs in general in the world at large. Right up and down the Rio Grande on both sides for almost a thousand miles the lonely cross upon some river-side, near to some thicket, or out in the wide plain, most generally is lettered "Killed by the Apaches," and in the game they played so long, and still held trumps in at the time I write of, they, too, paid for all errors, in their play, by death. But still it seemed a pity, savage as they were, that so much cunning, such stoical indifference to both death and life, should always finish as the warrior whom I saw hang by the feet from the huisaché, just where the road to Matehuala bifurcates, and the trail breaks off to El Jarral. And so we took our road, passed La Parida, Matehuala, El Catorce, and still the sterile plateau spread out like a vast sea, the sparse and stunted bushes in the constant mirage looming at times like trees, at others seeming just to float above the sand; and as we rolled along, the mules struggling and straining in the whitish dust, we seemed to lose all trace of the Apaches; and at the lone hacienda or rare villages no one had heard of them, and the mysterious hegira of the party, now reduced to three, left no more traces of its passing than water which has closed upon the passage of a fish.

Gomez Farias, Parras, El Llano de la Guerra, we passed alternately, and at length Saltillo came in sight, its towers standing up upon the plain after the fashion of a lighthouse in the sea; the bull-ring built under the Viceroys looking like a fort; and then the plateau of Anáhuac finished abruptly, and from the ramparts of the willow-shaded town the great green plains stretched out towards Texas in a vast panorama; whilst upon the west in the dim distance frowned the serrated mountains of Santa Rosa, and further still the impenetrable fastnesses of the Bolson de Mapimi.

Next day we took the road for Monterey, descending in a day by the rough path known as "la cuesta de los fierros," from the cold plateau to a land of palms, of cultivation, orange-groves, of fruit-trees, olive-gardens, a balmy air filled with the noise of running waters; and passing underneath the Cerro de la Silla which dominates the town, slept peacefully far from all thoughts of Indians and of perils of the road, in the great caravansary which at that time was the chief glory of the town of Monterey. The city with its shady streets, its alameda planted with palm-trees, and its plaza all decorated with stuccoed plaster seats painted pale pink, and upon which during both day and night half of the population seemed to lounge, lay baking in the sun.

Great teams of waggons driven by Texans creaked through the streets, the drivers dressed in a "défroque" of old town clothes, often a worn frock-coat and rusty trousers stuffed into cowboy boots, the whole crowned with an ignominious battered hat, and looking, as the Mexicans observed, like "pantomimas, que salen en las fiestas." Mexicans from down the coast, from Tamaulipas, Tuxpan, Vera Cruz and Guatzecoalcos ambled along on horses all ablaze with silver; and to complete the picture, a tribe of Indians, the Kickopoos, who had migrated from the north, and who occasionally rode through the town in single file, their rifles in their hands, and looking at the shops half longingly, half frightened, passed along without a word.

But all the varied peoples, the curious half-wild, half-patriarchal life, the fruits and flowers, the strangeness of the place, could not divert my thoughts from the three lone pathetic figures, followed by their dog, which in my mind's eye I saw making northward, as a wild goose finds its path in spring, leaving no traces of its passage by the way. I wondered what they thought of, how they looked upon the world, if they respected all they saw of civilized communities upon their way, or whether they pursued their journey like a horse let loose returning to his birthplace, anxious alone about arriving at the goal. So Monterey became a memory; the Cerro de la Silla last vanishing, when full five leagues upon the road. The dusty plains all white with alkali, the grey-green sage-bushes, the salt and crystal-looking rivers, the Indians bending under burdens, and the women sitting at the cross roads selling tortillas — all now had changed. Through oceans of tall grass, by muddy rivers in which alligators basked, by "bayous," "resacas," and by "bottoms" of alluvial soil, in which grew cotton-woods, black-jack, and post-oak, with gigantic willows; through countless herds of half-wild horses, lighting the landscape with their colours, and through a rolling prairie with vast horizons bounded by faint blue mountain chains, we took our way. Out of the thickets of "mesquite" wild boars peered upon the path; rattlesnakes sounded their note of warning or lay basking in the sun; at times an antelope bounded across our track, and the rare villages were fortified with high mud walls, had gates, and sometimes drawbridges, for all the country we were passing through was subject to invasions of "los Indios Bravos," and no one rode a mile without the chance of an attack. When travellers met they zigzagged to and fro like battleships in the old days striving to get the "weather gauge," holding their horses tightly by the head, and interchanging salutations fifty yards away, though if they happened to be Texans and Mexicans they only glared, or perhaps yelled an obscenity at one another in their different tongues. Advertisements upon the trees informed the traveller that the place to stop at was the "Old Buffalo Camp" in San Antonio, setting forth its whisky, its perfect safety both for man and beast, and adding curtly it was only a short four hundred miles away. Here for the first time in our journey we sent out a rider about half-a-mile ahead to scan the route, ascend the little hills, keep a sharp eye on "Indian sign," and give us warning by a timely shot, all to dismount, "corral" the waggons, and be prepared for an attack of Indians, or of the roaming bands of rascals who like pirates wandered on the plains. Dust made us anxious, and smoke ascending in the distance set us all wondering if it was Indians, or a shepherd's fire; at halting time no one strayed far from camp, and we sat eating with our rifles by our sides, whilst men on horseback rode round the mules, keeping them well in sight, as shepherds watch their sheep. About two leagues from Juarez a traveller bloody with spurring passed us carrying something in his hand; he stopped and held out a long arrow with an obsidian head, painted in various colours and feathered in a peculiar way. A consultation found it to be "Apache," and the man galloped on to take it to the governor of the place to tell him Indians were about, or, as he shouted (following the old Spanish catchword), "there were Moors upon the coast."

Juarez we slept at, quite secure within the walls; started at daybreak, crossing the swiftly-running river just outside the town, at the first streak of light; journeyed all day, still hearing nothing of the retreating Mescaleros, and before evening reached Las Navas, which we found astir, all lighted up, and knots of people talking excitedly, whilst in the plaza the whole population seemed to be afoot. At the long wooden tables set about with lights, where in a Mexican town at sundown an al fresco meal of kid stewed in red pepper, "tamales" and "tortillas," is always laid, the talk was furious, and each man gave his opinion at the same time, after the fashion of the Russian Mir, or as it may be that we shall yet see done during debates in Parliament, so that all men may have a chance to speak, and yet escape the ignominy of their words being caught, set down, and used against them, after the present plan. The Mescaleros had been seen passing about a league outside the town. A shepherd lying hidden, watching his sheep, armed with a rifle, had spied them, and reported that they had passed close to him; the woman coming last and carrying in her arms a little dog; and he "thanked God and all His holy saints who had miraculously preserved his life." After the shepherd's story, in the afternoon firing had been distinctly heard towards the small rancho of Las Crucecitas, which lay about three leagues further on upon the road. All night the din of talk went on, and in the morning when we started on our way, full half the population went with us to the gate, all giving good advice; to keep a good look-out, if we saw dust to be certain it was Indians driving the horses stolen from Las Crucecitas, then to get off at once, corral the waggons, and above all to put our trust in God. This we agreed to do, but wondered why out of so many valiant men not one of them proffered assistance, or volunteered to mount his horse and ride with us along the dangerous way.

The road led upwards towards some foothills, set about with scrubby palms; not fifteen miles away rose the dark mountains of the Santa Rosa chain, and on a little hill the rancho stood, flat-roofed and white, and seemingly not more than a short league away, so clear the light, and so immense the scale of everything upon the rolling plain. I knew that in the mountains the three Indians were safe, as the whole range was Indian territory; and as I saw them struggling up the slopes, the little dog following them footsore, hanging down its head, or carried as the shepherd said in the "she-devil's" arms, I wished them luck after their hegira, planned with such courage, carried out so well, had ended, and they were back again amongst the tribe.

Just outside Crucecitas we met a Texan who, as he told us, owned the place, and lived in "kornkewbinage with a native gal," called, as he said,

"Pastory," who it appeared of all the females he had ever met was the best hand to bake "tortillers," and whom, had she not been a Catholic, he would have made his wife. All this without a question on our part, and sitting sideways on his horse, scanning the country from the corner of his eye. He told us that he had "had right smart of an Indian trouble here yesterday just about afternoon. Me and my 'vaquerys' were around looking for an estray horse, just six of us, when close to the ranch we popped kermash right upon three red devils, and opened fire at once. I hed a Winchester, and at the first fire tumbled the buck; he fell right in his tracks, and jest as I was taking off his scalp, I'm doggoned if the squaw and the young devil didn't come at us jest like grizzly bars. Wal, yes, killed 'em, o' course, and anyhow the young 'un would have growed up; but the squaw I'm sort of sorry about. I never could bear to kill a squaw, though I've often seen it done. Naow here's the all-firedest thing yer ever heard; jes' as I was turning the bodies over with my foot a little Indian dog flies at us like a 'painter,' the varmint, the condemndest little buffler I ever struck. I was for shootin' him, but 'Pastory' — that's my 'kornkewbyne' — she up and says it was a shame. Wal, we had to bury them, for dead Injun stinks worse than turkey-buzzard, and the dodgasted little dog is sitting on the grave, 'pears like he's froze, leastwise he hasn't moved since sun-up, when we planted the whole crew."

Under a palm-tree not far from the house the Indians' grave was dug; upon it, wretched and draggled, sat the little dog. "Pastory" tried to catch it all day long, being kind-hearted though a "kornkewbyne"; but, failing, said "God was not willing," and retired into the house. The hours seemed days in the accursed place till the sun rose, gilding the unreached Santa Rosa mountains, and bringing joy into the world. We harnessed up the mules, and started silently out on the lonely road; turning, I checked my horse, and began moralizing on all kinds of things; upon tenacity of purpose, the futility of life, and the inexorable fate which mocks mankind, making all effort useless, whilst still urging us to strive. Then the grass rustled, and across an open space a small white object trotted, looking furtively around, threw up its head and howled, ran to and fro as if it sought for something, howled dismally again, and after scratching in the ground, squatted dejectedly on the fresh-turned-up earth which marked the Indians' grave.

Sidi Bu Zibbala

Religious persecution with isolation from the world, complete as if the Lebanon were an atoll island in the Paumotus group; a thousand years of slavery, and centuries innumerable of traditions of a proud past, the whole well filtered through the curriculum of an American missionary college, had made Maron Mohanna the strange compound that he was. Summer and winter dressed in a greasy black frock-coat, hat tilted on his head, as if it had been a fez; dilapidated white-topped mother-of-pearl bebuttoned boots, a shirt which seemed to come as dirty from the wash as it went there; his shoulders sloping and his back bent in a perpetual squirm, Mohanna shuffled through the world with the exterior of a pimp, but yet with certain aspirations towards a wild life which seldom are entirely absent from any member of the Arab race. So in his village of the Lebanon he grew to man's estate, and drifted after the fashion of his countrymen into a precarious business in the East. Half proxenete, half dragoman, servile to all above him and civil for prudence' sake to all below, he passed through the various degrees of hotel tout, seller of cigarettes, and guide to the antiquities of whatever town he happened to reside in, to the full glory of a shop in which he sold embroideries, attar of roses, embroidered slippers and all the varied trash which tourists buy in the bazaars of the Levant. But all the time, and whilst he studied French and English with a view to self-advancement, the ancient glories of the Arab race were always in his mind. Himself a Christian of the Christians, reared in that hot-bed of theology the Lebanon, where all the creeds mutually show their hatred of each other, and display themselves in their most odious aspects; and whilst hating the Mohammedans as a first principle of his belief, he found himself mysteriously attracted to their creed. Not that his reason was seduced by the teachings of the Koran, but that somehow the stately folly of the whole scheme of life evolved by the ex-camel-driver appealed to him, as it has oftentimes appealed to stronger minds than his. The call to prayers, the half-contemplative, half-militant existence led by Mohammedans; the immense simplicity of their hegemony; the idea of a not impossible one God, beyond men's ken, looking down frostily through the stars upon the plains, a Being to be evoked without much hope of being influenced, took hold of him and set him thinking whether all members of the Arab race ought not to hold one faith. And in addition to his speculations upon faith and race, vaguely at times it crossed his mind, as I believe it often crosses the minds of almost every Arab (and Syrians not a few), "If all else fail, I can retire into the desert, join the tribes and pass a pleasant life, sure of a wife or two, a horse, a lance, a long flint gun, a bowl of camel's milk, and a black tent in which to rest at night."

Little indeed are the chances of a young educated Syrian to make his living in the Lebanon. A certain modicum of the young men is always absorbed into the ranks of the various true faiths which send out missionaries to convert Arab-speaking races, and those so absorbed generally pass their lives preaching shamefacedly that which they partially believe, to those whose faith is fixed. Others again gravitate naturally to Cairo to seek for Government employment, or to write in the Arabic press, taking sides for England or for France, as the editors of the opposing papers make it worth their while. But the great bulk of the intellectual Syrian proletariat emigrates to New York and there lives in a quarter by itself, engaging in all kinds of little industries, dealing in Oriental curiosities, or publishing newspapers in the Arab tongue. There they pass much of their time lounging at their shop-doors with slippers down at heel, in smoking cigarettes, in drinking arrack, and in speculating when their native country shall be free.

To none of these well-recognized careers did Maron Mohanna feel himself impelled. Soon tiring of his shop he went to Egypt, worked on a newspaper, and then became a teacher of Arabic to Europeans; was taken by one of them to London, where he passed some years earning a threadbare livelihood by translating Arabic documents and writing for the press. When out of work he tramped about the streets to cheat his hunger, and if in funds frequented music-halls, and lavished his hard-earned money on the houris who frequent such places, describing them as "fine and tall, too fond of drink, and perhaps colder in the blood than are the women of the East." Not often did his fortunes permit him such extravagances, and he began to pass his life hanging about the City in the wake of the impossible gang of small company-promoters, who in the purlieus of the financial world weave shoddy Utopias, and are the cause of much vain labour to postmen and some annoyance to the public, but who as far as I can see live chiefly upon hope deferred, for their prospectuses seem to be generally cast into the basket, from which no share list ever has returned. But in the darkest of poor Maron Mohanna's blackest days, his dreams about the Arab race never forsook him, and he studied much to master all the subtleties of his native tongue, talking with Arabs, Easterns, Persians, and the like in the lunch-room of the British Museum, where scholars of all nations, blear-eyed and bent, eat sawdust sandwiches and drink lemonade, whilst wearing out their eyes and lives for pittances which a dock labourer would turn from in disgust. Much did the shivering Easterns confabulate, much did they talk of grammar, of niceties of diction, much did they dispute, often they talked of women, sometimes of horses, for on both all Easterns, no matter how they pass their lives, have much to say, and what they say is often worth attention, for in both matters their ancestors were learned when ours rode shaggy ponies, and their one miserable wife wrestled with fifteen fair-haired children in the damp forests where the Briton was evolved. How long Maron Mohanna dwelt in London is matter of uncertainty, to what abyss of poverty he fell, or if in the worst times he tramped the Embankment, sleeping on a bench and dreaming ever of the future of the Arab race, is not set down. The next act of his life finds him the trusted manager of the West African Company at Cape Juby. There he enjoyed a salary duly paid every quarter, and was treated with much deference by the employees as being the only man the company employed who could speak Arabic. Report avers he had embraced either the Wesleyan or the Baptist faith, as the chief shareholders of the affair were Nonconformists, whose ancestors having (as they alleged) enjoyed much persecution for their faith, were well resolved that every one who came within their power should outwardly, at least, conform to their own tenets in dogma and church government.

Established at Cape Juby, Maron Mohanna for the first time enjoyed consideration, and for a while the world went well with him. He duly wrote reports, inspected goods, watched the arrival of the *Sahara*, the schooner which came once a month from Lanzarote, and generally endeavoured to discharge the duties of a manager, with some success. The chiefs Mohammed-wold-el-Biruc and Bu-Dabous, with others from the far-distant districts of El Juf, El Hodh, and from Tishit, all flattered him, offering him women from their various tribes and telling him that he too was of their blood. So by degrees either the affinity of race, the community of language or the provoking commonness of his European comrades, drew him to seek his most congenial friends amongst the natives of the place. Then came the woman: the woman who always creeps into the life of man as the snake crept into the garden by the Euphrates; and Mohanna knowing that by so doing he forfeited all chance of his career, gave up his post, married an Arab girl, and became a desert Arab, living on dates and camel's milk in the black Bedouin tents. Children he had, to whom, though desert-born, he gave the names of Christians, feeling perhaps the nostalgia of civilization in the wilds, as he had felt before the nostalgia of the desert, in his blood. And living in the desert with his hair grown long, dressed in the blue "baft" clothes, a spear in his hand and shod with sandals, he yet looked like a European clerk in masquerade.

The bushy plains stretched like an ocean towards the mysterious regions of El Juf and Timbuctoo, Wadan, Tijigja, Atar and Shingiet, and the wild steppes where the Tuaregs veiled to the eyes roam as they roamed before they hastened to the call of Jusuf-ibn Tachfin to invade El Andalos and lose the battle at Las Navas de Tolosa: the battle where San Isidro in a shepherd's guise guided the Christian host. Men came and went, on camels, horses, donkeys and on foot; all armed, all beggars, from the rich chief to the poorest horseman of the tribe; and yet all dignified, draped in their fluttering rags, and looking more like men than those whom eighteen centuries of civilization and of trade have turned to apes. Men fought, careering on their horses on the sand, firing their guns and circling round like gulls, shouting their battle-cries; men prayed, turning to Mecca at the appointed hours; men sat for hours half in a dream thinking of much or nothing, who can say; whilst women in the tents milked camels, wove the curious geometric-patterned carpets which they use, and children grew up straight, active and as fleet of foot as roe.

Inside the factory the European clerks smoked, drank, and played at cards: they learned no Arabic, for why should those who speak bad English struggle with other tongues? Meanwhile the time slipped past, leaving as little trace as does a jackal when on a windy day he sneaks across the sand. Only Maron Mohanna seemed to have no place in the desert world which he had dreamed of as a boy; and in the world of Europe typified by the factory on the beach his place was lost. On marrying he had, of course, abjured the faith implanted in him in the Lebanon, and yet though now one of the "faithful" he found no resting-place. Neither of the two contending faiths had sunk much into his soul, but still at times he saw that the best part of any faith is but the life it brings. For him, though he had dreamed of it, the wild desert life held little charm; horses he loathed, suffering acutely when on their backs, and roaming after chance gazelles or ostriches with the horsemen of the tribe did not amuse him; but though too proud to change his faith again, at times he caught himself longing for his once-loathed shop in the Levant. So that clandestinely he grew to haunt the factory and the fort, as before, in secret, he had hung round the straw-thatched mosque, and loitered in the tents. His one amusement was to practise with a pistol at a mark, and by degrees he taught his wife to shoot, till she became a marksman able to throw an orange in the air and hit it with a pistol bullet three times out of five. But even pistol-shooting palled on his soul at last, and he grew desperate, not being allowed to leave the tribe or go into the fort except in company with others, and keenly watched as those who change their faith and turn Mohammedans are ever watched amongst the Arab race. But in his darkest hour fate smiled upon him, and the head chief wanting an agent in the islands sent him to Lanzarote, and in the little town of Arrecife it seemed to him that he had found a resting-place at last. Once more he dressed himself in European clothes, he handled goods, saw now and then a Spanish newspaper a fortnight old; talked much of politics, lounged in the Alameda, and was the subject of much curiosity amongst the simple dwellers in the little town. Some said he had denied his God amongst the heathen; others again that he suffered much for conscience' sake; whilst he attended mass occasionally, going with a sense of doing something wrong, and feeling more enjoyment in the service than in the days of his belief. His wife dressed in the Spanish fashion, wore a mantilla, sometimes indeed a hat, and looked not much unlike an island woman, and was believed by all to have thrown off the errors of her faith and come into the fold.

But notwithstanding all the amenities of the island life, the unlimited opportunities for endless talk (so dear to Syrians), the half-malignant pleasure he experienced in dressing up his wife in Christian guise, sending for monstrous hats bedecked with paroquets from Cadiz, and gowns of the impossible shades of apple-green and yellow which in those days were sent from Paris to Spain and to her colonies, he yet was dull. And curiously enough, now that he was a double renegade his youthful dreams haunted him once again. He saw himself (in his mind's eye) mounted upon his horse, flying across the sands, and stealthily and half ashamed he used to dress himself in the Arab clothes and sit for hours studying the Koran, not that he believed its teachings, but that the phraseology enchanted him, as it has always, both in the present and the past, bewitched all Arabs, and perhaps in his case it spoke to him of the illusory content which in the desert life he sought, but had not found.

He read the "Tarik-es-Sudan," and learned that Allah marks even the lives of locusts, and that a single pearl does not remain on earth by him unweighed. The Djana of Essoyuti, El Ibtihaj, and the scarce "Choice of Marvels" written in far Mossul by the learned Abu Abdallah ibn Abderrahim (he of Granada in the Andalos), he read; and as he read his love renewed itself for the old race whose blood ran in his veins. He read and dreamed, and twice a renegade in practice, yet remained a true believer in the aspirations of his youth. He sailed in schooners, running from island port to island port down the trade winds; landed at little towns, and hardly marked the people in the rocky streets, Spanish in language, and in type quite Guanche, and but a step more civilized than the wild tribesmen from the coast that he had left. Then thinking maybe of his sojourn in London, and its music-halls, frequented uninterestedly the house of Rita, Rita la Jerezana; sat in the courtyard under the fig-tree with its trunk coated with whitewash, and listened to the "Cante Hondo," saw the girls dance Sevillanas; and drinking zarzaparilla syrup, learned that of all the countries in the world Spain is the richest, for there even the "women of the life" cast their accounts in ounces.

Then growing weary of their chatter and their tales of woe, each one of them being, according to herself, fallen from some high estate, he wandered to the convent of the Franciscan friars. They saw a convert in him, and put out all their theologic powers; displayed, as they know how, the human aspect of their faith, keeping the dogma out of sight; for well they knew, in vain the net is spread in the sight of any man, if the fires of hell are to be clearly seen. Long hours Mohanna talked with them, enjoying argument for its own sake after the Scottish and the Eastern way; the friars were mystified at the small progress that they made, but said the renegade spoke "as he had a nest of nightingales all singing in his mouth." And all the time his wife, an Arab of the Arabs, sighed for the desert, in her Spanish clothes. The "Velo de toalla" and the high-heeled shoes, the pomps and miseries of stays, and all the circumstance and starch of European dress, did not console her for the loss of the black tents, the familiar camels kneeling in the sand, the goats skipping about the "sudra" bushes; and the church bells made her but long more keenly for the call to prayers, rising at evening from the straw-thatched mosque.

Her children, left with the tribe, called to her from the desert, and she too found neither resting-place nor rest in the quiet island life.

At last Maron Mohanna turned again to trade, and entered into partnership with one Benito Florez; bought a schooner, and came and went between the islands and the coast. All things went well with him, and in the little island town "el renegado" rose to be quite a prosperous citizen, till on a day he and his partner quarrelled and went to law. The law in every country favours a man born in the land against a foreigner; and the partnership broke up, leaving Mohanna almost penniless. Whether one of those sudden furies which possess the Arabs, turning them in a moment and without warning from sedate well-mannered men to raving maniacs frothing at the mouth, came over him, he never told; but what is certain is that, having failed to slay his partner, he with his wife went off by night to where his schooner lay, and instantly induced his men to put to sea, and sailed towards the coast. Mohanna drew a perhaps judicious veil of mystery over what happened on his arrival at the inlet where his wife's tribe happened to be encamped. One of the islanders either objecting to the looting of the schooner upon principle, or perhaps because his share of loot was insufficient, got himself killed; but what is a "Charuta" more or less, except perhaps to his wife and family in Arrecife or in some little dusty town in Pico or Gomera? Those who assented or were too frightened to protest found themselves unmolested, and at liberty to take the schooner back. Maron Mohanna and his wife, taking the boat rowed by some Arabs, made for the shore, and what ensued he subsequently related to a friend.

"When we get near the shore my wife she throw her hat." One sees the hideous Cadiz hat floating upon the surf, draggled and miserable, and its bunch of artificial fruit, of flowers or feathers, bobbing about upon the backwash of the waves. "She throw her boots, and then she take off all her clothes I got from Seville, cost me more than a hundred 'real'; she throw her parasol, and it float in the water like a buoy, and make me mad. I pay more than ten real for it. After all things was gone she wrap herself in Arab sheet and step ashore just like an Arab girl, and all the clothes I brought from Cadiz, cost more than a hundred real, all was lost." What happened after their landing is matter of uncertainty. Whether Mohanna found his children growing up semi-savages, whether his wife having thus sacrificed to the Graces, and made a holocaust of all her Cadiz clothes, regretted them, and sitting by the beach fished for them sadly with a cane, no man can tell.

Years passed away, and a certain English consul in Morocco travelling to the Court stopped at a little town. Rivers had risen, tribes had cut the road, our Lord the Sultan with his camp was on a journey and had eaten up the food upon the usual road, or some one or another of the incidents of flood or field which render travel in Morocco interesting had happened. The town lay off the beaten track close to the territory of a half-wild tribe. Therefore upon arrival at the place the consul found himself received with scowling looks; no one proceeded to hostilities, but he remained within his tent, unvisited but by a soldier sent from the Governor to ask whether the Kaffir, son of a Kaffir, wished for anything. People sat staring at him, motionless except their eyes; children holding each other's hands stood at a safe distance from his tent, and stared for hours at him, and he remarked the place where he was asked to camp was near a mound which from time immemorial seemed to have been the common dunghill of the town. The night passed miserably, the guards sent by the Governor shouting aloud at intervals to show their vigilance, banished all chance of sleep.

Cursing the place, at break of day the consul struck his camp, mounted his horse, and started, leaving the sullen little town all wrapped in sleep. But as he jogged along disconsolately behind his mules, passing an angle of the "Kasbah" wall, a figure, rising as it seemed out of the dunghill's depths, advanced and stood before him in the middle of the way. Its hair was long and matted and its beard ropy and grizzled, and for sole covering it had a sack tied round its waist with a string of camel's hair; and as the consul feeling in his purse was just about, in the English fashion, to bestow his alms to rid himself of trouble, it addressed him in his native tongue. "Good-morning, consul, how goes the world with you? You're the first Christian I have seen for years. My name was once Mohanna, now I am Sidi bu Zibbala, the Father of the Dunghill. Your poet Shakespeare say that all the world's a stage, but he was Englishman. I, Syrian, I say all the world dunghill. I try him, Syria, England, the Desert, and New York; I find him dung, so I come here and live here on this dunghill, and find it sweet when compared to places I have seen; and it is warm and dry."

He ceased; and then the consul, feeling his words an outrage upon progress and on his official status, muttered "Queer kind of fish," and jerking at his horse's bridle, proceeded doggedly upon his way.

La Pulperia

It may have been the Flor de Mayo, Rosa del Sur, or Tres de Junio, or again but have been known as the Pulperia upon the Huesos, or the Esquina on the Napostá. But let its name have been what chance or the imagination of some Neapolitan or Basque had given it, I see it, and seeing it, dismounting, fastening my "redomon" to the palenque, enter, loosen my facon, feel if my pistol is in its place, and calling out "Carlon," receive my measure of strong, heady red Spanish wine in a tin cup. Passing it round to the company, who touch it with their lips to show their breeding, I seem to feel the ceaseless little wind which always blows upon the southern plains, stirring the dust upon the pile of fleeces in the court, and whistling through the wooden "reja" where the pulpero stands behind his counter with his pile of bottles close beside him, ready for what may chance. For outward visible signs, a low, squat, mud-built house, surrounded by a shallow ditch on which grew stunted cactuses, and with paja brava sticking out of the abode *[sic = adobe]* of the overhanging eaves. Brown, sun-baked, dusty-looking, it stands up, an island in the sea of waving hard-stemmed grasses which the improving settler passes all his life in a vain fight to improve away; and make his own particular estancia an Anglo-Saxon Eden of trim sheep-cropped turf, set here and there with "agricultural implements," broken and thrown aside, and though imported at great trouble and expense, destined to be replaced by ponderous native ploughs hewn from the solid ñandubay, and which, of course, inevitably prove the superiority of the so-called unfit. For inward graces, the "reja" before which runs a wooden counter at which the flower of the Gauchage of the district lounge, or sit with their toes sticking through their potro boots, swinging their legs and keeping time to the "cielito" of the "payador" upon his cracked guitar, the strings eked out with fine-cut thongs of mare's hide, by jingling their spurs.

Behind the wooden grating, sign in the Pampa of the eternal hatred betwixt those who buy and those who sell, some shelves of yellow pine, on which are piled ponchos from Leeds, ready-made calzoncillos, alpargatas, figs, sardines, raisins, bread — for bread upon the Pampa used to be eaten only at Pulperias — saddle-cloths, and in a corner the "botilleria," where vermuth, absinthe, square-faced gin, Carlon, and Vino Seco stand in a row, with the barrel of Brazilian caña, on the top of which the pulpero ostentatiously parades his pistol and his knife. Outside, the tracks led through the biscacheras, all converging after the fashion of the rails at a junction; at the palenque before the door stood horses tied by strong raw-hide cabrestos *[sic=cabestros]*, hanging their heads in the fierce sun, shifting from leg to leg, whilst their companions, hobbled, plunged about, rearing themselves on their hind-legs to jump like kangaroos.

Now and then Gauchos rode up occasionally, their iron spurs hanging off their naked feet, held by a raw-hide thong; some dressed in black bombachas and vicuña ponchos, their horses weighted down with silver, and prancing sideways as their riders sat immovable, but swaying from the waist upwards like willows in a wind. Others, again, on lean young colts, riding upon a saddle covered with sheepskin, gripping the small hide stirrup with their toes and forcing them up to the posts with shouts of "Ah bagual!" "Ah Pehuelche!" "Ahijuna!" and with resounding blows of their short, flat-lashed whips, which they held by a thong between their fingers or slipped upon their wrists, then grasping their frightened horses by the ears, got off as gingerly as a cat jumps from a wall. From the rush-thatched, mud-walled rancheria at the back the women, who always haunt the outskirts of a pulperia in the districts known as tierra adentro (the inside country), Indians and semi-whites, mulatresses, and now and then a stray Basque or Italian girl turned out, to share the quantity they considered love with all mankind.

But gin and politics, with horses' marks, accounts of fights, and recollections of the last revolution, kept men for the present occupied with serious things, so that the women were constrained to sit and smoke, drink maté, plait each other's hair (searching it diligently the while), and wait until Carlon with Vino Seco, square-faced rum, cachaza, and the medicated log-wood broth, which on the Pampa passes for "Vino Francés," had made men sensible to their softer charms. That which in Europe we call love, and think by inventing it that we have cheated God, who clearly planted nothing but an instinct of self-continuation in mankind, as in the other animals, seems either to be in embryo, waiting for economic advancement to develop it; or is perhaps not even dormant in countries such as those in whose vast plains the pulperia stands for club, exchange, for meeting-place, and represents all that in other lands men think they find in Paris or in London, and choose to dignify under the style of intellectual life. Be it far from me to think that we have bettered the Creator's scheme; or by the substitution of our polyandry for polygamy, bettered the position of women, or in fact done anything but changed and made more complex that which at first was clear to understand.

But, be that as it may and without dogmatism, our love, our vices, our rendering wicked things natural in themselves, our secrecy, our pruriency, adultery, and all the myriad ramifications of things sexual, without which no novelist could earn his bread, fall into nothing, except there is a press-directed public opinion, laws, bye-laws, leaded type and headlines, so to speak, to keep them up. True, nothing of all this entered our heads as we sat drinking, listening to a contest of minstrelsy "por contrapunto" betwixt a Gaucho payador and a "matrero negro" of great fame, who each in turn taking the cracked "changango" in their lazo-hardened hands, plucked at its strings in such a style as to well illustrate the saying that to play on the guitar is not a thing of science, but requires but perseverance, hard finger-tips, and an unusual development of strength in the right wrist. Negro and payador each sang alternately; firstly old Spanish love songs handed down from before the independence, quavering and high; in which Frasquita rhymed to chiquita, and one Cupido, whom I never saw in Pampa, loma, rincon, bolson, or medano, in the Chañares, amongst the woods of ñandubay, the pajonales, sierras, cuchillas, or in all the land, figured and did nothing very special; flourished, and then departed in a high falsetto shake, a rough sweep of the hard brown fingers over the jarring strings forming his fitting epitaph.

The story of "El Fausto," and how the Gaucho, Aniceto, went to Buenos Ayres, saw the opera of "Faust," lost his puñal in the crush to take his seat, sat through the fearsome play, saw face to face the enemy of man, described[1] as being dressed in long stockings to the stifle-joint, eyebrows like arches for tilting at the wing *[sic = ring?]*, and eyes like water-holes in a dry river bed, succeeded, and the negro took up the challenge and rejoined. He told how, after leaving town, that Aniceto

[1] "Medias hasta la berija
   Con cada ojo como un charco,
   Y cada ceja era un arco
   Para correr la sortija."

mounted on his Overo rosao,[1] fell in with his "compadre," told all his wondrous tale, and how they finished off their bottle and left it floating in the river like a buoy.

The payador, not to be left behind, and after having tuned his guitar and put the "cejilla" on the strings, launched into the strange life of Martin Fierro, type of the Gauchos on the frontier, related his multifarious fights, his escapades, and love affairs, and how at last he, his friend, Don Cruz, saw on an evening the last houses as, with a stolen tropilla of good horses, they passed the frontier to seek the Indians' tents. The death of Cruz, the combat of Martin with the Indian chief — he with his knife, the Indian with the bolas — and how Martin slew him and rescued the captive woman, who prayed to heaven to aid the Christian, with the body of her dead child, its hands secured in a string made out of one of its own entrails, lying before her as she watched the varying fortunes of the fight, he duly told. La Vuelta de Martin and the strange maxims of Tio Viscacha, that Pampa cynic whose maxim was never to ride up to a house where dogs were thin, and who set forth that arms are necessary, but no man can tell when, were duly recorded by the combatants, listened to and received as new and authentic by the audience, till at last the singing and the frequent glasses of Carlon made payador and negro feel that the time had come to leave off contrapunto and decide which was most talented in music, with their facons. A personal allusion to the colour of the negro's skin, a retort calling in question the nice conduct of the sister of the payador, and then two savages foaming at the mouth, their ponchos wrapped round their arms, their bodies bent so as to protect their vitals, and their knives quivering like snakes, stood in the middle of the room. The company withdrew themselves into the smallest space, stood on the tops of casks, and at the door the faces of the women looked in delight, whilst the pulpero, with a pistol and a bottle in his hands, closed down his grating and was ready for whatever might befall. "Negro," "Ahijuna," "Miente," "carajo," and the knives flash and send out sparks as the returns de tic au tac jar the fighters' arms up to the shoulder-joints. In a moment all is over, and from the payador's right arm the blood drops in a stream on the mud

[1] "En un overo rosao, flete lindo y parejito,
    Cayo al bajo al trotecito, y lindamente sentao.
  Un paisano del Bragao, de apelativo Laguna,
    Mozo ginetazo ahijuna, como creo que no hay otro
  Capaz a llevar un potro a sofrenarlo en la luna."

floor, and all the company step out and say the negro is a "valiente," "muy guapeton," and the two adversaries swear friendship over a tin mug of gin. But all the time during the fight, and whilst outside the younger men had ridden races barebacked, making false starts to tire each other's horses out, practising all the tricks they knew, as kicking their adversary's horse in the chest, riding beside their opponent and trying to lift him from his seat by placing their foot underneath his and pushing upwards, an aged Gaucho had gradually become the centre figure of the scene.

Seated alone he muttered to himself, occasionally broke into a falsetto song, and now and then half drawing out his knife, glared like a tiger-cat, and shouted "Viva Rosas," though he knew that chieftain had been dead for twenty years.

Tall and with straggling iron-grey locks hanging down his back, a broad-brimmed plush hat kept in its place by a black ribbon with two tassels under his chin, a red silk Chinese handkerchief tied loosely round his neck and hanging with a point over each shoulder-blade, he stood dressed in his chiripa and poncho, like a mad prophet amongst the motley crew. Upon his feet were potro boots, that is the skin taken off the hind-leg of a horse, the hock-joint forming the heel and the hide softened by pounding with a mallet, the whole tied with a garter of a strange pattern woven by the Indians, leaving the toes protruding to catch the stirrups, which as a domador he used, made of a knot of hide. Bound round his waist he had a set of ostrich balls covered in lizard skin, and his broad belt made of carpincho leather was kept in place by five Brazilian dollars, and through it stuck a long facon with silver handle shaped like a half-moon, and silver sheath fitted with a catch to grasp his sash. Whilst others talked of women or of horses, alluding to their physical perfections, tricks or predilections, their hair, hocks, eyes, brands or peculiarities, discussing them alternately with the appreciation of men whose tastes are simple but yet know all the chief points of interest in both subjects, he sat and drank. Tio Cabrera (said the others) is in the past, he thinks of times gone by; of the Italian girl whom he forced and left with her throat cut and her tongue protruding, at the pass of the Puán; of how he stole the Indian's horses, and of the days when Rosas ruled the land. Pucha, compadre, those were times, eh? Before the "nations," English, Italian and Neapolitan, with French and all the rest, came here to learn the taste of meat, and ride, the "maturangos," in their own countries having never seen a horse. But though they talked at, yet they refrained from speaking to him, for he was old, and even the devil knows more because of years than because he is the devil, and they knew also that to kill a man was to Tio Cabrera as pleasant an exercise as for them to kill a sheep. But at last I, with the accumulated wisdom of my twenty years, holding a glass of caña in my hand, approached him, and inviting him to drink, said, not exactly knowing why, "Viva Urquiza," and then the storm broke out. His eyes flashed fire, and drawing his facon he shouted "Muera! . . . Viva Rosas," and drove his knife into the mud walls, struck on the counter with the flat of the blade, foamed at the mouth, broke into snatches of obscene and long-forgotten songs, as "Viva Rosas! Muera Urquiza dale guasca en la petiza," whilst the rest, not heeding that I had a pistol in my belt, tried to restrain him by all means in their power. But he was maddened, yelled, "Yes, I, Tio Cabrera, known also as el Cordero, tell you I know how to play the violin (a euphemism on the south pampa for cutting throats). In Rosas' time, Viva el General, I was his right-hand man, and have dispatched many a Unitario dog either to Trapalanda or to hell. Caña, blood, Viva Rosas, Muera!" then tottering and shaking, his knife slipped from his hands and he fell on a pile of sheepskins with white foam exuding from his lips. Even the Gauchos, who took a life as other men take a cigar, and from their earliest childhood are brought up to kill, were dominated by his brute fury, and shrank to their horses in dismay. The pulpero murmured "salvage" from behind his bars, the women trembled and ran to their "tolderia," holding each other by the hands, and the guitar-players sat dumb, fearing their instruments might come to harm. I, on the contrary, either impelled by the strange savagery inherent in men's blood or by some reason I cannot explain, caught the infection, and getting on my horse, a half-wild "redomon," spurred him and set him plunging, and at each bound struck him with the flat edge of my facon, then shouting "Viva Rosas," galloped out furiously upon the plain.

Higginson's Dream

The world went very well with Higginson; and about that time — say fifteen years ago — he found himself, his fortune made, settled down in Noumea. The group of islands which he had, as he said, rescued from barbarism, and in which he had opened the mines, made all the harbours, and laid out all the roads, looked to him as their Providence; and to crown the work, he had had them placed under the French flag. Rich, *décoré*, respected, and with no worlds to conquer in particular, he still kept adding wealth to wealth; trading and doing what he considered useful work for all mankind in general, as if he had been poor.

Strange that a kindly man, a cosmopolitan, half French, half English, brought up in Australia, capable, active, pushing, and even not devoid of that interior grace a speculative intellect, which usually militates against a man in the battle of his life, should think that roads, mines, harbours, havens, ships, bills of lading, telegraphs, tramways, a European flag, even the French flag itself, could compensate his islanders for loss of liberty. Stranger in his case than in the case of those who go grown up with all the prejudices, limitations, circumscriptions and formalities of civilization become chronic in them, and see in savage countries and wild peoples but dumping ground for European trash, and capabilities for the extension of the Roubaix or the Sheffield trade; for he had passed his youth amongst the islands, loved their women, gone spearing fish with their young men, had planted taro with them, drunk kava, learned their language, and become as expert as themselves in all their futile arts and exercises; knew their customs and was as one of them, living their life and thinking it the best.

'Tis said (Viera, I think, relates it) that in the last years of fighting for the possession of Teneriffe, and when Alonso de Lugo was hard pressed to hold his own against the last Mencey, Bencomo, a strange sickness known as the "modorra" seized the Guanches and killed more of them than were slain in all the fights. The whole land was covered with the dead, and once Alonso de Lugo met a woman sitting on the hill side, who called out, "Where are you going, Christian? Why do you hesitate to take the land? the Guanches are all dead." The Spanish chroniclers say that the sickness came about by reason of a wet season, and that, coming as it did upon men weakened by privation, they fell into apathy and welcomed death as a deliverer. That may be so, and it is true that in hill-caves even to-day in the lone valleys by Icod el Alto their bodies still are found seated and with the head bowed on the arms, as if having sat down to mourn the afflictions of their race, God had been merciful for once and let them sleep. The chroniclers may have been right, and the wet season, with despair, starvation and the hardships they endured, may have brought on the mysterious "modorra," the drowsy sickness, under which they fell. But it needs nothing but the presence of the conquering white man, decked in his shoddy clothes, armed with his gas-pipe gun, his Bible in his hand, schemes of benevolence deep rooted in his heart, his merchandise (that is, his whisky, gin and cotton cloths) securely stored in his corrugated iron-roofed sheds, and he himself active and persevering as a beaver or red ant, to bring about a sickness which, like the "modorra," exterminates the people whom he came to benefit, to bless, to rescue from their savagery, and to make them wise, just, beautiful, and as apt to differentiate evil from good as even he himself. So it would seem, act as we like, our presence is a curse to all those people who have preserved the primeval instincts of our race. Curious, and yet apparently inevitable, that our customs seem designed to carry death to all the so-called inferior races, whom at a bound we force to bridge a period which it has taken us a thousand years to pass.

In his prosperity, and even we may suppose during the Elysium of dining with sous-préfets in Noumea, and on the occasions when in Melbourne or in Sydney he once again consorted with Europeans, he always dreamed of a certain bay upon the coast far from Noumea, where in his youth he had spent six happy months with a small tribe, fishing and swimming, hunting, spearing fish, living on taro and bananas, and having for a friend one Tean, son of a chief, a youth of his own age. The vision of the happy life came back to him; the dazzling beach, the heavy foliage of the palao and bread-fruit trees; the grove of cocoa-nuts, and the zigzag and intricate paths leading from hut to hut, which when a boy he traversed daily, knowing them all by instinct in the same way that horses in wild countries know how to return towards the place where they were born. And still the vision haunted him; not making him unhappy, for he was one of those who find relief from thought in work, but always there in the same way that the remembrance of a mean action is ever present, even when one has made atonement, or induced oneself to think it was not really mean, but rendered necessary by circumstances; or, in fact, when we imagine we have put to sleep that inward grasshopper which in our bosoms, blood, brain, stomach, or wheresoever it is situated, is louder or more faint according to our state of health, digestion, weakness, or what it is that makes us hear its chirp.

And so it was that cheap champagne seemed flat to him; the company of the yellow-haired and faded *demi-mondaines* whom Paris dumps upon New Caledonia insipid; the villas on the cliff outside Noumea vulgar; and the prosperity and progress of the place to which he had so much contributed, profitless and stale. Not that for a single instant he stopped working, planning and improving his estates, or missed a chance to acquire "town lots," or if a profitable 10,000 acres of good land with river frontage came into the market, hesitated for a moment to step in and buy. Now, though by this time he had long got past the need of actually trading with the natives at first hand, and kept, as rich men do, captains and secretaries and lawyers to do his lying for him, and only now and then would condescend to exercise himself in that respect when the stake was large enough to make the matter reputable, yet sometimes he would take a cruise in one of his own schooners and play at being poor. Nothing so tickles a man's vanity as to look back upon his semi-incredible past, and talk of the times when he had to live on sixpence a day, and to recount his breakfast on a penny roll and glass of milk, and then to put his hands upon his turtle-bloated stomach, smile a fat smile and say, "Ah, those were the days, then I was happy!" although he knows that at that halcyon period he was miserable, not perhaps so much from poverty, as from that envy which is as great a curse to poor men as is indigestion to the rich.

So running down the coast of New Caledonia in a schooner, trading in pearls and copra, he came one evening to a well-remembered bay. All seemed familiar to him, the low white beach, tall palm-trees, coral reef with breakers thundering over it, and the still blue lagoon inside the clump of breadfruit trees, the single tall grey stone just by the beach all graven over with strange characters, all struck a chord long dormant in his mind. So telling his skipper to let go his anchor, he rowed himself ashore. On landing he was certain of the place; the tribe, about five hundred strong, ruled over by the father of his friend Tean, lived right along the bay, and scattered in palm-thatched huts throughout the district. Then he remembered a certain cocoa-nut palm he used to climb, a spring of water in a thicket of hibiscus, a little stream which he used to dam, and then divert the course to take the fish, and sitting down, all his past life came back to him. As he himself would say, "C'était le bon temps; pauvre Tean il doit être Areki (chef) maintenant; sa soeur peut-être est morte ou mariée . . . elle m'aimait bien . . ."

But this day-dream dispelled, it struck him that the place looked changed. Where were the long low huts in front of which he used to pass his idle hours stretched in a hammock, the little taro patches? The zigzag paths which used to run from house to house across the fields to the spring and to the turtle-pond were all grown up. Couch-grass and rank mimosa scrub, with here and there ropes of lianas, blocked them so that he rubbed his eyes and asked himself, Where is the tribe? Vainly he shouted, cooeed loudly; all was silent, and his own voice came back to him muffled and startling as it does when a man feels he is alone. At last, following one of the paths less grown up and obliterated than the rest, he entered a thick scrub, walked for a mile or two cutting lianas now and then with his jack-knife, stumbling through swamps, wading through mud, until in a little clearing he came upon a hut, in front of which a man was digging yams. As many of the natives in New Caledonia speak English and few French, he called to him in English, "Where black man?" Resting upon his hoe, the man replied, "All dead." "Where Chief?" And the same answer, "Chief, he dead." "Tean, he dead?" "No, Tean Chief; he ill, die soon; Tean inside that house." And Higginson, not understanding, but feeling vaguely that his dream was shattered in some way he could not understand, called out, "Tean, oh, Tean, your friend Johnny here!" Then from the hut emerged a feeble man leaning upon a long curved stick, who gazed at him as he had seen a ghost. At last he said, "That you, John? I glad to see you once before I die." Whether they embraced, shook hands, rubbed noses, or what their greeting was is not recorded, for Higginson, in alluding to it, always used to say, "C'est bête, mais le pauvre homme me faisait de la peine."

This was his sickness. "Me sick, John; why you wait so long? you no remember, so many years ago when we spear fish, you love my sister, she dead five years ago . . . When me go kaikai (eat) piece sugar-cane, little bit perhaps fall on the ground, big bird he come eat bit of sugar-cane and eat my life."

Poor Higginson being a civilized man, with the full knowledge of all things good and evil contingent on his state, still was dismayed, but said, "No, Tean, I get plenty big gun; you savey when I shoot even a butterfly he fall. I shoot big bird so that when you go kaikai he no eat pieces, and you get well again." Thus Higginson from his altitude argued with the semi-savage, thinking, as men will think, that even death can be kept off with words. But Tean smiled and said, "Johnny, you savey heap, but you no savey all. This time I die. You go shoot bird he turn into a mouse, and mouse eat all I eat, just the same bird." This rather staggered Higginson, and he felt his theories begin to vanish, and he began to feel a little angry; but really loving his old friend, he once more addressed himself to what he now saw might be a hopeless task.

"I go Noumea get big black cat, beautiful cat, all the same tiger — you savey tiger, Tean? — glossy and fat, long tail and yellow eyes; when he see mouse he eat him; you go bed sleep, get up, and soon quite well." Tean, who by this time had changed position with his friend, and become out of his knowledge a philosopher, shook his head sadly and replied, "You no savey nothing, John; when black man know he die there is no hope. Suppose cat he catch mouse, all no use; mouse go change into a big, black cloud, all the same rain. Rain fall upon me, and each drop burn right into my bones. I die, John, glad I see you; black man all die, black woman no catch baby, tribe only fifty 'stead of five hundred. We all go out, all the same smoke, we vanish, go up somewhere, into the clouds. Black men and white men, he no can live. New Caledonia (as you call him) not big enough for both."

What happened after that Higginson never told, for when he reached that point he used to break out into a torrent of half French, half English oaths, blaspheme his gods, curse progress, rail at civilization, and recall the time when all the tribe were happy, and he and Tean in their youth went spearing fish. And then bewildered, and as if half-conscious that he himself had been to blame, would say, "I made the roads, opened the mines, built the first pier, I opened up the island; ah, le pauvre Tean, il me faisait de la peine . . . et sa soeur morte . . . she was so pretty with a hibiscus wreath . . . ah, well, pauvre petite . . . je l'aimais bien."

Thirteen Stories

Calvary

Just where the River Plate, split by a hundred islands, forms a sort of delta, a tract of marshy land in Entre Rios, known as the Rincones of the Ibicuy, spreads out flat, cut by a thousand channels, heavily timbered, shut in upon the landward side by a long range of hills of dazzling sand, and buried everywhere in waving masses of tall grass.

Grass, grass, and yet more grass. Grass at all seasons of the year, so that the half-wild horses never know the scarcity of pasture which in the winter makes them lean and rough upon the outside plains. A district shut by its sand-hills and the great river from the outer world. A paradise for horses, cattle, tigers, myriads of birds, for capibaras, nutrias, and for the stray Italians who now and then come from the cities with a rotten boat, and miserable, cheap, Belgian gun, to slaughter ducks.

The population, sparse and indolent, a hybrid breed between the Gauchos and the Chanar Indians, who at the conquest retreated into the thickest swamps and islands of the River Plate. But still a country where life flows easily away amongst the cane-brakes, thickets of espinillo, tala and ñandubay, and where from out the pajonales the half-wild horses bound like antelopes, shaking their manes, their tails aloft like flags, snorting and frisking in the pride of strength, and lighting up the landscape with their variegated colours like a herd of fallow deer. A land of vegetation so intense as to bedwarf mankind almost as absolutely as we bedwarf ourselves with our machinery in a manufacturing town. Air plants upon the trees; oven-birds' earthen, gourd-like nests hanging from boughs; great wasp nests in the hollows of the trunks; scarlet and rose-pink flamingoes fishing in the shallow pools; nutrias floating down the streams, their round and human-looking heads appearing just awash; and the dark silent channels of the stagnant backwaters, so thickly grown with water weeds that by throwing a few branches on the top a man may cross his horse.

Commerce, that vivifying force, that bond of union between all the basest instincts of the basest of mankind, that touch of lower human nature which makes all the lowest natures of mankind akin, was quite unknown. Cheating was elementary, and rarely did much harm but to the successful cheat; at times a neighbour passed a leaden dollar on a friend, was soon detected, and was branded as a thief; at times a man slaughtered a neighbour's cow, and sold the hide, stole a good horse, or perpetrated some piece of petty villainy, sufficient by its transparent folly to reassure the world that he was quite uncivilized, and not fit by his exertions ever to grow rich.

Adultery and fornication were frequent, and, again, chiefly concerned the principals, as there were no self-instituted censors, eager to carry tales, and to revenge themselves upon the world for their own impotency.

All were apt lazoers, great with the bolas, and all rode as they had issued from their mothers' wombs mounted upon a foal, and grown together with him, half horse, half man — quiet and almost blameless centaurs, and as happy as it is possible for men to be who come into the world ready baptized in tears.

So much for man in the Rincones of the Ibicuy, and let us leave him quiet and indolent, fighting occasionally at the "Pulperia" for a quart of wine, for jealousy, for politics, or any of the so-called reasons which make men shed each other's blood.

But commerce, holy commerce, thrice blessed nexus which makes the whole world kin, reducing all men to the lowest common multiple; commerce that curses equally both him who buys and him who sells, and not content with catching all men in its ledgers, envies the animals their happy lives, was on the watch. Throughout the boundaries of the River Plate, from Corrientes to the bounds of Tucuman, San Luis de la Punta to San Nicholas, and to the farthest limits of the stony southern plains, nowhere were horses cheaper than in the close Rincones of the Ibicuy. Three, four, or five, or at the most six dollars, bought the best, especially if but half-tamed, and a convenient curve of the river allowed a steamboat to discharge or to load goods, tied to a tree and moored beside the bank.

Upon a day a steamer duly arrived, whistled, and anchored, and from her, in a canoe, appeared a group of men who landed, and with the assistance of a guide went to the chief estancia of the place. The owner, Cruz Cabrera, called also Cruz el Narigudo, came to his door, welcomed them, driving off his dogs, wondered, but still said nothing, as it is not polite to ask a stranger what is the business that brings him to your house. Maté went round, and gin served in a square-faced bottle, and drank *[sic]* out of a solitary wine-glass, the stem long snapped in the middle, and spliced by shrinking a piece of green cow-hide round a thin cane, and fastening the cane into a disc of roughly-shaped soft wood. "Three dollars by the cut, and I'll take fifty." "No, four and a half; my horses are the best of the whole district." And so the ignoble farce of bargaining, which from the beginning of the world has been the touchstone of the zero of the human heart, pursued its course.

At last the "higgling of the market" — God-descended phrase — dear to economists and those who in their studies apart from life weave webs in which mankind is caught, decreed that at four dollars the deal was to be made. But at the moment of arrangement one of the strangers saw a fine chestnut colt standing saddled at the door, and claimed him as a "sweetener," and to save talk his master let him go, and then, the money counted over, the buyer, prepared to give a hand to catch the horses, and to lead them singly to the boat. Plunging and snorting, sweating with terror, and half dead with fear, kicked, cuffed, and pricked with knives, horse after horse was forced aboard, and stood tied to a ring or stanchion, the sweat falling in drops like rain from legs and bellies on the deck. Only the chestnut stood looking uneasily about, and frightened by the struggles and the sound of blows falling upon the backs of those his once companions in the wild gallops through the forest glades, who had been forced aboard.

Then Cruz Cabrera cursed his folly with an oath, and getting for the last time on his back made him turn, passage, plunge, and started and checked him suddenly, then getting off unsaddled him, and gave his halter to a man to lead him to the ship. The horse resisted, terrified at the strange unusual sight, and one of the strangers, raising his iron whip, struck him across the nose, exclaiming with an oath, "I'll show you what it is to make a fuss, you damned four dollars' worth, when once I get you safe aboard the ship." And Cruz Cabrera, gripping his long knife, was grieved, and said much as to the chastity of the stranger's mother, and of his wife, but underneath his breath, not that he feared to cut a "gringo's" throat, but that the dollars kept him quiet, as they have rendered dumb, priests, ministers of state, bishops and merchants, princes and peasants, and have closed the mouths of three parts of mankind, making them silent complices in all the villainies they see and hate, and still dare not denounce, fearing the scourge of poverty, and the smart lash which

Don Dinero flourishes over the shoulders of all those who venture even remotely to express their thoughts.

Quickly the Ibicuy melted into the mist, as the wheezy steamer grunted and squattered like a wounded wild duck, down the yellow flood. Inside, the horses, more dead than alive, panted with thirst, and yet were still too timid to approach the water troughs. They slipped and struggled on the deck, fell and plunged up again, and at each fall or plunge, the blows fell on their backs, partly from folly, partly from the satisfaction that some men feel in hurting anything which fate or Providence has placed without the power of resistance in their hands. Instinct and reason; the hypothetic difference which good weak men use as an anæsthetic when their conscience pricks them for their sins of omission and commission to their four-footed brethren. But a distinction wholly without a difference, and a link in the long chain of fraud and force with which we bind all living things, men, animals, and most of all our reasoning selves, in one crass neutral-tinted slavery. Who that has never put his bistouri upon the soul, and hitherto no vivisectionist (of men or animals) can claim the feat, shall say who suffers most — the biped or the four-footed animal? I know the cant of education, the higher organism, and the dogmatics of the so-called scientists which bid so fair to worthily replace those of the theologians, but who shall say if animals, when suddenly removed from all that sanctifies their lives, do not pass agonies far more intense than such endured by those whose education or whose reason — what you will — still leaves them hope?

By the next morning the wheezy, wood-fired steamer was in the roads of Buenos Ayres, the exiles of the Ibicuy with coats all starring, flanks tucked up, hanging their heads, no more the lightsome creatures of but yesterday.

Steam launches, pitching like porpoises in the shallow stream, whale-boats manned by Italians girt with red sashes, and with yellow shirts made beautiful with scarlet horse-shoes, and whose eyes glistened like diamonds in their roguish, nut-coloured faces, came alongside the ship. Lighters, after much expenditure of curses and vain reaches with boat-hooks at the paddle-floats, hooked on, and dropped astern. The donkey-engine started with a whirr, giving the unwilling passengers another tremor of alarm, and then the work of lowering them into the flat-bottomed lighters straight began. Kickings and strugglings, and one by one, their coats all matted with the sweat of terror, they were dropped into the boat. One or two slipped from the slings, and landed with a broken leg, and then a dig with a "facon" ended their troubles, and their bodies floated on the shallow waves, followed by flocks of gulls. Puffing and pitching, the tug dragging the lighter reached the ocean-steamer's side. Again the donkey-engine rattled and whirred, and once again the luckless animals were hoisted up, stowed on the lower deck in rows in semi-darkness, and after a due interval the vessel put to sea.

"Who would not sell a farm and go to sea?" the sailor says, and turns his quid remarking, "Go to sea for pleasure, yes, and to hell for fun." The smell of steam, confinement, the motion of the ship, monotony of days, time marked but by the dinner-bell, a hell to passengers who in their cabins curse the hours, and kill the time with cards, books, drink and flirtation, and yet find every day a week. But to the exiles of the Ibicuy, stricken with terror, too ill to eat, parching, and yet afraid to drink, hopeless and fevered, sick at heart, slipping and falling, bruised with each motion of the ship, beaten when restless, and perhaps in some dim way conscious of having left their birthplace, and foreseeing nothing but misery, who shall say what they endured during the passage, in the hot days, the stifling nights, and in the final change to the dark skies and chilling breezes of the north? Happiest those who died without the knowledge of the London streets, and whose bruised carcasses were flung into the sea, their coats matted with sweat and filth, legs swelled, and heads hanging down limply as they trailed the bodies on the decks.

The docks, the dealer's yard, the breaking in to harness, and the sale at Aldridge's, and one by one they were led out to meet no more; as theologians who have blessed man with hell, allow no paradise to beasts. Perhaps because their lives being innocent, they would have filled it up so that no man could enter, for what saint in any calendar could for an instant claim to be admitted if his life were compared to that of the most humble of his four-footed brethren in the Lord? Docked duly, to show that nature does not know how to make a horse, bitted and broken, the chestnut colt, once Cruz Cabrera's pride, started on cab work, and for a time gave satisfaction to his owner, for, though not fast, he was untiring, and, as his driver said, "yer couldn't kill 'im, 'e was a perfect glutton for 'ard work."

Streets, streets, and yet more streets, endless and sewer-like, stony and wood-paved, suburbs interminable, and joyless squares, gaunt stuccoed crescents, "vales," "groves," "places," a perfect wilderness of bricks, he trotted through them all. Derbies and boat-races, football matches, Hurlingham and the Welsh Harp, Plaistow and Finchley, Harrow-on-the-Hill, the wait at theatres, the nightly crawl up Piccadilly watching for fares, where men and women stop to talk; rain, snow, ice, frost, and the fury of the spring east wind, he knew them all, struggled and shivered, baked, shook with fatigue, and still resisted. But time, that comes upon us and our horses, stealthily creeping like Indians creep upon the war trail without a sign, loosening the sinews of our knees, thickening their wind, and making both of us useless except for worms, began to tell. The chronic cough, the groggy feet, the eye covered with a cloud, caused by a flick inside the blinkers, and the staring coat, soon turned the chestnut, from a cab with indiarubber tyres, celluloid fittings, and a looking-glass upon each side (for fools to see how impossible it is that they can ever have been made after God's image), to a night hack, and then the fall to a fish-hawker's cart was not too long delayed.

Blows and short commons, sores from the collar, and continued overwork, slipping upon the greasy streets, struggling with loads impossible to move, finished the tragedy; and of the joyous colt who but a year or two ago bounded through thickets scarcely brushing off the dew, nothing was left but a gaunt, miserable, lame, wretched beast, a very bag of bones, too thin for dog's meat, and too valueless even to afford the mercy of the knacker's fee. So, struggling on upon his Via Crucis, Providence at last remembered, and let him fall, and the shaft entering his side, his blood coloured the pavement; his owner, after beating him till he was tired, gave him a farewell kick or two; then he lay still, his eyes open and staring, and white foam exuding from his mouth.

The scent of horse dung filled the fetid air, cabs rattled, and vans jolted on the stones, and the dead horse, bloody and mud-stained, formed, as it were, a sort of island, parting the traffic into separate streams, as it surged onward roaring in the current of the streets.

A Pakeha

Rain, rain, and more rain, dripping off the sodden trees, soaking the fields, and blotting out the landscape as with a neutral-tinted gauze. The sort of day that we in the land "dove il doce Dorico risuona" designate as "saft." Enter along the road to me a neighbour of some fifty to sixty years of age, one Mr. Campbell, a little bent, hair faded rather than grey, frosty-faced as we Scotsmen are apt to turn after some half a century of weather, but still a glint of red showing in the cheeks; moustache and whiskers trimmed in the fashion of the later sixties; "tacketed" boots, and clothes, if not impervious to the rain, as little affected by it as is the bark of trees. His hat, once black and of the pattern affected at one time by all Free Church clergymen, now greenish and coal-scuttled fore and aft and at the sides. In his red, chapped, dirty, but grey-mittened hands a shepherd's stick — long, crooked, and made of hazel-wood.

"It'll maybe tak' up, laird."

"Perhaps."

"An awfu' spell o' it."

"Yes, disgusting."

"Aye, laird, the climate's sort o' seekenin'. I mind when I was in New Zealand in the sixties, aye, wi' a surveyor, just at the triangulation, ye ken. Man, a grand life, same as the tinklers, here to-day and gane to-morrow, like old Heather Jock. Hoot, never mind your dog, laird, there's just McClimant's sheep, puir silly body, I ken his keel-mark. Losh me, a bonny country, just a pairfect pairadise, New Zealand. When I first mind Dunedin it wasna bigger than the clachan there, out by. A braw place noo, I understan' and a' the folk fearfu' took up wi' horse, driving their four-in-hands, blood cattle, every one of them. There's men to-day like Jacky Price — he was a Welshmen, I'm thinking — who I mind doing their day's darg just like mysel' aboot Dunedin, and noo they send their sons hame to be educated up aboot England.

"When? 'Oo aye, I went oot in the old *London* wi' Captin Macpherson. He'd bin the round trip a matter o' fifteen times, forbye a wee bit jaunt whiles after the 'blackbirds' (slaves, ye ken, what we called free endentured labourers) to the New Hebrides. The *London*, aye, 'oo aye, she foundered in the Bay (Biscay, ye ken) on her return. It's just a special providence I wasna a passenger myself.

"Why did I leave the country? Eh, laird, ye may say. I would hae made my hame out there, but it was just the old folks threap, threaping on me to come back, I'm telling ye. A bonny toon, Dunedin, biggit on a wee hill just for a' the wurrld like Gartfarran there, and round the point a wee bit plain just like the Carse o' Stirling. Four year I wrocht at the surveyin', maistly triangulation, syne twa at shepherdin', nane o' your Australlian *[sic]* fashion tailing them a' day, but on the hame system gaen' aboot; man, I mind whiles I didna see anither man in sax weeks' time."

"Then you burned bricks, you say?"

"Aye, I didna' think ye had been so gleg at the Old Book. Aye, aye, laird, plenty of stra', or maybe it was yon New Zealand flax stalk. The awfiest plant ye ever clapt your eyes on, is yon flax. I mind when I first landed aff the old *London* — she foundered in the Bay. It was just a speecial interposition . . . but I mind I telt ye. Well, I just was dandering aboot outside the toon, and hettled to pu' some of yon flax; man, I wasna fit; each leaf is calculated to bear a pressure of aboot a ton. The natives, the Maories, use it to thack their cottages. A bonny place, New Zealand, a pairfect pairadise — six-and-thirty years ago — aye, aye, 'oo aye, just the finest country in God's airth.

"Het? Na, na, nane so het as here in simmer, a fine, dry air, and a bonny bright blue sky. Dam't, I mind the diggings opening tae. There were a wheen captins. Na, na, not sea captins, airmy captins, though there were plenty of the sea yins doon in the sooth; just airmy captins who had gone out and ta'en up land; blocked it, ye ken, far as frae here to Stirlin'. Pay for it, aye, aboot a croon the acre, and a wee bit conseederation to the Government surveyor just kept things square. Weel, when the diggins opened, some of them sold out and made a fortune. Awfu' place thae diggins, I hae paid four shillin' a pound for salt mysel', and as for speerits, they were just fair contraband.

"And the weemen. Aye, I mind the time, but ye'll hae seen the Circassian weemen aboot Africa. Weel, weel, I'm no saying it's not the case, but folk allow that yon Circassians are the finest weemen upon earth. Whiles I hae seen some tae, at fairs, ye ken, in the bit boothies, but to my mind there's naething like the Maories, especially the half-casted yins, clean-limbed, nigh on six feet high the maist o' them. Ye'll no ken Geordie Telfer, him that was a sojer, he's got a bit place o' his ain out by Milngavie. Geordie's aye bragging, bostin' aboot weemen that he's seen in foreign pairts. He just is of opeenion that in Cashmere or thereaboots there is the finest weemen in the warld. Black, na, na, laird, just a wee toned and awfu' tall, ye ken. Geordie he says that Alexander the Great was up aboot Cashmere and that his sojers, Spartans I think they ca'ed them, just intromitted wi' the native weemen, took them, perhaps, for concubines, as the Scriptures say; but ye'll ken sojers, laird; Solomon, tae, an awfu' chiel yon Solomon. The Maori men were na blate either, a' ower sax fut high, some nigh on seven fut, sure as death, I'm tellin' ye. Bonny wrestlers, tae; man, Donald Dinnie got an unco tirl wi' ane o' them aboot Dunedin, leastwise if it wasna Dinnie, it was Donald Grant or Donald McKenzie, or ane of they champions frae Easter Ross. Sweir to sell their land tae they chaps, I mind the Government sent out old Sir George Grey, a wise-like man, Sir George, ane o' they filantrofists. Weel, he just talkit to them, ca'ed them his children, and said that they shouldna resist legeetimate authority. Man, a wee wiry fella', he was the licht-weight champion wrestler at Tiki-Tiki, just up and said, 'Aye, aye, Sir George,' though he wasna gi'en him Sir George, but just some native name they had for him, 'we're a' your children, but no sic children as to gie our land for naething.' Sir George turnit the colour of a neep, ane o' yon swedes, ye ken, and said nae mair."

"How did they manage it?"

"The Government just arranged matters wi' the chiefs. Bribery, weel a' weel, I'll no gae sae far as to impute ony corruption on them, but a Government, a Government, ye ken, is very apt to hae its way.

"Dam't, 'twas a fine country, a pairfect pairadise. I mind aince going oot with Captin Brigstock, Hell-fire Jock they ca'ed him, after they bushrangers. There was ane Morgan frae Australlia *[sic]* bail't up a wheen folks, and dam't, says Captin Brigstock, ye'll hae to come, Campbell. Shot him, yes, authority must be respected, and the majesty o' law properly vendeecated, or else things dinna thrive. It was in a wood of gora-gora we came on him about the mouth of day. Morgan, ye ken, was boiling a billy in a sort o' wee clearin', his horse tied to a tree close by, when Brigstock and the others came upon him. Brigstock just shouted in the name o' the law and then let fly. Morgan, he fell across the fire, and when we all came up says he, 'Hell-fire, ye didna gie me ony chance,' and the blood spouted from his mouth into the boiling pan.

"Deid, 'oo aye, deid as Rob Roy. I dinna care to mind it. But a fine life, laird, nae slavin' at the plough, but every ane goin' aboot on horseback; and the bonny wee bit wooden huts, the folk no fashed wi' furniture, but sittin' doon to tak' their tea upon the floor wi' their backs against the wall. That's why they ca'ed them squatters. They talk aboot Australlia [*sic*] and America, but if it hadna been for the old folks I would hae made my hame aboot a place ca'ed Paratanga, and hae taken up with ane o' they Maori girls, or maybe a half-caste. Married, weel, I widna say I hae gane to such a length. Dam't, a braw country, laird, a pairfect pairadise, I'm telling ye;" and then the rain grew thicker, and seemed to come between us as he plodded on towards the "toon."

Victory

Ranks upon ranks of rastaquoères, Brazilians, Roumanians, Russians, Bulgarians, with battalions of Americans, all seated round the "piazza" of the Grand Hotel. Ladies from Boston, Chicago, and New York, their heels too high, their petticoats too much belaced, their Empire combs bediamonded so as to look almost like cut-glass chandeliers, as in their chairs they sat and read the latest news from Tampa, Santiago, and how Cervera's Squadron met the fate which they (the ladies) reckoned God prepares for those who dare to fight against superior odds.

Outside upon the boulevards, cocottes, guides, cabmen, and androgynous young men, touts, and all those who hang about that caravansary where the dulcet Suffolk whine, made sharper by the air of Massachusetts, sounds, passed and repassed.

Smug-faced, black-coated citizens from Buffalo and Albany, and from places like Detroit and Council Bluffs, to which the breath of fashion has not penetrated, scanned the *New York Herald*, read the glorious news, and, taking off their hats, deigned publicly to recognize the existence of a God, and after standing reverently silent, masticating their green cigars in contemplation of His wondrous ways, to take a drink.

Aquatic plants and ferns known only to hotels, and constituting a sub-family of plants, which by the survival of the ugliest have come at last to stand gas, dust, saliva, and an air befogged with Chypre, grew in the fountain where, in the tepid water, gold fish with swollen eyes, and blotched with patches of unhealthy white, swam to and fro, picking up crumbs and rising to the surface when some one threw a smoked-out cigarette into the basin, in the midst of which a fig-leaved Naiad held a stucco shell.

The corridors were blocked with Saratoga trunks; perspiring porters staggered to and fro, bending beneath the weight of burdens compared to which a sailor's chest is as a pill-box.

All went well; the tapes clicked off their international lies, detailing all the last quotations of the deep mines upon the Rand, the fall in Spanish Fours; in fact, brought home to those with eyes to see, the way in which the Stock Exchange had put a rascals' ring around the globe.

Waiters ran to and fro, their ears attuned to every outrage upon French, seeking to find the meaning of the jargons in which they were addressed.

Majestic butlers in black knee-breeches, and girt about the neck with great brass chains, moved slowly up and down, so grave and so respectable that had you laid your hands upon any one of them and made a bishop of him he would have graced the post.

Mysterious, well-dressed men sat down beside you, and after a few words proposed to take you in the evening to show you something new.

Women walked to and fro, glaring at one another as they had all been tigresses, or again, catching each other's eyes, reddened, and looked ashamed, as if aware, though strangers, that they understood the workings of the other's heart.

Burano chandeliers and modern tapestry, with red brocade on the two well-upholstered chairs, imparted beauty and a look of wealth, making one feel as if by striking an electric bell a door would open and a troop of half-dressed women file into the court, after the fashion of another kind of inn.

Outside the courtyard Paris roared, chattered, and yelped, cycles and automobiles made the poor *piéton's* life a misery, and set one thinking how inferior after all the Mind which thought out Eden was to our own.

Upon the asphalt the horizontales lounged along, pushing against the likely-looking passer-by like cats against a chair.

Cabs rattled, and the whole *clinquant* town wore its best air of unreality, which it puts off alone upon the morning of a revolution.

Through boulevards, parvis, cités, along the quays, in the vast open spaces which, like Saharas of grey stone, make the town desolate, in cafés, brothels, theatres, in church and studio, and wherever men most congregate, groups stood about reading the news, gesticulating, weeping, perspiring, and agog with a half-impotent enthusiastic orgasm of wildest admiration for Spain, Cervera, and the men who without bunkum or illusion steamed to certain death. And, curiously enough, the execration fell not so much upon Chicago as on "ces cochons d'Anglais," who by their base connivance had wrought the ruin of the Spanish cause.

Yankees themselves read and remarked with sneers that England's turn was coming next, and after "Kewby," that they reckoned to drag the British flag through every dunghill in New York; then one winked furtively and said, "We need them now, but afterwards we'll show Victoria in a cage for a picayune a peep, and teach the Britishers what to do with their old Union Jack," thinking no doubt of the ten-cent paper which is sold in every city of the States, stamped with the Spanish flag.

And as I sat, musing on things and others — thinking, for instance, that when you scratch a man and see his blood you know his nature by the way he bears his wound, and that the Spaniards, wounded to the death, were dying game (after the fashion of the English in times gone by, before Imperialism, before the Nonconformist snuffle, the sweating system, and the rest had changed our nature), and that the Yankees at the first touch cried out like curs, though they had money, numbers, and everything upon their side — I fell a-thinking on the Spain of old. Iñigo Lopez de Mendoza, el Gran Capitan, Cortes (not at the siege of Mexico, but in the rout before Algiers) came up before me, and I thought on the long warfare, extending over seven hundred years, by which Spain saved the southern half of Europe from the Moors; upon Gerona, Zaragoza, and, most of all, upon Cervera, last of the Quixotes, Vara de Rey, Linares, and the poor peasants from Galician hills, thyme-scented wastes in Lower Aragon, Asturian mountains, and Estremenian oak-woods, who, battling against superior numbers, short of food, of ammunition, and bereft of hope, were proving their descent from the grim soldiers of the Spanish "Tercios" of the Middle Ages, and making the invaders of their country pay for their piracy in blood.

Blood is the conqueror's coin the whole world over, and if the island which Columbus found for Spain pass into other hands, let those who take it pour out their blood like water to inaugurate their reign of peace.

Where the connection between the senses and the brain comes in, which influences first, and how, or whether a wise Providence, always upon His guard (after the fashion of an operator in a Punch and Judy show), influences each man directly, as by celestial thought suggestion, I cannot tell.

All that I know is, that once walking on the rampart gardens which in Cadiz overhang the sea and form the outside rim of the "Taza de Plata," as the Spaniards call the town, I on a sudden saw the River Plate. The Gauchos, plains, wild horses, the stony wastes, the ostriches (the "Alegria del Desierto"), came up before me, and in especial a certain pass over a little river called the Gualiyan; the sandy dip, the metallic-looking trees, the greenish river with the flamingoes and white herons and the black-headed swans; the vultures sitting motionless on the dead trees, and most of all the penetrating scent of the mimosa, known to the natives as the "espinillo de olor."

Turning and wondering why, I saw a stunted tree with yellow blossoms duly ticketed with its description "Mimosa" this or that, and with its "habitat" the warmer district of the River Plate.

I leave these things to wise philosophers and to those men of science who seem to think mankind is worth the martyrdom of living dogs and cats; or who, maybe, drag out the entrails of their quivering fellow-mortals merely to stimulate their senses or erotic powers.

But the "dwawm" over, looking about, fenced in by swarms of overjoyed Americans, all talking shrilly, reading out the news, exultant at the triumph of their fleet, puffed up and arrogant as only the descendants of the Puritans can be, I saw a Spaniard sitting with his daughter, a girl about nineteen.

Himself a Castellano rancio, silent and grave, dressed all in black, moustache waxed to a point, square little feet like boxes, brown little hands, face like mahogany, hair cropped close, and with the unillusional fatalistic air of worldly wisdom mixed with simplicity which characterizes Spaniards of the older school.

Being a Christian, he spoke no tongue but that which Christians use, was proud of it, proud of his ignorance, proud (I have no doubt) of his descent.

No doubt he saw everything through the clear dazzling atmosphere of old Castille, which Spaniards of his kind seem to condense and carry off with them for use in other climes.

Seeing so clearly, he saw nothing clear, for the intelligence of man is so contrived as to be ineffective if a mist of some sort is not interposed.

The daughter fair, fair with the fairness of a Southern, blue-eyed, and skin like biscuit china, hands and feet fine, head well set on, and yet with the decided gestures and incisive speech, the "aire recio," and the "meneo" of the hips in walking, of the women of her race.

They sat some time before a pile of newspapers, the father smoking gravely, taking down the smoke as he were drinking it, and then in a few minutes breathing it out to serve as an embellishment to what he said, holding his cigarette meanwhile fixed in a little silver instrument contrived like two clasped hands.

The Spanish newspapers were, of course, all without news, or said they had none, and as the daughter read, the old man punctuated with "Valiente," "Pobrecitas," and the like, when he heard how before El Caney, Vara de Rey had died, or how the Americans had shot the three Sisters of the Poor whose bodies were found lying with lint and medicine in their hands.

"Read me the papers of the Americans, hija de mi corazon," and she began, translating as she read.

Reading of the whole agony, choking but self-possessed, she read: the *Vizcaya*, *Almirante Oquendo*, and the rest; the death of Villamil, he who at least redeemed the promise made to the Mother of his God in Cadiz before he put to sea.

And as she read the old man gave no sign, sitting impassive as a fakir, or like an Indian warrior at the stake.

She went on reading; the fleet steamed through the hell of shot and shell, took fire, was beached, blew up, and still he gave no sign.

Cervera steps on board the conqueror's ship, weeping, gives up his sword, and the old man sat still.

When all was finished, and the last vessel burning on the rocks, slowly the tears fell down his old brown cheeks, and he broke silence. "Virgen de Guadalupe, has not one escaped?" and the girl, looking at him through her now misty eyes, "No, papa, God has so willed it. . . . What is wrong with your moustache?"

Then, with an effort, he took down his grief, said quietly, "I must change my hairdresser," got up, and offering his daughter his arm, walked out impassible, through the thick ranks of the defeated foe.

Thirteen Stories

Rothenberger's Wedding

Short and broad-shouldered, with the flaxen hair and porcelain-coloured eyes of the true man of Kiel or Koenigsberg, Dr. Karl Rothenberger prided himself on being a townsman of the Great Kant, "who make the critique of pure sense." For him in vain the modern mystic spread his nets; his mass, his psychological research, his ethics based on the saving of his own gelatinous soul, said nothing to the man of Koenigsberg. His work to minister by electricity to the rheumatic, the gouty; to those who had loved perhaps well, but certainly in a vicarious and post-prandial fashion; his passion fishing with a float; a "goode felawe," not too refined, but yet well educated; his literary taste bounded by idealistic novels about materialistic folk, and the drum-taps of the bards of Anglo-Saxon militarism; the doctor looked on the world as a vast operating theatre, sparing not even his own foibles in his diagnosis of mankind. All sentiment he held if not accursed, yet as superfluous, and though he did not pride himself exactly on his opinions, knowing them well to be but the result of education, and of a few molecules of iron, more or less, in the composition of his blood, yet would deliver them to all and sundry, as he were lecturing to students in a university. Women he held inferior to men, as really do almost all men, although they fear to say so; but again, he said, "de womens they have occupy my mind since I was eighteen years."

So after many wanderings in divers lands, he came, as wise men will, to London, and set up his household gods in a vast plane-tree-planted square (with cat ground in the middle called a garden), and of which the residents each had a key, but never walked in, sat in, or used in any way, though all of them would have gone to the stake rather than see a member of the public enter into its sacred precincts, or a stray child play in it, unless attended by a nurse.

Honours and fees fell thick on Rothenberger, and he became greatly belettered, member of many a learned, dull society. He duly purchased a degree; and squares and crescents quite a mile away sent out their patients, and were filled with the sonorous glory of his name. One thing was wanting, and that one thing troubled him not a little; but he yet saw it was inevitable if he would rise to Harley Street or Saville Row, and the sleek pair of horses which (without bearing-reins) testify to a doctor's status in the scientific world. A wife, or as he said, a "real legitimate," to prove to all his patients that he was a moral man. Strange that the domestic arrangements of a public man should militate for or against him; but so it is, at least in England, where even if a man cheat and spread ruin to thousands, yet he may find apologists, chiefly, of course, amongst that portion of the public who have not suffered by his delinquencies, so that his life be what is known as pure. Morals and purity in our group of islands seem to condone drunkenness, lies, and even theft (so that the sum stolen be large enough), and to have crystallized themselves into a censorship of precisely the very thing as to which no man or woman has the right to call another to account.

So Rothenberger, looking about for a vessel by means of which to purify himself (and push his business), lit on a girl with money, living, as he said, "oot by Hampstead way;" went through the process known as courting, in a mixture of German and of English, eked out with Plaat-Deutsch, and finally induced the lady to fix the day on which to make him pure. Science and business jointly having so taken up his time that he had learnt but little English, he was at some loss, and left arrangements to the family of his intended wife.

Not knowing English customs, he had written asking in what costume he should appear on the great day, and received a letter telling him to make his appearance at the church duly dressed in a tall hat, light trousers, and a new frock coat. Frock coat he read as "frac," and ordered wedding garments such as he thought suitable, with the addition of a brand-new evening coat. The wedding breakfast having been ordered at the Hôtel Metropole, he there transferred himself, proposing to pass the night before his final entry into moral life quietly and decently, as befits one about to change his state. But as he said, "God or some other thing was of another mind, for when I was arriving at the place, mein head feel heavy, and I was out of sorts, and when I ring the bell, a housemaid answer it wit a hot-water jug, and came into the room. Himmel, what for a girl, black hair like horse's tail, great glear plue eyes, and tall and fat, it was a miracle. I fall in love wit her almost at once, but I say nothings, only wink little at her with my eye. All the night long I could not schleep, thinking part of the housemaid, part of mein wife, and part if perhaps I was not going to do a very silly ding. When it was morning I have quite forgot the church, but still remember what the clergyman was like. So I go to the porter (he was a landsman of my own), and ask him to get me a cab, and then explain, I was to be married oot by Hampstead way, that morning at eleven and half o'clock. The porter say what church shall I tell the schelm to drive to, but mein Got I have forgot. So I say, go to Hampstead, and I will go to all the churches and ask if a German is to be married, till I find the right one out. The cabman think that I was mad, and I get into the cab dressed in clear trousers, white waistcoat, and plue necktie, mit little spot; shiny new boots that hurt me very much; with yellow gloves three-quarter-eight in size, and with my new "frac" coat, so that I think myself, eh, Rothenberger, was that really you? The cabman wink mit de porter, and we start away. We drive and drive, first to one church and then another, and I always ask, is it in this church that a German is to be marry at half twelve o'clock? Dey grin at me, and every one say no. De dime approach, and I was sweating in the cab, not knowing what they say if at half twelve o'clock I not turn up to time. At last looking out from the window I see the clergyman walking along the street mit a big hymn-book in his hand. I cry to him, Ach Himmel, it is I, Karl Rothenberger, that you must marry at half twelve o'clock. He stop, and shomp into the cab, and then we drive to church.

All was so glad to see me, for I hear one say, I thought the German must have change his mind. I ran into the church, and my wife say, What for a costume is it that you have? Frock coat and clear grey pants, dat is not wedding dress; so I say I know dat, but why you write to me, mind and buy a new "frac coat"?

They mumble out their stuff, and when the clergyman ask me if I want this woman for mein wife, I say, all right, and all the people laugh like everythings. Then when he say, I, Karl, do promise and etcetera, I say, dat is so, and de people laugh again. At last it all was done, and we drive off to the hotel to have the breakfast, and mein wife look beautiful in her new travelling dress. At the hotel the company was met, and I go up to mein apartment to change the dam frac coat, to wash mein hands, and put a little brillantine on my moustache, whilst mein wife mit the bridesmaids go to another room, and all the company was waiting down below.

I want hot water, so I rang the bell, and the stout pretta chambermaid she bring it in a jug. How the thing pass I never knew till now, but I wink at her, and she laugh, and then — she put down the jug, just for a moment, — for the company, mein wife, her father, and the bridesmaids, all was waiting down below. So I come down and make mein speech, talk to the bridesmaids, and we eat like anythings, and then we drive away to pass our honeymoon, and somehow I feel mein head much lighter than before. Marriage is good for man, it sober him, it bring him business, and it bring him children, and . . . I am happy mit my wife . . . The housemaid, oh yes, ach Got, I hear that some one take from the place to live mit him, and it is not a wonder, for she was so tall, so stout, have such black hair, and such great eyes, it was a pity that she spend her life answering the bell, and bringing up hot water in a jug.

La Clemenza de Tito

The hotel paper had a somewhat misguiding "Comfort" as its telegraphic address. Upon the walls were reproductions of sporting prints by Leech, depicting scions of the British aristocracy taking their pleasures not so very sadly after all, and easily demonstrating their superiority to several smock-frocked rustics by galloping close past them, and shouting "Tally-ho," holding their left ear between their thumb and finger to emphasize the note. Apollinaris and whisky splits, Fritz Rupprecht's "Special," with other advertisements of a like nature, filled up the blanks between the oleographs. *Iron* and *Commerce*, with the *Cook's Excursionist* and *Engineering*, lay untouched upon the tables, serving to show that if some books be not real books at all, there are newspapers which are, as it were, but dummies, holding no police news, football specials, murders, assaults on women, divorce cases, and other items which the educated public naturally expects within their sheets. Slipshod and futile, but attentive German waiters, went about bringing hot whisky, whisky and soda, whisky and lemonade, and whisky neat to the belated customers. Upon the tables glasses had made great rings, commercial travellers had left their pigskin satchels in a heap, and, by the fire, a group of travellers sat silently drinking after the Scottish fashion, and spitting in the grate. Twelve o'clock, half-past twelve, then one by one they dropped away murmuring good-night, and setting down their glasses with an air of having worked manfully for a good night's repose.

Still I sat on gazing into the fire, and almost unaware that on the other side sat a companion of my vigil, till at last he said, "Do you know Yambo, sir?" and to my vague assent rejoined, "Yambo on the Arabian coast, just opposite Hodeida, where vessels in the pilgrim trade discharge their 'niggers.' It's the port for Mecca, that is, the 'Sambaks' used to put in there, but now we do the traffic right from Mogador." I looked with interest at the man, liking his Demosthenic style of opening remarks. Tall and broad-shouldered, dressed in navy blue, boots like small packing-cases, and a green necktie in which was stuck a cairngorm pin; he wore a silver watch-chain with a small steering-wheel attached to it; not quite a sailor, yet a look of the sea about his clothes; he had a face open and innocent, yet wrinkled round the eyes like a young elephant, and struck me as being, perhaps not foolish, certainly not wise, but with a tinge of worldly wisdom gathered in seaport towns, at music-halls, and other places where those who go down to the sea in ships gain their experience of life. "Yambo," I said; "I thought that Jeddah was the port the pilgrims landed at." "Well, so it is," he said, "but I was thinking about Yambo, been there a many times, used to run arms for the tribes to fight the Turks, when I was fourth engineer in the old *Pyramus*. Yes, yes, I've been at sea most all my life, though my old dad keeps a slap-up hotel at Weston-super-Māre. No need to go to sea, no, but you know some folks would go to hell for pleasure, and I suppose I'm one. Dad, you know — now were you ever at Weston-super-Māre? — is fond of literature, does a bit himself, Chambers you know; mostly upon the conchology and the fossils of the South Devon coast; awfully fond of it, and so am I, nothing I like better than, after getting out of the engine-room, to lie on deck and read one of Bulwer's books or Dickens's, both of them stunning. No, I never write myself. Can't make out what set me thinking about Yambo. What! you won't? Well, waiter, waiter, Garçong, as we used to say at Suez, another whisky, slippy, you know. I've always been a temperate man, but like a nightcap before turning in. Perim ain't so far off from Yambo; ah yes, now I remember what it was I had to say. You know them Galla girls? prime, ain't they? But Perim, I remember being Shanghaed *[sic]* there, nothing to do, a beastly hole; sand, beastly, gets in your socks, gets in your hair, makes you feel dirty, no matter how you wash. Well, you know, there were about two hundred of us there, some kind of Government work was going on, and I was left there out of my ship, kind of loaned off, you see, to help the Johnnies at the condensing works. I've been at Suez, Yambo as I told you, Rangoon, down at Talcahuano on the Chilian coast, wrecked in Smythe's Channel, and been about a bit, but Perim fairly takes the cake, not even a sheet of blotting-paper between it and hell. As I was saying, then, we were cooped up, and not a woman in the place; even the Government saw it at last, thought maybe worse would happen if they did nothing, and sent and got six of them Galla girls. Leastwise, if they didn't send for them, they let a Levantine, Mirandy was his name, introduce them on the strict Q.T. Well, you know, the thing was like this, sir — you know them Galla girls, black as a boot and skins always as cool as ice, even in

a khamsin; some people says they are better than white girls; but not
in mine; but anyhow they've got no 'Bookay d'Afreek' about them, it
always turns me sick. As I was saying, I thought I'd have a 'pasear' one
evening, so I lemonaded up to the 'Mansion,' and began talking to one
of them girls, sort of to pass the time. Serpent upon the rocks, eh? well,
that old Solomon knew something about girls. Now here comes in the
curious thing, it always strikes me just as if I'd read it in a book; Dickens
now or Thackeray could have 'andled it, Bulwer would 'ave made it a
little loosious. Just as the gal was taking off her things — oh, no offence,
captain, I'm telling you the thing just as it happened — I saw she had
a crucifix a-hanging round her neck. Papist? Oh no, not much; father,
he sat under Rev. Hiles Hitchens, light of the Congregationalists. No,
no, nothing to do with Rome, never could bear the influence of the
confessor in a family. A little free myself, especially below latitude forty,
but at 'ome and in the family I like things ship-shape. Well, as I said,
round her black neck she had a silver crucifix, contrast of colour made
the thing stand out double the size. Ses I, 'What's that?' and she says,
'Klistian girl, Johnny, me Klistian all the same you.' That was a stopper
over all, and I just reached for my hat, says, 'Klistian are yer,' and I gave
her two of them Spanish dollars and a kiss, and quit the place. What
did she say? Why, nothing, looked at me and laughed, and says, 'You
Klistian, Johnny, plenty much damn fool.' No, I don't know what she
meant, I done my duty, and that's all I am concerned about.

"Another half, just a split whisky and Apollinaris. Well, if you won't,
good-night;" and the door slammed, leaving me gazing at the fast-
blackening fire.

Sohail

Sohail is the Arabic name of the star Canopus, to which a curious belief belongs. It appears that in some fashion, known alone to Allah, the fate of the Arab race is bound up with the star. Where it sheds its light their empire flourishes, and there alone. Wherefore or why the thing is so, no true believer seems to know, but that it is so he is well aware, and that suffices him.

Questionings and doubts, changes of costume and religion, striving for ideals, improvements, telegraphs and telephones, are well enough for Christians, whose lives are passed in hurry and in hunting after gold. For those who have changed but little for the last two thousand years, in dress, in faith and customs, it is enough to know it is a talismanic star. Let star-gazers and those who deal in books, dub the star Alpha (or Beta) Argo, it is all one to Arabs. If you question knowledge, say the Easterns, it falls from its estate. If this is so the empiric method has much to answer for. Knowledge and virtue and a horse's mouth should not pass through too many hands. Knowledge is absolute, and even argument but dulls it, and strips it of its authenticity, as the bloom of a ripe peach is lost, almost by looking on it.

Of one thing there can be no doubt. When in the Yemen, ages before the first historian penned the fable known as history, the Arabs, watching their flocks, observed Sohail, it seems to have struck them as a star differing from all the rest.

Al-Makkari writes of it on several occasions. The Dervish Abderahman Sufi of Rai, in his *Introduction to the Starry Heavens*, remarks that, at the feet of Sohail is seen, in the neighbourhood of Bagdad, a "curious white spot." The "curious white spot" astronomers have thought to be the greater of the two Magellan clouds. Perhaps it is so, but I doubt if the Arabs, as a race, were concerned about the matter, so that they saw the star.

From wandering warring tribes Mohammed made a nation of them. Mohammed died and joined the wife in paradise, of whom he said, "By

Allah, she shall sit at my right hand, because when all men laughed she clave to me." Then came Othman, Ali, and the rest, and led them into other lands, to Irak, Damascus, El Hind, to Ifrikia, lastly to Spain, and still their empire waxed, even across the "black waters" of the seas, and still Sohail was there to shine upon them. In the great adventure, one of the few in which a people has engaged; when first Tarik landed his Berbers on the rock which bears his name; at the battle on the Guadalete where the king, Don Roderick, disappeared from the eyes of men, leaving his golden sandals by a stream; to Seville, Cordoba, and Murcia, the land of Teodmir ben Gobdos, to which the Arabs gave the name of Masr, right up to Zaragoza, Sohail accompanied the host. A curious host it must have been with Muza riding on a mule, and with but two-and-twenty camels to carry all its baggage. From Jativa to Huesca of the Bell, where King Ramiro, at the instigation of Abbot Frotardo (a learned man), cut off his nobles' heads as they were poppies in a field, they followed it across the Pyrenees, halting at the spot where from his "Camp in Aquitaine" Muza dispatched a messenger to Rome to tell the Pope that he was coming to take him by the beard if he refused Islam. Then the wise men (who always march with armies), looking aloft at night, declared the star was lost. Although they smote the Christian dogs, taking their lands, their daughters, horses, and their gold, on several occasions as Allah willed it, yet victory was not so stable as in Spain. Perhaps beyond the mountains their spirits fell from lack of sun, or their horses sickened in the fat plains of France.

Then the conquering tide had spent itself and flowed back into Spain; at Zaragoza the first Moorish kingdom rose. Al-Makkari writes that at that time Sohail was visible in Upper Aragon, but low on the horizon. Again the Christians conquered, and the royal race of Aben Hud fled from the city. Ibn Jaldun relates that, shortly afterwards, Sohail became invisible from Aragon. The Cid, Rodrigo Diaz, he of Vivar (may God remember him), prevailed against Valencia, and from thence the star, indignant, took its departure. And so of Jativa, Beni Carlo, and Alpuixech.

Little by little Elche, with its palm-woods, and even Murcia bade it good-bye, as one by one, in the centuries of strife, the Christians in succession conquered each one of them. At last the belief gained ground that, only at one place in Spain, called from the circumstance Sohail, could the star be seen. At Fuengirola, between Malaga and Marbella, still stands the little town the Arabs called Sohail, lost amongst sand-hills, looking across at Africa, of which it seems to form a part; cactus and olive, cane-brake and date palms, its chiefest vegetation; in summer, hot as Bagdad, in winter, sheltered from the winds which come from Christendom by the Sierras of the Alpujarra and Segura. Surely there the star would stop, and let the Arab power flourish under its influence, and there for centuries it did stand stationary. The City of the Pomegranate was founded, the Alhambra, with its brilliant court, the Generalife; and poets, travellers, and men of science gathered at Granada, Cordoba, and at Isbilieh. Ab-Motacim, the poet king of Cordoba, planted the hills with almond trees, to give the effect of snow, which Romaiquia longed for. He wrote his *Kasidas*, and filled the courtyard full of spices and sugar for his queen to trample on, when she saw the women of the brickmakers kneading the clay with naked feet, and found her riches but a burden to her. Averroes and Avicenna, the doctors of medicine and of law, laid down their foolish rules of practice and of conduct, and all went well. Medina-el-Azahra, now a pile of stones where shepherds sleep or make believe to watch their sheep, where once the Caliph entertained the ambassador from Constantinople, showing him the golden basin full of quicksilver, "like a great ocean," rose from the arid hills, and seemed eternal. Allah appeared to smile upon his people, and in proof of it let his star shine. Jehovah though was jealous. A jealous God, evolved by Jews and taken upon trust by Christians, could not endure the empire of Islam. Again town after town was conquered, Baeza, Loja, Antequera, Guadix and Velez-Malaga, even Alhama (Woe is me, Alhama), lastly Granada. Then came the kingdom of the Alpujarra, with the persecutions and the rebellions, Arabs and Christians fighting like wolves and torturing one another for the love of their respective Gods. Yet the star lingered on at Fuengirola, and whilst it still was seen hope was not lost. A century elapsed, and from Gibraltar — from the spot where first they landed — the last Moors embarked. In Spain, where once they ruled from Jaca to Tarifa, no Moor was left. Perhaps about the mountain villages of Ronda a few remained, but christianized by force, the sword and faggot ever the best spurs to the true faith. But they were not the folk to think of stars or legends, so that no one (of the true faith) could say whether Sohail still lingered over Spain.

Trains, telegraphs, and phonographs, elections and debates in parliament, with clothes unsuited to the people they deform, give a false air of Europe to the land. The palm-trees, cactus, canes, and olives, the tapia walls, the women's walk and eyes, the horses' paces, and the fatalistic air which hangs on everything, give them the lie direct. The empire of the Arabs, though departed, yet retains its hold. The hands that built the mosque at Cordoba, the Giralda, the Alhambra, and almost every parish church in Southern Spain, from ruined aqueduct and mosque, sign to the Christian half derisively. So all the land from the gaunt northern mountains to the hot swamps along the Guad-el-Kebir (stretching from Seville to San Lucar) is part of Africa. The reasons are set forth lengthily by the ethnographers, economists, and the grave foolish rout of those who write for people who know nothing, of what they do not understand themselves.

But the star's lingering is the real cause, and whilst it lingers things can never really go on in Spain as they go on in England, where gloom obscures all stars. The Arabs, issuing from the desert like the khamsin, came, conquered, and possessed, their star shone on them, and its rays sank deep into the land. Their empire waned, and they, retreating, disappeared into the sands from whence they sprang. Spain knows them not, but yet their influence remains. Only at Cadiz can the talisman be seen, shining low down on the horizon, and still waiting till the precession of the equinoxes takes it across the Straits. Let it recross, and shine upon the old wild life of the vast plains, upon the horsemen flying on the sands, whirling and circling like gulls, whilst the veiled women raise the joyous cry which pierces ears and soul; upon the solemn stately men who sit and look at nothing all a summer's day, and above all upon the waveless inland sea men call the Sahara.

There may it shine forever on the life unchanged since the Moalakat, when first the rude astronomers observed the talisman and framed the legend on some starry night, all seated on the ground.

Success

R. B. Cunninghame Graham

To my mother

The author has to thank the editors of the "Saturday Review" and "Justice" for permission to republish some of the sketches.

Introduction

In the Preface to *Success* Cunninghame Graham shows his real excitement about writing and engaging the reader. He compares himself to a gladiator fighting for his artistic life. Writers and artists, he alleges, feel contempt for their readers because they could not do what they do – but they fear their readership because, like the Roman overlords, they have the power to judge and condemn them. It is natural for there to be tension between the writer and the reader because both think that they are right. It is, he says, the writer's job to convince the reader, and when he feels he has done so the spice goes out of the argument. However, there are more readers than writers, so in the end the readers will always win and the writer has to start afresh each time with new arguments and ideas. Like the gladiator when his work receives the "thumbs down" he must smile and press on.

The seventeen stories and sketches which make up this volume, which is dedicated to Graham's mother, Mrs Bontine, explore ideas of what constitutes success. Typical of Cunninghame Graham, they show a wide range of settings. Two are set in his beloved Argentina, two in North Africa and one in Southern Spain. Six are set in London, two in Scotland, one in Northern Ireland. Two have biblical/allegorical settings whilst the very first item is a disquisition on the nature of success itself.

"Success" contains no narrative element. It argues that it is those who fail rather than those who succeed who are remembered by posterity – people like Hannibal, Alcibiades, and Mary Queen of Scots. Success is simply a recognition that you are better than others. Successful nations are boring. Failures, on the other hand, keep themselves free of vulgarity, and by illustration we are left with the pathetic image of the skeleton of a defeated Spanish General in the tattered rags of his uniform sitting in a chair looking out to a Cuban sea, a topical image relating to the recent defeat of Spain by the USA. The General's bleached bones "were of themselves more interesting than were his living conquerors with their cheap air of insincere success."

"The Gualichu Tree" is a haunting picture, supposedly obtained from a Jesuit priest, of a solitary tree in the remoteness of the Colorado desert in Argentina. Gualichu is the Indian God of evil and to the Indians the tree "was but an altar on which they placed their free will offerings". The gauchos, on the other hand, feared it believing the God to inhabit the tree. In this remote desert it also served as a landmark for travellers. Used as such on one occasion by a Christian ostrich hunter he was, sadly, disappointed in his hope of obtaining water from fellow travellers there and died of thirst beneath it.

Again set in Argentina on the pampas of the River Plate, a wild area "where the passions have full play," "Los Seguidores" is a dramatic story full of the elemental starkness of world of the black brothers of the Cauldstaneslap in R L Stevenson's *Weir of Hermiston*. It tells of two brothers Cruz and Froilan, complete opposites in temperament and attitude. Cruz is considered to be relatively moral and upright and Froilan a libertine. Both start to have feelings for their much younger stepsister. Eventually Cruz can control his anger for his rival brother no longer and attacks him with a knife. Ironically he slips and stabs himself. In his dying moments he asks his brother to make sure his sister marries a decent man. A fascinating and integral aspect of the story is the beautiful description of the brothers' horses (los seguidores, the followers) which are trained in pairs to follow one another, the second always being unmounted so that it can carry heavy loads. At the end of the story, the body of Cruz, the once dominant brother, is propped up on the saddle of the second horse to become the "follower", led by his brother to his burial place.

"Un Infeliz" is set in an unnamed town in Algeria and is a blend of travelogue and story. Having described the inhabitants and architecture of this French-controlled place the narrator is approached with obsequious politeness by a man seeking a lift in his carriage to his copper mine some thirty miles away. He has the appearance of some pathetic sea-beaten boulder, worn hollow by the beating of the waves of life ... "he bore upon his face the not to be mistaken mark of failure: that failure which alone makes a man interesting and redeems him from the vulgarity of success. He is a Frenchman who has failed to make his fortune at home and has come to try his luck in Algeria but, in spite of his education and culture, has had mere crass success." When the carriage nears the mine and its surrounding village the scene is one of dilapidation and misery. When the man leaves the carriage his faded grey clothes merge with the boulders and he becomes indistinguishable from his surroundings.

Also set in North Africa in the city of Marrakech in Morocco is "From the Mouth of the Sahara". In this sketch there is no narrative as such, rather what we have is a brilliant description of the heaving chaos of the city centre with its bazaars, its street entertainers, its trades-people, its beggars and its animals. Everyone makes their way to the horseshoe gate to view the procession of the desert Arabs who are leaving the city. They are invested "with a kind of sanctity" by the city dwellers because, in spite of their great poverty and lack of sophistication, they represent the uncorrupted purity of the Arab race – the prototype of their people. At the end of the procession as night descends comes the holy man whom all reverence.

"At Utrera" describes a railway station near Seville in Southern Spain. The people of this region are much poorer and much less sophisticated than the people of the north of the country. Their concerns are with the major and basic issues of life, like love and hatred, rather than the material diversions which preoccupy the prosperous northerners. This is illustrated in the graphic description of the straightforward, honest and unpretentious behaviour of the passengers congregating in the station at Utrera. These people might be considered underprivileged by some but, Graham seems to be asking, are they therefore inferior?

The next six pieces are set in London. "Might, Majesty and Dominion" describes the scene at the death of Queen Victoria. The narrator describes her as the mother of the nation and how the country is enveloped in grief at her passing. He describes too the tremendous progress that has been made during her reign. And yet at the end, ironically, a poor man scavenges for food among the leftovers discarded by the crowd. Lastly, a man grown old in the long reign of the much-mourned monarch, whose funeral procession had just passed, stumbled about, slipping upon the muddy grass, and taking up a paper from the mud fed ravenously on that which two dogs had looked at with disdain.

The title "Sursum Corda" is taken from the Preface of the Latin Mass and is usually translated "Lift up your hearts". The piece is mainly a disquisition on the rich value of speech as a means of human expression and fulfilment. It concludes with an illustrative anecdote about prisoners who derive real happiness when they get the opportunity to express themselves through the words of a hymn in the prison chapel on a Sunday. This "breaks the dull monotony of weeks and days, and lets men feel for a brief space they are men once more."

"The Pyramid" is a cynical view of a night at the circus. It concludes with the description of the contribution of La Famiglia Sinigaglia. First they put on a tumbling display, then the five girls of the family make up a human pyramid. The youngest girl, who takes her place at the top of the human tower, clearly dislikes her work and looks down on the audience with a mixture of hatred and contempt. The audience, however, clap "being aware that acrobats live on its breath and counting it as righteousness they were not stinted in their food". The act was a technical success but the young acrobat did not like it and the audience clapped out of a sense of benign superiority and condescension.

"Terror" paints a vivid and eerie picture of Belgravia at night with its poverty, its drunks and its prostitutes. The focus shifts to the body of a dead cat which is described in minute detail. Another cat, fascinated by this corpse, returns to and flees from it several times – until the corpse is disfigured by the wheel of a passing carriage. The spell is broken and the inquisitive cat disappears. "Normality" returns.

"Postponed" is a story about a priest's dilemma. A widowed Anglican priest converts to Catholicism and later becomes a Catholic priest. He has two daughters whom he puts into the care of a Mrs Macnamara. He is convinced for reasons of orthodoxy that his decision to be ordained in the Catholic Church is the proper course of action for him but he misses his daughters and feels enormous guilt for abandoning them. Eventually he plucks up the courage to visit them and, after an agonising effort, he arrives at the house where they live – but Mrs Macnamara will not let him see his children. After an emotional conversation she convinces him that this is in their best interests. He leaves relieved and cheerful: "God bless you! I think I'll wait to see them till the Judgment Day. " A solution has been found. But is it a real success? Was it in the best interests of the children? Were other solutions possible?

"London" describes the pathetic fate of a Cingalese child who is named after the place of her birth. She grew up in London – and her poor relatives back home in Ceylon may have thought that she was fortunate to do so. But she never became a truly integrated Londoner: "London remained a sort of 'exhibition' gipsy, always a foreigner wherever she might go." She made a living giving public exhibitions of the crafts of her native culture, married a Zulu, had a deformed child and died young. Finally "the thin body of the Earl's Court Cingalese lay in the mortuary, the knees and elbows making sharp angles in the covering sheet." Only those at home in Ceylon might have thought her life a success.

"Beattock for Moffat" is a wonderful piece. It is the story of a Scot exiled in London returning to his family home in Moffat to die. The long tense train journey through the night is vividly described as Andra and his cockney wife and Calvinist brother make their way north. Andra is mortally ill but desperate to reach his native soil before his end and, when they reach the Border, his spirits lift and he seems to get extra strength. But the optimism is short lived. They alight at Beattock station from where it is a short journey by horse-drawn vehicle to Moffat. But it is not to be and he expires on a bench on the station platform with the words of the porter "Beattock for Moffat" ringing in his ears. His brother Jock praises his fortitude and his strong determination to get home and with grim and understated humour concedes that there has been some gain in his arduous journey: "Weel, weel, he'll hae a braw hurl onyway in the new Moffat hearse."

"A Fisherman" is a well observed portrait of an eccentric "goin' aboot body", a Highlander from the island of Mull. The narrator encounters him on a steamer sailing from Loch Fyne to Largs in the Clyde estuary and on to Greenock. He is clutching a geranium wrapped in a newspaper. He corners the narrator and belabours him with a monologue of his life story. He is clearly a restless gangrel. He comes from a family of fishermen, is constantly attracted to the sea and cannot settle anywhere. At the end he tells the narrator that, although he has brought his geranium with him all the way from Tobermory on Mull, he knows that it will not find Greenock congenial. It is a symbol of his own life.

"The Impenitent Thief" asks us to examine the final words of Dimas and Gestas, the two thieves crucified on Golgotha with Christ – although, ironically, we cannot be sure which name belongs to the "good" and which to the "bad" thief. We are asked to consider that the "bad" thief, to whom tradition has always given a bad press, may be merely a petty criminal, perhaps a horse thief, condemned to capital punishment by over-stringent Eastern laws. He may be merely trying to make a living as best he can and is honestly unrepentant. He is much more dignified than "some cold-hearted scoundrel who as solicitor, banker, or confidential agent, swindles for years, and in the dock recants and calls upon his God to pardon him." We are then asked to reflect on the "good" thief who did repent and whom we have been taught to admire. He may not have been so good after all: he may have told lies about his crime to make it seem more honourable, he may have thought that his last words on the cross were the truth when they were not, he may have testified that Jesus was their king merely to defy the Jews. Repentance, retrospection and remorse, Graham tells us, are problematic.

The next piece is called, ironically, "The Evolution of a Village". This is a little morality story set in a rural village in Northern Ireland. There is some superficial religious tension between Catholics and Protestants, but by and large, though life is very basic, people are happy, easy going and contented – there is no pernicious rivalry and they are mutually supportive. But the village had water power and the injection of a little capital could transform it, it was suggested, into a "paradise". Eventually that capital is injected and a water mill is built. But instead of enhancing the standard of living of the villagers, it does the opposite. The area soon becomes industrialised and debased physically and morally. People from the surrounding area flood in looking for work and the villagers have to compete for employment on their own land. Instead of growing wealthier they become poorer. They become "slaves to the 'steam hooter's' call to work in the dark winter mornings". The villagers become the victims of the success of Capital.

Finally, "Castles in the Air" is another morality piece, part disquisition part anecdote. The narrator argues his preference for the spiritual to the material: castles in the air are worth more than material castles. He then tells the story of a master builder, a competent craftsman, who was also a dreamer who built his own castles in the air.

One day, however, he loses his job and has to take to road to look for work. After endless searching he fails to find any and revolts against God for this great injustice.

Soon after he comes to a black oily river outside a manufacturing town, the waters thick and greasy, and at night looking like Periplegethon, when iron works belch out their fires and clouds of steam creep on the surface of the flood. Workers on the night shift in one of the factories encounter him ask him what he does for a living. He replies, "Castles, castles in the air". Against the backdrop of this hellish town he realises again their value.

R B Cunninghame Graham's "Success" is a fascinating collection. It contains many brilliantly observed descriptions of places and people and reveals many penetrating insights into human behaviour. The reader is challenged in each story to define exactly the nature of the success being described in it – and to consider whether the failures are in fact more interesting than the success.

(RWR)

Contents

Preface

It is not to be thought that gladiators, when they advanced before the imperial loggia, with their "*Ave Cæsar, te morituri*," &c., had any great respect or love for the purple-wearing critic of their deeds.

But whatever they may have felt for the emperor himself, it is probable that their feelings for the grimacing crowd were definite enough. Spanish "espada," Roman gladiator, acrobat, actor, politician, author, and even "authoress," when they behold, or think of the grinning faces of the respectable public, must all be filled with feelings of contempt and fear. Contempt of those they feel cannot, even badly, perform that upon which they have to give a verdict, and fear because the verdict (even of unintelligent, or, at the best, of half comprehending men) is to them final, and has no appeal. Has no appeal, for who but madmen (in a mad world) would not a thousand times rather submit himself to Philip drunk, than seek the verdict of the same Philip, with the whole folly of his unwine-filled brain active and all agog.

If a man tells you that he has a mystery to show, you instantly suspect either a fool or knave. In the same way, when the poor gymnast in the music-hall, advances clothed in trunk hose and tights, and wreathed in smiles, to risk his neck, the tender-hearted Christians in the stalls and pit all secretly hope something untoward may befall. If they did not, those who ride bicycles down iron wires, stretched at an angle of some thirty-five degrees from the roof, into a water tank, would have no vogue.

So that, bereft of verbiage, that verbiage by means of which we put a fig leaf over the realities of life, hiding them from our view, although we know that they are there in all their natural indecency, the tight-rope dancer, gladiator, author, and seller of corn plaisters at a fair, look upon those that they grimace before, both with contempt and awe. Upon the one side, all the performers, whether of bodily or mental lofty tumbling, are quite aware of their own feelings towards the great gelatinous, but yet Olympian entity, who from its depths or heights (for depth and height are really all the same) surveys their tricks, whether of suppleness of joint or mind.

But now comes in the rub; the humour, without which all tragedy is incomplete, especially the tragedy of life. The great, good-humoured public, secure in its brute strength (and in the main good humour comes from sense of power), looks on the pigmies who contort themselves before it, with benevolency *[sic]*, and though it fails to comprehend all that they do, just as a tourist, stuck at double price in a "sun" seat, applauds a bull-fighter, who by a hair's breadth vaults the barrier before the bull, not knowing what he does, it still extends its kindly patronage. Who that has not been weak, and here (with or without its leave) I will presume to turn the great panjandrum into its component parts, each part of which is merely man, having a soul to save and a posterior to be kicked, but must have felt the horror of benevolency? *[sic]*

A tyrant, who as the Spaniards used to say of one of their worst kings, is "mucho rey," who cuts your head off, and acts as inconsiderately as if he were a God, one can respect, even though hating him. But for the tyrant, who yet as fickle as is providence, still pats your head, what words suffice?

I think the monster looks upon us all, oh brothers of the show, brush, pen, and forceps, paring knife, and soiled silk tights, as worshippers all bowing down, and praying day and night for the proud privilege of adoring their liege lord. Strange that in every act of human life one kisses, and the other reaches out the cheek. So we in England talk with fond unction of America — our flesh and blood beyond the seas, our cousins, brethren of the Anglo-Saxon race, who joined to us could rule the world, we roar and write, almost believe, through iteration damnable, whilst from the other side, the Yankee squirts out tobacco juice, and sticks his tongue into his cheek.

Still, that the feeling of antagonism should exist between the writer and the man who reads, or between listener and composer, and the like, is natural, when it is understood. Write but on subjects light as air and trifling in themselves, such as political economy, which in a decade becomes antiquated, and is consigned to railway lavatories, and perforce all that you write, let it be even as commonplace as all right-thinking men could wish, is different in essence and in form to the ideas of every living man. Thus, as all men are gods unto themselves, born as is he who writes above the rest of all mankind, superior to them in intelligence, wit, humour, beauty, and morality (morality that makes hypocrites of all men who breathe), it follows that another man's ideas cannot be made acceptable, without a fight.

By so much, therefore, as the man who writes, composes, paints, or speaks, has anything to say, so is the battle with his heaven-sent readers and the rest more keen. So the poor book, sonata, picture, or what not goes forth like "Athanasius contra mundum," and few but will admit that Athanasius, even though a saint, cannot but have looked out upon the world with feelings partly of terror, partly of dislike. Let but the creed be once accepted, and for all I know, the case is changed; but when that happens all the interest of the fight is gone, and the poor writer, painter, or what not, either sinks into the Nirvana of neglect, or, worse, becomes a classic, and in tree calf, well tooled, and with gilt edges, serves as a resting place for flies in scholars' libraries.

So, be the upshot of the unequal struggle what it may, the real victory is as usual to the big battalions, and what remains to writer, painter, or to acrobat, is but to wipe the saw-dust from his hair, and try again. But as he wipes, let him by all means clear, if possible, the cobwebs from his mind, and view the question as it really is, making himself no spiced conscience, as to the very real antagonism betwixt himself and those who may (by accident) chance to peruse his book.

As for myself, I sit in a neglected orange garden, in which all day the doves coo in the trees, and water murmurs in cemented rills; in which the grass grows long and lush, making an everglade in miniature, through which cats (loved of Mohammed) steal like tigers, and over which a stork sits sentinel, calling to prayers, in the true way, at intervals, and when he feels inclined.

I sit and write this preface, to my slight tales, not seeking to turn off your criticism, but remembering that in the amphitheatre, when the "respectable" turned down its thumb, it could take away the gladiator's life, but still, for all its power and its might, could not prevent the dying man from turning up his eyes, and smiling as he passed.

R. B. Cunningham Graham.
Fez, 1st July, 1902.

"*Hoot awa' lads, hoot awa',*
Ha' ye heard how the Ridleys and Thirwalls and a'
Ha' set upon Albany Featherstonhaugh,
And taken his life at the Deidman's haugh.
Hoot awa' lads, hoot awa'."

Border Minstrelsy

Success

Success, which touches nothing that it does not vulgarise, should be its own reward. In fact, rewards of any kind are but vulgarities.

We applaud successful folk, and straight forget them, as we do ballet-dancers, actors, and orators. They strut their little hour, and then are relegated to peerages, to baronetcies, to books of landed gentry, and the like.

Quick triumphs make short public memories. Triumph itself only endures the time the triumphal car sways through the street. Your nine days' wonder is a sort of five-legged calf, or a two-headed nightingale, and of the nature of a calculating boy — a seven months' prodigy, born out of time to his own undoing and a mere wonderment for gaping dullards who dislocate their jaws in ecstasy of admiration and then start out to seek new idols to adore. We feel, that after all the successful man is fortune's wanton, and that good luck and he have but been equal to two common men. Poverty, many can endure with dignity. Success, how few can carry off, even with decency and without baring their innermost infirmities before the public gaze!

Caricatures in bronze and marble, and titles made ridiculous by their exotic style we shower upon all those who have succeeded, in war, in literature, or art; we give them money, and for a season no African Lucullus in Park Lane can dine without them. Then having given, feel that we have paid for service rendered, and generally withhold respect.

For those who fail, for those who have sunk still battling beneath the muddy waves of life, we keep our love, and that curiosity about their lives which makes their memories green when the cheap gold is dusted over, which once we gave success.

How few successful men are interesting! Hannibal, Alcibiades, with Raleigh, Mithridates, and Napoleon, who would compare them for a moment with their mere conquerors?

The unlucky Stuarts, from the first poet king slain at the ball play, to the poor mildewed Cardinal of York, with all their faults, they leave the stolid Georges millions of miles behind, sunk in their pudding and prosperity. The prosperous Elizabeth, after a life of honours unwillingly surrendering her cosmetics up to death in a state bed, and Mary laying her head upon the block at Fotheringay after the nine and forty years of failure of her life (failure except of love), how many million miles, unfathomable seas, and sierras upon sierras separate them?

And so of nations, causes, and events. Nations there are as interesting in decadence, as others in their ten-percentish apogee are dull and commonplace. Causes, lost almost from the beginning of the world, but hardly yet despaired of, as the long struggle betwixt rich and poor, which dullards think eternal, but which will one day be resolved, either by the absorption of the rich into the legions of the poor, or vice versâ, still remain interesting, and will do so whilst the unequal combat yet endures.

Causes gone out of vogue, which have become almost as ludicrous as is a hat from Paris of ten years ago; causes which hang in monumental mockery quite out of fashion, as that of Poland, still are more interesting than is the struggle between the English and the Germans, which shall sell gin and gunpowder to negroes on the Coast.

Even events long passed *[sic]*, and which right-thinking men have years ago dismissed to gather dust in the waste spaces of their minds, may interest or repel according as they may make for failure or success.

Failure alone can interest speculative minds. Success is for the millions of the working world, who see the engine in eight hours arrive in Edinburgh from London, and marvel at the last improvement in its wheels. The real interest in the matters being the forgotten efforts of some alchemist who, with the majesty of law ever awake to burn him as a witch, with the hoarse laughter of the practical and business men still ringing in his ears, made his rude model of a steam engine, and perhaps lost his eyesight when it burst.

On a deserted beach in Cuba, not far from El Caney, some travellers not long ago came on a skeleton. Seated in a rough chair, it sat and gazed upon the sea. The gulls had roosted on the collar bones, and round the feet sea-wrack and dulse had formed a sort of wreath. A tattered Spanish uniform still fluttered from the bones, and a cigar-box set beside the chair held papers showing that the man had been an officer of rank. One of these gave the password of the day when he had lost his life, and as the travellers gazed upon the bones, a land crab peeped out of a hole just underneath the chair.

All up and down the coast were strewn the remnants of the pomp and circumstance of glorious war. Rifles with rusty barrels, the stocks set thick with barnacles, steel scabbards with bent swords wasted to scrap iron, fragment of uniforms and belts, ends of brass chains and bones of horses reft from their wind-swept prairies to undergo the agonies of transport in a ship, packed close as sardines in a box, and then left to die wounded with the vultures picking out their eyes. All, all, was there, fairly spread out as in a kindergarten, to point the lesson to the fools who write of war, if they had wit to see. Gun carriages half silted up with sand, and rusted broken Maxims, gave an air of ruin, as is the case wherever Titan man has been at play, broken his toys, and then set out to kill his brother fools.

Withal nothing of dignity about the scene; a stage unskilfully set out with properties all got up on the cheap; even the ribs and trucks of the decaying ships of what once had been Admiral Cervera's fleet stood roasting in the sun, their port-holes just awash, as they once roasted in the flames which burned them and their crews. Nothing but desolation, in the scene, and yet a desolation of a paltry kind, not caused by time, by famine, pestilence, or anything which could impart an air of tragedy, only the desolation made by those who had respectively sent their poor helots out to fight, staying themselves smug and secure at home, well within reach of the quotations of the Stock Exchange.

So in his mouldering chair the general sat, his pass-word antiquated and become as much the property of the first passer-by as an advertisement of "liver pills." His uniform, no doubt his pride, all rags; his sword (bought at some outfitter's) long stolen away and sold for drink by him who filched it; but yet the sun-dried bones, which once had been a man, were of themselves more interesting than were his living conquerors with their cheap air of insincere success.

The world goes out to greet the conqueror with flowers and with shouts, but first he has to conquer, and so draw down upon himself the acclamations of the crowd, who do not know that hundreds such as the man they stultify with noise have gloriously failed, and that the odium of success is hard enough to bear, without the added ignominy of popular applause. Who with a spark of humour in his soul can bear success without some irritation in his mind? But for good luck he might have been one of the shouters who run sweating by his car; doubts must assail him, if success has not already made him pachydermatous to praise, that sublimate which wears away the angles of our self-respect, and leaves us smooth to catch the mud our fellows fling at us, in their fond adoration of accomplished facts. Success is but the recognition (chiefly by yourself) that you are better than your fellows are. A paltry feeling, nearly allied to the base scheme of punishments and of rewards which has made most faiths arid, and rendered actions noble in themselves mere huckstering affairs of fire insurance.

If a man put his life in peril for the Victoria Cross, or pass laborious days in laboratories tormenting dogs, only to be a baronet at last, a plague of courage and laborious days. Arts, sciences, and literature, with all the other trifles in which hard-working idle men make occupations for themselves, when they lead to material success, spoil their professor, and degrade themselves to piecework at so many pounds an hour.

Nothing can stand against success and yet keep fresh. Nations as well as individuals feel its vulgarising power. Throughout all Europe, Spain alone still rears its head, the unspoiled race, content in philosophic guise to fail in all she does, and thus preserve the individual independence of her sons. Successful nations have to be content with their success, their citizens cannot be interesting. So many hundred feet of sanitary tubes a minute or an hour, so many wage-saving applications of machinery, so many men grown rich; fancy a poet rich through rhyming, or a philosopher choked in banknotes, whilst writing his last scheme of wise philosophy. Yet those who fail, no matter how ingloriously, have their revenge on the successful few, by having kept themselves free from vulgarity, or by having died unknown.

A miner choked with firedamp in a pit, dead in the vain attempt to save some beer-mused comrade left behind entombed, cannot be vulgar, even if when alive he was a thief. Your crass successful man who has his statue set up in our streets (apparently to scare away the crows), and when he dies his column and a half in penny cyclopædias, turns interest to ashes by his apotheosis in the vulgar eye.

But the forgotten general sitting in his chair, his fleshless feet just lapping in the waves, his whitening bones fast mouldering into dust, nothing can vulgarise him; no fool will crown him with a tin-foiled laurel wreath, no poetaster sing his praise in maudlin ode or halting threnody, for he has passed into the realm of those who by misfortune claim the sympathy of writers who are dumb.

Let him sit on and rest, looking out on the sea, where his last vision saw the loss of his doomed country's fleet.

An architype [*sic*] of those who fail, let him still sit watching the gulls fly screaming through the air, and mark the fish spring and fall back again with a loud crash, in the still waters of the tropic beach.

The Gualichu Tree

Just where the Sierra de la Ventana fades out of sight, a mere blue haze on the horizon; close to the second well in the long desert travesia between El Carmen and Bahia Blanca, upon a stony ridge from which to the north the brown interminable Pampa waves a sea of grass, and to the south the wind-swept Patagonian stone-strewed steppes stretch to the Rio Negro, all alone it stands. No other tree for leagues around rises above the sun-browned, frost-nipped grass, and the low scrub of thorny carmamoel and elicui. An altar, as some think, to the Gualichu, the evil spirit, which in the theogony of the wandering Indian tribes has so far hithero prevailed over the other demon who rules over good, that all the sacrifices which they make, fall to his lot. An espinillo, some have it; a tala, or a chañar, as others say; low, gnarled, and bent to the north-east by the continual swirl of the Pampero which rages on the southern plains, the tree, by its position and its growth, is formed to have appealed at once to the imagination of the Indian tribes. Certain it is that in the days before the modern rifle slew them so cowardly (the slayers, safe from the weak assaults of lance and bolas by the distance of their weapons' range, and rendered as maleficent as Gods, by the toil of men in Liege or Birmingham, who at the same time forged their own fetters, and helped unknowingly to slay men they had never seen), no Araucanian, Pampa, Pehuelche, or Ranquele passed the Gualichu Tree, without his offering. Thus did they testify by works to their belief both in its power, its majesty, and might.

The Gauchos used to say the tree was the Gualichu incarnated. They being Christians by the grace of God, and by the virtue of some drops of Spanish blood, spoke of the Indians as idolators. The Indians had no idols, and the Gauchos now and then a picture of a saint hung on the walls of their low reed-thatched huts, to which a mare's hide used to serve as door. So of the two, the Gauchos really were greater idolators than their wild cousins, whom they thus contemned, as Catholics and Protestants condemn each other, secure in the possession of their church and book, and both convinced the other must be damned.

So all the Gauchos firmly held the Indians thought the Tree a God, not knowing that they worshipped two great spirits, one ruling over good, and the more powerful over evil, as is natural to all those who manufacture creeds.

Before a Gaucho passed below the mountains of Tandil, the Jesuits knew the tribes, and Father Falkner has written of the faiths of the Pehuelches and the other tribes who roamed from Cholechel to Santa Cruz, round the Salinas Grandes, about the lake of Nahuel-Huapi, and in the apple forests which fringe the Andes on their southern spurs.

Of all the mountains which faith can, but hitherto has not attempted, to remove, the monstrous cordillera of misconception of other men's beliefs is still the highest upon earth. So, to the Gauchos, and the runagates (forged absolutely on their own anvils), who used to constitute the civilising scum which floats before the flood of progress in the waste spaces of the world, the Gualichu Tree was held an object half of terror, half of veneration, not to be lightly spoken of except when drunk, or when ten or a dozen of them being together it was not worthy of a man to show his fear.

Among the Indians, and in the estimation of all those who knew them well, the Tree was but an altar on which they placed their free-will offerings of things which, useless to themselves, might, taking into account the difference of his nature from their own, find acceptation, and be treasured by a God.

So fluttering in the breeze it stood, a sort of everlasting Christmas tree, decked out with broken bridles, stirrups, old tin cans, pieces of worn-out ponchos, bolas, lance-heads, and skins of animals, by worshippers to whom the name of Christian meant robber, murderer, and intruder on their lands. No Indian ever passed it without suspending something to its thorny boughs, for the Gualichu, by reason of his omnipotent malevolence, was worth propitiating, although he did not seem to show any particular discernment as to the quality of the offerings which his faithful tied upon his shrine. Around the lone and wind-swept Tree, with its quaint fruit, has many a band of Indians camped, their lances, twenty feet in length, stuck in the ground, their horses hobbled and jumping stiffly as they strayed about to eat, what time their masters slew a mare, and ate the half-raw flesh, pouring the blood as a libation on the ground, their wizards (as Father Falkner relates) dancing and beating a hide-drum until they fell into the trance in which the Gualichu visited them, and put into their minds that which the Indians wished that he should say.

The earliest travellers in the southern plains describe the Tree as it still stood but twenty years ago; it seemed to strike them but as an evidence of the lowness of the Indians in the human scale. Whether it was so, or if a tree which rears its head alone in a vast stony plain, the only upright object in the horizon for leagues on every side, is not a fitting thing to worship, or to imagine that a powerful spirit has his habitation in it, I leave to missionaries, to "scientists," and to all those who, knowing little, are sure that savages know nothing, and view their faith as of a different nature from their own. But, after all, faith is not absolutely the sole quality which goes to make belief. No doubt the Indians saw in the Tree the incarnation of the spirit of their race, in all its loneliness and isolation from any other type of man. Into the Tree there must have entered in some mysterious way the spirit of their own long fight with nature, the sadness of the Pampa, with its wild noises of the night; its silent animals, as the guanaco, ostrich, mataco, the quiriquincho, and the Patagonian hare; its flights of red flamingoes; the horses wild as antelopes, and shyer than any animal on earth; the rustle of the pampas grass upon the watercourses, in which the pumas and the jaguars lurk; the birth of spring covering the ground with red verbena, and the dark leaden-looking grass which grows on the guadal; the giant bones of long-extinct strange animals which in some places strew the ground; all the lone magic of the summer's days, when the light trembles, and from every stem of grass the fleecy particles, which the north wind blows, tremble and quake, whilst over all the sun beats down, the universal god worshipped from California to Punta Arenas by every section of their race.

To Christians too the tree had memories, but chiefly as a landmark, though few of them, half in derision, half in the kindliness which comes of long communication (even with enemies) who would pass without an offering of an empty match-box, a dirty pocket-handkerchief, a brimless hat, or empty sardine tin — something, in short, to bring the beauty of our culture and our arts home to the Indians' minds. One Christian at least had offered up his life beneath its boughs — an ostrich hunter who, finding ostriches grow scarce, the price of ostrich feathers fall, or being possessed with a strange wish for regular, dull work, had hired himself to carry mail bags from Bahia Blanca to Carmen de Patagones, the furthest settlement in those days, towards the south. As all the country which he travelled was exposed to Indian raids, and as he generally, when chased, had to throw off his saddle and escape barebacked ("en pelo", as the Gauchos say), by degrees he found it too expensive to make good the saddles he had lost. So all the eighty leagues he used to ride "en pelo", use having made him part and parcel of his horse. An ostrich hunter from his youth up, aware one day that he would die the ostrich hunter's death, by hunger, thirst, or by an Indian's lance, well did he know the great green inland sea of grass in which men used to sleep with their faces set towards the way they had to go, knowing that he who lost the trail had forfeited his life, unless by a hard, lucky chance he reached an Indian tolderia, there to become a slave. Well did the ex-ostrich hunter know the desert lore, to take in everything instinctively as he galloped on the plain, to mark the flight of birds, heed distant smoke, whether the deer or other animals were shy or tame, to keep the wind ever a-blowing on the same side of his face, at night to ride towards some star; but yet it fell upon a day, between the first well and the Rio Colorado, his horse tired with him, and as his trail showed afterwards, he had to lead it to the second well, which he found dry. Then after long hours of thirst, he must have sighted the Gualichu Tree, and made for it, hoping to find some travellers with water skins; reached it, and, having hung his mail bags on it to keep them safe, wandered about and waited for relief. Then, his last cigarette smoked and thrown aside (where the belated rescuers found it on the grass), he had sat down stoically to meet the ostrich hunter's fate. A league or two along the trail his horse had struggled on, making for the water which he knew must be in the river Colorado, and like his master, having done his best, died in the circle of brown withered grass which the last dying struggle of an animal upon the Pampa makes.

Landmark to wandering Gauchos, altar or God to all the Indian tribes, a curiosity of nature to "scientists," who, like Darwin, may camp beneath its boughs, and to the humourist [*sic*] looking half sadly through his humour at the world, a thorny Christmas tree, but scarce redeemed from being quite grotesque, when, amongst its heterogeneous fruit, it chanced to bear a human hand, a foot, or a long tress or two of blue-black hair, torn from some captive Christian woman's head, long may it stand.

You in the future who, starting from Bahia Blanca pass the Romero Grande, leave the Cabeza del Buey on the right hand, and at the Rio Colorado exchange the grassy Pampa for the stony southern plains, may you find water in both wells, and coming to the tree neither cut branches from it to light your fire, or fasten horses to its trunk to rub the bark. Remember that it has been cathedral, church, town-hall, and centre of a religion and the lives of men now passed away; and, in remembering, reflect that from Bahia Blanca to El Carmen, it was once the solitary living thing which reared its head above the grass and the low thorny scrub. So let it stand upon its stony ridge, just where the Sierra de la Ventana fades out of sight, hard by the second well, right in the middle of the travesia — a solitary natural landmark if naught else, which once bore fruit ripened in the imaginations of a wild race of men, who at the least had for their virtue constancy of faith, not shaken by unanswered prayer; a tombstone, set up by accident or nature, to mark the passing of light riding bands upon their journey towards Trapalanda; passing or passed; but all so silently, that their unshod horses' feet have scarcely left a trail upon the grass.

Success

Los Seguidores

Only the intimate life of man with the domestic animals which takes place upon the pampas of the River Plate could have produced "Los Seguidores."

Brothers, or trained to be as brothers by being tied together by the neck till they had conquered the repugnance which every animal, including man, has for his fellow, this was the name the Gauchos gave two horses which to their owner were as one. The followers (los seguidores) on the darkest night trotted along, the loose horse following the mounted brother, as it had been a shadow on the grass. At night, when one was picketed to feed, the other pastured round about him like a satellite, and in the morning sometimes the two were found either asleep or resting with their heads upon each other's necks. When saddled for a march, the owner mounting never even turned his head to look, so sure he was that the loose horse would follow on his trail. Even in crossing rivers, after the first deep plunge which takes the rider to his neck, one swam behind the other, spurting out water like a whale, or biting at the quarters of the ridden horse, and on emerging, both of them shook themselves like water dogs, and the unmounted follower patiently waited for the start, and then after a plunge or two, to shake the water from his coat, trotting along contentedly behind his brother, on the plain.

Such a pair I knew, the property of one Cruz Cabrera, a Gaucho living close to the little river Mocoretá which separates the province of Entre Rios from that of Corrientes, to the north. Both horses were picazos, that is, black with white noses, and so like each other that it was a saying in the district where he lived, "Like, yes, as like as are the two picazos which Cruz Cabrera rides." In a mud rancho, bare of furniture save for a horse's head or two to sit upon, an iron spit stuck in the floor, a kettle, a bed, made scissors-wise of some hard wood with a lacing of raw hide thongs, an ox's horn in which he kept his salt, and a few pegs on which he hung his silver reins and patent leather boots with an eagle worked in red thread upon the legs, the owner of the seguidores lived. A mare's hide formed the door, and in a corner a saddle and a poncho lay, a pair or two of bolas, and some lazos; raw hide bridles hung from the rafters, whilst in the thatch was stuck a knife or two, some pairs of sheep shears and a spare iron spit. Outside his rancho fed a flock of long-haired, long-legged sheep resembling goats, two or three hundred head of cattle, and some fifty mares, from which the celebrated seguidores had been bred.

His brother Froilan lived with him, and though only a year separated them in age, oceans and continents were set between them in all the essential qualities which go to make a man.

The elder brother was a quiet man; hard working too, when he had horses on which to work, and peaceable when no one came across his path, and when at the neighbouring pulperia he had not too incautiously indulged in square-faced gin (Albert Von Hoytema, the Palm Tree brand), on which occasions he was wont to forget his ordinary prudence, and become as the profane. But, in the main, an honourable, hard-riding man enough, not much addicted to brand his neighbour's cows, to steal their horses, or to meddle with their wives, even when military service or the exigencies of ordinary Gaucho life called men out on the frontier, or made them seek the shelter of the woods.

Froilan never in all his life had done what is called honest work. No cow, no horse, no sheep, still less a "China" girl, ever escaped him; withal, a well-built long-haired knave before the Lord, riding a half-wild horse as if the two had issued from the womb together as one flesh. A great guitar player, and what is called a "payador" — that is, a rhymester — for, as the Gauchos say, "The townsman sings, and is a poet, but when the Gaucho sings he is a payador." A lovable and quite irresponsible case for an immortal soul, about the possession or the future state of which he never troubled himself, saying, after the fashion of his kind, "God cannot possibly be a bad man," and thus having made, as it were, a full profession of his faith, esteeming it unworthy of a believing man to trouble further in so manifest a thing.

In fact, a pagan of the type of those who lived their lives in peace, content with nature as they found her, in the blithe days before Mohammedanism and Christianity, and their mad myriad sects, loomed on the world and made men miserable, forcing them back upon themselves, making them introspective, and causing them to lose their time in thinking upon things which neither they nor anyone in the ridiculous revolving world can ever solve, and losing thus the enjoyment of the sun, the silent satisfaction of listening to the storm, and all the joys which stir the natural man when the light breeze blows on his cheek as his horse gallops on the plain.

But still the neighbours (for even on the pampa man cannot live alone, although he does his best to separate his dwelling from that of his loved fellow human beings) preferred Froilan before his elder brother, Cruz. Their respect, as is most natural, for respect is near akin to fear, and fear is always uppermost in the mind towards those who have a severer code of life than we ourselves (and hatred ever steps upon its heels), was given to Don Cruz. He was a serious man and formal, complying outwardly with all the forms that they themselves were disregardful of, and so religious that it was said, once in Concordia he had even gone to mass after a drinking bout. But as the flesh is weak — as is but just when one reflects upon the providential scheme, for without its weakness where would the due amount of credit be apportioned to the Creator of mankind — Cruz would when all was safe fall into some of the weaknesses his brother suffered from, but in so carefully concealed and hidden fashion that the said weaknesses in him, seemed strength. Still the two brothers loved one another after the fashion of men who, living amongst unconquered nature, think first of their daily battle with a superior force, and have but little leisure for domestic ties. Love, hate, attachment to the animals amongst whom they lived, and perhaps a vague unreasoned feeling of the beauty of the lonely plains and exultation in the free life they led, were the chief springs which moved the brothers' lives.

The elementary passions, which moved the other animals, and which, though we so strenuously deny their strength, move all of us, despite of our attempts to bury them beneath the pseudo duties and the unnecessary necessities of modern life, acted there directly, making them relatively honest in their worst actions, in a way we cannot understand at all, in our more complicated life. With the two brothers all went well, as it so often does with those who, neither honest nor dishonest, yet keep a foot in either camp, and are esteemed as estimable citizens by those in office, and are respected by dishonest men as having just enough intelligence to guard their own. Their flocks and herds multiplied steadily, and when the locusts did not come in too great quantities or the green parroquettes refrained from eating the green corn, the patch of maize which Cruz grew, partly for an occasional dish of "mazamorra," and more especially to keep the "seguidores" in condition during winter, was duly reaped by the aid of a Basque or a Canary Islander, and stored in bunches hanging from the roof of a long straw-thatched shed. Before their house upon most days of every year stood a half-starved and much tucked-up young horse, enduring the rough process known as "being tamed," which consisted in being forcibly thrown down and saddled on the ground, then mounted and let loose, when it indulged in antics which, as the Gauchos used to say, made it more fit for a perch for a wild bird than for the saddle of a Christian man.

The "seguidores," the greatest objects of the brothers' love, were black as jet, with their off fore and the off hind feet white, so that the rider, riding on a cross, was safe from the assaults of evil fiends by night, and from ill luck which makes its presence felt at every moment when the Christian thinks himself secure. Both of the horses were so round you could have counted money on their backs; their tails just touched their pasterns, and were cut off square; their noses both were blazed with white, and in addition one had a faint white star upon his forehead, and the other one or two girth marks which had left white hairs upon his flank. Both had their manes well hogged, save for a mounting lock, and on the top of the smooth arch made by the cut-off hair, castles and crosses were ingeniously cut, giving them both the appearance of having been designed after the pattern of the knight at chess. Both horses were rather quick to mount, not liking to be kept a moment when the foot was in the stirrup iron, and both of them, well trained to lazo work, could keep a strain upon the rope when once a bull was caught, so that their master could get off and, creeping up behind, despatch the animal, thus lassoed, with a knife. Rather straight on the pasterns, and a little heavy in the shoulder, they could turn, when galloping, in their own length, their unshod feet cutting the turf as a sharp skate cuts ice when a swift skater turns at topmost speed. Full-eyed, flat-jointed, their nostrils red and open, their coats as soft as satin, and their gallop easy as an iceboat's rush before the wind, the two picazos were as good specimens of their race as any of the breed between Los Ballesteros and the Gualeguay, or from San Fructuoso to the mountains of Tandil.

In the mud-reed-thatched hut, or to be accurate, in another hut beside it, dwelt the mother of the two brothers and their half-sister Luz. The mother, dried by the sun and cured by the smoke of sixty years (which blackened all the thatch, polishing it as it had been japanned), loved her two sons in the submissive fashion in which a mare may love her colts when they are grown to their full strength. Seated upon a horse's head, she watched the meat roast on a spit, boiled water for the perpetual *maté*, and seldom went outside the house. A Christian, if simple faith, convinced of all things hard to believe and quite impossible to understand, can make one such, she was. Although the nearest church was twenty leagues away, and in her life she had been but a few times there, she knew the dogmas of her faith to the full as well as if communion with the church and the free use of books had placed hell fire always in her view. Octaves, novenas, and the rest she never missed, and on the rare occasions when some neighbouring women rode over to take *maté* and eat mazamorra with her, she acted as a sort of fugle-woman, leading the hymns and prayers out of a tattered book, which, in times past, she had partly learned to read. Outside religion, she was as strict in her materialism as the other women of her race, making herself no spiced conscience about any subject upon earth. From her youth upwards she had seen blood shed as easily as water; had seen the uncomplaining agony of the animals under the knife, observing "pobrecito" when a lamb's throat was slowly cut, and then (being a Christian, and thus of a different flesh to that of beasts) hurrying up quickly to assist in taking off its skin. Like most of us, of her own impulse she was pitiful, but yet not strong enough to stand against the universal cruelty which habit has rendered second nature to the most tender-hearted and the kindest of mankind. Spanish and Indian blood had made her look at things without the veil, which northern melancholy has cast over them, and thus she clearly looked at all, without hypocrisy, just as she saw the locusts moving in a cloud, the dust storms whirling in the air, and all the other wild phenomena of life upon the plains. She saw the human beast in all his animalism, and thought it no disgrace to admit that in essentials all his actions sprang from the motives which influenced all the other links in the same chain of which she formed a part. Seeing so clearly, she saw that Luz, although their sister, was an object of desire to both her brothers, and the old woman knew that fire and tow are safe *[Sp. seguro=safe]* to make a blaze if they are brought too close. Much did she muse upon the problem, muttering to herself proverbs which spoke of the necessity of a stone wall between a male and female saint, and she resolved to keep Luz from her brothers as far as it was possible within the narrow limits of the hut. The girl herself, like many "Chinas"* when just grown up, was pretty, and attractive as a

* China is the term applied to the Gaucho girls of Indian blood. It is also used in Peru and the Habana, why, no one seems to know.

young deer or colt may be attractive, by its inexperience and youth. In colour, something like a ripe bamboo, with a faint flush of pink showing through upon the cheeks and palms; round faced, and dark eyed, dressed in a gay print gown made loose, and round her neck a coloured handkerchief, Luz was as pretty as a girl upon the pampas ever is, for being semi-civilised and Christian she lacked the graces of a half-clothed Indian maid, and yet had not resources which in a town make many a girl, designed by nature to scrub floors and suckle fools, a goddess in the eyes of those who think a stick well dressed is more desirable than Venus rising naked from the foam.

She, too, having seen from youth the tragedy of animal birth, love, and death displayed before her eyes, was not exactly innocent; but yet, having no standard of false shame to measure by, was at the same time outspoken upon things which in Europe old women of both sexes feign to be reticent about, and still was timid by the very virtue of the knowledge which she had. The life of women on the pampa, or, for that matter, in all wild countries, is of necessity much more circumscribed than that of those their sisters who in other lands approach more nearly to their more godlike brothers by the fact of wearing stiffly starched collars and most of the insignia of man's estate. Philosophers have set it down that what is known as sexual morality is a sealed book to women, and that, whilst outwardly conforming, most of them rage inwardly at the restrictions which men, to guard their property, have set upon their lives. This may be so, for who can read what passes in the heart of any other man, even if he has felt its closest beat for years? And it may well be that the most Puritan of happy England's wives chafe at the liberty their husbands all enjoy, and from which they, bound in their petticoats, stays, flounces, furbelows, veils, bonnets, garters, and their Paisley shawls, are impiously debarred.

But speculations upon sex problems did not greatly trouble Luz, who, when she thought, thought chiefly of the chance of going into town, buying new clothes, attending mass, and meeting her few friends, and so it never came into her head but that her two half-brothers, both of them far older than herself, regarded her but as their sister and a child. Some say the heart of man is wicked from his birth, and so it may be to those men who, reading in their own, see naught but mud. But if it is so, then either the framer of man's heart worked on a faulty plan, or those who furbish for us codes of morality, have missed his meaning and misunderstood his scheme. As the brothers never thought, most likely never had heard in all their lives about morality, which in despite of theorists seems not to be a thing implanted in mankind, but supergrafted mainly with an eye to the consecration of our property, they found themselves attracted towards Luz after a fashion which, had it happened in regard to any other girl, they could have understood. Certain it is, that both of them felt vaguely that she was near to them in blood, and neither of them perhaps had formulated in his mind exactly what he felt. They watched each other narrowly, and neither cared to see the other alone with Luz, but neither Cruz or Froilan spoke to their half-sister or to each other, but by degrees they grew morose and quarrelsome, making their mother miserable, and their half-sister sad at their changed temper both to each other and to her. Their mother, with the experience of her sixty years, saw how the matter lay, and recognised that on the pampa strange things did take place, for, as she said, "El Cristiano macho (the male Christian) is the hardest to restrain of all God's beasts," having had no doubt experience of his ways with her two husbands in the days gone by. So, whilst the petty tragedy was brewing, so to speak, nature, serene, inimitable and pitilessly sad, but all unconscious of the puny passions of mankind, unrolled the panorama of the seasons as quietly as if no human souls hung trembling in the scales. Night followed day, the scanty twilight scarcely intervening, the hot sun sinking red upon the low horizon as at sea, and in an instant the whole world changed from a yellow sun-burnt waste to a cool shadow, from the depths of which the cries of animals ascended to the unhearing sky which overhung them like a deep blue inverted bowl flecked with a thousand stars. The frogs croaked with a harsh metallic note, and from the thorny trees great drops of moisture hung, or dripped upon the roofs. Again night yielded up its mysteries to the dawn, advancing, conquering and flushed with power. So by degrees the summer melted insensibly to autumn, and the vast beds of giant thistles, with stems all frosted over with their silver down, began to vanish, and the thin animals wandered about, or perished in the sand, as the Pampero whistled across the plains. But winter too faded before the inexorable unfelt turning of the world; the red verbenas spread like carpets, covering the earth as with a blanket, the shoots of pampas grass shot up green spikes almost between the dusk and dawn, and on their little meeting places outside their towns, biscachos *[sic=biscachas]* sat and looked out on the world, and found it good, whilst the small owls which keep them company nodded their stupid looking, wise, little heads, and gave assent.

The horses played upon the edges of the woods, rearing and striking at each other with their fore feet, and some who in the autumn had been left thin and tired out suddenly thought upon their homes, and, throwing up their heads, snorted, and, trotting round a little, struck the home trail as surely as a sea-gull finds its way across the sea.

But all the magic of the perpetual kaleidoscopic change of season, which ought to interest any man a million times more keenly than his own never-changing round of sordid cares, brought no distraction to the brothers, who had grown to look upon each other partly as rivals, and partly with astonishment that the same thoughts which tortured each one were present in the other's mind. But the mere fact of feeling the identity of thought confirmed them in their purpose, and in a measure served to confirm them in their course, for men catch thoughts from one another as they take diseases, by contagion with the worst particles of the sick man they touch.

Upon the pampa, where the passions have full play, quite unrestrained by the complexity of life which in more favoured lands imprisons them in bands of broadcloth and of starch, it was impossible that in the compass of a little hut the situation could endure for long. No doubt it might have been more admirable had one or both the brothers seen the error of their ways, repented, and in chivalry and ashes gone their respective ways to do their duty in the counting-house of life. No doubt in many of the neighbouring farms girls lived as pretty as their half-sister Luz — girls whom they might have loved without a qualm, and made the mothers of their dusky, thievish children, with or without the blessing of a priest. They might have told their guilty love, and been stricken to the earth by the outraged majesty of their sister's womanhood, or felled to the ground with a bullock's head swung by the nervous hand of her who gave them birth. But chance, that orders everything quite in a different way from that we think should be the case, had ordered otherwise, and the simple tragedy upon the Mocoretá was solved more quickly and as effectually as if justice or outraged public feeling had seen fit to intervene.

How it occurred, up to his dying day Froilan was never sure, but, seated in the semi-darkness, cutting some strips of mare's hide to mend a broken girth, their mother and their sister sitting by, high words broke out between the brothers without apparent cause. Cruz, passing, in Gaucho fashion, in an instant from a grave, silent man, to a foaming maniac, rushed on his brother, a long thin-bladed knife clutched in his hand. Almost before Froilan had had time to draw his knife, or stand on guard, his brother tripped and fell, and the knife piercing his stomach, he lay on the mud floor with but a short half hour of agonising life. Pressing the knife into the wound, he beckoned to his brother with the other hand, asked his forgiveness, made him swear to see their sister married to some honourable man, and promise that his own body should be laid in consecrated ground. Then, turning to his mother, he asked her blessing, and, summoning his last strength, drew the knife from the wound, and in an instant bled to death. His mother closed his eyes and then with Luz broke out into a death wail, whilst Froilan stood by half stupidly, as if he had not comprehended what had taken place.

The simple preparations over, the short but necessary lie arranged, the alcalde duly notified, and the depositions of the chief actor and the witnesses painfully put on record in a greasy pocket-book, nothing remained but to carry out the wish of the dead man, to lie in consecrated earth. At daybreak Froilan had the two seguidores duly tied before the door, saddled and ready for the road. The neighbours helped to tie the dead man upon his saddle, propping him up with sticks. When all was ready, Froilan mounted his own horse, and took the road to Villaguay, the dead man's horse cantering beside his fellow as if the rider that he bore had been alive.

Their mother and their sister watched them till they sank into the plain, their hats last vanishing as a ship's top sails sink last into the sea. Then, as she drew her withered hand across her eyes, she turned to Luz, and saying gravely, "The male Christian is the wildest thing which God has made," lifted the mare's hide hung before the door and went into the hut.

Success

Un Infeliz

During the somewhat fragmentary meal, I had watched him, seeing a difference between him and the usual French Algerian types. Dressed all in grey, his clothes of that peculiar substance which seems specially constructed for Algeria, Morocco, and the Levant, and which, intended to look like English tweed, yet is as different from its prototype as is "kincob," his shirt of greenish flannel, his boots apparently made by a portmanteau maker, his scanty hair a yellowish grey, and his thin beard a greyish yellow, he gave you the idea of some pathetic seabeaten boulder, worn hollow by the beating of the waves of life.

As the smart Spanish-looking, but French-speaking, daughter of the landlady brought round the dishes, in which sea-slieve, stewed in high-smelling oil, made the air redolent, and over which myriads of flies kept up a pandemoniac concert, or yielded up their lives in the thick oleaginous black sauce, he paid her all those futile, yet kindly compliments, which only men, who in their youth have never known that ginger may be hot in the mouth, pay womankind. She easily accepted them, whilst smiling at the commercial travellers, who, with napkins tucked into their waistcoats, performed miraculous feats of sleight of hand, taking up pease [sic] as dexterously with the broad-pointed, iron-handled knives, as does an elephant transfer the buns which children give him at a travelling circus, from his proboscis to his mouth. Loose-trousered officers of the Chasseurs d'Afrique sat over the high-smelling foods talking regretfully of Paris, and of "les petites" who there and elsewhere had fallen victims to their all-compelling charms. Detailing all the points both physical and moral of the victims, they pitied them, and spoke regretfully of what they had been, so to speak, impelled to do by the force of circumstances, but still with that well-founded yet chastened pride with which a horseman, once the struggle over, depreciates the efforts of a vicious horse.

Outside, the sandy street, shaded by bella sombra and by China trees, was full of Arabs straying aimlessly about, existing upon sufferance in their own country, each with his hand ready to raise at once to a military salute and his lips twitching with the salutation of "Bonne chour, Mossi," if the most abject member of the ruling race should deign to greet him as he passed. Dogs, thin and looking like cross-breeds between a jackal and a fox, slunk furtively about, their ears raw with mange, the sores upon their bodies all alive with flies, squirmed in and out between the people's legs, receiving patiently or with a half-choked yelp, blows with the cudgels which all country Arabs use, or kicks administered between their ribs from seedy, unvarnished patent-leather boots with drab cloth tops. At the corners of the streets, horses blinked sleepily, their high and chair-like saddles sharply outlined against the white-washed walls in the fierce glare of the Algerian sun. The hum compounded of the cries of animals and men, not disagreeable and acute as is the noise which rises from a northern crowd, but which throughout the East blends itself into a sort of chant, rose in the air, and when it ceased, the grating of the pebbles on the beach, tossed in the ceaseless surf, fell on the ear in rhythmic cadences. In all the spaces and streets of the incongruous North-European-looking town, the heterogeneous population lounged about lazily, knowing full well that time was the commodity of which they had the most. Riffians in long white haiks, carrying the sword-shaped sticks with which their ancestors attacked the Roman legionaries, strode to and fro, their heads erect, their faces set like cameos, impassable except their eyes, which lighted for a second in a blaze when a French soldier pushed them roughly, and then became deliberately opaque. Their women with their chins tattooed like Indians, dressed in sprigged muslins, their jet black hair hanging in plaited tails upon their shoulders, walked about staring like half-wild horses at the unfamiliar shops. Wearing no veils, their appearance drew from the wealthier Mohammedans pious ejaculations as to their shamelessness, and aphorisms such as "the married woman is best with a broken leg at home," and others more direct and quite unfitted for our European taste, as we have put a veil of cotton wool before our ears, and count all decent, so that we do not hear.

Over the insubstantial French provincial houses hung that absorbing eastern thin white dust, which in Algeria seems to mock the efforts of the conquering race to Europeanise the land, no matter howsoever mathematically correct they build the spire of Congregational Gothic church or façade of the gingerbread town hall. The streets all duly planted with the most shady-foliaged trees, the arms of the Republic, looking as dignified as the tin plates of fire insurance offices upon "les monuments," even the pomp and circumstance of the military band, crashing out patriotic airs upon the square, were unavailing to remove the feeling that the East was stronger than the West here in its kingdom, and that did some convulsion but remove the interlopers, all would fall back again into its time-worn rut.

Musing upon the instability of accepted facts, and wondering whether after all, if both the English and the French were expelled from India and Algeria, they would leave as much remembered of themselves as have the makers of the tanks in Kandy, or the builders of the walls of Constantine: in fact, having fallen into that state, which we in common with the animals fall into after eating, but which we usually put down to the workings of the spirit when it is nothing but the efforts of digestion, a voice fell on my ear.

"Would I be good enough to share my carriage with a gentleman, an engineer who wanted to regain his mine some thirty miles away, upon the road."

The stranger was my dissonance in grey, a blot upon the landscape, an outrage in his baggy trousers amongst the white-robed people of the place. He bore upon his face the not to be mistaken mark of failure: that failure which alone makes a man interesting and redeems him from the vulgarity of mere crass success. Gently but with prolixity, he proffered his request. All the timidity which marks the vanquished of the world exhaled from his address as he politely — first tendering his card — apologised both for existence and for troubling me to recognise the fact. I had the only carriage in the town, the diligence did not run more than once a week, and he was old to make the journey on a mule, besides which, though he had been for five and thirty years a dweller in the province of Oran, he spoke but little Arabic, and it was dull to be obliged for a long day to talk in nothing but "le petit nègre."

Most willingly I gave consent, and shortly the miserable conveyance drawn by a starveling mule and an apocalyptic horse, and driven by a Jew, dressed in a shoddy suit of European clothes, surmounted by a fez, holding in either hand a rein and carrying for conveniency *[sic]* his whip between his teeth, jangled and rattled to the door. We both stood bowing after the fashion of Don Basilio and Don Bartolo, waving each other in, and making false preparatory steps, only to fall back again, until I fairly shoved my self-invited guest into the carriage, shut to the door, and called upon the Jew to start. He did so, dexterously enveloping his miserable beasts with a well-executed slash of his whip and a few curses, without which no animal will start in any colony, ill-use him as you may.

In a melancholy, low-pitched, cultivated voice my fellow-traveller pointed out the objects of chief interest on the road. Here such and such an officer had been led into an ambush and his men "massacred" by Arabs posted on a hill. Their tombs, with little cast-iron crosses sticking in the sparse sandy grass, were hung with immortelles, and the shaky cemetery gate, guarded by a plaster lion modelled apparently from a St. Bernard dog, was there to supplement his history. A palm tree grew luxuriantly outside, "its roots in water and its head in fire," as if to typify the resistance of the land to all that comes from Europe, whilst within the walls exotic trees from France withered and drooped their heads, and seemed to pine for their lost rain and mist. The road, well made and bridged, and casting as it were a shadow of the cross upon the land, wound in and out between a range of hills. At intervals it passed through villages, built on the French provincial type, with a wide street and pointed-steepled church, a "mairie," telegraph station, and a barracks for the troops. An air of discontent, begot of "maladie du pays" and absinthe, seemed endemic in them all: no one looked prosperous but the two Arab soldiers, who on their horses, sitting erect and motionless, turned out to see the passage of the coach.

Long trains of donkeys and of mules passed on the road, driven by men dressed in mere bundles of white rags, or by Mallorcans or Valencians, who, with their sticks shoved down between their shirts and backs, urged on their beasts with the loud raucous cries which throughout Spain the Moors have left to their descendant muleteers, together with their pack saddles, their baskets of esparto, and the rest of the equipment of the road. Occasionally camels passed by, looking quite out of place on the high road, but still maintaining the same swaying pace with which their ancestors from immemorial time have paced the desert sands.

And as we jangled noisily upon our path, my guest detailed his life, with circumstance, quoting his "acte de naissance," telling the number of his family, his adventures in the colony, on which he looked half with affection, half with dislike, after the fashion of one mated to a loud-tongued wife, who in recounting all his sufferings never forgets to add, "But still she was a splendid housekeeper," thus hoping to deceive his audience and himself.

"The country it is good, you see (he said), but still unsuited for most kinds of crops. Either it rains in torrents and the corn is washed away, or else the drought lasts years, so that the colonist is always grumbling; not that our countrymen as a general rule are agriculturists, no, that they leave to the Mallorcans and Valencians, but still they grumble at their relatively prosperous life." A comfortable doctrine and a true; for grumbling is as sauce to the hard bread of poverty; without it riches would be bereft of half their charm, and life be rendered tasteless and a mere dream of stertorous content.

As we drove on, the road emerged from woods of greenish-grey Aleppo pine into rough hills clothed with lentiscus and wild olives, and thicketed with cistus and dwarf rhododendrons. Partridges flew across the path continually, occasionally wild boars peeped out, grunted and wheeling back, dived into the recesses of the scrub. Parties of mounted Arabs, their haiks and selhams floating in the wind, carrying hooded hawks on their gloved hands or balancing upon their horses' croups, passed us impassible, making their stallions rear and passage; their reins held high and loosely as they raised themselves almost upright upon their horses' backs. We passed outlying farms, sun-swept and desolate, without the charm of mystery of a ranche *[sic]* in Texas or in Mexico, but looking rather more like bits of railway stations, cut off in lengths, and dropped upon the hills. I learned that most of them were held by officers and soldiers who had served in times gone by against "les indigenes," and that some of them had grown quite rich by waiting till civilisation had spread up to them; a kind of unearned increment which even dogmatists in points of economics could not be hard on, taking into consideration the time and dulness *[sic]* the owners had endured. Gourbis of Arabs, mud-built ksour with now and then black goats'-hair tents, each with its horse feeding in front of it, were dotted on the hill sides or on the plains green with palmettos and with camel-thorn. Occasionally white little towns glittered upon the mountain sides or nestled in the corries of the hills. The untiring sun beat down and blended all in one harmonious whole of brown: brown dusty roads, brown shaggy hills and rocks; the animals were all coated with the bright brown dust, and men, scorched copper-coloured, stood leaning on their sticks playing reed pipes and watching goats and sheep, so motionless that they seemed tree-trunks from which floated sound.

Little by little I learned all my companion's life. His college days, his triumphs, medals, and his entry to the world, wise as he said in scientific knowledge, but a child in the mean necessary arts without which no one can achieve success.

"I was," he said, "bête comme tous les chastes, and therefore fell a victim to the first pretty face . . . I married and adored her, working day and night to make a home, a stupid story of a stupid man, eh? . . . well, well, the usual thing, the husband all day out, planning and striving, and the devil, no not the devil, but the idle fool, who flattered . . . and the nest empty when the working bird came home. So I forswore all women, and lived miserably, came to this colony, and thought I saw an opening, and then married again, this time an honest woman almost a peasant, and have passed my life, the wolf ever just howling close to the door, but not quite entering the house.

"A happy life, yes happy, for you see I knew that I was born a simple, and holy writ says that we simples are to inherit all the earth . . . well so we do, for we maintain all our illusions green, and after all illusions are the best riches, so I have been rich, that is until a month ago. Not rich, you know, in money, though I have had my chances, but never took them, as when the Germany company offered me fifty thousand francs to discover copper in a mine, where since the beginning of the world no copper ever was. I have seen friends grow rich and have not envied them, for till a month ago I had a treasure in my wife. Yes, a good woman, always equal *[Sp. igual=same]*, ever the same, good year, bad year, smiling but sensible, hard-working, and with just that worldly sense I ever wanted . . . yet looked up to me for my scant book learning . . . . No, no . . . I have not wept much, for I have work to do; not that work deadens grief, as you in England say, but that you cannot work and weep.

"The mine is not a rich mine, ten or twelve Spaniards, the foreman and myself, the sole inhabitants. Dull life, you say. . . . Yes, but no duller than in Paris: life is life, no matter where you have to live. No I do not shoot; why should one shoot? rabbits and hares are under every tuft of grass; the Spanish workmen kill them now and then with stones. Ah, there is the mine, that yellowish mark upon the hill, those tunnels, and the huts."

We rattled down the hill, the miserable jades both galloped for their lives, the carriage bounding after them, checked but by a rusty Arab stirrup fastened to a chain, which acted as a drag. We pulled up sharply, and the drag chain breaking left the stirrup stranded on the road. As the driver went to retrieve it, and to repair the damage, I had full time to contemplate the mine. Twelve or thirteen kilometres from the nearest house just perched above the road, it seemed as if some giant rabbit had burrowed in the hill. Two or three tunnels, one of which vomited yellowish water underneath the road, two or three workings, open-cast and left deserted, two or three heaps of cinders, and a pumping engine broken and left to rust, together with the ten or a dozen cottages flanked by the dreary unsuccessful gardens which in all countries miners seem to own, were its chief features. An iron water tank upon a pile of masonry, and several heaps of coal dumped in the bushes which grew between the dark grey boulders with which the hill was strewn, served as embellishments toward the melancholy scene. Slatternly women washed their husbands' clothes, or stood and looked out listlessly into the driving mist; a mangy goat or two grazed on the prickly shrubs, and a keen wind, whistling and screeching through the gullies of the hills, made the coarse skirts and flannel petticoats crack in the air like whips. The sort of place which might have had a kind of grandeur of its own had not the mine been there, but which disfigured and made vulgar as it was became more desolating than a slum outside a town. The engineer collected his few traps, his carpet bag and shoddy plaid, his bulgy umbrella and his new hat carefully carried in a handbox all the journey on his knee: he tendered me his card, large, limp, and shiny, and with his "noms," his "prénoms," and his "titres," duly set forth upon it.

Then, having thanked me with prolixity, he took his leave of me, and slinging all his things upon his back, struck into a small footpath up the hill, winding his way amongst the boulders, looking so like them in his worn grey clothes that it appeared all were identical, only that one was moving on the ground. I called and waved my hand, but he went upwards towards the huts without once turning, and when I looked again, the bent grey moving figure had disappeared amongst the stones.

Success

From the Mouth of the Sahara

Up from the Arab market comes a hum of voices as the white-robed figures shuffle noiselessly about the sandy open space.

The saddles of the kneeling camels stand out like islands in some prehistoric sea, outlined against the background of the white-washed walls. A yellowish red glow towards the north bathes palm trees and the long line of tawny hills in the declining light. To the south the white-topped sierras of the Atlas are all flushed with pink. The Kutubieh tower stands up four square, a deserted lighthouse in the ebbing ocean of Islam; Marrakesh, wrapt in a shroud of mystery, the houses blended together in the grey violet haze of twilight, stretches out, silent and looking like some Babylonian ruin of the past. Horses neigh shrilly now and then, and camels grumble; the muezzin calls to prayers, fatiguing the bewildered Allah with his cry, whilst the unbelievers day by day push back the faithful and usurp their lands. A whirring sound as of a city inhabited by human insects fills the ear, and from the beggars sitting blind besides the gates rises the cry, Oh! Abd-el-Kader el Jilani, Ah! Abd-el-Kader el Jilani, the invocation to the saint of far Jilan, he who forty years besieged the Lord with prayers for the poor. From tortuous bazaars and narrow streets sunk deep below the houses, as they were gullies in a hill, the noiseless crowds emerge, all pressing forward to the Jamal-el-Fanar, the centre space in which converges all the life and movement of the town. There, jugglers play, swallowing their swords, twisting themselves into strange shapes, and walking on the tight rope after the fashion of the Eastern juggler from the time of Moses to the present day. Five deep the listeners stand, as a man tells stories from the Arabian nights [sic], whilst horsemen with one leg across the saddle-bow, and with one hand grasping the gun and rein, the other playing with a rosary, sit silently, occasionally sententiously ejaculating, Allah, as the artist tells of the enchanted princess and her adventures with Ginoun. In the middle of the listening crowd the tale unfolds itself, accompanied by gesture and by change of voice that in another land would make the teller's fortune on the stage. He starts and turns, whilst tears rise to his

177

eyes, he laughs, and with him start and weep his audience, although he never for a moment misses an opportunity as he rests for breath, to urge a boy to make his rounds, holding a wooden bowl or battered white enamelled coffee cup for pence. Then, when the offertory is done, resumes his tale, the hearers standing fascinated, though they have heard it all a thousand times. All the wild life of ancient civilisation, further removed from us by far than is the life of savages who soon assimilate all that is worst of progress, was in full swing as it has been since Haroun-er-Raschid went forth in Bagad, tired of the dulness *[sic]* of his palace life, to listen to the secrets of the poor who then as now were nearer nature and more interesting than cultured dullards in their pride of books. It may be that the railway, which has obliterated most of ancient life, which was but half-a-century ago unchanged in all essentials from remotest times, will work its trumpery transformation on the city of Yusuf-ibn-Tachfin. Before its smoke the world grows grey. Its whistle crumbles down the walls of every Jericho, even as it puffs along the plain, making the whole world but a replica of Leeds. Caste, dignity, repose, the joy even in a hard life, all vanish in the rush to catch a train. The Bedouin draped in blue rags, his sandals on his feet, seated upon a hide-bound "wind-drinker," or perched upon a camel, with his long gun or spear in his hand, retains an air of dignity, such as might grace a king. The same man, waiting at a railway station for a train, becomes a beggar, and as you pass him, bound in your hat and hosen, and with your umbrella in your hand, you hold your travelling rug away, so that it may not touch his rags. So does our progress make commercial travellers of us all, and take away the primeval joy in sun, in wind, in divine idleness, the first and greatest gift that nature ever gave to man.

Still in Marrakesh the world wags as in the days of the Arabian nights *[sic]*, and though the Sultan buys balloons and motor cars, these are as much outside the national life as literature and painting are outside the life of England.

Balloons and literature, painting and motor cars, are but in England and Morocco forms of sport for the cultured few; trifles by means of which the well-to-do pass idle hours, and which the bulk of business and God-fearing men do not reject, as they are quite outside their lives, but do without, deeming them childish, dangerous, or effeminate, anti-Mohammedan, or un-English as the case may be. But in Marrakesh, before the flush upon the tapia walls had died away, before the muezzin from the innumerable mosque towers had called to evening prayer the crowds, which from the remotest quarters of the town had poured towards the sandy square, were packed, like sardines in an esparto basket, waiting to see the procession of the desert men, who with the Sultan's gifts were to pass out to camp just underneath the walls. Throughout Morocco, and the Arab portion of the east, the desert dweller is invested with a kind of sanctity. This only he himself in person ever entirely dissipates, in the same fashion as the sight of Rome was said to dissipate the fervour of the neophyte. Let but the Saharawi or the Bedouin but keep at home and ride his camels in the sand, and he is still a sort of link with pre-historic times. His unshorn head, with curled and well oiled locks bound round the temples with a string of camel's hair, his purity of speech, his nomad life, and freedom from contamination by the infidel, make him, amongst the dwellers in the town, a sort of prototype. Knowledge, they say, is in the Sahara, and in a certain way it is; that is, the knowledge which in remotest times, the Arabs bought *[sic. ?brought]* with the camels and the horses from the Yemen and from Hadramut. There in the desert the traditions of the race are better kept than in the towns, or in the "tiresome Tell," where men are so much lost to self respect (sons of the shameless mothers), that they use horses in the plough, set them to carry packs upon their backs, and thus degrade the animal the prophet loved, and which Allah himself gave to the Ishmaelites to ride to war. Certain it is that in the Sahara, your man-ennobling toil is looked on as the primeval curse, and who so impious as to try with sophistry and argument, to prove that that which Allah laid on men for chastisement is but a paltry blessing in disguise. What reasonable man with an immortal soul, a healthy body, and an intelligence with which to cheat, who cares for blessings when they come in a disguise? As soon may children like the medicine lurking in black-currant jam, or sea-sick folk, writhen and pallid in their paroxysm, listen with equanimity to him who tells them it will do them good, as Arabs understand the meaning of a blessing which is hid. The sun, the wind which blows across the sea and bends the suddra bushes till they work patterns on the sands, the hours of idleness stretched in the goats' hair tents, whilst women play the gimbry and the hot air quivers and shakes outside upon the plain, all these are blessings — blessings which Allah gives to those his Arabs whom he loves.

There in the Sahara the wild old life, the life in which man and the animals seem to be nearer to each other than in the countries where we have changed beasts into meat-producing engines deprived of individuality, still takes its course, as it has done from immemorial time. Children respect their parents, wives look at their husbands almost as gods, and at the tent door elders administer what they imagine justice, stroking their long white beards, and as impressed with their judicial functions as if their dirty turbans or ropes of camels' hair bound round their heads, were horse hair wigs, and the torn mat on which they sit a woolsack or a judge's bench, with a carved wooden canopy above it, decked with the royal arms.

Thus, when the blue baft-clad, thin, wiry desert-dweller on his lean horse or mangy camel comes into a town, the townsmen look on him as we should look on one of Cromwell's Ironsides, or on a Highlander, of those who marched to Derby and set King George's teeth, in pudding time, on edge. Not that the town-bred Arabs look at the desert man with reverence, but with a curiosity mixed with respect, as upon one who though a fool — for everyone who does not live as we do is a fool — yet as the prototype of what he was himself and would be now, but for the special care which fate has had of him, and the exertion of his individual powers.

The throngs who all the afternoon had listened to the story-tellers, or watched the tumblers, went to swell the crowd. The grave and silent men who sitting in wooden box-like shops, with high up-lifted flap, suspended by a string fixed to a wooden peg stuck in the wall, careless about their sales, and yet as eager for a farthing should a sale occur, as an Italian or a Scotchman, all joined the crowd and slowly walked towards the Jamal-el-Fanar. Along the walls blind beggars sat with wooden bowls; flies clustered round their eyes, and as the people passed they clamoured in the self same way that orientals pray, seeking to force their wishes on Allah, just as in times gone by blind Bartimæus sat beside the gate, and no doubt as he sat kept up a constant cry for alms. Grave sheikhs rode past, mere bundles of white fleecy wrappings, as they sat high on their pacing mules. If they were holy, that is descended from Mohammed, and rich men, a true believer now and then, when their mules halted in the crowd, and the attendants on the sheikh parted the press with cries of "balak," "balicum," stepped up and kissed their robes. Had they been twice as well descended and been poor, 'tis ten to one no one had had sufficient faith to see the holy blood as it ran through the veins beneath the dirty rags. Faith is not absolute either in east or west, and those who have it, enjoy it as they do good teeth, without volition of their own, and even then they hold it, so to speak on sufferance, and a too strenuous stretching may in a moment break the strings. Wild Berbers from the hills, their heads shaved all but a love or war lock, call it what you will, with scanty beards and Mongol-looking eyes, went trotting by in bands. And as they ran they held each other's hands, for those who dwell in cities are sons of devils, and it is wise to keep together in a town. So running hand in hand, their clubs beneath their arms or stuck into their waist-belts, or between their orange-eyed achnifs and their bare backs, they passed towards the Jamal-el-Fanar. Long trains of camels at the cross streets blocked the way, the planks they carried trailing on the ground. Loud rose the cries of "balak," and as the camels stood, whilst dogs and children ran between their legs, and men on donkeys which they guided with a club, made themselves flat against the walls and glided past, the donkeys' tripping feet just brushing on the ground, the riders sitting so steadily they might have carried in their hands a bowl of water without spilling it, they stretched their necks towards the piles of dates, which in a solid mass, made living by the myriads of flies, lay piled up in the shops. A smell of spices, mingled with horsedung, hung in the air, as from the shops the bags of asafoetida, bundles of cinnamon, attar of roses, tamar-el-hindi, and the like gave out their various scents to mingle with the acrid odours of the crowd. Occasionally a madman in an old sack, his hair like ropes hanging upon his shoulders, and in his hand a stick, his eyes staring about or wrapt *[sic]*, stalked by. The people murmured devoutly as he walked, for madness is a proof of Allah's love, and those we shut in prisons, all well sanitated and with electric light, to save our eyes the unpleasant spectacle of seeing those whose blood flows to the brain too slowly or in too great force, the Easterns cherish and allow to roam about the streets, believing that Allah made all things according to his will, and not presuming to step in and help him in the details of the plan. Pigeons strolled in and out amongst the throng, walking as gravely as if they too were slaves of the one God, and no man harmed them, either in their walk, or when they sat upon the matting stretched across the street, well within reach of those who passed along. Brown boys, half naked, and with stomachs swollen like tubs, formed up in bands, and danced the "heidus," stamping and clapping hands to a half rythmic *[sic]* chant coeval with the times when the first chimpanzee, after due cogitation, thought he had a soul. Within the square, soldiers who looked unmitigated pimps, and dressed in ragged uniforms of pink or red, struggled to keep a passage in the throng, as with their rifles stacked they smoked and sang, and one of them, a tray hung from his neck, sold sweetstuff, calling as he sold upon Edris, Muley Edris, the patron of the sweetmeat sellers and of all those who use the sugar of the cane. The officers, each dressed according to his will, but generally in clean white Arab clothes, riding fat horses which passed sidling through the crowds, tossing their heads, and ready to say Ha, did trumpets sound, leisurely got the soldiers into line. A thrill of expectation moved all hearts, and then from underneath a horseshoe archway at the furthest corner of the square the desert men appeared.

Our Lord the Sultan had been gracious to them, and they had stood before him seeing his face, and listening to his words conveyed to them by the court herald, he who speaks before the King. Horses and pacing mules, with gold embroidered saddles, somewhat the worse for wear, cloth cloaks and shoes, some rifles, though probably with cartridges made for another bore, and jars of butter, which makes glad the heart of man, spices, and watches of the Christians, bearing the mystic name of Waterbury, God's caliph had bestowed upon his Saharowis, with many gifts even more valuable, for their headman, the holy Ma-el-ainain. Horsemen dressed all in indigo, with naked arms and legs dyed blue with the baft clothes they wore, filed in irregular procession slowly across the square. Olive in colour and wild eyed, their hair unshorn and streaming down their backs, or thick with mutton fat sticking out like a bush, well knit and nervous, with small hands and feet, they looked a race pure and unmixed with any other blood. Some rode their mules as they were camels, with their hands held on a level with their mouths, their guns stuck upright on their saddle-bow, as they were spears, and their quick eyes embracing everything, or fixed and seeing nothing, looking out on the distance after the way of those who live in lands of vast horizons and of unbounded space. Others on foot led horses by the reins, some rode their camels with their faces veiled in blue, their eyelids painted with collyrium, and as the camels paced, they swayed about, backwards and forwards, as ships sway about at sea. So did their ancestors, the Almohades, called by the Spanish chroniclers, "those of the veils," ride when they crossed the narrow straits, which they knew as the "gate of the road," from Hisnr-el-Mujaz, the castle of the crossing, to invade the Andalos, and introduce again the worship of "the one," which with the Moors in Spain had been obscured by contact with the Christians, and too much study of the Greeks.

The crowd stood silent watching them, half in respect, and half inclined to jeer at their bad horsemanship, for desert men are better on a camel than a horse, but still they murmured as the procession took its way, "these men indeed be Arabs," as who should say, would we were like them in their customs and their faith. Faith certainly they had, and of such quality as to be able not only to remove a mountain, but to erect a sierra out of a grain of sand. Beside them rode men of the Sultan's bodyguard, all horsemen from their birth, drawn from the Arab tribes, and now and then they charged across the square regardless of the people in their way, wheeling their horses as birds wheel upon the wing, standing erect an instant in their saddles, twisting their silver-mounted guns above their heads, then stopping short and firing, whilst from the housetops all around the square the women raised the curious shrill cries which the old Spaniards knew as "Alelies," sharp and ear-piercing as a jackal's bark or the wild cry of the coyoté in New Mexico.

A dense white dust hung over everything, which in the waning light looked grey and ghastly on the dark blue clothes the Saharowis wore. At length, and just before the last red gleam of sunset sunk *[sic]* into grey and violet tints on the brown tapia walls, and tinged the palm trees which like a sea for leagues embower Marrakesh in a sea of green, the holy man appeared.

Mounted upon a fat white pacing mule, veiled to the eyes, and with a mass of charms depending from his turban like horses' trappings streaming down his face, dressed all in spotless white, except a dark blue cloak, flung over his left shoulder, and guarded from the vulgar by a band of desert youths, who trotted on beside his mule like dogs, he slowly hove in sight.

The crowd closed in anxious to kiss his clothes, to get the holy "baraka" which clings about the person of a saint. Ma-el-Ainain, 'tis he, the crowd exclaimed, the saint of saints, the man our Lord the Sultan honours above all, and as they pressed to touch his stirrups or his clothes, he rode impassible taking all as his due, and slowly pacing through the throng, took his way desertwards, under the horseshoe gateway at the corner of the square.

Then night descended on the town, and the last gleams of sunlight flickering on the walls, turned paler, changed to violet and to grey, and the pearl-coloured mist creeping up from the palm woods outside the walls enshrouded everything.

Success

At Utrera

"Do you think," says Gonzalo Silvestre, in the "Florida" of Garcilaso de la Vega, to a starving comrade who was complaining of his hunger, "that in this desert we shall find delicacies (manjares) or Utrera cakes?"

This little sentence in the enchanting history of the old half Inca prince, half Spanish gentleman, has always made Utrera, for me, an entity. True that I have often seen the place, often waited wearily at it for the compulsory forty minutes for breakfast, in the heat and dust. But I knew it only as an unnecessary junction outside Seville, a station, amongst others, between Las dos Hermanas and El Arrahal, until I read that line. Most towns we pass upon a journey have no real being for us. Even if we stopped at them, they would perhaps have as little to distinguish them from their immediate neighbours as have the majority of the educated voters of the world. But let a writer, such as Garcilaso, mention them, but cursorily, and they become as it were alive, and have a real existence of their own, ten times as real as the existence which their streets, their churches, dust-heaps, prosperity, and all the want of circumstance of their municipality, seem to impart. So much more vital is the pen of genius than is the simulacrum of vitality, which is called actual life. Not that in southern towns there does not still exist a real life, far more intense than that which northerners enjoy. We in the north have quite obscured the actors in the setting of the piece. Our interest in the welfare of mankind — an interest which our modern and unwise philosophers declare is to be centered [sic] in the future, and that mankind to-day is in such keen necessity of everything, that it becomes unwise to meddle with it — renders us dwellers as it were in a camera obscura, wherein we see ourselves as people sitting at a play. So have we lost our sense of being players, which the Southerners still have, and go about our lives, trying by sport, athletics, and the like to make believe we live.

All that makes life worth having we neglect or relegate back to the middle distance of our minds, as cabs and omnibuses passing in the street, appear to float in space, fata morganas in the panes of the black mirror window in West Halkin Street. So that life's mainsprings, if not quite unknown (for every animal, northern and southern, man, wolf, and bull, feel in a measure hatred and love), are so beset with property, convention, and so be-fig-leaved, as to be relegated from the first place they should enjoy, to that of waiters on prosperity; for in the lands where County Councils rule, no one has time for either love or hate till his position is assured, and he begins to feel the ache between the shoulder blades. But in the countries of the sun a man's best property is after all his life, and power of love and hate, and therefore he becomes a child in things which we think all important, and a profound philosopher in those other things, as hate, love, well-filled idleness, and indifference to care, to which no one of us attains.

Except in dress, the people at Utrera could not have greatly changed since when Silvestre sailed from San Lucar in some high-pooped ship, or caravel small as La Pinta, from the rail of which a sailor sitting fishing had his leg bitten by a shark in the first voyage that Columbus made. An iron wheel or two, a water tank from which the wheezing engine fills its boilers twice a day, a telegraph which, if it works, is used alone for things in which the general public have no share, have not vitality enough to alter greatly or at all the single race of Europe which has remained unspoiled. Even the railway, which in other lands bends people to its will, in Spain is changed and puts on some of the graces of a bullock cart. About the station, looking at the train, but with its thoughts turned inward on itself, the lazy crowd of olive-coloured, under-sized, but well-knit men, in tightly-fitting trousers, low-crowned, broad-brimmed hats, each with his cigarette alight or burnt out in his lips, as it had been part of his system at his birth, strolled gravely up and down, looking the women as they passed full in the face, and being in their turn severely scrutinised by their black unflinching eyes. The heterogeneous mass of bundles, the corded, hairy, cowskin trunks, and cotton umbrellas, which form the bulk of luggage at a southern railway station, lay on the platform blistering in the sun. The electric bell twittered and chattered like a grasshopper, whilst the grave station-master, arrayed in white, strolled up and down, absorbed in the full emptiness of mind which gives an air of seriousness to southern folk. In the refreshment-room the waiters lounged round the table bearing stews yellow with saffron, pilaffs of rice, salads and fruit, smoking the while, and exchanging their ideas on politics and things in general with the company they served. The company itself, seated without a vestige of class separation, talked as unconstrainedly as they had all been intimate with one another from their youth. The gentlemen all had an air of having been at one time bull-fighters, or at least "intelligents" (inteligentes), and the stray bull-fighters looked like gentlemen who pursued their calling from the love of sport. The ladies, dressed in the extreme of Paris fashions, still looked like "chulas" in disguise; the "chulas" gave you the impression that were they painted with more art, and dressed in Paris, they could straight pose as ladies, and be successful in their part. Not that the ladies were not ladies, or that the "chulas" aped their ways, or envied their position, but yet, the type was so alike in each, that outwardly all the distinction was in dress. Both of them heard without resentment compliments of the most violent kind, accepted them at their true value, and recognised, perhaps by instinct and without reasoning, but clearly all the same, that the first duty that their sex owed to itself was to be women, thus conquering without an effort the respect which it has taken northern women centuries of struggle to achieve.

Outside the station, donkeys and mules and horses nodded their heads, tied to a bar between two posts by esparto ropes, their woollen-covered saddles, striped red and purple, looking almost Oriental against the background of the sand. Men slept in corners close to their horses, mere brown bundles, their olive riding-sticks stuck down between their naked backs and ragged shirts, and standing up stiffly, or projecting out fantastically beyond their heads in the intense abandonment of life, which seemed to come upon them in their sun-steeped sleep.

Over the whole incongruous meeting of the powerful semi-Oriental life with the sour breath of the new-fangled and progressive world as typified in the cheaply run-up station and the Belgian engine snorting on the track, the sun shone down, fiery and merciless, exposing all the shams of life, and making men more simple in their villainy and their nobility than it is possible to be in the dim regions of electric light.

Trains came and went, the passengers scaling their steps from the level of the line, after the fashion of a soldier mounting the deadly imminent breach, the men ascending first, and holding out their hands to the women, who were shoved behind by any passing stranger, and dumped like bales of goods upon the carriage floor. The water-sellers, with their Andujar pottery water-coolers, called out their merchandise so gutturally, that their cry seemed Arabic, and the sellers of fruit and toasted ground-nuts, crawled along the platform seemingly quite unconcerned about a sale. Boys climbed the windows, and whined for halfpence, turning their blessings into curses if they were refused. All the bright, lazy, virile elements of southern Spanish life passed swaying on their hips, and looking fixedly with unblinking eyes, whilst in the middle of the line a tame white pigeon walked about, picking up grains of corn, and diving in and out between the carriage wheels, to the terror of the country-women, who after their custom attached a sort of sanctity to it, because it was so white.

Strange that the qualities which endear both animals or men to us are all inherent and impossible to be acquired. No study, education, striving, nor a whole life of wishing, will give beauty or a sweet disposition to an ugly fool. A pigeon born of another colour, by a whole century of self-sacrifice cannot attain to whiteness, so perhaps those who in that tint see sanctity, are right, for anything that is attainable by work is of its very nature common, and open to us all. So underneath the wheels, and on the line, playing at hide and seek with death, the holy whiteling walked, occasionally picking an insect from its feathers with its coral beak, as naturally as if it had been black, slate-coloured, or a mere speckled ordinary bird. Trains came and went, clanging and rattling, and the passengers proceeded on their way packed in the sweltering carriages, contented, almost as patient in their endurance of the miseries of transit, as they had all of them been born without the vaunted power of reasoning, which takes away from man the placid dignity which animals possess.

Men rolled their cigarettes between their fingers browned with tobacco juice, and women fanned themselves, using their fans as they had come into the world with a small fan stuck in their baby hands, ready for future use. All talked incessantly, and as they talked, and smoked, and fanned, the tame white pigeon wove its way in and out amongst the wheels. All the bright comedy of southern life displayed itself, cheap, careless, philosophic, and intent to enjoy the world it lives in; heedless of pain, of suffering, of life itself; trembling at the idea of death when spoken of, and yet prepared to meet it stoically at its real approach. Simple, yet subtle in trivialities, convinced that none but they themselves had grace, wit, beauty, or intelligence, and yet not greatly self-exalted by the fee simple of the only qualities which make men loveable, but taking all as their own due, the people accepted everything that was, and looked upon the trains, the station, the electric bells, the telegraph, and the grave Catalonian engine-drivers perspiring in the sun upon their engines, with lumps of cotton waste in their strong dirty hands, as things sent into the glad world by Providence on their behalf. An attitude which after all may be as good as that of northerners, who, thinking that all the planets turn round their own particular place of abode, yet hold that they themselves in some mysterious way are half accountable for every revolution that they make, and if they stopped but for a moment in their efforts, or but withdrew a tittle of their countenance, that the whole solar system would crumble on their heads.

Seated upon the platform drinking coffee, and thinking listlessly on things, the "chicas," the coming bull fight, if the Madrid express would ever come, and if Silvestre, if he came to life, would find much difference, beyond the railway, in Utrera, I saw the local train start with a puffing, jangling of couplings, banging of doors, and belching forth of smoke. The two grave gendarmes got into their van, belated passengers worked themselves along the footboard to their seats, and in a cloud of dust engine and carriages bumped off upon their way. Clinkers and straws were wafted in my face, the multitudinous last words floated in the still air, and on the line lay something which at first sight appeared a newspaper, but that it seemed alive, and here and there was flecked with red; it flapped a little feebly, turned over once or twice, and then lay motionless upon the six-foot way.

Success

Might, Majesty, and Dominion

A nation dressed in black, a city wreathed in purple hangings, woe upon every face, and grief in every heart. A troop of horses in the streets ridden by kings; a fleet of ships from every nation upon earth; all the world's business stilled for three long days to mourn the passing of her who was the mother of her people, even of the poorest of her people in the land. The newspapers all diapered in black, the clouds dark-grey and sullen, and a hush upon the islands, and upon all their vast dependencies throughout the world. Not only for the passing of the Queen, the virtuous woman, the good mother, the slave of duty; but because she was the mother of her people, even the poorest of her people in the land. Sixty odd years of full prosperity; England advancing towards universal Empire; an advance in the material arts of progress such as the world has never known; and yet to-day she who was to most Englishmen the concentration of the national idea, borne on a gun-carriage through the same streets which she had so often passed through in the full joy of life. Full sixty years of progress; wages at least thrice higher than, when a girl, she mounted on her throne; England's dominions more than thrice extended; arts, sciences, and everything that tends to bridge space over, a thousand times advanced, and a new era brought about by steam and electricity, all in the lifetime of her who passed so silently through the once well-known streets. The national wealth swollen beyond even the dreams of those who saw the beginning of the reign; churches innumerable built by the pious care of those who thought the gospel should be brought home to the poor. Great battleships, torpedo boats, submarine vessels, guns, rifles, stinkpot shells, and all the contrivances of those who think that the material progress of the Anglo-Saxon race should enter into the polity of savage states, as Latin used to enter schoolboys' minds, with blood. Again, a hum of factories in the land, wheels whizzing, bands revolving so rapidly that the eye of man can hardly follow them, making machinery a tangled mass of steel, heaving and jumping in its action, so that the unpractical looker-on fears that some bolt may break and straight destroy him, like a cannon ball.

Success

All this, and coal mines, with blast furnaces, and smelting works with men half-naked working by day and night before the fires. Infinite and incredible contrivances to save all labour; aerial ships projected; speech practicable between continents without the aid of wires; charities such as the world has never known before; a very cacoethes of good doing; a sort of half-baked goodwill to all men, so that the charities came from superfluous wealth and the goodwill is of platonic kind; all this and more during the brief dream of sixty years in which the ruler, she who was mother of her people, trod the earth. All these material instances of the great change in human life, which in her reign had happened, and which she suffered unresistingly, just as the meanest of her subjects suffered them, and as both she and they welcomed the sun from heaven as something quite outside of them, and, as it were, ordained, her people, in some dull faithful way, had grown into the habit of connecting in some vague manner with herself. For sixty years, before the most of us now living had uttered our first cry, she held the orb and sceptre, and appeared to us a mother Atlas, to sustain the world. She left us, almost without a warning, and a nation mourned her, because she was the mother of her people, yes, even of the meanest of her people in the land.

So down the streets in the hard biting wind, right through the rows of dreary living-boxes which like a tunnel seemed to encase the assembled mass of men, her funeral procession passed. On housetops and on balconies her former subjects swarmed like bees; the trees held rookeries of men, and the keen wind swayed them about, but still they kept their place, chilled to the bone but uncomplainingly, knowing their former ruler had been the mother of them all.

Emperors and kings passed on, the martial pomp and majesty of glorious war clattering and clanking at their heels. The silent crowds stood reverently all dressed in black. At length, when the last soldier had ridden out of sight, the torrent of humanity broke into myriad waves, leaving upon the grass of the down-trodden park its scum of sandwich papers, which, like the foam of some great ocean, clung to the railings, round the roots of trees, was driven fitfully before the wind over the boot-stained grass, or trodden deep into the mud, or else swayed rhythmically to and fro as seaweed sways and moans in the slack water of a beach.

At length they all dispersed, and a well-bred and well-fed dog or two roamed to and fro, sniffing disdainfully at the remains of the rejected food which the fallen papers held.

Lastly, a man grown old in the long reign of the much-mourned ruler, whose funeral procession had just passed, stumbled about, slipping upon the muddy grass, and taking up a paper from the mud fed ravenously on that which the two dogs had looked at with disdain.

His hunger satisfied, he took up of the fragments that remained a pocketful, and then, whistling a snatch from a forgotten opera, slouched slowly onward and was swallowed by the gloom.

Success

Sursum Corda

There is a plethora of talk, which seems to stop all thought, and by its ceaseless noise drive those who wish to think back on themselves. All talk, and no one listens, still less answers, for all must swell the general output of the chatter of the world. Bishops and Deans, with politicians, agitators, betting men, Women's Rights Advocates, members of Parliament, lawyers, nay even soldiers, sailors, the incredible average man, and most egregious superior person, must all be at it for their very lives. Still, talking serves a purpose, if only that of saving us from the dire tedium of our thoughts. Tobacco, sleep, narcotics, dice, cards, drink, horse racing, women, and religion, with palmistry, thought reading, the "occult," athletic sports, politics, all stand out ineffectual as consolers when compared to speech. What triumphs in the world can be compared to those speech gives ?

The writer writes, toils, waits, publishes, and succeeds at last, but feels no flush of triumph like to that which the "cabotin," preacher, pleader, or mob orator enjoys when he perceives the eyes of the whole audience fixed upon him like a myriad of electric sparks; their ears drink in his words, and men and women, rich, poor, old, young, foolish, and wise alike, are bound together by the spell of speech. So after all it may be that, though silence is of silver, speech is purest gold. Pity that, being golden, it should be abused; but still to what base uses gold is put, and so of speech.

But be that as it may, let speech be only silver, silence gold, take but away our speech, chain us within the terror of ourselves by silence long enforced, and the most abject drivel of the sound business man, whose every thought is abject platitude, whose mind has never passed from the strict limits of his villa and his counting-house, becomes as sweet as music to our ears. Let those who doubt try for a month to keep strict silence, never to speak, to hear and never dare to answer, to enchain their thoughts, their wishes, their desires, passions, anxieties, affections, regrets, remorses, anger, hatreds, loves — in brief, to leave the gamut of that inner life which makes a man, with all the notes untouched.

Whilst listening to a painful preacher, sitting out a play, endeavouring to understand in Parliament what a dull speaker thinks he means to say, the thought creeps in, why teach the dumb to speak? Why rive away from them that which at first sight seems the chief blessing, want of speech, and so enable them to set their folly forth and talk themselves down fools. Then comes experience, experience that stands as a divinity to reasoning men, and clamours out, Nay, let them speak although they know not what they say; their speech may strike a chord they know not of in some man's heart.

Think on a silent world, a world in which men walked about in all respects equipped with every organ, every sense, but without speech. They might converse by signs as Indians do upon the trail, but I maintain no city of tremendous night could be more awful than the horror of a speechless world. Never to speak, only to find our tongues in agony of fear, as horses tied within a burning stable, dumb idiots in great peril of their lives, or, as the animal under curare, upon the vivisector's bench (calling to man who should be as his God), give out occasionally some horrid sound, and even then know it would be unheard. Shepherds upon the hills, men in a cattle "puesto" in La Plata, hut keepers in Australia, the Gambusino straying amongst the valleys of the Sierra Madre, Arab rekass, monks, fishermen, lighthouse-keepers, and the poor educated man lost in the crowded solitude of London, all know of silence and its fears. Still they can talk if only to themselves, sing, whistle, speak to their animals, look at the sea, the desert, scan the immeasurable brown of pampas, the green of prairie, or the dull duskiness of bush, or if in London launch into objurgation on mankind, knowing that if they objurgate enough some one will answer, for we Britons cannot stand reproaches, knowing that we are just. An inward something seems to assure us of our righteousness, and all we do is never done as it is done in other and less favoured lands, from impulse, prejudice, or hurriedly, but well thought out, and therefore as inexorably unjust in the working as is fate itself. Let speech be golden, silver, diffusive, tedious, flippant, deceptive, corrupting, somnolent, evasive, let it be what you will, it is the only medium by which we can assert that majesty which some folks tell us is inherent in mankind, but which the greater part of us (from democratic sentiment perchance) rarely allow to creep into the light of day; it is the only humanizing influence innate in men, and thus it seems unwise to put restraint upon it, except in Parliament. Chained dogs, parrots in cages, squirrels within their stationary bicycles, gold fish in globes, wild animals behind their bars, monkeys tied to an organ dressed in their little red woollen gowns (the fashion never changes), bears fastened to a Savoyard, camels on which climb multitudinous bands of children, elephants accompanied by a miserable "native" tramping about with tons of tourists on their backs, move me to wrath, and set me thinking what is it they can have done in an anterior state to undergo such treatment, and whether they were men who must as beasts thus expiate their crimes of *lèse-majesté* against the animals. Yet they are not condemned to silence, and perchance may fabulate at night or when their keepers sleep, or lie drunk, and in their ratiocination exhale their cares.

No, silence is reserved for men who have offended against the hazy principles of right and wrong, or over-stepped that ever-shifting frontier line, never too well defined, and which advancing toleration — that toleration which shall some day lighten life — may soon obliterate, or, if not quite obliterate, yet render the return across the line more feasible than now. When one considers it, how crass it is to shut men up in vast hotels, withdrawing them from any possible influence which might ever change their lives, and to confine them in a white-washed cell, with windows of Dutch glass, gas, and a Bible, table, chair, little square salt-box, wooden spoon, tin pan, schedule of rules, hell in their hearts, a pound of oakum in their hands, condemned to silence and to count the days, pricking them off under the ventilator with a bent nail or pin!

Well was it said, the only humanizing influence in a prison comes from the prisoners. Let the officials do their duty as they think they should, the governor be humane, the doctor know a little of his work, the chaplain not too inept, still prisoners of whatever rank or class, imprisoned for whatever crime, offence, or misdemeanour, look on each other as old friends after a day or two within the prison walls. Day follows day with "skilly," exercise, with chapel, with dreary dulness [sic], and with counting hours. Night follows night, and when the light goes out the tramping up and down the cells begins, the rappings, and the mysterious code by which the prisoners communicate, sound through the building like an imprisoned woodpecker tapping to be free; tremendous nights of eight and forty hours, a twisting, turning, rising oft, and lying down to rise again, of watching, counting up to a million, walking about and touching every separate article; of thinking upon every base action of one's life, of breaking out a cursing like a drab; then falling to a fitful, unrefreshing sleep which seems to last but for a minute, and then the morning bell.

Happier by far the men who, in my youth in Spain, fished with a basket from the window for alms from passers by, smoked, drank, and played at cards, talked to their friends; whose wives and sisters brought them food in baskets, sat talking to them from outside, talked all day long, and passed the time of day with other citizens who walked the streets, read newspapers, and were known to other men as the "unhappy ones." A hell on earth you say, contaminating influences, murderers and petty thieves, with forgers, shop-lifters and debtors all together. At most a hell within a hell, and for the influence for good or ill, I take it that the communion of the sinners was at least as tolerable as we can hope to find (should we attain it) the communion of the saints. Philosophers can theorize to good effect as to the probability of other worlds, the atmosphere of Mars, the Delphic E, the Atomic Theory, the possible perfectibility of the pneumatic tyre, on form, style, taste, or forms of government, on Socialism, Anarchy, the Trinity, on Cosmic Theism, Gnosticism, or the cessation of direct divine interposition in affairs sublunary, discuss their theories and the muzzling of their dogs, weave their philosophies (no man regarding them), invent their faiths, destroy them, and set to work again in the construction of new faiths just as ridiculous as the faiths destroyed; but when they come to theorize upon the treatment of mankind, all their acumen straight evaporates.

But leaving theorists weaving the ropes to hang themselves, spun from the cobwebs of their minds, and coming back to practice and to common sense — that common sense which makes so foolish most things that we do. A recent essayist fresh from his Malebolge has set forth all that men suffer shut within the silence of themselves, has written down the lessons that a man gains from the companionship of those who no doubt are in general not much more guilty than judges, gaolers, their chaplains, warders, or than ourselves who sit forgetting that our neglect entailed on them the lack of opportunity.

Well has he spoken of the humility of prisoners, their cheerfulness, compassion for one another, well described the circling miserable ring of lame folk, aged men, those on the sick list, and the rest, who in the prison yard revolve in a small circle round a post, too feeble to keep pace with the robuster rogues at exercise. I see them, too (can do so any time I close my eyes), in their long shoddy greatcoats, thin, pale, abject as dogs, purposeless, shiftless, self-abased, down-eyed, and shuffling in the prison shoes; expectorating, coughing, and a jest to those who trot around the ring stamping and cursing underneath their breath, what time the warders stand blowing their fingers, side arms belted on, stiff and immovable, and on the watch to pounce upon a contravention of the rules. But whilst the quondam humourist *[sic]* now turned moralizer has left his faithful picture of the misery of those he lived amongst for two long years, he has omitted to set down the one event of prison life which breaks the dull monotony of weeks and days, and lets men feel for a brief space that they are men once more.

The dull week over, oakum all duly picked, cells well swept out, the skilly and brown bread discussed, beds all rolled up, the inspection over, faces all washed, with clean checked handkerchiefs (coarse as the topsail of a sugar droger) duly served out to last the week, the terrors of the bath encountered, the creepy silence of the vast unmurmuring hive is broken by the Sabbath bell. Then cells give up their dead, and corridors are full of the pale skilly-fed shuffling crowd, each headed by its warder, and every man with something of anticipation in his eye, ready to march to church. To the vast chapel streams the voiceless crowd, and soon each seat is filled, a warder duly placed at each bench end to see the worshippers do not engage in speculations as to the nature of the Trinity, but stand and kneel and sit, do everything in fact that other congregations do, omitting only the due dumping of the threepenny bit into the plate, and not forgetting that when two or three are gathered thus to pray, their Creator stands amongst them, although they all are thieves. And thus assembled in their hundreds, to make their prayer before the God of Prisons, the congregation sits — prisoners and captives, shut within themselves, and each man tortured by the thought that those outside have lost him from their minds. The chapel built in a semicircle, with the back seats gradually rising, so that all may be in view, the pulpit made of deal and varnished brown, the organ cased in deal, and for all ornament, over the altar the Creed, Lord's Prayer, and Ten Commandments, and those last look at the congregation as if ironically, and seem designed to fill the place of prison rules for all mankind. Furtively Bill greets Jack, and 'Enery, George: " 'Ow are yer blokes? Another bloomin' week gone past." "I ain't a-talkin', Sir, 'twas t' other bloke," and a mysterious twitch makes itself felt from bench to bench till the whole chapel thus has said good-day. Loud peals the voluntary, the convicted organist — some thievish schoolmaster or poor bank clerk having made (according to himself) a slight mistake in counting out some notes — attacks an organ fugue, making wrong notes, drawing out all the stops alternately, keeping the vox humana permanently on, and plays and plays and plays till a grim warder stalks across the floor and bids him cease. "Dearly Beloved" seemed a little forced, our daily skilly scarce a matter worth much thanks, the trespasses of others we forgave thinking our own were all wiped out by our mere presence in the place, the Creed we treated as a subject well thrashed out, "Prisoners and Captives" made us all feel bad, the litany we roared out like a chant, calling upon the Lord to hear us in voices that I feel He must have heard; epistle, gospel, collects we endured, sitting as patiently as toads in mud, all waiting for the hymn. The chaplain names it, and the organ roars, the organist rocks in his chair, on every brow the perspiration starts, all hands are clenched, and no one dares to look his neighbour in the eyes; then like an earthquake the pent-up sound breaks forth, the chapel quivers like a ship from stem to stern, dust flies, and loud from every throat the pious doggerel peals. And in the sounds the prison melts away, the doors are opened, and each man sits in his home surrounded by his friends, his Sunday dinner smokes, his children all clean washed are by his side, and so we sing, lift up our hearts and roar vociferously (praising some kind of God), shaken inside and out, yelling, perspiring, shouting each other down. Old lags and forgers, area sneaks, burglars, cheats, swindlers, confidence trick men, horse thieves, and dog stealers, men in for rape, for crimes of violence, assault and battery, with "smashers," swell mobsmen, blackmailers, all the vilest of the vile, no worse perhaps if all were known than are the most immaculate of all the good, made human once again during the sixteen verses of the hymn, and all the miseries of the past week wiped out in the brief exercise of unusual speech. The sixteen verses over, we sit down, and for a moment look at one another just in the same way as the worshippers are wont to do in St. Paul's, Knightsbridge, or St. Peter's, Eaton Square.

"Does you good, No. 8, the bloomin' 'ymn," an old lag says, but for the moment dazed by the ceasing of the noise, as Bernal Diaz says he was when the long tumult ended and Mexico was won, I do not answer, but at length deal him a friendly kick and think the sixteen verses of the hymn were all too short.

So in a side street when the frequent loafer sidles up, and says mysteriously "Gawd bless yer, chuck us arf a pint; I was in with you in that crooil plaice," I do so, not that I think he speaks the truth nor yet imagine that the prison, large though it was, contained two million prisoners, but to relieve his thirst and for the sake of those condemned to silence, there "inside," and for the recollection of the "bloomin' 'ymn."

The Pyramid

Fat, meretricious women in evening gowns had sung their ballads, their patter songs, their patriotic airs, in sentimental or in alcoholic tones. Comedians in checked clothes and sandy wigs, adorned with great red whiskers, and holding either short canes or bulgy umbrellas, had made the whole "Pretoria" laugh, till the vast music hall seemed to rock, as a volcano in activity is shaken with its interior fire.

Women and men had hung head downward from trapezes, had swung across the audience and been caught by the feet or hands by other "artistes" swinging to meet them suspended by one foot. Tottering and miserably anthropomorphous dogs had fired off cannons, and cats had tremblingly got into baskets with fox terriers; a skinny, sallow French "divette" had edified the audience with indecencies, rendered quite tolerable because half understood. Men dressed in evening clothes had bawled about the empire, holding a champagne glass in one hand whilst with their other hand they pressed a satin opera hat against their epigastrum; and as the songs became more patriotic or more obscene, and as each trick of the equilibrists, trapezists, wire-walkers and the rest became more dangerous, the public — the respectable, the discerning, the sovereign public — had testified its joy in shouts, in clappings, and in stampings, and by thumping with its sticks and umbrellas on the floor.

Over the auditorium, tobacco smoke hung like a vulgar incense in the shoddy temple of some false and tinsel god. In the great lounges the women sat at tables, dressed in a caricature of the prevailing styles; their boots too pointed, their gowns too tightly laced, their hair too curled or too much flattened to the head; and talked to youths in evening dress; to men who had the mark of husbands out on strike; to padded and painted elders, who whispered in their ears and plied them with champagne. Others who, out of luck, had found no man to hire them, walked up and down in pairs, pushing against such men as looked like customers, laughing and joking to one another, or singly stalked about, bored and dejected, and their legs trailing along imprisoned in their rustling skirts,

enduring all the martyrdom of the perpetual walking which is the curse
entailed upon their class. Behind the bars, the barmaids, painted and
curled, kept up a running fire of half indecent chaff with the intelligent
consumers of American drinks, of whisky-splits, or lemon-squashes,
returning change for half a sovereign if the drinker was too far gone in
liquor to observe it was a sovereign he put down.

Cadaverous and painted youths, with hothouse flowers in their
buttonholes, paraded up and down, as it seemed for no particular
purpose, speaking to no one, but occasionally exchanging glances with
the women as they passed upon their beat.

In fact, the great, the generous, public was represented in all its phases,
of alcoholic, of bestial, brutal, lustful, stupid, and of commonplace.
Yet each one knew he was a part and parcel of a great empire, and was
well convinced that in his person in some mysterious way he made for
righteousness. The soldier sitting with his sweetheart in the gallery; the
rich young idler about town, with his dressed-up and bejewelled mistress
in the stalls; the betting men — made, it is well not to forget, in their
creator's image — each, all, and every one, knew he was not as men of
other nations, but in some way was better, purer, and more manly than
the best citizen of any foreign race. And so they sat, confident that all
the performers, of whatever class, lived on their approbation, as it was
certain they existed on their entrance fee. No trick so dangerous as to
awake their pity, no song quite vile enough to make them feel ashamed
to see a man or woman publicly prostitute their talents for their sport.
Brutal, yet kindly folk they were, quite unappreciative of anything but
fun and coarse indecency; of feats on which the performer's life hung on
a hair; but still idealistic, sentimental souls, easily moved to tears with
claptrap sentiment, and prone to clench their fists, and feel an ardour as
of William Tell, when from the stage a man waved a small Union Jack or
sang of Britain and her Colonies, ending each verse of his patriotic chant
with a refrain of "hands across the sea."

And so the evening wore away. The performer on the fiddle with one
string was succeeded by the quick-change "artiste," who in an instant
appeared as a life-guardsman, walked across the stage and came on as a
ballet dancer or an archdeacon, a costermonger, or lady from a cathedral
city, and still in every change of costume looked the clever humorous
Italian that he was.

Footmen in gorgeous liveries removed the numbers from the wings,
and stuck up others, doing their duty proudly, being well aware their

noble calves saved them from ridicule. The orchestra boomed and thumped through German waltzes, popular songs, and Spanish music, with the Spanish rhythm all left out, so that it sounded just as common as it were made at home.

Between eleven and twelve, turn number seventeen, the début of "La Famiglia Sinigaglia" stood announced. Carpenters came and went upon the stage, and reared a kind of scaffold some fifteen feet in height. Then the "Famiglia Sinigaglia" came upon the scene — the father, mother, two children under ten years old, and five tall girls ranging from sixteen up to five-and-twenty years. The father, of some fifty years of age, was stout and muscular, his eyes as black as sloes, moustache and chin-tuft waxed to points, hair gone upon the crown, which shone like ivory, but still clinging to the occiput like sea weed to a rock. Those who had been responsible for what they did had called him at his baptism Anibale, which name he bore as conscious of the responsibility it laid on him, half modestly and half defiantly, with a perception of the ludicrous in life which yet did not distract him an iota from his profession, which he esteemed the noblest in the world.

"Altro Signore, ours is reality, not like the painters and the poets, with the musicians and the actors, who, if they miss their tip, can try again; but we, per Baccho, when we miss, straight to the Campo Santo, Corpo del Bambin."

The mother, stout and merry-looking, was flaccid from the waist upwards, and had legs as of a mastodon, into the skin of which her high blue satin boots seemed to embed themselves, and to become incorporated. The children passed from hand to hand like cricket balls, being projected from Anibale to his wife La Sinigaglia, behind his back, flying between his legs, alighting on her shoulders or her head like birds upon a bough. Watching this tumbling stood the five daughters in a row. All dressed in tights, with trunks so short, they seemed to cut into their flesh, and so cut open on the hips, that it seemed marvellous what kept them in their place. They were all muscular, especially the eldest, who bid fair to be a rival to her mother in flesh and merriness; her eyes, roving about the theatre, smiled pleasantly when they met anyone's, after the fashion of a Newfoundland dog. The others, slighter in form, were replicas of her at stated intervals. The youngest, thinner than the rest, seemed less goodnatured, and with her brown bare arms folded across her chest stood rather sullenly looking at nothing, smoothing down her tights, crossing her feet, and then uncrossing them, and now and then, raising her head, looked out into the theatre, half frightened, half defiantly. The tumbling of the children done, the father lying on his back threw the fattest of his girls from his feet towards the mother who caught her with her feet right in the middle of the back, after a somersault. The public knowing the trick was dangerous applauded joyfully, and then the five tall girls stepped out to build the pyramid. The eldest, straddling her legs, folded her arms, after saluting right and left with the "te morituri" gesture, which perhaps the modern acrobat has had straight from the gladiator. Her sister climbed upon her shoulders and stood upright, waving her arms a minute, smiling as the applause broke out from the spectators in the theatre. Taking a lace-edged pocket-handkerchief from some mysterious hiding place, she wiped her hands, and bending down signed to another sister, who clambered up, and in her turn stood on her shoulders. The fourth succeeded, and as they stood, the lowest sister staggered a little, and took a step to get her balance, making the pyramid all rock, and causing Anibale to swear beneath his breath, and mutter to his wife.

"Su Gigia," and the fifth sister ran up the staging like a monkey, and stepping from it stood on the topmost sister's hands in the attitude of John of Bologna's Mercury, one arm uplifted, and her eyes turned upwards to the roof. The supporting sister staggered a pace or two into the middle of the stage, the perspiration dripping from her face, and then saluted cautiously with her right hand, and the three others broke into a smile which they had learned together with their tricks.

The audience burst into applause, Anibale and La Sinigaglia looked at each other with content, knowing their turn had taken on, and from the top of the high pyramid the youngest sister glared at the applauders with hatred and contempt, opening her eyes so that the pupils almost seemed to burst, but as she glared the public kept applauding, being aware that acrobats live on its breath, and counting it as righteousness they were not stinted in their food.

Terror

The scent of horse-dung filled the summer air; the whispering trees stood out black menacing masses in the moonlight; the stuccoed houses frowned respectably upon the streets, looking like artificial cliffs bounding some silent and exclusive sea. Belgravia lay asleep, steeped in the pseudo-moonbeams of the electric light; the roar of traffic, which by day-time deafens and renders by degrees the ear incapable of hearing anything but noise, was dulled, or only rumbled fitfully in the far-off streets, whilst in the silent squares a breeze shook the dust-powdered trees, and rained the first dry summer leaves upon the ground. At corners, a stray prostitute or two still lingered, lying in wait for the belated diner-out.

At the opening of a mews, a knot of stablemen, in shirt-sleeves, with their braces hanging down their backs, girt with broad webbing belts, stood talking about horses, but seriously and without emotion, as befits the solemn nature of their theme. The strange and ragged loiterers who at night parade the streets, coming out silently from the nothingness of misery, "dossing" in the park, and at the first approach of dawn sinking again into the misery of nothingness which is their life, were all abroad. Women, who seemed mere bundles of black rags in motion, and men in greasy, old frock-coats and trousers with a fringe behind the heels, passed one another silently, ships on a sea of failure, without a salutation or a sign.

Mechanically they scratched themselves, their hands like claws of mangy vultures, raking amongst their rags. Munching a hunch of dirty bread, they passed into the night, a silent menace to their well-fed brothers in the Lord. All that by day is hidden from our sight, was out, giving the lie to optimists, to statisticians, and to all those who make pretence to think that progress makes for happiness, and that the increase of wealth acts as a sort of blotting-pad on poverty, and sucks up grief.

Dressed in their blue-serge jumpers, and sweating in the thick blue trousers and the ammunition boots which a paternal government deals out to them, so that their lightest step shall thunder on the pavement and give ill-doers a fair chance of stealing themselves away to safety, the police stood at the crossings and conversed in pairs, or, leaning against some iron railings, courted the servant girls, as they watched for the welfare of the sleeping town. A homing cab or two lurched wearily along, the horse and driver nodding in their respective situations, each of them conscious of having earned his meed of beer or corn. The bicyclist's sharp bell startled the swinkt pedestrian at the crossings, as the machine, vanguard of those which will soon sweep pedestrians from all streets, slipped noiselessly along and vanished in the distance, its rider seeming to be suspended in the air as his legs worked like wings.

From the windows of a distant house, the music of a valse floated out fitfully; the shadows of the dancers turned as in a mist behind the glass; outside, the group of waiting footmen lounged, and waifs and strays, leaning against the railings of the square, completed the gradations of society, thus seeming, by their presence, at the same time to act as foil to those inside, and yet unite them in the bonds of brotherhood and faith.

The happy, rich, successful, vulgar-looking city, after the toils of business and of fashion, seemed to be taking its well-earned repose. A light night-breeze just stirred the dust upon the leaves of the black walnuts in the oblong square, shut at one end by the bulk of the long, cake-like church, with bell-tower pepper-box and portico, upon the steps of which the high-heeled boots of fashionable worshippers had left the imprints of the first stage upon their journey towards their self-appointed place.

Nothing on all the face of the quiet, well-regulated town seemed to be out of joint, for tramps and prostitutes have each their proper place in the Chinese puzzle of society, and it is possible, were they but removed, that institutions men deem honourable might find themselves without a place. But nature, pitiless and ever on the watch, and seemingly intent to lower our pride whenever we look round complacently upon our puny so-called scientific triumphs, by linking us inexorably to the other animals in all our passions and our feelings, was not asleep.

Between some iron railings and a stretch of bare and stuccoed wall, some smoke-stained lilacs grew, their roots a lurking-place for cats and a receptacle for bones and empty tins, straws, and the scraps of newspapers which act as banners to our progress, driven by the wind. Right opposite this urban jungle, close to the curbstone, its head upon some horse-dung and its legs stretched out upon the little waves and inequalities of hardened mud left by the rain, lay the dead body of a white-and-yellow cat. Upon its staring coat, each individual hair, stiff with dry sweat and mud, stood out like frozen grass protruding from the snow. Its eyes stared glassy and distended, its legs and tail had taken the rigid forms of feline death, rendered more horrible by contrast with the subtle grace of life. Its body, swollen to twice its proper size, seemed just about to burst.

Killed by a passing cab, or worried by a dog, or perhaps slain out of pure joy in death and love of field-sports by some sportsman to whom the joys of shooting elephants and giraffes were unattainable through lack of means, it lay, pending the arrival of the dust-cart, as a *memento mori* to the young guardsman sauntering home in evening dress, his coat upon his arm, but one step lower than the angels in the estimation of himself and of his friends.

The grimy lilacs rustled and parted, and through the iron railings was stuck out a head. A body followed, squirming like a snake, and, with a squeal, a small black-and-white cat bounded upon the pavement, and stood staring at the body in the street.

Poised lightly on its feet, arching its back a little, and its tail quivering as it slowly lashed its sides, it stood and gazed. With bristling hair and crouching low upon the ground, slowly it crawled towards the stiff dead cat, as if drawn by a magnet irresistibly; its whiskers touched the body, and, as if horrified, it bounded back. Slowly it made a circuit, swelling, and visibly distraught with fear; then, with a spring or two, took refuge on the pavement, but always looking at the object of its dread and quivering with fear. Backing, and with its eyes wide staring, it sought the shelter of the lilacs, but in an instant, with a squeal, bounced out again and rushed away, only to stop and once again to steal along up to the dead with every limb aquake,

A fascination, such as seems to draw the eyes of women to some sight their nerves abhor, possessed it, and it lay down, purring, close to the corpse, stretched out a paw in horror, felt the cold flesh, and, shrieking, fled again into the street. Five or six times, it ventured close and shrunk away, unable, as it seemed, to leave the spot; then lightly leaped from side to side, alighting with its legs as stiff as posts, like a horse buck-jumping, and, lastly, crouching once more its belly to the ground, retired into the shrubs.

A drunkard howled a song, three or four semi-Hooligans *[sic]* lurched down the street, a carriage rattled by the kerb, the wheel crushing the body of the dead yellow cat, causing its entrails to protrude; the spell was broken, the fascinated and terror-stricken black-and-white little cat ran swiftly up a wall, and, with a last long look into the street, was gone.

Success

Postponed

Conviction, one might think, cometh neither from the east nor from the west. In fact, in many cases, it is a mere matter of digestion. Be that as it may, the Rev. Arthur Bannerman, a widower with two little girls, abruptly forsook the Anglican Communion and fell away to Rome. What were his real motives, perhaps even he himself could not have quite explained. A love of continuity; doubts as to the true and apostolical succession of orders transmitted at the Nag's Head; a lingering fear that the laity, if once admitted to the cup, might still exceed after the fashion of the early Christians at their feasts — these causes may have accounted for the step. Or, again, they may have had but little influence, for most conversions spring from impulse rather than a due reasoning out of motives for the change of faith.

The Rev. Bannerman (as most of his parishioners styled him) though a good man, was of a mean presence, with the fair hair, blue eyes, and freckled skin which, with a stutter and a shamble, fit a man for ministration to his fellows, or might enable him to burlesque himself with great effect upon the stage. Good and ridiculous, but lovable, he had a heart whose workings, obfuscated by the foibles of the outward man, beat like a bull-dog's. Some men seem born for heroes; so tall, so straight are they, their eyes so piercing and their gait so free, that it appears impossible when one learns that they are stockbrokers or chiropodists. Having run all the gamut of parochial duties in the English Churches, presided at the mothers' meeting, visited the poor, worn vestments, dabbled in the outskirts of Theosophy, and dallied with Spiritualism, Mr. Bannerman yet had found his life not full enough of sacrifice. By degrees his parsonage (twined round with roses, and with its glebe stretching away beyond the Saxon church into the lush meadows of the squire), his Jersey cow, even his cob, the faithful sharer of his rambles while studying the fossils of the neighbouring downs, the bobs and curtseys of the village children, the waving salutation of the smock-frocked boy who was "woful tired a'scaring o' birds," all grew to be distasteful, and seemed chains which but attached him to a material world.

How many men before the Rev. Arthur Bannerman have failed to see that there is nothing so materialistic as the mystic and the supernatural, and that the dullest duties of the dreariest parish are in reality more transcendental than the dreams of the theologist?

But into speculations of this nature he did not enter. Seeing his duty — that is, his inclination — straight ahead, he embraced it and the Roman Church. Then after the due steps (for once a Levite is to be a Levite to the end, no matter how wide apart is set the new faith from the old), he became a priest, more or less after the order of Melchizedek. A priest and still ridiculous — never in time at Mass, stumbling about the confessional with furtive gait — he seemed a tree transplanted from a cold soil into another hardly less uncongenial which stunts it in its growth. Still, the reliance on a hierarchy, the consciousness that he was (so to speak) in telephonic rapport with St. Peter and St. Paul, by way of Constantine, Charlemagne, Bernard of Clairvaux, the blessed bloody Mary, and the seminary priests slain by that paragon of virgins, stout Queen Bess (who wished to show that she was as zealous for her faith as was her sister), brought comfort to his heart. That is, to his intellectual heart; for now and then he thought upon his children, given away to a pious lady and brought up far from him with a view to convents, as if the marriage of their father before he knew the truth had rendered them unclean for ordinary intercourse with fellow beings, and only fit for God. So, in his communings with himself, at times his natural love strove strongly with his artificial and dogmatic instincts; and after the fashion of all those who strive to conquer nature by the force of reason, he always thought that he did something praiseworthy when he choked down his tears, his longings, and everything which really, being natural, makes for righteousness. The children, far from their father, grew up half-bastard, half-legitimate, knowing their father's name, yet not allowed to mention him, as if their very being was a tacit scandal upon themselves and him. The pious lady loved them in a way, feeding them heavily, as kind-hearted but religious people always do; making their lives a round of prayer, half looking on them as a scandal to the faith, and half regarding them as material evidence of her own strength of mind and freedom from all petty prejudice. The children, duly called after Anglo-Saxon saints (having been baptized before the time when their father's eyes were opened), meekly bore the names of Edelwitha and Cunegunde and, though they loved their father, thought of him with the easy contempt accorded by the female sex to those who act on principle or form their conduct upon abstract lines.

Seated among the other shavelings in his clergy-house, Mr. Bannerman was regarded as in the world one looks upon a man whose conduct in his youth has been a little wild — that is, with reprobation tempered by envy and respect. His fellows talked with him about the glorious days when England once again should own the Papal sway, the poor be fed at the monastery gate, the so-called Reformation be held a thing accursed, and statues be erected (at the national expense) to the twin saints of Smithfield, Bonner and Gardiner, of pious memory and of Christian renown.

Much did the priest employ himself in parish work, having found that his conversion had changed the collar, but left the load as heavy as before; much did he read the Fathers of the Church; much muse upon the Jesuits and all their works, and on the mystics of the Church in Spain, St. Peter of Alcantara, St. John of the Cross, St. Francis Borgia, and all the glorious band grouped round the Saint of Avila, who, as a colonel of artillery, ought to have been at Santiago when Cervera's fleet steamed from its "bottle" to destruction by the unbelievers' guns.

The assiduity of the Church impressed him — the missions in Alaska, in China, those of the Franciscans in Bolivia; the curious rechristianisation of the faithful in Japan, those who without their priests maintained their faith two hundred years, until the faithful from the West revisited them. All the romance and mysticism of the sole enduring Christian sect amazed and strengthened him, entering into his spirit, and making him feel part and parcel of something stable, so pitched inside and out with such authority, that against its strength all the assaults of reason were foredoomed to fail.

But still, the human virus in his blood, against whose promptings even churchmen at times have found their teaching no avail, simmered and effervesced, troubling his soul, and prompting questions whether his duty lay with his children rather than with the souls of men. After writhing all the night in tears, he would descant upon the wonders of the Church, and dwell (as converts who have left their hearts outside the Church, owing conversion to a reason or a sentiment, will do) upon the comfort that he felt, the blessed calm of mind, the joy it was to know he could not doubt, and generally cheat himself with words, after the fashion of mankind, who always have from the first ages sought relief from facts and theories in rhapsodies, in mysticism, striving to build a wall of cobwebs up between that which they knew, and that they wished to be the case. What wall so strong as cobwebs, or what so easily renewed when broken down? The substance, equally applicable to a cut finger and to a broken heart, is your best mental hint.

But, when a Protestant charity girls' school passed by, robed in their shoddy capes and scanty skirts, and sheltered by their pre-Victorian brown straw hats, with pale blue ribbons hanging down their backs — or when a nurse, with children bowling hoops, walked down the streets — the Rev. Arthur Bannerman found his cross heavy on his neck, and hoped the road to Golgotha was short. But yet he steeled himself; thinking that, as a year or two had passed, the children must have forgotten him; hoping that time would bring relief both to himself and them. Then, after the way of good and foolish men, he thought himself to blame, exclaimed aloud upon his weakness, redoubled work and prayers, and threw himself in agony of spirit upon the ground, grasping his cross after the fashion of the penitents in early Flemish pictures, but without finding rest.

At times he wandered passed *[sic]* the villa where, in the odour of respectability, his children lived, half hoping to catch sight of them, and half expecting that a miracle would keep them from his sight; and then, becoming suddenly aware of his transgression, would hurry through the street as if the whole world depended on his arriving at some place whose whereabouts he could not ascertain. By degrees he grew still more eccentric, still more ridiculous; for sorrow seldom gives dignity, but, on the contrary, brings out our petty foibles, and makes us sport for fools, as if the whole world had been created in a fit of spleen, and a malignant demon looked out mockingly upon our woes. Occasionally the priest would start his mass in English, break off and stop, and then begin on a wrong note, taxing the gravity of the choir and of the faithful in the Church, and drawing from the Irish worshippers who clustered round the door, in the sort of "leper's squint" in which the economies of the Church usually give them places, the remark that "The Divil had put a mortial spraddle on his Riverence's spache." At times in the confessional his memory played him false; and girls who had accused themselves of gluttony, of telling falsehoods, or any other futile uninteresting sin of youthful and inexperienced penitents, were rebuked with sternness, told to repent and make their peace with outraged husbands, and sent giggling away. These lapses did not detract a whit from the affection in which his congregation (especially the children, and those who are to inherit all the earth while millionaires lie howling) held him; for they all knew the priest for a kind poor soul, even as a horse discounts an indifferent rider before the man has got upon his back.

At last the Rev. Arthur Bannerman found his strength waning; and on a day he approached the villa where the lady who had taken the care of his two children on herself dwelt, in the glories of plate-glass, an araucaria (imbricata), trim gravel walks, and yellow calceolarias, all duly separated from the next-door neighbour by a wall blinded by a privet hedge. Twice did he pace the street, passing through vistas of plate-glass and araucarias; reading the styles and titles of the houses, as "Beau Sejour," "Sea View," and "Qui Si Sana"; admiring the imagination of the nomenclature as a condemned criminal may admire the judge's wig and the paltry sword of justice over the bench, or as a patient, seated in the dental surgeon's chair, scans the heraldic figures on the window, which reflects a bluish glare upon his face, while he, gripping the arms of the chair, perspires in terror, as the dentist fumbles for his tools. Twice did he catch himself entering at the wrong gate; and when at last he stood before the hedge of bay trees and euonymus which, like a fig leaf, covered the mysteries of the interior garden plot of Beau Sejour from the public gaze, he trembled and perspired.

On the exterior gate the name was writ in brass above the letter-box, a wire communicating with the inside forming (as it were) a telegraph between the outer world and the interior graces of the house. He paused and chewed a dusty bay leaf, and then rang fitfully and waited at the gate. Three times he rang, waiting while butcher boys passed the time of day with bakers cycling their daily bread to residents along the street. At last the gate flew open suddenly, surprising him, and causing him to drop his umbrella in the mud. Then, advancing on the crunching gravel path, he passed between the stucco urns in which twin iron cactuses bloomed perennially, and gained the porch, the housemaid waiting with the door half-opened in her hand. Ushered into the dining-room, and left to contemplate the horsehair sofa, and the plated biscuit-box embedded in its woolly mat upon the sideboard, the black slab clock upon the mantelpiece, the views of Cader Idris and the Trossachs in washy water-colours on the walls, he sat expectant, thinking each moment that his children might rush in, or that at least he might catch their footsteps on the stairs, or hear them singing in the upper regions of the house.

The interval which passed while Mrs. Macnamara was employed in preparation of mind and body for the interview seemed to him mortal. The lady rustled in, perturbed, but kindly; and the poor priest began to tell her of his struggles, and the consuming longing which had come over him to see his children, and to hold them on his knee. After much weeping on both sides, and offers of clean pocket-handkerchiefs ("For yours is so damp, ye'll get a cold with using it"), the priest became more calm. Then did the kindly Irishwoman reason with him, and put before him that it was better to let things take their course, telling him that the girls were happy, and that she loved them as they had been her own, and pointing out to him what would ensue if he persisted in his wish.

Some time he pondered on her words, straining his ears as a horse strains when listening for a distant sound, to catch even a footstep of the children on the stairs. Then, calm, but snuffling, he choked down his tears, and with an effort said, "God bless you! I think I'll wait to see them till the Judgment Day."

He took his leave, and left the house composed and cheerful, whistling a lively air, all out of tune, and, passing by the Irish beggar-woman at her customary post, gave her a half-penny, which she received with thanks and a due sense of the benefit which alms bring down upon the soul of him who gives. Then looking after him, she broke into professional blessings, and exclaimed, "By the holy Paul, his Riverence looks so cheerful, sure the 'good people' must have been with him this morning, just at the birth of day."

London

"Buddha wishes the child health, riches, and prosperity, that she may have no enemies, enjoy good fortune, and be a comfort to her parents in their old age. May she be as pure and as lovely as these flowers; and I the headman of the Cingalese here present, after the custom of our country, call the child after the city she was born in, London."

Then the mother knelt before a figure of Buddha, and the headman sprinkled her with rose leaves, which fell upon her like flakes of scented snow; and all around an Earl's Court crowd, composed of what is styled the "general public," looked on and gaped. The little band of Cingalese no doubt were part and parcel of the general public of Ceylon. They formed a brownish-whitish group, dressed in their unsubstantial hot-country clothes; their thin brown hands, and semi-prehensile feet, unused to boots, contrasting strangely with the hands and feet of all around them.

In the midst the little London, about as big as a young monkey, with large black eyes as preternaturally grave as are the eyes of all the Eastern races, who never emerge from childhood all their lives. Not that their eternal childhood keeps them free from lies and theft, for these are attributes of children, but it preserves them largely from hypocrisy, and from commerce, the worst of all the crimes that mankind suffers from; that is, of course, *successful* , for the commerce of the East is so entirely futile in its villainy as to be almost harmless, even to those it cheats.

At Kandy, or Colombo, or by some village hidden in the forests, or on the margin of a rice-swamp, the relatives all in good time will learn the news, and how the child was named; and they will know of all the wonders of the great city, seen, so to speak, without perspective, and distorted through the medium of the teller's mind. A stucco city, where it is always dark, upon a river which flows liquid mud, and yet so rich the very beggars have their three meals a day. The residence of the great Queen, she who is Empress; and of Madame Tussaud, the great magician, who makes copies of all men and women, just as they are in life, and by her art preserves them, so that they never die — that is, those who are once included in her palace never die, for it costs sixpence to enter and to see, and those who write have entered (after the payment) and have seen.

Much they will hear about the wondrous Western life, so different to their own, and framed apparently without regard to anything that they consider common-sense. The streets of houses forming great stucco drains, the noise which ceases not; the atmosphere impregnated with particles of coal and horse-dung; the rush, the hurry, the sameness of the people, all so alike, that to a Cingalese they all seem brothers; the curious justice so ingeniously contrived as to appear the grossest tyranny, or at best a nightmare — all will in the due fulness *[sic]* of the post arrive, and will be read by the letter-writer in the evening under the mango trees. Girls carrying water in long earthen jars, the wandering beggars, the herdsmen bringing home the kine, the elders of the place, the monkeys seated on the neighbouring trees, all will give ear and comment (the monkeys loudest and with perhaps more emphasis than all the rest), and then, the letter ended, silence and the sadness of the evening will descend on all. These things, such a strange country, and the lucky child, will be the themes of conversation for many days, until the salt-tax, the want of water, the failing crops, the locusts, or that standing topic in the East, the price of bread, will once again hold sway.

But in the wondrous West, London, and all her family, going from town to town, from hideous capital to hideous capital, will sit in "exhibitions," and make believe to spin, to weave, to carve, or exercise some of the simple Eastern arts; all preternaturally grave, all marking everything they see in a distorted way, like faces seen in water, or like a landscape in a black mirror with the shadows all reversed. Nothing so saddening as to see an animal mewed in a public garden in a cage, walking about and turning at the corner of his den with a quick whirl, whilst the intelligent spectators read his Latin name and grin at him; except it be the miserable "native," giving, on a rainy day, within the fetid atmosphere of an "exhibition" (admission sixpence), a counterfeit presentment of arts and industries which should be carried on in the full blaze of sun.

So in the various towns, and in the stifling exhibitions, growing up, squatted at sham work before the eternal crowds of unintelligent and unappreciative civilised spectators, the little London expanded gradually from the almost simian childhood of the Easterns into precocious womanhood. And in Ceylon, upon the rare occasions when the cares of daily life left time for conversation, and thoughts of those who in the magic West were coining gold, no doubt a vision of the growing London haunted her kinsfolk as of a countrywoman of their own, but rich, both in possessions and the wondrous knowledge of the West. A glorious vision of a being knowing how telegraphs and telephones are worked, and how the power is lent by steam to iron carriages, those devil-invented engines which snort through the forests, and, best of all, respected by, almost an equal of, the Europeans amongst whom she lived. A vision of a glorious half Eastern, half European London (oh, the strange name!) appeared to them. But in the atmosphere of eternal fog she grew up neither a European nor an Eastern, chattering cockney English and bad French, blanched for the want of sun, as orchids grown in greenhouses are blanched, and never look the least like what they appear when clinging to the trees in Paraguayan or in Venezuelan wilds. Knowledge, of course, she had, especially of evil, for the "exhibition" is, in its interior human view, chiefly remarkable as a meeting place of the most diverse races of mankind, all thrown together without the restraining influence of their respective fetishes. But though the school board, benevolent and wooden-headed, had done its task up to some standard of obligatory non-excellence, still little London remained a doubtful native, yet, after the fashion of a rare hot-country weed reared in an English garden as a flower, and become wild again in some half favourable soil.

Not quite an Eastern, and still less a European, without the Oriental grace, and with the European stolidity, which, with the northern races, makes up for cunning and quick wittedness, London remained a sort of "exhibition" gipsy, always a foreigner wherever she might go. An Oriental in all prejudices, and in appearance, but so to speak only at second-hand, and a true European but as regards her clothes, and the accomplishments of reading, writing, and the like, forced on her by the school board, and acquired against her will, and in despite of the opposition of her family to such unwomanly pursuits. Thin and still undeveloped, with the unstable-looking bust of Oriental women when dressed in European clothes, and the small, simian feet which in her case were not a beauty, but in her cheap, ill-fitting shoes only ridiculous, she grew to womanhood.

The impertinence of those who, from the theological fortress of their black rusty clothes, presumed to talk about a thing so ethereal as should be a soul, rendered her life at times a misery. These would-be savers of her soul had no idea that in such matters Eastern women have no part; for souls and philosophical discussions, with shoemaking and bullock-driving, are affairs of men, and women have their work in other ways, spinning and weaving, bearing their children, and doing that which since the beginning of the (Eastern) world has always been their lot. But yet the fact of being noticed, to an outcast such as perforce must be the exhibition-bred transplanted Oriental, is better than neglect. And so she passed her life, superior in knowledge to her parents, and inferior to them in manual dexterity at the trade at which they worked.

Then came the fitful fever of the blood which humorists call love. Love, the ennobling, the passion which takes us out of our common nature, and raises us to heights of self-abnegation; love, the magician, the strongest passion in our nature, sung of by poets, etherealised by writers, and which has given our men of science so many opportunities for pathologic study in our hospitals and streets. Cupid revealed himself to London, as he reveals himself so often, in a disguise, perhaps because most women cannot well bear the god's full blaze of beauty, or perhaps because the god himself takes many incarnations and strange shapes. So her brief union with a Zulu brought her no joy, and left her with a monstrous child, stamped from its birth with the misshapen limbs which children born of such ill-assorted parents generally have.

Desertion and the streets, drink and disease, and then the hospital — and the thin body of the Earl's Court Cingalese lay in the mortuary, the knees and elbows making sharp angles in the covering sheet. The headman's blessing, perhaps from having been pronounced outside the influence, or on uncongenial soil to Buddha, had been ineffectual, and the Western life too powerful for the Oriental born within its pale. The flickering corpse-candle of the brief life had failed in the full glare of the electric light.

All in good time the news of her decease was duly notified to the surviving relations in their village in Ceylon. They read it, apathetic but incredulous, being aware that no one ever dies, but is absorbed in the air of the place wherein the body and soul separate. So in the vast conglomerate of villages, the stucco labyrinth, built on the clay where day and night the myriads come and go, as little conscious of each other's presence as of the footprints on the pavement, which all of them must leave, where the foul atmosphere of sweat and dust and the scent rising from millions of animals and men commingle in the air, no doubt some particles of little London float. Or it may be (for after all it is but faith) her soul looks down contentedly upon the dingy crowd, and surveys happily the butcher-boys, the nursery-maids, and all the waifs and strays who flatten their bodies on the rails and crane their heads to view the police recruits being drilled upon the guards' parade-ground, whilst a few drummer boys stand by and criticise.

Success

Beattock for Moffat

The bustle on the Euston platform stopped for an instant to let the men who carried him to the third class compartment pass along the train. Gaunt and emaciated, he looked just at death's door, and, as they propped him in the carriage between two pillows, he faintly said, "Jock, do ye thing I'll live as far as Moffat? I should na' like to die in London in the smoke."

His cockney wife, drying her tears with a cheap hem-stitched pocket handkerchief, her scanty town-bred hair looking like wisps of tow beneath her hat, bought from some window in which each individual article was marked at seven-and-sixpence, could only sob. His brother, with the country sun and wind burn still upon his face, and his huge hands hanging like hams in front of him, made answer.

"Andra," he said, "gin ye last as far as Beattock, we'll gie ye a braw hurl back to the farm, syne the bask air, ye ken, and the milk, and, and — but can ye last as far as Beattock, Andra?"

The sick man, sitting with the cold sweat upon his face, his shrunken limbs looking like sticks inside his ill-made black slop suit, after considering the proposition on its merits, looked up, and said, "I should na' like to bet I feel fair boss, God knows; but there, the mischief of it is, he will na' tell ye, so that, as ye may say, his knowledge has na commercial value. I ken I look as gash as Garscadden. Ye mind, Jock, in the braw auld times, when the auld laird just slipped awa', whiles they were birlin' at the clairet. A braw death, Jock . . . do ye think it'll be rainin' aboot Ecclefechan? Aye . . . sure to be rainin' aboot Lockerbie. Nae Christians there, Jock, a' Johnstones and Jardines, ye mind?"

The wife, who had been occupied with an air cushion, and, having lost the bellows, had been blowing into it till her cheeks seemed almost bursting, and her false teeth were loosened in her head, left off her toil to ask her husband "If 'e could pick a bit of something, a porkpie, or a nice sausage roll, or something tasty," which she could fetch from the refreshment room. The invalid having declined to eat, and his brother having drawn from his pocket a dirty bag, in which were peppermints, gave him a "drop," telling him that he "minded he aye used to like them weel, when the meenister had fairly got into his prelection in the auld kirk, outby."

The train slid almost imperceptibly away, the passengers upon the platform looking after it with that half foolish, half astonished look with which men watch a disappearing train. Then a few sandwich papers rose with the dust almost to the level of the platform, sank again, the clock struck twelve, and the station fell into a half quiescence, like a volcano in the interval between the lava showers. Inside the third class carriage all was quiet until the lights of Harrow shone upon the left, when the sick man, turning himself with difficulty, said, "Good-bye, Harrow-on-the-Hill. I aye liked Harrow for the hill's sake, tho' ye can scarcely ca' yon wee bit mound a hill, Jean."

His wife, who, even in her grief, still smarted under the Scotch variant of her name, which all her life she had pronounced as "Jayne," and who, true cockney as she was, bounded her world within the lines of Plaistow, Peckham Rye, the Welch 'Arp ('Endon way), and Willesden, moved uncomfortably at the depreciation of the chief mountain in her kosmos, but held her peace. Loving her husband in a sort of half antagonistic fashion, born of the difference of type between the hard, unyielding, yet humorous and sentimental Lowland Scot, and the conglomorate *[sic]* of all races of the island which meet in London, and produce the weedy, shallow breed, almost incapable of reproduction, and yet high strung and nervous, there had arisen between them that intangible veil of misconception which, though not excluding love, is yet impervious to respect. Each saw the other's failings, or, perhaps, thought the good qualities which each possessed were faults, for usually men judge each other by their good points, which, seen through prejudice of race, religion, and surroundings, appear to them defects.

The brother, who but a week ago had left his farm unwillingly, just when the "neeps were wantin' heughin' and a feck o' things requirin' to be done, forby a puckle sheep waitin' for keelin'," to come and see his brother for the last time, sat in that dour and seeming apathetic attitude which falls upon the country man, torn from his daily toil, and plunged into a town. Most things in London, during the brief intervals he had passed away from the sick bed, seemed foolish to him, and of a nature such as a self-respecting Moffat man, in the hebdomadal enjoyment of the "prelections" of a Free Church minister could not authorise.

"Man, saw ye e'er a carter sittin' on his cart, and drivin' at a trot, instead o' walkin' in a proper manner alangside his horse?" had been his first remark.

The short-tailed sheep dogs, and the way they worked, the inferior quality of the cart horses, their shoes with hardly any calkins worth the name, all was repugnant to him.

On Sabbath, too, he had received a shock, for, after walking miles to sit under the "brither of the U.P. minister at Symington," he had found Erastian hymn books in the pews, and noticed with stern reprobation that the congregation stood to sing, and that, instead of sitting solidly whilst the "man wrastled in prayer," stooped forward in the fashion called the Nonconformist lounge.

His troubled spirit had received refreshment from the sermon, which, though short, and extending to but some five-and-forty minutes, had still been powerful, for he said:

"When yon wee, shilpit meenister — brither, ye ken, of rantin' Ferguson, out by Symington — shook the congregation ower the pit mouth, ye could hae fancied that the very sowls in hell just girned. Man, he garred the very stour to flee aboot the kirk, and, hadna' the big book been weel brass banded, he would hae dang the haricles fair oot."

So the train slipped past Watford, swaying round the curves like a gigantic serpent, and jolting at the facing points as a horse "pecks" in his gallop at an obstruction in the ground.

The moon shone brightly into the compartment, extinguishing the flickering of the half-candle power electric light. Rugby, the station all lit up, and with its platforms occupied but by a few belated passengers, all muffled up like race horses taking their exercise, flashed past. They slipped through Cannock Chase, which stretches down with heath and firs, clear brawling streams, and birch trees, an out-post of the north lost in the midland clay. They crossed the oily Trent, flowing through alder copses, and with its backwaters all overgrown with lilies, like an "aguapey" in Paraguay or in Brazil.

The sick man, wrapped in cheap rugs, and sitting like Guy Fawkes, in the half comic, half pathetic way that sick folk sit, making them sport for fools, and, at the same time, moistening the eye of the judicious, who reflect that they themselves may one day sit as they do, bereft of all the dignity of strength, looked listlessly at nothing as the train sped on. His loving, tactless wife, whose cheap "sized" handkerchief had long since become a rag with mopping up her tears, endeavoured to bring round her husband's thoughts to paradise, which she conceived a sort of music hall, where angels sat with their wings folded, listening to sentimental songs.

Her brother-in-law, reared on the fiery faith of Moffat Calvinism, eyed her with great disfavour, as a terrier eyes a rat imprisoned in a cage.

"Jean wumman," he burst out, "to hear ye talk, I would jist think your meenister had been a perfectly illeeterate man, pairadise here, pairadise there, what do ye think a man like Andra could dae daunderin' aboot a gairden naked, pu'in soor aipples frae the trees?"

Cockney and Scotch conceit, impervious alike to outside criticism, and each so bolstered in its pride as to be quite incapable of seeing that anything existed outside the purlieus of their sight, would soon have made the carriage into a battle-field, had not the husband, with the authority of approaching death, put in his word.

"Whist, Jeanie wumman. Jock, dae ye no ken that the Odium-Theologicum is just a curse — pairadise — set ye baith up — pairadise. I dinna' even richtly ken if I can last as far as Beattock."

Stafford, its iron furnaces belching out flames, which burned red holes into the night, seemed to approach, rather than be approached, so smoothly ran the train. The mingled moonlight and the glare of iron-works lit the canal beside the railway, and from the water rose white vapours as from Styx or Periphlegethon. Through Cheshire ran the train, its timbered houses showing ghastly in the frost which coated all the carriage windows, and rendered them opaque. Preston, the catholic city, lay silent in the night, its river babbling through the public park, and then the hills of Lancashire loomed lofty in the night. Past Garstang, with its water-lily-covered ponds, Garstang where, in the days gone by, catholic squires, against their will, were forced on Sundays to "take wine" in Church on pain of fine, the puffing serpent slid.

The talk inside the carriage had given place to sleep, that is, the brother-in-law and wife slept fitfully, but the sick man looked out, counting the miles to Moffat, and speculating on his strength. Big drops of sweat stood on his forehead, and his breath came double, whistling through his lungs.

They passed by Lancaster, skirting the sea on which the moon shone bright, setting the fishing boats in silver as they lay scarcely moving on the waves. Then, so to speak, the train set its face up against Shap Fell, and, puffing heavily, drew up into the hills, the scattered grey stone houses of the north, flanked by their gnarled and twisted ash trees, hanging upon the edge of the streams, as lonely, and as cut off from the world (except the passing train) as they had been in Central Africa. The moorland roads, winding amongst the heather, showed that the feet of generations had marked them out, and not the line, spade, and theodolite, with all the circumstance of modern road makers. They, too, looked white and unearthly in the moonlight, and now and then a sheep, aroused by the snorting of the train, moved from the heather into the middle of the road, and stood there motionless, its shadow filling the narrow track, and flickering on the heather at the edge.

The keen and penetrating air of the hills and night roused the two sleepers, and they began to talk, after the Scottish fashion, of the funeral, before the anticipated corpse.

"Ye ken, we've got a braw new hearse outby, sort of Epescopalian lookin', we' *[sic = wi']* gless a' roond, so's ye can see the kist. Very conceity too, they mak' the hearses noo-a-days. I min' when they were jist auld sort o' ruckly boxes, awfu' licht, ye ken upon the springs, and just went dodderin' alang, the body swinging to and fro, as if it would flee richt oot. The roads, ye ken, were no nigh hand so richtly metalled in thae days."

The subject of the conversation took it cheerfully, expressing pleasure at the advance of progress as typefied *[sic]* in the new hearse, hoping his brother had a decent "stan' o' black," and looking at his death, after the fashion of his kind, as it were something outside himself, a fact indeed, on which, at the same time, he could express himself with confidence as being in some measure interested. His wife, not being Scotch, took quite another view, and seemed to think that the mere mention of the word was impious, or, at the least, of such a nature as to bring on immediate dissolution, holding the English theory that unpleasant things should not be mentioned, and that, by this means, they can be kept at bay. Half from affection, half from the inborn love of cant, inseparable from the true Anglo-Saxon, she endeavoured to persuade her husband that he looked better, and yet would mend, once in his native air.

"At Moffit, ye'd 'ave the benefit of the 'ill breezes, and that 'ere country milk, which never 'as no cream in it, but 'olesome, as you say. Why yuss, in about eight days at Moffit, you'll be as 'earty as you ever was. Yuss, you will, you take my word."

Like a true Londoner, she did not talk religion, being too thin in mind and body even to have grasped the dogma of any of the sects. Her Heaven a music 'all, her paradise to see the king drive through the streets, her literary pleasure to read lies in newspapers, or pore on novelettes, which showed her the pure elevated lives of duchesses, placing the knaves and prostitutes within the limits of her own class; which view of life she accepted as quite natural, and as a thing ordained to be by the bright stars who write.

Just at the Summit they stopped an instant to let a goods train pass, and, in a faint voice, the consumptive said, "I'd almost lay a wager now I'd last to Moffat, Jock. The Shap, ye ken, I aye looked at as the beginning of the run home. The hills, ye ken, are sort 'o heartsome. No that they're bonny hills like Moffat hills, na', na', ill-shapen sort of things, just like Borunty tatties, awfu' puir names too, Shap Fell and Rowland Edge, Hutton Roof Crags, and Arnside Fell; heard ever ony body sich like names for hills? Naething to fill the mooth; man, the Scotch hills jist grap ye in the mooth for a' the world like speerits."

They stopped at Penrith, which the old castle walls make even meaner, in the cold morning light, than other stations look. Little Salkeld, and Armathwaite, Cotehill, and Scotby all rushed past, and the train, slackening, stopped with a jerk upon the platform, at Carlisle. The sleepy porters bawled out "change for Maryport," some drovers slouched into carriages, kicking their dogs before them, and, slamming to the doors, exchanged the time of day with others of their tribe, all carrying ash or hazel sticks, all red faced and keen eyed, their caps all crumpled, and their great-coat tails all creased, as if their wearers had laid down to sleep full dressed, so as to lose no time in getting to the labours of the day. The old red sandstone church, with something of a castle in its look, as well befits a shrine close to a frontier where in days gone by the priest had need to watch and pray, frowned on the passing train, and on the manufactories, whose banked up fires sent poisonous fumes into the air, withering the trees which, in the public park, a careful council had hedged round about with wire.

The Eden ran from bank to bank, its water swirling past as wildly as when "The Bauld Buccleugh" and his Moss Troopers, bearing " the Kinmount" fettered in their midst, plunged in and passed it, whilst the keen Lord Scroope stood on the brink amazed and motionless. Gretna, so close to England, and yet a thousand miles away in speech and feeling, found the sands now flying through the glass. All through the mosses which once were the "Debateable Land" on which the moss-troopers of the clan Graeme were used to hide the cattle stolen from the "auncient enemy," the now repatriated Scotchman murmured feebly "that it was bonny scenery" although a drearier prospect of "moss hags" and stunted birch trees is not to be found. At Ecclefechan he just raised his head, and faintly spoke of "yon auld carle, Carlyle, ye ken, a dour thrawn body, but a gran' pheelosopher," and then lapsed into silence, broken by frequent struggles to take breath.

His wife and brother sat still, and eyed him as a cow watches a locomotive engine pass, amazed and helpless, and he himself had but the strength to whisper "Jock, I'm dune, I'll no' see Moffat, blast it, yon smoke, ye ken, yon London smoke has been ower muckle for ma lungs."

The tearful, helpless wife, not able even to pump up the harmful and unnecessary conventional lie, which after all, consoles only the liar, sat pale and limp, chewing the fingers of her Berlin gloves. Upon the weather-beaten cheek of Jock glistened a tear, which he brushed off as angrily as it had been a wasp.

"Aye, Andra' " he said, "I would hae liket awfu' weel that ye should win to Moffat. Man, the rowan trees are a' in bloom, and there's a bonny breer upon the corn — aye, ou aye, the reid bogs are lookin' gran' the year — but Andra', I'll tak' ye east to the auld kirk yaird, ye'll no' ken onything aboot it, but we'll hae a heartsome funeral."

Lockerbie seemed to fly towards them, and the dying Andra' smiled as his brother pointed out the place and said, "Ye mind, there are no ony Christians in it," and answered, "Aye, I mind, naething but Jardines," as he fought for breath.

The death dews gathered on his forehead as the train shot by Nethercleugh, passed Wamphray, and Dinwoodie, and with a jerk pulled up at Beattock just at the summit of the pass.

So in the cold spring morning light, the fine rain beating on the platform, as the wife and brother got their almost speechless care out of the carriage, the brother whispered, "Dam't, ye've done it, Andra', here's Beattock; I'll tak' ye east to Moffat yet to dee."

But on the platform, huddled on the bench to which he had been brought, Andra' sat speechless and dying in the rain. The doors banged to, the guard stepping in lightly as the train flew past, and a belated porter shouted, "Beattock, Beattock for Moffat," and then, summoning his his last strength, Andra' smiled, and whispered faintly in his brother's ear, "Aye, Beattock — for Moffat?" Then his head fell back, and a faint bloody foam oozed from his pallid lips. His wife stood crying helplessly, the rain beating upon the flowers of her cheap hat, rendering it shapeless and ridiculous. But Jock, drawing out a bottle, took a short dram and saying, "Andra', man, ye made a richt gude fecht o' it," snorted an instant in a red pocket handkerchief, and calling up a boy, said, "Rin, Jamie, to the toon, and tell McNicol to send up and fetch a corp." Then, after helping to remove the body to the waiting room, walked out into the rain, and, whistling "Corn Rigs" quietly between his teeth lit up his pipe, and muttered as he smoked "A richt gude fecht — man aye, ou aye, a game yin Andra', puir felly. Weel, weel, he'll hae a braw hurl onyway in the new Moffat hearse."

A Fisherman

The steamer scrunched against the pier, the gangway plank was drawn back slowly, and with as great an effort as it had weighed a ton, by the West Highland tweed-clad semi-sailors, semi-longshore men. The little groups of drovers separated, each following its fugleman to the nearest public-house. The ropes were cast off from the belaying pins, and whisked like serpents over the slippery slime-covered boards: a collie dog holding on to one of them by its teeth was dragged to the very edge, amongst a shower of Gaelic oaths.

Then with a snort and plunge the "Islesman" met the south-west swell coming up past Pladda from the Mull. The wandering Willie, with his fiddle in a green baize bag, stripped off its cover, and got to work in the wild wind and drizzling rain, at reels, strathspeys, laments, and all the minor music which has from immemorial time been our delight in Scotland, although, no doubt, it is as terrifying to the Southern as when the bagpipes skirl. His dog beside him, a mere mongrel, looking like a dirty mop, and yet with something half pathetic, half ridiculous about him, sat holding round his neck a battered can for pence. The fiddler, bandy-legged and dressed in heather mixture tweed, which gave out fumes of peat reek, snuff, and stale whisky, stood by the forebits, and round him clustered all the heterogeneous "heids and thraws" of the population of the West Highlands, Glasgow and Greenock, and the other towns upon the Firth of Clyde. Gently the steamer glided through the Kyles of Bute, left Toward Point on her port bow, and headed for Dunoon. And as she steamed along, passing the varied scenery of mist-capped mountain, and of stormy loch, the peaks of Arran in the distance like a gigantic saddle hung outlined in the clouds. The passengers, for the most part, seemed to see nothing but each other's clothes and personal defects, after the fashion of so many travellers, who, with their shells of prejudice borne on their backs as they were snails, go out to criticise that which they could have seen to just as great advantage in their homes. Amongst them was a man dressed in a greasy "stan' o' black," who, at first sight, appeared to be what we in Scotland call a "goin' aboot body," and recognise as having quite a status in the land. His clothes, originally black, had borne the labour, whisky, and the rain of many a funeral. He did not seem a townsman, for he had that wizened, weather-beaten look which, once a sailor, never leaves a man this side the grave. At once you saw that he had made his bread in ships, or boats, or in some way upon that element on which those who go down to it in brigs "smell hell," as the old shellback said who heard the passage in the Bible on the wonders of the deep.

Hard bread it is; damned hard, as the old admiral told his sacred majesty, the fourth William, who asked him whether he had been bred up to the sea.

The nondescript, at least, cared not an atom for the others on the boat, but seemed to know each inlet, stone, and islet on the coast. He carried a geranium cutting in a little pot, hedged round with half a newspaper to shield it from the wind, and as the sun fell on the hills of "Argyle's bowling-green," broke out into a rhapsody, half born of whisky and half of that perfervidness which is the heritage of every Scot.

" 'There shall be no more sea,' na a wise like saying of John, though he was sort o' doited in Patmos; what had the body got against the sea?"

"I followed it myself twal year. First in an auld rickle o' a boat, at Machrihanish, and syne wi' the herrin' fishers about Loch Fyne. Man, a gran' life the sea. Whiles I am sorry that I left it; but auri sacra fames, ye mind. Nae mair sea! Set John up. But the mountains, the mountains, will remain. Thank the Lord for the mountains."

No one responding to his remarks, he turned to me, observing that I looked an "eddicated man."

"Aye, ou aye, I mind I made a matter of five hundred pund at the herrin' fishin', and then, ye ken, I thocht I saw potentialities (gran' word, potentiality) of being rich, rich beyond the dreams of avarice, as that auld carle, Dr. Johnson, said. Johnson, ye ken, he that keepit a skule, and ca'ed it an academy, as auld Boswell said. A sort o' randy body yon Boswell, man, though he gied us a guid book. Many's the time I hae lauched over it. Puir, silly deevil, but with an eye untill him like a corbie for detail. Details, ye ken, are just the vertebrae of the world. Ye canna do without detail. What did I do? Losh me, I had most forgot. Will ye tak' an apple ? It'll keep doun the drouth. Scotch apples are the best apples in the world, but I maun premise I like apples sour, as the auld leddie said.

"Na — weel, ye're maybe right, apples are sort o' wersh without speerits. Bonny wee islands, yon Cumbraes, the wee yin just lik a dunter's heid, the big yin, a braw place for fishin'.

"Whitin' Bay, ye ken, just beyond where the monument for they puir midshipmen stands. An awfu' coast, I mind three laddies, some five and thirty year syne, from up aboot England gaein' oot in a lugsail boat from the Largs. Ane o' they easterly haars cam' on. They just come doon like a judgment of God on this coast — ye canna escape them, nor it. Aye weel, I'll no say no, a judgment, a special judgment o' divine providence, just fa's like a haar, fa's on the just and the unjust alike. Na, na, I'm no meanin' any disrespeck to providence, weel do I ken which side my bannock's buttered. . . . The laddies, the easterly wind just drave them aff the coast, in a wee bit boatie, and had it no' been ane o' them was a sailor laddie, they would ne'er a' won back. Wondrous are His ways, whiles He saves those that never would be missed, and whiles. . . . Do I no believe in the efficacy o' prayer. Hoots aye, that is I'm no sure. Whiles a man just works his knees into horn wi' prayin' for what might profit him, that is, profit him in this world ye see, and providence doesna steer for a' his prayin'. Whiles a man just puts up a sipplication for some speeritual matter, and the Lord just answers him before the man is sure he wants the object of his prayer.

"The Cumbraes, sort o' backlyin' islands, but the folk that live on them hae a guid conceit. Sort o' conceity, the bit prayer, the minister in Millport used to pit up for the adjawcent islands o' Great Britain and Ireland, ye'll mind it, ye that seem to be a sort o' eddicated man.

"Yer lookin' at the bit gerawnium. Sort of tragical that gerawnium, if you regard the matter pheelosophically. I tell't you that I aince made a bit o' money at the herrin' fishin'. Shares in a boat or twa. Man, I was happy then, a rough life the fishin', but vera satisfyin'. Just an element o' gambling aboot it that endears it to a man. Aye, ou aye, the sea, I ken it noo, I see why I lik't the life sae weel. I felt it then though, just like a collie dog feels the hills, although he doesna ken it. I always fancy that collies look kind o' oot o' place in Glesca.

"A collie dog, ye ken, would rather hear a West Hielandman swear at him in Gaelic than an English leddy ca' him a' the pets in the world. It's no his fault, it's no the swearin' that he likes, but just the tone o' voice. A gran' language the Gaelic, profanity in it just sounds like poetry in any other tongue.

"Weel, a fisherman is just like a collie dog, he'd rather hear the tackle run through the sheaves o' the blocks than a' the kists o' whistles in the Episcapalian churches up aboot Edinburgh. And then the sea, dam't I canna tell why I still ettle to get back to it. It took ma fayther, maist o' ma brithers, and the feck o' a' ma folk. It's maybe that, it's the element o' uncertainty there again, but dam't I dinna right know what it is, except that when ye aince get the salt doon into the soul ye ken, ye canna get it oot again. That is, no' on this side the grave. I wouldna have left it, had it not been ma mither, threep, threepin' on me . . . aye, and the auri sacra fames.

" . . . Bonny the Largs looks, eh? Gin its *[sic]* no the view of Cuchullin, the hills of Arran frae the Largs is the brawest view in Scotland. That is for a man that likes the sea. But I see I'm wearyin' ye wi' ma clash. Ye'd maybe like to see the *Herald.* . . I hae Bogatsky in my bawg; Bogatsky's 'Golden Treasury,' but maybe its *[sic]* no greatly read in your body. Fine old-fashioned book Bogatsky, nae taint o' latter-day Erastianism aboot it. Na, na, I'se warrant ye the man compiled Bogatsky gied his congregation mony a richt shake abune the pit. Tophet, ye ken, the real old, what I might ca' the constitutional Tophet, before they hung thermometers aboot the walls, in case the temperature should gae ower high."

The steamer, after plunging uneasily beside the pier at Largs for sufficient time to let a knot of drovers, each with his dog led by a piece of twine, and holding in their hands hooked hazel sticks, reel off towards the town, and to allow the passengers (who did not mark it) space to view the beauties of the place, the little river brawling through the town, and the long bit of sea-swept grass on which goats pasture fixed to chains, and get a living on the scanty herbage, eked out with bottles, bones and sardine tins, turned eastward once again towards the Clyde.

She ran past Fairlie, with its cliffs all clothed in oak and hazel copse. The passengers by this time being "michtily refreshed," as was the chairman of the curling Club at Coupar-Angus, after his fifteenth tumbler, threw sandwich bags and bottles overboard, and took to dancing on the deck. The elders gathered into knots, talked politics, religion, or with much slapping of red hands upon their knees, enjoyed indecent tales, after the fashion of the Puritan, who though his creed enjoys a modest life, yet places no embargo on the speech. So it is said an Irishman in Lent, meeting a friend who remarked that he was drunk, rejoined, "Sure, God Almighty never set a fast upon the drink."

My philosophic friend and I watched the athletic sports, and when the lassies skirled as partners pinched them, or in the joy of life, which manifests itself in divers ways, and usually in some unseemly fashion when the two sexes meet, he wagged a moralising head, and freely poured out his philosophy.

"Man Rabbie, . . . ye'll hae Burns . . . Rabbie kenned his countrymen. A fine, free, fornicatin', pious folk we are. Man, Rabble kent us better than he kent himsel', I sometimes think. Aye, ou aye, ye canna mak' a saint o' Rabbie. Saints, ye ken, are weel enough in books, but sort o' weary bodies to live wi', they must hae been, the feck o' them. I didna tell ye though aboot the bit gerawnium. I hae it in the cabin, for fear they cattle micht sit doon on it; ye mind auld Walter Scott, the time he pouched the glass George IV drank oot o', and then fair dang it into flinders on the road hame? Kind o' weak o' Scott, pouchin' yon glass; a bonny carle, yon George, to touch folk for the King's evil . . . but ou aye, the gerawnium, I mind it.

"Ye see a' my potentialities of growing rich werena just realised. I wrocht twa year in Glesca, ane in Edinburgh, syne sax in Brig o' Weir, whiles takin' a bit flutter on the Stock Exchange. Rogues they fellies on the Exchange, ettlin' to mak' their siller without honest toil. Na, na; I ken what ye're goin' to say — if I had won, I wouldna' hae misca'ed them. Pairfectly reasoned, sir; but then ye ken when a man loses, the chap that get his siller is aye a rogue. Weel, weel, many's the time I wished masel back at Tobermory in the bit boat, wi' the bonny wee-tanned lug, fishin', aye, fishin', like the Apostles. Weel, I ken why the Lord found His first followers amongst fishermen. Simple folk, ye see, and wi' the gamblin' element weel developed; no like yer hinds — slave, slavin' at the ground — but oot upon the lake, yon sea of Galilee, ye mind; a sort o' loch, just like Loch Fyne, as I ae thocht. When ye sit in the boat, keepin' her full and by, fechtin' the sea, your eye just glancin' on the waves, it kind o' maks ye gleg to risk a wee. Nae fears we'll get another preacher like the Lord; but if we did, there wouldna be a fisherman, from Tobermory doun to the Cruives o' Cree that wouldna follow him. I'se warrant them. Dour folk, the fishers, but venturesome; and a' the time I wrocht aboot thae stinkin' towns, I ettled to get back. I aye went aince a year to see our mither; she just stops aboot twa mile west of Tobermory, and I aye tak back ane of they gerawniums in a pot. Why do I no stop there when I win back, ye say? Aye, there's the mystery of it, the sort o' tragedy as I was tellin' ye when we cam through the Kyles.

"Ye see . . . spot yon lassie wi' the sunset hair, ane o' the lang backit, short-leggit West Highland kind, built like a kyloe, just gars me think upon yon woman of Samaria . . . I'm haverin' . . . weel, the fack is I canna stop at hame. Tak' a West Hielan' stirk, and put him in a park, doon aboot Falkirk, or in the Lothians, and maybe, at the first, he doesna' thrive, misses the Hielan' grass maybe, and the gran' wind that blaws across the sea. Syne, he gets habeetuated, and if ye take him back to the north, maybe he couldna bide. That's just ma ain case, sir.

"Weel do I mind the auld braw days; a herrin' never tastes sae weel as just fresh caught and brandered in the boat. I mind yon seinin' too, sic splores we had, aye and a feck o' things come back to me when I am in the toon. The peat reek, and a' the comfortable clarty ways we had; the winter nights, when the wind blew fit to tak' aff the flauchter feals o' the old cottage. I mind them a'. That is, I dinna care to mind."

And as we talked, the steamer slipped past Wemyss Bay, left the Cloch Lighthouse on the left hand, and passed by Inverkip, slid close by Gourock, and then opened up the valley of the Clyde. Greenock with all its smoky chimneys rose in view, sending a haze of fog into the air. The timber in the ponds upon the shore surged to and fro against the railings as the steamer's swell lifted it slowly, and then settled down again to season in the mud. Dumbarton Rock showed dimly, and the river narrowed; the fairway marks showing the channel like a green ribbon winding through mud banks, as the vessel drew towards the pier.

Gathering their packages and parcels, and smoothing out their clothes, the passengers passed down the gangway, laughing and pushing one another in their haste to get away.

The man with the geranium in the pot still lingered, looking back towards the sea. Then, gathering up his traps and tucking his umbrella underneath his arm, prepared to follow them.

"Good-bye," he said, "we hae had a pleasant crack, I'll just be off and daunder up the toon. Doddered and poor, and a wee thing addicted to strong drink, strong drink, ye ken, speerits, that maketh glad the heart o' man; neither a fisher nor a townsman, a sort o' failure, as ye may say, I am. Good-bye, ye seem a sort o' eddicated man. . . . Na, na, I will na drop it, never fear. I broacht it a' the way from Tobermory, and ye ken, sir, Greenock is no' a guid place for gerawniums after all."

He stumbled out along the gangway plank, his rusty "stan o' black" looking more storm-worn and ridiculous than ever in the evening sun. Holding his flower-pot in his hand, wrapped round with newspaper, he passed out of my sight amongst the crowd, and left me wondering if the flower in the pot would live, and he return, and die in Tobermory, by the sea.

The Impenitent Thief

Dimas or Gestas, Gestas o Dimas, who can say which, when even monkish legends disagree?

At any rate, one of the two died game.

Passion o' me, I hate your penitents.

Live out your life: drink, women, dice, murder, adultery, meanness, oppression, snobbery (by which sin the English fall); be lavish of others' money, and get thereby a name for generosity. Bow down to wealth alone, discerning talent, beauty, humour (the most pathetic of all qualities), wit, courage, and pathos, only in gilded fools.

Keep on whilst still digestion waits on appetite, and at the first advance of age, at the first tinge of gout, sciatica, at the first wrinkle, crow's-foot, when the hair grows thin upon the temples, the knees get "schaucle," when the fresh horse seems wild, the jolting of the express crossing the facing points makes you contract your muscles, and when all life seems to grow flat, stale, and unprofitable outside the library, forsake your former naughty life, and straight turn traitor on your friends, ideas, beliefs, and prejudices, and stand confessed apostate to yourself. For the mere bettering of your spiritual fortunes leaves you a turncoat still. It is mean, unreasonable, and shows a caitiff spirit, or impaired intellect in the poor penitent who, to save his paltry soul, denies his life.

Dimas or Gestas, whiche'er it was, no doubt some unambitious oriental thief, a misappropriator of some poor bag of almonds, sack of grain, bundle of canes, some frail of fruit, camel's hair picket rope, or other too well considered trifle, the theft of which the economic state of Eastern lands makes capital, had given him brevet rank amongst the world's most honoured criminals, set up on high to testify that human nature, even beside a coward and a God, is still supreme.

Perhaps again some sordid knave, whipped from the markets, an eye put out, finger lopped off, nose slit, ears cropped, and hoisted up to starve upon his cross as an example of the folly of the law, crassness of reason, to appease the terrors of the rich, or, perhaps, but to exemplify that Rome had a far-reaching arm, thick head, and owned a conscience like to that enjoyed by Rome's successor in the empire of the world.

Dimas or Gestas, perhaps some cattle thief from the Hauran, some tribesman sent for judgment to Jerusalem, black bearded, olive in colour, his limbs cast like an Arab's, or a Kioway's twisted in agony, his whole frame racked with pain, his brain confused, but yet feeling, somehow, in some vague way, that he, too, suffered for humanity to the full as much as did his great companion, who to him, of course, was but a Jewish Thaumaturgist, as his adjuration, "If thou be the Son of God, save us and thyself," so plainly shows.

And still, perhaps, impenitent Gestas (or Dimas) was the most human of the three, a thief, and not ashamed of having exercised his trade. How much more dignified than some cold-hearted scoundrel who, as solicitor, banker, or confidential agent, swindles for years, and in the dock recants, and calls upon his God to pardon him, either because he is a cur at heart, or else because he knows the public always feels tenderly towards a cheat, having, perhaps, a fellow-feeling, and being therefore kind.

I like the story of the Indian who, finding his birch canoe caught in the current, and drifted hopelessly towards Niagara, ceased all his paddling when he found his efforts vain, lighted his pipe, and went it, on a lone hand, peacefully smoking, as the spectators watched him through their opera glasses.

And so perhaps this stony-hearted knave, whom foolish painters bereft of all imagination, have delighted to revile in paint, making him villainous in face, humpbacked, blind of one eye, and all of them drawing the wretched man with devils waiting for his poor pain-racked soul, as if the cross was not a hell enough for any act of man, may have repented (of his poor unsuccessful villainies) long years ago. He may have found no opportunity, and being caught red-handed and condemned to death, made up his mind to cease his useless paddling, and die after the fashion he had lived. This may have been, and yet, perhaps again, this tribesman, as the night stole on the flowers, the waters, and the stones, all sleeping, reckoned up his life, saw nothing to repent of, and thought the cross but one injustice more. As gradually hope left his weakening body, he may have thought upon the folded sheep, the oxen in their stalls, the camels resting on their hardened knees, men sleeping wrapped up in their "haiks" beneath the trees, or at the foot of walls, mere mummies rolled in white rags, under the moonbeams and the keen rays of El

Sohail. No one awake except himself and the two figures on his either hand, during the intolerable agony of the long hours, when jackals howl, hyenas grunt, and as from Golgotha, Jerusalem looked like a city of the dead, all hushed except the rustling of the palm trees in the breeze. Then may his thoughts have wandered to his "duar" on the plains, and in his tent he may have seen his wives, and heard them moan, heard his horse straining on his picket rope and stamping, and wept, but silently, so that his fellow sufferers should not see his tears.

And so the night wore on, till the tenth hour, and what amazed him most was the continual plaint of Dimas (or of Gestas) and his appeals for mercy, so that at last, filled with contempt and sick with pain, he turned and cursed him in his rage.

Repentance, retrospection, and remorse, the furies which beset mankind, making them sure of nothing; conscious of actions, feeling they are eternal, and that no miracle can wipe them out. They know they forge and carry their own hell about with them, too weak to sin and fear not, and too irrational not to think a minute of repentance can blot out the actions of a life.

Remorse, and retrospection, and regret; what need to conjure up a devil or to invent a place of torment, when these three were ready to our souls. Born in the weakness (or the goodness) of ourselves, never to leave us all our lives; bone of our bone and fibre of our hearts; man's own invention; nature's revenge for all the outrages we heap upon her; reason's despair, and sweet religion's eagerest advocates; what greater evils have we in the whole pack with which we live, than these three devils, called repentance, retrospection, and regret ?

But still the penitent upon the other side was human too. Most likely not less wicked in his futile villainy than his brother, whom history has gone out to vilify and to hold up as execrable, because he could not recognise a god in him he saw, even as he himself, in pain, in tears, and as it seemed least fit to bear his suffering, of the three. Repentance is a sort of fire insurance, hedging on what you will — an endeavour to be all things to all men and to all gods.

Humanity repentant shows itself *en deshabille*, with the smug mask of virtue clear stripped off, the vizor of consistency drawn up, and the whole entity in its most favourite Janus attitude, looking both ways at once. The penitent on the right hand, whom painters have set forth, a fair young man, with curly golden hair, well rounded limbs, tears of contrition streaming from his eyes, with angels hovering around his head to carry off his soul, whom writers have held up for generations as a bright instance of redeeming faith duly rewarded at the last, was to the outward faithless eye much as his brother thief.

Perhaps he was some camel driver, who, entrusted with a bag of gold, took it, and came into Jerusalem showing some self-inflicted wounds, and called upon Jehovah or Allah to witness that he had received them guarding the money against thieves. That which he said upon the cross he may have thought was true, and yet men not infrequently die, as they have lived, with lies upon their lips. He may have seen that in his fellow sufferer which compelled respect, or yet again he may have, in his agony, defied the Jews by testifying that the hated one was king. All things are possible to him who has no faith.

So, when the night grew misty towards dawn, and the white eastern mist crept up, shrouding the sufferers and blotting out their forms, the Roman soldiers keeping watch, had they looked up, could not have said which of the thieves was Gestas and which Dimas, had they not known the side on which their crosses stood.

The Evolution of a Village

I knew a little village in the North of Ireland — call it what you please. A pretty, semi-ruinous, semi-thriving place. In it men did not labour over much. All went easy (*aisy* the people called it); no man troubling much about the sun or moon; still less bothering himself about the fixed stars or planets, or aught outside the village bounds. All about the place there was an air of half-starvation, tempered by half content. Few ever hurried; no one ever ran. Each hedge was shiny, for the people had cut seats in them, which they called "free sates." The able-bodied occupied them all day long, for they served to prop men up as they discoursed for hours on nothing. Cows marched up and down the lanes: and sometimes children led them by a string, or, seated on the ground, they made believe to watch them as they ate, much in the same way, I suppose, that shepherds watched their flocks upon the night the star shone in the East near Bethlehem, or as the people do in Spain and in the East to-day. Goats wandered freely in and out of all the houses. Children raggeder, and happier, and cunninger [*sic*] than any others on the earth, absolutely swarmed, and Herod (had he lived in those parts) could have made an awful *battue* of them, and they would not have been missed. Children, black-haired, grey-eyed, wild-looking, sat at the doors, played with the pigs, climbed on the tops of cabins, and generally permeated space, as irresponsibly as flies.

Trees there were few. The people said the landlords cut them down. The landlords said the people never left a tree alone. However, let that pass. Creeds there were, two — Catholic and Protestant. Both sides claimed to have a clear majority of sheep. They hated one another; or they said so, which is not the same thing, by the way. Really, they furnished mutually much subject of entertainment and of talk, for in this village no one really hated very much, or very long. All took life quietly.

On the great lake folk fished lazily, and took nothing save only store of midge-bites. The roads were like pre-Adamite tracks for cattle: nothing but the cow of the country could cope with them; and even that sometimes sustained defeat. Still, given enough potatoes, the people were not miserable; far from it. Wages were low — but yet they were not driven like slaves, as is the artizan *[sic]* of more progressive lands.

In the morning early, out into the fields they went, to while away the time and lounge against the miniature round towers that serve for gate-posts.

Those who did not go out remained at home, and, squatting by the fire at ease, looked after their domestic industries, and through the "jamb-wall hole" kept a keen eye on foreign competition, or on the passing girls and women, and criticised them freely as they passed. Still there was peace and plenty, of a relative degree. No factories, no industries at all, plenty of water power running to waste, as the Scotch agent said, and called on God to witness that if there were only a little capital in the town, it would become a paradise. What is a paradise? Surely it is a land in which there is sufficiency for all; in which man works as little as he can — that is to say, unless he likes to slave — which no one did, or he would have been looked on as a madman, in the village by the lake. Men reaped their corn with sickles, as their forefathers did, in lazy fashion, and then left the straw to rot. Agriculture was all it never should have been. Sometimes a woman and an ass wrought in one plough — the husband at the stilts.

Men were strong, lazy, and comfortable; women, ragged, as lazy, and, when children did not come too fast, not badly off. The owner of the soil never came near the place. Patriot lawyers talked of liberty, and oppressed all those they got within their toils; but still the place was happy, relatively. Those who did not like work (and they were not a few) passed through their lives without doing a hand's turn, and were generally loved. Any one who tried to hurry work was soon dubbed tyrant. Thus they lived their lives in their own way.

If they were proud of anything, it was because their village was the birthplace of a famous hound. In my lord's demesne his monument is reared — the glory of the place. Master Magrath — after the Pope, King William, Hugh Roe O'Neill, or Mr. Parnell — he seemed the greatest personage that ever walked the earth. "Himself it was that brought prosperity amongst us. Quality would come for miles to see him, and leave their money in the place. A simple little thing to see him: ye had never thought he had been so wonderful. The old Lord (a hard old naygur!) thought the world of him. 'Twas here he used to live, but did his business (winning the Waterloo Cup) over on the other side." England seemed as vague a term as China to them, and quite as far removed. Master Magrath, the Mass, the Preaching, the price of cattle at the fairs, and whether little Tim O'Neil could bate big Pat Finucane — these were the subjects of their daily talk. A peaceful, idle, sympathetic, fightingly-inclined generation of most prolific Celto-Angles or of Anglo-Celts.

Agiotage, Prostitution, Respectability, Morality and Immorality, and all the other curses of progressive life, with them had little place.

Not that they were Arcadians; far removed enough from that. Apt at a bargain, ready to deceive in little things. In great things, on the whole, "dependable" enough. Had there but been enough to eat, less rent to pay, one faith instead of two, a milder whiskey, and if the rain had cleared off now and then, the place had been about as happy as it is possible to be, here in this vale of tears. Little enough they recked of what went on in Parliament, upon the stock exchange, or in the busy haunts of men.

Once in a way a Home Rule speaker spoke in the village hall. The folk turned out to cheer with all their might, and in a week or two an Orangeman came round, and, if possible, the cheers were louder than before. In fact, they looked upon the rival Cheap Jacks as travelling entertainments sent by Providence on their behalf.

Except on Pitcairn's Island, Tristan d'Acunha, or in some group of islets in the South Seas before the advent of the missionaries, I doubt if anywhere men fared better on the whole.

But still a change was floating in the air.

One day a traveller from Belfast came to the village, and it struck him — "What a place to build a mill! Here there is water running all to waste, the land is cheap, the people vigorous and poor; yes, we must have a mill."

The priest and minister, the local lawyer, and the Scotch land-agent, all approved the scheme. All that they wanted was but capital.

The want of capital is, and always has been, so they said, the drawback of the land. Had we but capital, we should be rich, and all become as flourishing as over there in England, where, as all know, the streets are paved with gold.

Alas! they never thought that on the golden pavements rain down floods of tears that keep them always wet, hiding the gold from sight. They never dreamt how the world crushes and devours those who leave little villages like this, and launch the vessel of their lives upon its waves. They could not see children perished and half-starved; they did not know the smug sufficiency of commerce; and had never heard the harlot's ginny laugh. Therefore, the proposition seemed to them a revelation straight from God. Yes, build a mill, and all will turn to gold. The landlord will get his rents, the minister his dues, the priest his tithes, the working man, instead of being fed on buttermilk and filthy murphies, will drink tea (they called it *tay*), feast upon bacon, and white bread, and in due course will come to be a gentleman. Wages will rise, of course; our wives and children, instead of running bare-foot or sitting idle at the doors, will wear both shoes and stockings, and attend Mass or preachment "dacent," carrying their parasols.

The syndicate of rogues, with due admixture of fools and dupes, was got together; the mill was built. The village suffered a great and grievous change. All day long a whirr and whiz of wheels was heard. At daybreak a long string of girls and men tramped along the dreary streets, and worked all day. Wealth certainly began to flow; but where? Into the pockets of the shareholders. The people, instead of sturdy, lazy rogues, became blear-eyed, consumptive weaklings, and the girls, who formerly were patterns of morality, now hardly reached eighteen without an "accident" or two. Close mewing up of boys and girls in hot rooms brought its inevitable result. Wages did not rise, but on the contrary, rather inclined to fall; for people flocked from the country districts to get employment at the far-famed mill.

The economists would have thrown their hats into the air for joy had not their ideas of thrift forbidden them to damage finished products, for which they had to pay. The goods made in the mill were quoted far and wide, and known for their inferior quality throughout two hemispheres.

Yet still content and peace were gone. The air of the whole place seemed changed. No longer did the population lounge about the roads. No longer did the cows parade the streets, or goats climb cabin-roofs to eat the house leek. The people did not saunter through their lives as in the times when there was lack of capital, and therefore of advancement, as they thought. They had the capital; but the advancement was still far to seek. Capital had come — that capital which is the dream of every patriotic Irishman. It banished idleness, peace, beauty, and content; it made the people slaves. No more they breathed the scent of the fields and lanes, but stifled in the mill. There was a gain, for savages who did not need them purchased, at the bayonet's point, the goods the people made. The villagers gained little by the traffic, and became raggeder as their customers were clothed. Perhaps the thought that savages wore on their arms or round their necks the stockings they had made, consoled them for their lost peaceful lives. Perhaps they liked the change from being wakened by the lowing of the kine, to the "steam hooter's" call to work in the dark winter mornings — calling them out to toil on pain of loss of work and bread, and seeming, indeed, to say: "Work, brother! Up and to work; it is more blessed far to work than sleep. Up! leave your beds; rise up; get to your daily task of making wealth for others, or else starve; for Capital has come!"

Success

Castles in the Air

Your castles in the air are the best castles to possess, and keep a quiet mind. In them no taxes, no housemaids, no men-at-arms, no larders bother, and no slavery of property exists. Their architecture is always perfect, the prospect of and from them always delightful, and, in fact, without them the greater part of humanity would have no house in which to shield their souls against the storms of life. It is prudent, therefore, to keep these aerial fortalices in good repair, not letting them too long out of our mind's eye, in case they vanish altogether into Spain.

Good business men, and those who think that they are practical merely because they lack imagination, have maintained that castles such as these are but the creation of the brain, and that as fancy is but an exercise of the mind, its creations can have no existence in mere fact. To each man after his demerits; to some daybooks, ledgers, cash-boxes, and the entire armour of the Christian business man. Let them put it on, taking in their hands the sword of covetousness, having on their arms the shield of counterfeit, the helmet of double-dealing upon their heads, till they are equipped fully at all points to encounter man's worst enemy, his fellowman. Let them go forth, prevail, destroy, deceive, opening up markets, broadening their balances and their phylacteries; let them at last succeed and build their stucco palace in Park Lane; to them the praise, to them the just reward of their laborious lives; to them blear eyes, loose knee joints, rounded backs, and hands become like claws with holding fast their gold.

But let your castle builders in the perspective of the mind have their life, too; let them pursue their vacuous way, if but to serve as an example of what successful men should all avoid. Buoys in safe channels, lighthouses set up on coasts where no ships pass; preachers who preach in city churches where no congregation ever comes except the beadle, a deaf woman, and a child or two; Socialist orators who do "Ye Men of England" to a policeman and an organ-grinder — all have their uses, and may serve some day if coral insects build their reef, the "Flying

Dutchman" should put in for rest, a shower fill the church, or men grow weary of the strife of parties, and why not those who dream? They have their uses, too, because the castles that they build are permanent and suffer no decay. Tantallon, Hermitage, Caerlaverock, Warwick, and Kenilworth must crumble at the last, a heap of stones, grey ruined walls grown green with moss, and viper's bugloss springing from the crevices, some grassy mounds, a filled-up ditch to mark the moat, a bank or two to show the tilting ground, and a snug lodge, in which the lodge-keeper sits with gold-laced hat to take the tourists' sixpences — to that favour must they all come, even if masonry be fathoms thick, mortar as hard as adamant, and the men who built have builded *[sic]* not on the modern system, but like beavers or the constructors of the pyramids.

Your visionary castle, though, improves with time, youth sees its bastions rise, and each recurring year adds counterscarps, puts here a rampart or a mamelon, throws out a glacis or contructs a fosse, till middle age sees the whole fort impregnable. But as imagination commonly improves with years, old age still sees the castle untaken and entire; and when death comes, and the constructor passes away to sleep beside the million masons of the past, young builders rise to carry on the work; so that, considered justly, air is the best foundation on which a man can build; so that he does not wish to see his ashlar scale, mortar return to lime, and to be bothered all his life with patching that which with so much pains in youth he built. The poor man's shelter in the frosts of life; the rich man's summer house, to which he can retire and ease himself of the tremendous burden of his wealth; the traveller's best tent; the very present refuge of all those who fail — your visionary castle rears its head, defying time itself.

Often so real is the castle in the air, that a man sells his own jerry-built, stuccoed mansion in the mud, to journey towards his castle, as travellers have sold their lands to see the deserts in which other people live. Think what a consolation to the outcast in the crowded street, on the wet heath, straying along the interminable road of poverty, to bear about with him a well-conceived and well-constructed dream house, pitched like the ark, inside and out, against not only weather, but the frowns of fortune — a place in which to shelter in against the tongues of fools, refuge in which to sulk under the misery of misconception, half-comprehension, unintelligent appreciation, and the more real ills of want of bread — for well the Spaniards say that every evil on God's earth is less with bread.

How few can rear a really substantial castle in the clouds: poets, painters, dreamers, the poor of spirit, the men of no account, the easily imposed upon, those who cannot say No, the credulous, the simple-hearted, often the weak, occasionally the generous and the enthusiastic spirits sent into the world to shed as many tears as would float navies; these generally are famous architects of other peoples' fortunes. They rear palaces set in the middle distance of their minds, compared to which the Alhambra, the Alcazar, the Ambraz, Windsor and Fontainebleau, and the mysterious palaces in Trapalanda, which the Gauchos used to say were situated somewhere in the recesses of the Andes, beyond the country of the Manzaneros, are heavy, over-charged, flat, commonplace, ignoble, wanting in all distinction, and as inferior as is the four-square house in Belgrave Square, just at the corner of Lower Belgrave Street, to an Italian palace of the rinascimento, or the old "Casa de Mayorazgo," in the plaza at Jaen.

I read of such a master builder once in a newspaper. He was, I think, a mason, and whilst he worked bedding the bricks in lime, or underneath his shed hewing the stone with chisel and the bulbous-looking mallet masons use, the white dust on his clothes and powdering his hair, or on the scaffold waiting whilst the Irish hodman brought him bricks, he used to think of what some day he would construct for his own pleasure in the far off time when money should be made, wife found, house of his own achieved, and leisure to indulge his whims assured. Needless to say he was not of the kind who rise; master and mates and foreman used to call him dreamy and unpractical. His nickname was "The Castle Builder," for those who had to do with him divined his mind was elsewhere, though his hands performed their task. Still, a good workman, punctual at hours, hard working, conscientious, and not one of those who spend the earnings of a week in a few hours of booze at the week's end. Tall, fair, blue-eyed, and curley-haired, a little loose about the knees, and in the fibre of the mind; no theologian; though well read, not pious, and still not a *revolté*, thinking the world a pleasant place enough when work was regular, health good, hours not too long, and not inclined to rail on fortune, God, nature, or society for not making him a clerk. Things, on the whole, went pretty well with him; during the week he worked upon the hideous cubelike structures which men love to build; and Sunday come, he walked into the fields to smoke his pipe and muse upon his castles in the air. Then came an evil time — lockout or strike, I can't remember which — no work, plenty of time to dream, till money flew away, and the poor mason started on the tramp to look for work. Travelling, the Easterns say, is hell to those who ride, and how much more than hell for those who walk. I take it that no desert journey in the East, nor yet the awful tramp of the man who left afoot walks for his life, on pampa or on prairie, is comparable in horror to the journey of the workman out of work. On the one hand the walker fights with nature, thirst, hunger, weariness, the sun, the rain, with possible wild beasts, with dangers of wild men, with loss of road; sleeping he lies down with his head in the direction he intends to take on rising, and rising tramps towards the point he thinks will bring him out; and as he walks he thinks, smokes, if he has tobacco, takes his pistol out, looks at the cartridges, feels if his knife is safely in his belt, and has a consciousness that if all goes right he may at last strike houses and be saved.

But on the other hand, the wanderer has houses all the way; carriages pass by him in which sit comfortable folk; children ride past on ponies, happy and smiling, bicycles flit past, cows go to pasture, horses are led to water, the shepherd tends his sheep, the very dogs have their appointed place in the economy of the world, whilst he alone, willing to work, with hands made callous by the saw, the hammer, file, the plough, axe, adze, scythe, spade, and every kind of tool, a castaway, no use, a broken cogwheel, and of less account than is the cat which sits and purrs outside the door, knowing it has its circle of admirers who would miss it if it died.

Oh, worse than solitude, to wander through a thicket of strange faces, all thorny, all repulsive, all unknown; no terror greater, no nightmare, no creeping horror which assails you alone at night in a strange house, so awful as the unsympathetic glare of eyes which know you not, and make no sign of recognition as you pass. And so the mason tramped, lost in the everglade of men who, like trees walking, trample upon all those who have no settled root. At first, thinking a mason must of necessity be wanted, either to build or work amongst the stone, he looked for labour at his trade. Then, finding that wheresoe'er he went masons were plentiful as blackberries upon an autumn hedge, he looked for work at any trade, conscious of strength and youth and wish to be of use in the great world which cast him out from it as a lost dog, to stray upon the roads.

Past villages and towns, along the lanes, by rivers and canals he wandered, always seeking work; worked at odd jobs and lost them, slept under railway arches and in the fields, in barns and at the lea of haystacks, and as he went along he dreamed (though now more faintly) of his castles in the air. Then came revolt; he cursed his God who let a workman, a stonemason, starve, with so much work to do, stone to be hewn and houses built, churches to rear, docks to be made, and he alone it seemed to him, of all mankind, condemned to walk for ever on the roads. At last, tired of his God's and man's injustice, faint from want of food, and with his castle scarcely visible, he sat him down just on the brink of a black, oily river outside a manufacturing town, the water thick and greasy, and at night looking like Periphlegethon, when iron-works belch out their fires and clouds of steam creep on the surface of the flood.

And seated there, his feet just dangling in the noxious stream, the night-shift going to a factory found him, and as they asked him what he did, he murmured, "Castles, castles in the air," and rested from his tramp.

Progress, and Other Sketches

R. B. Cunninghame Graham

To Joseph Conrad

The author has to thank the Editors of *The Saturday Review*, *The Speaker* and *Justice* for permission to use some of the sketches.

Introduction

The Preface to *Progress* is a reflection on the nature of prefaces. For Graham what is important in a preface is not the description of a person's actions but rather of what he thinks, says and writes: "A preface is an apologia, autobiography, book of confessions, and a diary, all combined, of a man's mind and his opinions of the world of thought" [in *Progress*, page 264] – and he cites as excellent examples Cervantes' introduction to the second part of *Don Quixote* and the foreword to the King James translation of the Bible. Modern prefaces, on the other hand, are more perfunctory. Often they are mere "puffs" and adverts for the adjoining subject matter. But, Graham tells us, we must follow the behest of the modern Goddess Progress. The modern writer at least is not controlled by the dictates of critics and wealthy patrons. Relations between the modern writer and the press and public are much more harmonious.

Progress contains eighteen stories and sketches. Of these two are set in Mexico and two in Argentina; five in Morocco and one in Saudi Arabia; one in the North of England and five in Scotland; one in Africa which deals with a Scottish minister; and one in France.

The first story, "Progress", which gives its name to the whole collection, is very long, almost a novella. In it the writer purports to be recounting an event he has read about in a book by one Heriberto Frias, a person completely unknown to him but who subsequently became a personal friend. It is the heartrending story of the fate of the village of Tomochic in the State of Chihuahua in Mexico. The poverty-stricken village has failed to pay its taxes and the Government prepares to punish this negligence and sends in a troop of soldiers. The village itself is controlled by a religious fanatic called Cruz Chaves who has infected all the inhabitants with his zeal. For some time the villagers heroically withstand invasion but gradually the army wears them down until the remaining survivors inhabit only the church and Cruz's house. The church is set on fire and its inhabitants are mercilessly consumed in the flames. Finally, after the release of emaciated and wounded women and children, the last seven survivors, including Cruz, are brought to be shot.

The last man to die, full of the religious fervour which characterised the village, shouts: "Long live the Power of God". The brutality in this story is recounted graphically, starkly and dispassionately and is summed up with devastating irony:

Of the hundred men of Tomochic fit to bear arms none had escaped, and of a thousand soldiers only four hundred now remained.

About a hundred women and some children had been spared and the great cause of progress and humanity had gained a step.

Set in Argentina, "San José" is a skilfully crafted account of the life and death of General Don Justo José de Urquiza, the last of the gaucho leaders. The piece begins with a description of his house on a low hill surrounded by trees and outhouses which accommodate his gaucho bodyguards. Inside, its gaudy furnishings culminate in a tasteless ballroom. The general himself is then described. He is a complete autocrat. Infringers of his laws are subject to frightening punishments. When he is transported around his territory in his private coach the local peasants are happy if "the Supreme" does not stop. On the occasions when he did he

talked and chaffed pleasantly, after the fashion of an Eastern potentate, with all his subjects, between whom and himself there was slight difference but the power of death, which power he wielded easily, and almost with an air of jocularity, which well became the place.

Then comes the moral. As long as he keeps his people in fear the general is safe. But, as often happens in old age, when a tyrant repents for his bloody sins and seeks to live a quiet life doing as much good as possible, "politicians under the guise of patriotism assassinate him to advance themselves, under the pretext of the welfare of mankind". In a highly charged and gruesome scene a band of assassins enter his home and hack him mercilessly to death before the eyes of his daughter in his tasteless ballroom.

Again set in Argentina the next story opens with the description of a ruined house, "La Tapera", which the local people superstitiously avoid. Two gauchos happen to meet near it and one them divulges its tragic history. The Reds and Whites, political factions, are constantly at war in the area. The narrator, a Red, tells how one day a group of his people decided to plunder this then prosperous ranch because the owner was a White. But one of their number, Pancho Pajaro, disclosed that his father was its owner. At once the Reds abandoned their plans to loot the place: its ownership by the family of one of their number made it sacred. However, as they were departing, they were attacked by a group of Whites. They retaliated and put them to flight. Pancho brought down the last of the retreating horsemen and stabbed him through the back – inadvertently he had killed his brother! Knowing he would be cursed by God he went into exile with the Indians. His father died and, without his sons, the ranch decayed. The house was doomed.

"A Chihuahueño" is the portrait of an old Mexican from Chihuahua. His conversation contained many aphorisms and he sang and played the guitar badly. He was an expert on Indian lore, had been an officer in the army and had contempt yet admiration for the Indians. (Mexicans, we are told, were frequently just as barbaric.) He had a great gift as a story teller and loved to tell the tale of Alexander the Great taming his steed Bucephalus. He had two wives with whom he had no offspring, but he had an illegitimate son by an Indian squaw of whom he said:

the little rogue, son of an Indian harlot, he must have taken may a Christian's scalp by this time if has turned out such as his dam.

In "From the Stoep" the narrator is positioned on a *stoep* or platform vantage point on the Morocco side of the Straits of Gibraltar. From there he describes the tantalising view at dusk at the same time evoking the intimate atmosphere:

... evening deepened, and the purple haze crept on the town and hill, flattening them out till they appeared to rise out of the water like a gigantic whale left high and dry by time.

He describes the activities of the people who pass close to him, then his gaze extends gradually outwards to the nearby harbour, to "the stream of country people coming from market towards the mountain valleys", to the mountain ranges of Morocco which merge with those of Spain and to the ships sailing through the Straits. Finally, his gaze returns to his immediate location where a beggar and two local women pass – and, last of all, a dog.

"Mariano Gonzalez" is the portrait of a Spaniard who came to live in Marrakech in Morocco. Graham suggests that only those who abandon the pursuit of material success and the "rat race" really understand the true value of life. They pass their existence without the bitterness of thinking of what might have been. Such a person was Mariano Gonzalez. He lives with the Jewish people in their part of the city. Once a veterinary surgeon, he has now become a doctor to the whole community but, having adopted the local culture, he does not become over-stressed about the accuracy of the drugs he prescribes since all is ultimately in the hands of Allah. He had hoped to be buried in his native Spain, but this was not to be.

"Faith" is a folk tale beautifully told through the mouth of one Hamed-el-Angeri about the unwavering sense of purpose of an old woman in Saudi Arabia. She lives near Medina and makes a pilgrimage to Mecca to ask the Prophet Mohammed why after all her sex had endured and the faith they had shown they were excluded from Paradise. The story describes vividly the trials and tribulations of her epic journey. At last she reaches Mecca and discovers the whereabouts of the Prophet. Eventually she manages to obtain an audience with him and asks her question. After some delay Mohammed replies:

"Allah has willed that no old woman enter paradise, therefore depart ..."

Then, seeing her distress, he stretches out his hand and says:

"Mother, Allah has willed it as I declared to you, but as his power is infinite, at the last day, it may be he will make you young again, and you shall enter into the regions of the blessed, and sit beside the Perfect Ones, the four, who of all women have found favour in his sight."

Set in Morocco, "His Return" tells of the anti-climax of a soldier's return to the *dúar* (rural encampment) of his family after his period of military service has expired. Bu'Horma is in the Sultan's army which is engaged in the siege of the *kásbah* (castle) of a *kaid* (local chieftain) who has become too powerful. A graphic description of the siege follows. The Sultan's troops ultimately triumph, the castle is plundered and the women divided among the conquering soldiers. Bu'Horma is given an Arab girl who had been ravished by others but whom he treats with respect. When he sets off for Fez, the Sultan's headquarters, despite her pleas, he refuses to take her with him but gives her all the money he has looted from the siege. He remains stationed in Fez and after many years of longing is finally allowed to return to his home and family in their *dúar*. But something is missing in his life there and he cannot settle. Under cover of darkness he slips away back to his life in the city of Fez. He cannot put the clock back.

"El Khattaia-es-Salaa" is a tale again set in Morocco and again put into the mouth of the storyteller Hamed-el-Angeri. It is in the tradition of the beast fable and is an aetiological myth explaining why animals cannot talk. At one time, we are told, they could all speak Arabic. But they had to pray regularly or they would lose this gift – and we are presented with a magnificent picture of the animal world at prayer. In spite of this devotion, however, a capricious Allah decrees that their power of speech be removed and this causes huge lamentation – and thanksgiving for past privileges – throughout the animal world. Then at evening prayer the decree of dumbness is sung and all the animals let out a huge roar:

Then lifting up their heads, a roar as of the sea which breaks upon the outer islands of the Hebrides filled the air.

From then on all are dumb. But a lizard, too taken up with its daily pursuits, inadvertently did not give thanks. When it realises its sin of omission it is convulsed with grief. In an endeavour to avoid the wrath of Allah it climbs to the roof of the mosque and scratches on it the words "Allah Ackbar" and thus saves itself from Allah's wrath by showing its faith. From then on the lizard was known as *Khattaia-es-Salaa*, the prayer-scratcher.

"A Renegade" is set in Spain and Morocco. It tells of a Northern Englishman, Si Abdul Wáhed, who abandoned his former way of life and culture to become a Muslim. He did not, however, become a renegade from conviction or necessity. One day in Seville he saw a tile covered with writing in the Cufic (Moorish) alphabet. That was incentive enough. He immediately moved to Tlemcen in Morocco and at once became a Moor and married an Arab girl. But he always looked awkward in his Arab clothes and could not disguise his Englishness. Indeed, he often reviled his neighbours and his adopted creed. Why he became a renegade is not clear. Perhaps *tedium vitae* was the cause. Perhaps he simply liked the slower pace of life.

For the next sketch, "A Yorkshire Tragedy", Graham takes us to the north of England itself, to a run-down village blackened by coal dust.

Even the surrounding countryside is tarnished by this substance. But that is not all. There is a strange quietness in the village. Men look afraid yet also resentful. There has been a miners' strike and one of their number has been shot by "the Government" after the Riot Act had been read. His miserable funeral procession from the village to the local cemetery is described in all its pathos and sombreness.

"McKechnie *v.* Scaramanga" is the portrait of a self-made man. A Scots-speaking Aberdonian, he has worked his way up through his industry until he has become a shipping magnate with a large fleet of cargo ships. He has acquired the nickname of Andrew Granite, speaks broad Scots and has become an elder in Milngavie United Presbyterian Church. He thrives on litigation and disputes in maritime matters and is a great believer in the legal concept of "general average". He tells a story to his friends of how one of his ships on its voyage to Smyrna in Turkey broke down and had to be towed into Salonika in Greece. His lawyers informed him that his firm would be penalised for the late delivery of the freight he was transporting, so he chartered a Greek schooner to take the freight on to Smyrna. Immediately after the captain of the vessel, one Scaramanga, put to sea, a storm blew up. Terrified that his vessel would sink he promised the Madonna (a shrine to whom he had on board) that he would sacrifice something very valuable in gratitude if his ship and crew were saved. And they did indeed arrive safely. Whereupon Scaramanga decided to sacrifice the mainsail of his ship – and burnt it on the beach. He then claimed the value of the mainsail back from McKechnie. To the latter's astonishment under "the law o' general average" Scaramanga's plea was upheld by the court in Smyrna because in enlisting the help of the Madonna he had done all he could to save his vessel. And McKechnie had to pay up!

Set in Africa, "A Convert" tells of the Reverend Archibald Macrae, a grim, dour, Scots-speaking missionary. He was very unpopular and very self-righteous. "Conviction should follow reasonable airgument," he would proclaim. Monday Flatface, a local chief, had resolutely refused to be converted, but some years later an odd respect is discernible between the two men and Macrae has clearly mellowed. Eventually he explains what happened. On one occasion Flatface had come to Macrae seeking help for his very sick wife. Macrae goes to her. He gives her quinine and prays for her. But there is no improvement. Then the chief makes a sacrifice for his wife to his God: he cuts off one finger. Then another.

And then, when hope seems past, she recovers. Macrae does not know why. Was it the quinine? The prayers? The amputated fingers? He has no idea, but the experience changes him:

"Ah ... Flatface, weel no, he's still a heathen, though we are friends, and whiles I think his God and mine are no so far apart as I aince thocht."

After seeing the chief's faith and sacrifice Macrae becomes a kinder and more sympathetic man. He realises that argument is not always so important: God has

"made me see the error of my ways, that is, has shown me that there are things man's reason canna touch."

The next two pieces with their exquisite lyrical beauty could be described as prose poems. "The Laroch" (Gaelic for "The Ruin") describes the deserted land with its own wild beauty around the remains of a dwelling near Glenfinnan at the head of Loch Shiel and laments the fate of its Highland inhabitants who had been forced, like so many of their people, to take refuge in the New World because of their loyalty to the defeated Jacobite Charles Edward Stuart. "Snow in Menteith" is a beautiful idyll describing with sensitive detail the snow lying on the land bordering Gartmore House in Stirlingshire, Cunninghame Graham's family home. The writer describes the beauty of the snow on trees and woodland, the variety of animal tracks which mysteriously appear on the white fields and the wonder of the snow-covered Flanders Moss:

Flanders Moss that once had been a sea became an ocean, for as the peat-hags and the heather turned to waves, and as the sun lit up their tips with pink, they seemed to roll as if they wished once more to wash the skirts of the low foothills of the carse.

"Pollybaglan" and "A Traveller" are also set in Stirlingshire and describe two properties and their tenants on the Gartmore Estate. Pollybaglan is a remote small-holding on the wide Flanders Moss. That land had been reclaimed from peat bog in the eighteenth century and, whilst much of it has become very fertile, the land of Pollybaglan is still far from good. A tenant works it – barely at subsistence level – but, nonetheless, exists happily there. "A Traveller" describes a shepherd who was the tenant of

Tombreak, a hill farm above the village of Buchlyvie. He was a tough and independent man, whose life revolved around sheep and "travellin'". He was never overtly optimistic but was, nevertheless, expert at his work and every inch the countryman. To the narrator, in this case Graham himself, he seemed indestructible. His death was sad and unexpected.

This collection concludes with "A Vestal", the sad story of a dignified and devoted Spanish lady of mature years who lives in a pretentious hotel in a French seaside resort. Her accommodation is restricted, uncomfortable and unwelcoming although she clearly gains comfort from the presence of a number of religious objects. It emerges that she had been brought there as "half mistress and half nurse" by an older Spanish gentleman called Don Fulano and they had lived there contentedly until his death. Clearly because they had not been married they were disapproved of by the other guests. Such, however, is the nature of hypocrisy that, because the gentleman was wealthy, the management never asked them to leave. When Don Fulano died (a very Catholic death) she was left nothing. The family, however, agreed to pay to allow her to stay on in the hotel. For the following ten years every day of her life revolved around a visit to her partner's grave. Eventually the family agreed that she could be buried alongside him but, in spite of her loyal devotion, they refused to allow her name, Ines, to be incised on the memorial cross above the grave. Cynically, the narrator suggests that St Anthony, to whom the lady showed great devotion, might arrange to have her name put on the cross for, after all, in spite of the family's snobbery, "'Fulano' but means 'So-and-So'".

As can be seen from the above, *Progress* contains a wide and varied collection of sketches and stories. Their subject matter ranges from tragedy, to perceptive character analysis, to social criticism, to highly accomplished descriptions of landscape and the natural world and to some beautiful reflections. Above all, this collection shows R. B. Cunninghame Graham's deep understanding of, and affection for, his fellow human beings.

(RWR)

Contents

Progress

Preface

To the Progressive Reader

When a man writes an apology *pro vita sua*, or his confessions, for no one with a spark of humour could in cold blood describe his proper "Life and Miracles" in set biography, the task cannot be hard. For in the main he has to deal with actions, with events, and how he has been influenced by other men, or influenced them. I do not speak of those who with the outward fallible pen describe the spiritual and inner life, which the interior and invisible eye alone can see and focus; for in their case invention, as a general rule, exceeds imagination, and the palaces in which their souls expatiate are not unfrequently *[sic]* as heavy, dull, and overloaded as were the mansions with which Vanbrugh oppressed the earth.

There are exceptions, such as St. John, he of the Cross, in whom imagination and invention flourished together, like the ivy and the oak, without the one oppressing or the other feeling the weight of gratitude for its support.

But these are rare. So, casting back again to writing of the exterior life, I say that it is easy — that is, of course, if the man writing has no humour, the lack of which no wit supplies; for wit is but a varnish on the mind, a brightness and an exterior polish, bringing out, no doubt, the colour; but humour is the recompense which man made for himself after the fall and when first sorrow came into the world.

So he who writes the preface to his book describes his own interior life, or, without wishing, lets it peep out from the depths of his own being, without the shield of faith which the *illuminati* hold upon their arms, protected only by his humour from the world.

What is important (as it seems to me) is not the actions of a man, which may be caused by circumstances, and which, rightly considered, are as immaterial as are the atoms dancing in a sunbeam, seen by the eye and not collated by the brain; but what he thinks, and, more important still, that which he says and writes. So that, as guineas in a purse get light by rubbing one against the other, so do the tissues of the soul decrease by frequent stripping off the outward panoply of indifference and mistrust, which we all wear about our hearts as a protection from man's enemy — mankind. For, rightly apprehended (as I take it), a preface is an apologia, autobiography, book of confessions, and a diary, all combined, of a man's mind and his opinions of the world of thought. This naturally does not apply to all those three-percentling "forewords" (I think they call the things), in which a writer gets a friend to puff his wares and play Autolycus at second hand, with an eye on the generous, appreciating public's purses for their joint benefit, no doubt, not without mutual back-scratching and "ca' me, ca' thee."

Still less to those long catalogues of quite unnecessary works of unknown and perhaps justly forgotten writers whose remains worms have long eaten, and whose spirits hover round Grub Street, seeking again to incarnate themselves in scribblers up-to-date, which masquerade as prefaces, like a misshapen maiden at a fancy ball who dresses up as Mary Queen of Scots. Your real and right preface should resemble Cervantes' introduction to his second part, in which he put his life's blood and his soul; or the last effort which he penned, his foot just resting in the stirrup (as he says), which none can read without a tightening at the heart.

These be your prefaces, *in excelsis et per sæcula*, worthy for true nobility of thought and style to place beside the best of all our English forewords, that to the translation of the Bible, dedicated to that bright boreal star, King Jamie First and Sixth.

After these masterpieces, what can your modern preface-monger do? For him there is no prince, no patron to address: nothing remains except the reading public, which quite naturally, when it has spent its eighteen pence upon a book, desires to be amused; for books exist to while away a tedious hour when travelling, or to be read in a dull country house or Swiss hotel, or when one is not up to polo, cricket, or the weather is too rough to take one's gun and slay the maize-fed pheasant at the corner of a wood. Who in his senses would attempt to captivate the public in the way the writers of the past endeavoured to propitiate the noble patrons to whom they dedicated books? The public, as I see the matter, likes advertisement, taking all men as it takes patent medicines, on their face value, and not stopping to inquire as to interior graces, exterior form, or anything but price.

So that it has come to be believed that prefaces, when they exist, are written to explain or puff the book, whereas, if rightly comprehended, a mere book is but a peg on which to hang a preface, for in it alone a man is free to write that which he thinks, unfettered by the subject, which has confined your writers since the world began. Who does not love the rambling preface of the past, in which a man displayed his knowledge both of mankind and things, brought forth his erudition, and speculated on the movement of the spheres whilst quoting freely from the classics and telling you about himself, his tastes, dislikes, and why it was he wrote. Such revelations of a man, made incidentally and, as it were, upon the way (of life), are worth a thousand storehouses of facts. Mere facts are in the reach of any fool to prose about, inflicting on a long-enduring world his knowledge gained at second hand, gleaned from encyclopædias and mugged up at museums, and then set forth with circumstance and at unnecessary length. But knowledge of mankind is precious, and the half-conscious revelations that a man makes of himself, above all price, either in rubies or in pearls.

Thus it is sometimes good to stray with preface-makers of an older world — a world of books bound all in leather, well printed, and with due license, and to be had at publishers in little streets, all long destroyed and now replaced by lofty phalansteries built of red brick and plastered with cement.

But, old or modern, your preface-monger, in the parturition of his thoughts, must, as I take it, suffer; for, at the birth of what he writes, something has left him, far beyond recall, which leaves him poorer, and perhaps enriches no one; for your writer oftentimes sows seed which now and then yields wheat, but just as often grain of another sort, as mustard or rank tares.

And so it is, progressive reader, that, as natural shame prevents a man from speaking of his natural deeds, so does humanity itself render it just as hard for him (or harder) when he must speak of thoughts and of opinions, both of which are more important and more intimate than actual things, and which no one but mere politicians, debt collectors, public officials, pimps, and procuresses can bear to touch upon without some loss of human dignity.

To write at all is in some measure but a prostitution of the soul, and we must all fain hope that scribblers may creep in for judgment upon All Saints' Day, when mercy is abroad, and so gain pardon from the offended readers, for from themselves it is in vain that they should look for grace or gramercy.

So as a bather stands upon the brink, dipping his toes as delicately as Agag into the water, we in a preface, O progressive crowd, to whom we sell ourselves at so much (with a reduction net), care not to come too speedily to close grips with you, fearing your dire Half Nelson, and being well convinced that you regard our antics with the just measure of contempt with which the purchaser regards the seller, and which the seller pays him back full measure, in dislike.

But as the Goddess Progress, who from the horse-dung of the streets ascended up on high, and sits enthroned within the hearts of all her votaries, beckons us onward, we must arise and follow where she leads.

Times change, and if the writers of the past could look up from the pit where they, no doubt, now expiate their sins against the spirit of the age in which they lived, they would congratulate the world upon its march.

In the dire days in which they scribbled, wearing the stones of Fleet Street slippery as ice with their patched shoes, and trotting humbly up and down to sell their wares; waiting on patrons with the lackeys at their doors, dining but fitfully, and oft dependent on a charitable publisher for an advance against the harvest of their brains, their lot was hard.

Painters and poets in the days of which I write were the sworn foes of critics, and they, like toads beneath a harrow, wrote in terror of their lives, to please the press, and to propitiate the powerful and the rich.

Wealth was all powerful, and the successful man, patting his stomach, looking at the world, affirmed it perfect, putting gilt cotton wool into his ears to bar out criticism. Barbed wire entanglements of gold hedged round the realm of thought, which was set thick with pitfalls for the trespasser, who, if he did not fall into them, was dubbed stark mad or envious, a common atheist, and a mere railer at accepted facts from sheer malignancy.

A sunless world it was, under an eighteen-carat sky set with sham diamonds for stars, as different from the earth in which we live as chalk from cheese, or as a millionaire fresh from Johannesburg from a mere dabbler in the South Sea Stock or Darien Company.

Now all is altered, and the progressive leaven working in our hearts has softened us. All feuds are over, wounds are healed, and writers and the press, laying all prejudice aside, embrace the public, who in its turn has pressed them to its heart. Progress is justified of works, . . . because they say so, and all unite to glorify success.

Self-praise is progress, and self-sufficiency the measure of success; all things are due to all men, all views tolerable, and the most ginny harlot worthy of her hire.

R. B. Cunninghame Graham
Ardoch, 15th October 1904.

Progress

A friend in Mexico sent me the other day a little book.

The author, Heriberto Frias, was quite unknown to me, but has become a friend.

It is asserted that some have been the hosts of angels unawares, a proposition most difficult of proof (or of disproof), for angels in the self-same way as ghosts are seen with the interior eye. But; the book lies before me, in all the poverty of its cheap paper, and the faint, eye-searing print, which Spain apparently has left among its legacies to the republics which once were "jewels in her crown."

Printed in Mexico (Mancier Brothers, I° del Relox), it has upon its outside cover a vignette of a little village in the Sierra Madre, known as Tomochic. A river runs in front, slow flowing, and its margin set about with tamarisks. It further is adorned with the presentment of a soldier of the republic that Porfirio Diaz rules; a rifle in his hand, his bandolier crossing his chest, his chin-strap stuck beneath his nose, and on his face, an air of Mexico expects each man to look his best.

On a small scroll there is a vignette of a poblana girl, wearing her hair in the old Spanish fashion in a long thick plait, and with a cross and rosary, sinister, sable, displayed upon a ground of rather sickly gules. But the keynote is given on the left corner of the page where a strange figure sits. Dressed all in grey, with deerskin sandals on his feet, kept on by straps which, like the garterings of Malvolio, or those worn by a pifararo, rise to his knee, with his hands crossed upon his Winchester, two bandoliers upon his chest, and one about his waist fastened by a long silver cross, he sits and looks out on the world, with all the realism that a bad portrait sometimes has in a supreme degree. His bushy beard and thick moustache, long and dishevelled hair, and hat thrown back almost to form an aureole, show the religious monomaniac or enthusiast (for all the difference in the term is but the exit of the enterprise), at the first glance.

A curious cloak, which rises almost to his ears in two peaked wings, completes the picture, which may, for all that I know, have been taken from the life. Upon the other outside covering of the work are some perfunctory advertisements of books, most of them translations from the French, setting forth the *Vida de Jesus*, by E. Renan, *Mi Madre*, by one Hugo Conway, and lastly, *La Señorita Giraud mi Mujer*, by Adolphe Belot.

These, with some works by Chateaubriand and Daudet, together with the beautiful *Maria*, especially described as a "novela americana" by Jorge Isaacs, pretty well make up the list — a list which, for its catholicity of taste, does honour to the house that issues it.

Thus with prolixity I have set forth the outside of my little book sent from Tenochtitlan, as when it came to me it did not strike me that I should be much moved by its contents.

Nobody knows or cares in what part of the world is situated the state and town known as Chihuáhuá.

Somewhere in South America would be the general answer to the question, and so it is not to be thought that the heroic struggle and the destruction of the remote and quite unfriended village of Tomochic should excite even a passing qualm, for we are worshippers of the accomplished fact.

But still it sometimes rises in my mind, what profits it although a man, in the attempt to gain his soul, should be successful and should lose the world, if the same soul when gained should prove to be so shrivelled and so hide-bound that it were better to have lost it gallantly and kept humanity intact?

Who with a spark of kindliness or feeling for humanity, having hit in his travels on some island lost in an undiscovered archipelago, on which the inhabitants lived in their own way, even although they had not heard of hell, but would not make it his first duty to forget its latitude and banish all remembrance of its longitude out of his head? Only by doing so could he fend off the servitude of taxes and of creeds from the poor islanders, the introduction of corruption, gin, and syphilis, and all the thousand woes that islanders endure from the misguided zeal of honest missionaries. Who does not feel as if a slug was crawling on his soul on reading in some missionary report of all their misdirected labours and their sufferings, and of the perils that they have endured, to turn some fine free race of savages, interesting to us by their customs and their relation to ourselves, into bad copies of our lowest class, waddling about in ill-made clothes and claiming kindred with us as brother "Klistians" in the Lord?

Our author paints the village for us with some art, and tells, half-sympathisingly, how the full misery of progress and of modern life passed over it, as avalanches fall upon a hamlet in the hills, destroying church and houses, men, women, children, cattle, and the crops, and leaving nothing living in their track.

The wicked villagers believed in God and in His power, and in especial held in esteem the works of Santa Teresa, her of Avila. Their favourite exclamation was, "Long live the power of God!" which they preferred to "Damn me!" or to any of the forms of phallic exclamation which their countrymen had ever in their mouths.

But though the President, Porfirio Diaz, he whom the travelling globe-trotter beslavers with his praise for having rooted out the highway robbers and enthroned the sweaters in their place, did not much care about the pious objurgations of the Tomoches, one article of their belief was sure to cut him to the quick. Taxes, they held, were only due to God, and thus at the first step they placed themselves outside the pale of Christianity. This was the way the matter seemed to strike "Don Porfi," the imperial President.

The book begins with the impressions of a young officer who had been sent to join his regiment in the advance against the ruffians who had withheld their taxes, and passed their time in glorifying Santa Teresa and their God. We meet the callow officer, Miguel Mercado, in one of those rustic restaurants which form a feature of the life of northern Mexico, after a long march.

Smoking tamales[1] and leathery tortillas,[2] roast kid and turkey cooked with red peppers in a savoury stew, with dishes of black beans (*frijoles*) cooked in bacon fat, comprised the fare. The wine was that of Parras, mezcal made from maguey,[3] and its superior variety Tequila, were the stronger drinks.

---

1 Tamales are masses of chopped meat, generally chicken or turkey, mixed with maize meal, and cooked in a maize leaf to keep in the juice.
2 The tortilla is a leathery flat cake made of maize bruised on a stone called a metate. It was the bread of the ancient Mexican, and resembles the Indian chupatty in leathery consistency and in the strain it puts upon the degenerate digestive organs of the civilised man.
3 Maguey is the Mexican name for the aloe. From it is also made pulque, and from its fibre cordage.

Here he finds all the officers of the regiment he has to join engaged at lunch. He learns that in the interior of the Sierra Madre a town composed of madmen had "pronounced." [1]

To his astonishment, his comrades tell him that the forces of the Government have been twice driven back with heavy loss, and that a number of their officers and a lieutenant-colonel had been taken prisoners.

No one can tell him why the little sierra-built town has set itself like Athanasius against the world.

Still, all the people of Chihuáhuá were loud in admiration of the valour of the villagers and of their skill in arms. They showed a mute antipathy for the soldiers and against the central government. All that the Chihuáhueños knew about Tomochic was that their chief was called Cruz Chaves, and that he preached a strange religion full of mysticism and a sanctity of life unknown to clergymen, mixed with wild ideas of communism unfit for the conversing of good business men.

Orders to march, however, came at once, and the troops, with a quick-firing gun, struck into the vast arid prairies which stretch right from the Rio Grande to the foothills of the great mountain range which runs all through the State. [2] As they advanced across the steppe, its scanty vegetation white with alkali, in the far distance antelopes scudded away down wind, pillars of dust arose, and overhead vultures and eagles soared, whilst now and then the soldiers plodded through villages of prairie-dogs, who, seated on their mounds, looked at the approaching force, and as they neared their towns squeaked and rushed down into their holes, whilst the grave little owls, their fellow-dwellers in the waste, after a widening flight, alighted on the hillocks and blinked their eyes at the unusual sight. The icy wind whistling down from the hills chilled to the bone, and as they passed a few lone ranches, it was seen that all the sympathy of the inhabitants was dead against the troops.

Beside the soldiers walked their women and their wives, shod with *huaraches*,[3] and having on their backs their cooking-pots. As they marched before the troops they looked (says Heriberto Frias) like some tribe of cannibals

1 To "pronounce" is to set up the standard of rebellion. It is an adaptation, much used in America, from the Spanish word *pronunciamiento*, meaning to declare an action (of rebellion).
2 Chihuáhuá
3 The *huarache* is a kind of moccasin, usually made of cow-hide with the hair on.

upon the march. Throughout the day the officers, as is the custom in the high plains of Mexico, did all they could to stop the soldiers drinking at the wells, knowing that drinking heated, at such altitudes, is almost certain death; but now and then the women, running up behind, contrived to slip a gourd of water into their hands, which they drank as they walked, in spite of every risk. And as they marched the women told them stories of the strange place that they were to attack, gleaned from the ranches that they passed upon the way.

Santa Teresa, it appeared, had blessed the rifles of her worshippers[1] so that each shot would have a victim, and no bullet fired, fall useless to the ground.

At last the column reached Guerrero and camped upon the alameda of the town, the peaks of the far mountains of the Sierra Madre showing sharp and blue, and seeming only a league or two away.

When the young officer Miguel Mercado had got some supper and began to talk with his companions of the day, news came that the lieutenant-colonel who had been taken prisoner by the men of Tomochic had been set free without conditions, and had rejoined their force. This naturally astonished every one, and when it then leaked out that the whole body of the fighting men of Tomochic reached to a hundred, and that each man, given his knowledge of the country and his skill in arms, was worth three soldiers, Miguel observed that it appeared as if a breath of icy wind had passed across the faces of his friends.

During his supper Mercado had observed a pretty girl who came into the rustic restaurant which, in a tent, is ready every evening in the frontier towns. As often happens when a man is just about to risk his life, his every sense was strung to breaking point. The image of the girl possessed him, and as he wandered up and down in the acute and bitter cold, he passed a cottage where he thought he would go in and ask if they had any drink to sell.

Just as he passed the threshold he heard a voice calling for coffee, with an oath. He went in, and on a rough camp-bed made of strips of ox-hide nailed to a wooden frame, from out a bundle of *sarapes*,[2] saw a head appear. It was that of a man of middle age, the hair was long and turning grey, the nose hooked, and the eyes piercing and red with drink.

1 This she could do without indiscretion, as she is a colonel of artillery in Spain.
2 *Sarape* is the Mexican word for a blanket, which is used as a cloak by the Mexicans of the poorer class.

271

Before him stood a girl half-dressed, with eyes cast down and trembling, and in an instant Mercado saw that she was the same girl who had occupied his thoughts. As he gazed at her the man called, "Julia, hurry up and bring my boots." The young man looked at her and saw that she was pretty and about fifteen. What was his horror and disgust, when the rough, long-haired giant had got up, to see her turning down the bed to find her handkerchief, and to remark that on the mattress she had left the impress of her body on the side next the wall.

He looked at her, and though (as Heriberto Frias says, with the simplicity and directness of the Spanish race) he was not handsome, yet he was young, and as his eyes met Julia's she turned red. Pointing towards a woman making tortillas just outside the door, Mercado said, "Is that your mother?" "No, my stepmother," the girl replied. "Ah, I thought she was your mother," said Mercado. "And this ogre of a man?" "My uncle — but he is also — that is to say, we are not married, for the woman is his wife." Then she would say no more, and to Mercado's question of why she did not leave her husband-uncle, answered, "It is my father's wish. He is a saint, but does not know his brother. Santa Teresa sanctified him, and though they shot him, he rose from the dead, just as did Christ." "But you, who are you?" "I am the daughter of José Carranza, and I come from Tomochic."

Here Heriberto Frias breaks off into a description of Tomochic and of the causes which led to the revolt, which might as well have been at the commencement of the book. But who shall quarrel with an author, unless it be a critic (and there are few of them in the Sierra Madre), as to the method which he uses to let us know what he is going to impart. We take it all on trust, as we do sermons, rain, and Acts of Parliament. Reading all that he writes, one cannot but believe that the Tomochitecos[1] must have all been mad.

It appears that Tomochic had been a frontier town always in warfare with the Apaches, and that once the immediate danger over, the inhabitants had settled down to the enjoyment of a kind of peace with arms. All carried guns, and used them frequently. All were religious, and in the parish church for many generations all the chief notables had been interred.

One sees the place dazzling with whitewash in the clear blue sky, or brown with sun-dried bricks, but as to this our author gives no details, so I will make it white.

---

[1] People of Tomochic sometimes. Heriberto Frias uses the form Tomoche, and sometimes Tomochitecos.

The little sandy streets crossed one another at right angles, and emerged upon the plaza, where was built the church. All round the square stood seats of stucco painted in yellow ochre or in blue. Above them waved some straggling China trees, or ashes of Japan. The windows all had gratings of wrought iron; the doors were solid, and were studded thick with nails. Outside the actual town extended maize fields set with *jacáls*[1] in which the cultivators lived. The church was built of brick, daubed over white with stucco, and no doubt had been the chapel of some Franciscan mission, so many of which are to be seen upon the frontiers both of Texas and of Mexico. Horses stood blinking saddled all the day at every door, and men wrapped in sarapes lounged so constantly against the sides of every house that all the angles of the walls were polished, and it seemed that the houses certainly would fall if the hard-working loungers were to move suddenly away.

There may have been some little shops in which some fly-blown wares were kept, with boxes of sardines, some macaroni, raisins of the sun, and bottles of mescal, Tequila, whisky of the Americanos, boots, girths, cigarettes, and general stores, called *abarrotes* by the Mexicans, although the real meaning of the word is "dunnage," and signifies the packing used for the cargo of a ship. And yet an air of melancholy hung all about the place: an air of melancholy, but mingled with distrust, so that, when men heard noises in the night, their hands grasped pistol-butts laid ready to their beds; and in the daytime hearing anything unusual, they stopped their conversation with their eyes and ears strained open, as a coyoté or a mustang listens when a twig crackles or a distant neigh is borne along the wind.

Lost in the mountains, far from roads, distrustful and distrusted, with its taxes dwindling and its offertory almost illusory, what wonder that Tomochic was neglected both by the Church and State?

But suddenly a wave of wild religion, which not infrequently breaks out in desert places, as at Mecca, or in Omán, where El Waháb essayed the last Mahommedan reform, swept on Tomochic and made it known, at least in Mexico.

The Governor of Chihuáhuá, one Carillo, having passed by the place, admired the pictures in the church and wished to take them to the capital. The inhabitants, who probably had never given them a thought before,

---

1 *Jacál* the Mexican word for a small cottage. It appears to be of Indian origin.

rose as one man in their defence, and from that time the Governor and all
the satellites of the dread majesty of law became anathema to the religious
townsfolk in the hills. Usually all revolts arise from insufficient causes; the
people bearing real evils as patiently as mules bear loads, or donkeys riders
upon Hampstead Heath.

A girl from Tomochic having fallen in love with a good-looking
minion of the law was left despairing, with a young solicitor, to face the
world. The people, who no doubt were not more strict in matters sexual
than ordinary hypocrisy demands, found themselves outraged, and at
the moment that the times required, a man from God appeared.

His name was Don José Carranza — the Don no doubt mere courtesy,
as is the case throughout America, where, as they say, "the treatment
(*tratamiento*) is general in our republics."

News came that on a day he would arrive and set to work to prove his
thaumaturgic skill. He came, and proved to be an old and feeble man,
but with him brought a wife a great deal younger than himself. He also
brought a brother, one Bernardo, who had long left the village, having
been expelled for theft.

But now he came triumphant and half-drunk, carrying a rifle in his
hand, and giving out that he was now a soldier under Jesus Christ, and
quite regenerate.

Saints, as it often happens with rude peoples, seem to be chosen for
their lack of wit. This does not mar their saintship, for there is usually
to hand some man, either fanatical or scheming, to take them under his
protection and stand between them and the world.

This was the case in Tomochic, for there lived there a family called
Chaves, Indian fighters to a man, withal religious, straight shooters,
charitable, honest, and much respected in the town. The oldest was
called Cruz, and he appears to have been a natural leader, and a man
illuminated, as Mahommed was — a preacher and a rifle shot, some
forty years of age, tall, dark, and with the steady eyes which show a spirit
obstinate and bold.

After the "saint" had made his entrance with his edifying brother and
his train of devotees, the vicar, who seems to have had some few remains
of common sense, preached to the people, and exhorted them to turn
away from folly, when suddenly Cruz Chaves rose in the body of the
church, and, walking to the pulpit, thus addressed the priest:

"In the name of the great power of God, I, His poor policeman, tell
you to withdraw."

The priest, alone and unsupported, naturally withdrew.

Then, so to speak, was the abomination of desolation set up on the altar, and Saint José Carranza reigned supreme.

But he did more than this, for some one having told him that he was really Saint Joseph risen from the dead, he got into his head that in all things he must assimilate his conduct to that his prototype pursued. So calling up his brother Bernardo, the convicted thief, he gave him all his property, and, not content with that, his wife, although this second gift may perhaps have been not so great a sacrifice as at first sight it would appear. His daughter Julia he had intended for a holy virgin, who should work miracles and cast out Lucifer, but she, too, he gave to the convicted thief. Then, either pushed by madness or religious zeal, or set on by his brother, he held, as it were, a family council, and informed his people that he was tired of being but a saint, and now intended to be God.

So far the movement would appear to have been the work of idiots and of rogues, but underneath them lay a real fund of true fanaticism.

The Chaves family, which seems to have been composed of honest but pig-headed mystics, took the reins, and soon Tomochic grew to be respected as a place where men, although they paid no taxes, practised a sort of rough and ready justice, and recognised no other power than God's, for the poor "saint" soon fell into a state of stupid drunkenness.

But as the world which, though it commonly affects to obey God's laws, can never bear to see its theories really put in practice, soon began to kick. The Government in Mexico, which could not understand God's laws without man's taxes, promptly endeavoured to reduce the erring villagers by force of arms. The first attempt proved unsuccessful, and an enormous booty fell into the hands of Chaves, who acted as God's general in the fight. The people of Tomochic grew to be known as honourable men throughout Chihuáhuá, and the trains of mules with silver coming from the mines passed all unguarded near the village, knowing that not a man would try to stop them on the way.

The schism grew, and soon showed signs of spreading through the State, until the Government was forced to take the matter up for its own credit, and sent the expedition in which Mercado found himself, and which was now upon the march.

Bernardo and his two wives had been sent off by Chaves, who feared his bad example on the people of Tomochic, to spy upon the enemy at Guerrero, the younger woman passing as his daughter, to avoid scandal amongst the weaker brethren who had not chosen to accept the prophet of the Sierra as a god.

Between him and Mercado a curious friendship rose, half brought about through the attraction which repulsive men and things occasionally exercise, and partly because it gave Mercado opportunities of seeing and of talking to the girl.

Little by little the inevitable occurred.

At first the gentle language and kind manners of the young officer attracted her, until at last one day he kissed her suddenly, and then (it is not I but Heriberto Frias who philosophises) there awoke in her the natural sensuality of youth, which the brutality of her tyrant had banished utterly.

Soon came the order for the column to advance, and after a wild meeting of the younger officers to celebrate the march, Mercado sallied out at night, wrapped in his cloak, to bid farewell to Julia before he set out for the fight.

These same good-byes are always perilous; but yet who would forgo them with all they mean and lead to, for human nature loves to reason out the dangers of a thing and then confront them, and when the worst has come, console itself with saying that the flesh is weak.

Miguel and Julia did not make the exception which is said to prove the rule, although of all the follies which mankind has crystallised in speech, surely this aphorism bears the palm. He went, as Holy Scripture says the adulterer goes, by night, wrapped in the cloak of darkness, saying no man will see, found the door shut, and knocking, it was opened by Julia in her shift, thinking that he who knocked was Don Bernardo, who in fact had remained drinking in the town.

There is a Scottish story of a doctor of old days who having bought a mare essayed to ride her, and what happened was related by his servant, thus: "The first kick landed the puir doctor on the pommel, the next between the mare's lugs; from thence his subsequent transition to the ground did not tak' long."

When about midnight Mercado left the rancho, conscious that he had perhaps but added to the miseries of Julia's life, he recollected that the column marched at daybreak, and, wrapping himself in his cloak, lay down beneath a tree upon the outskirts of the town, to sleep. The bugle woke him, as it seemed, almost before he had well closed his eyes. Struggling already dressed upon his feet, he ran to place himself upon the right flank of his company. As usually occurs in all campaigns, the column did not march at the time ordered, and Miguel had time to think upon his brief possession of the girl.

He saw her trembling and ashamed, loving and yet afraid to give herself to him because of her disgrace, himself imploring and Julia resisting, and then his taking her almost by force amidst her tears.

Vaguely he recalled that she had told him all her story, and that her monstrous husband was a spy sent by the people of Tomochic to tell them what was passing at the camp. He felt himself a traitor, both to his country and the girl, and drawn insensibly to see her once again on some pretext, stepped off to the *jacál*. He found it empty, with nothing left of its inhabitants but a lame donkey, which silently stood in the corral alone, its head hanging down sadly almost to the ground.

Then came the preparations for the march, and once again the column struck into the steppe.

Little by little from Guerrero the road ascends towards the enormous bulk of the backbone of Mexico. One seems to march for ever, and still the Sierra Madre looks as far away as at the beginning of the day. The thick white dust lies thick upon the dwarf mezquita and Huisaché trees, and makes the scattered cactuses loom like gaunt spectres on the plain.

Most of the streams are salt; the pasture salitrose,[1] over all the sun glares down as it were made of brass. Nightfall just caught the column, which numbered over five hundred men and a quick-firing gun, at "La Generala," a point at which the road begins to pass through pine woods and gigantic blocks of stone.

The soldiers, who had brought provisions from the town, were still in spirits, and the dull feeling which invades tired troops, making them fall at once to sleep, not even cooking food unless obliged, had not come over them. With songs and conversation round the fires they passed away the evening, and daylight found them once more on the road. Little by little they began to mount; the track wound in and out between great rocks and overhung the streams, becoming here and there so narrow that ten men could stop a thousand; the soldiers marched in Indian file, and wondered why the enemy did not attack in such a favourable place to lay an ambuscade.

But the Tomochitecos, though they knew the Sierra better than any one in Mexico except the Indians, thought it beneath their dignity to

1 Salitrose, which is my adaptation of the Spanish word "salition," *[sic]* seems to me a better word than the English "salitrinous."

leave their town, which they considered sacred, and to defend which all had determined to devote their lives. At one o'clock they halted at "La Peña Agujerada," a great rock, and rested till the evening, when once again in the bright moonlight they struggled up the track.

The peaks and needles of the rocks shone in the moonbeams like great organ-pipes. The precipices looked more awful, and the tired men, footsore and carrying their provisions on their backs, stumbled along, oft falling like the Christian on life's track, and oft blaspheming as they fell, as even Christians will when obstacles and pitfalls bar the way. The frightened horses' eyes gleamed bright as phosphorus, as most unwillingly they picked their way, choosing each footstep and snorting wildly now and then as they passed torrents or the pine boughs waved like phantoms in the night.

They camped at Rio Verde, more than half way, with great precautions, fearing a surprise; but nothing happened, and the night passed quietly away.

The next day's journey from Rio Verde to Las Juntas only took three hours, and left them but two leagues to march before they reached the town.

Though short, the march was mortal, as it was all uphill and through a country where they could get no water, so that, as usually occurs, they were tired out before the fight began, and lay about the fire wrapped in their blankets sleeping like marmots; but still the enemy did not attack them, so they slept on till nearly daybreak, when the sergeants wakened them silently and prepared them for the fray.

The cold was glacial as the men stood in the ranks waiting until the sun rose, for the guides were not quite certain of the direction of the town. A black descent yawned right in front of them, into which they plunged. Scouts were thrown out, and in the semi-dark they stumbled down the trail, till the stars paled and all the sky grew white. The dawn, scarlet and orange coloured, showed them they had come to a small open space, whence once again the rough track mounted to the clouds. There all the officers dismounted, leaving their horses with the rear-guard, and the men set themselves for the last and steepest climb up the rough road which ran through pine woods which closed black above their heads. The officers, who all had left their kepis with the baggage, had put on grey felt hats with but a strip of bright red ribbon to distinguish them.

Mercado, like the rest, marched silently, feeling the tightening at the stomach which creeps over most men when in peril of their lives, and hoping that the soldiers could not guess his feelings, when suddenly some desultory shots were heard, and the scouts fell back in confusion and the quick-firing gun advanced. Once more the path descended, and they heard but could not see the enemy. Shouts of "Long live the power of God!" "Long live the Blessed Virgin!" and of "Death to Lucifer!" resounded from the recesses of the pine woods and the rocks.

The soldiers, taken at disadvantage, could not see where to direct their fire, and suddenly a man close to Mercado's side opened his arms, let fall his rifle, and with an "Ay Jesus" fell dead, remaining open-mouthed with a thin streak of blood staining his dark blue tunic and trickling down into the sand. Then there stepped out from underneath the pine trees a tall figure with a steeple-crowned straw hat, and standing on a rock shouted his war-cry of "Long live the power of God!" and firing rapidly in quick succession, killed three soldiers and struck the bugle from the bugler's mouth. It fell with a dull clang upon the stones, and the heroic fanatic, pierced by a dozen bullets, subsided slowly from his rock, his rifle rolling down the hill close to Mercado's feet.

The column of the troops, attacked on every side by enemies they could not see, slowly retreated with considerable loss, leaving on every side their dead and dying, and at length in great confusion returned to camp, just where they started from some hours ago.

All the time that the fight was taking place, Cruz Chaves, full of religious ardour or fanaticism, for ardour and fanaticism are terms which interchange on victory or defeat, was fortifying to the best of his ability the town which he imagined that he held against the world, for God.

His own house was a veritable fort, entrenched with lines of loopholes pierced for musketry.

In it there lived his brothers José and Manuel with all their families. Built of adobés of the hardest make, a tangle of barbed wire and a strong palisade encircled it. Between it and two other blockhouses, in one of which were kept some fifty prisoners taken in former fights, stood a pedestal of white-washed stone, a cross with linen streamers floating from its arms. The other blockhouse served as a store for arms and cartridges, and close behind it stood a little oratory which also was the study and the bedroom of Cruz Chaves, the self-appointed prophet and the priest of the community.

As he sat by the fire drinking his coffee and meditating on his plans, Bernardo entered, having ridden all the night to bring his news of the advance upon the place. Rising, he said, "It does not matter, for none can strive against the soldiers of the Lord. God will protect us, let us go and pray." Prayer without whisky probably was not much to Bernardo's taste, but silently he followed Cruz down a small winding stair which came out at the church. The porch was full of men, their rifles in their hands, their cartridge-belts all full, all dressed in deerskin or in velveteen. Their hats were felt or straw, high in the crown and heavy, and round them they wore the heavy sausage-shaped silver bands, known as toquillas, which all Mexicans affect.

Those who were seated on the steps arose respectfully as Cruz drew near. Tall and majestic looking, his wandering eyes and matted hair gave him the look with which convention has endued the prophet, and which is not uncommon in a lunatic asylum.

He walked across the tombstones which formed the flooring of the porch, his deerskin moccasins dulling his footsteps, and giving him an air of mystery as he seemed to glide without a sound.

Entering the aisle, his hat upon his head, he went up to the altar, and turning round towards the body of the church, waited until his followers came in and ranged themselves.

When all had entered, he took up his parable. "Brothers in Jesus Christ and in His Mother, prepare yourselves, confident in the great power of God, to fight the impious sons of Lucifer who are advancing to destroy us and impose their laws. They treat us all as beasts; they take away our saints, our money, and now our Government is sending soldiers here to kill us all. But we fight for God's kingdom, and we cannot die. If we fall wounded and appear as dead, we shall arise again, as did our Lord, on the third day; we shall all conquer by the great power of God."

He paused, and an Amen low and intense ran through the church. Outside, the women and the children looked through the porch as horses grazing on the Essex marshes gaze at a hay-barge floating down the tide. Then, taking from the pocket of his blouse some papers, he untied them, and, altering his tone, began to read his disposition for the fight. Then once again resuming a sacerdotal tone, and raising up one hand, he said, "Kneel down," and stood a moment motionless, fixing the people with a glance of steel.

All knelt except Bernardo, till Cruz looked towards him frowning, when he turned pale and fell upon his knees.

Lastly Cruz blessed the company in God's name and that of all the Trinity combined. In silence the fanatics left the church, and Cruz remained to draw up with his officers the plan of the attack which had forced back the troops.

The women had the task assigned of making loopholes, baking tortillas, preparing lint, and making rations of pinole[1] and tasajo[2] for the men.

At six o'clock all the men capable of bearing arms drew up before his house, where he examined all their rifles, and then their scapularies and the brass medals which they carried round their necks. The women and the girls went to the church to pass the night in prayer, leaving Cruz Chaves and his family alone. He, after having visited the prisoners, sat down before the fire in his own house, his wife and sisters sitting near, but without daring to address him as he sat.

At eight o'clock he rose and said, "Come, let us pray," and the whole family knelt silently before the battered image of a saint, whilst he poured forth a rhapsody of prayer and praise. This finished, he retired to his own room and shut the door, leaving the women silent and miserable, all gazing at the fire.

A silence that seemed preternatural pervaded everything; even the dogs, which in a frontier town in Mexico render the night harmonious, were all silent, and hearing not a sound, forgot to howl. Silent before the fire the women sat, the wife of Cruz, his sisters, Julia, and some girls, chewing the cud of bitterness and smothering down their grief.

Suddenly shots echoed through the hills, and a loud knocking nearly broke down the door. They opened it, and a man wrapped in a blanket, carrying his rifle in his hand, came in and asked for Cruz. Cruz came out of his room and took the stranger into the little oratory which served him for his study, and then heard that more troops were coming from Sonora, and bringing with them more than two hundred Indians, Pimas and Ópatas, men known through Mexico as famous rifle-shots.

Although he must have known his fate was sealed, taken as he was between two forces, each of which was three or four times larger than his own, yet he gave no sign, but, taking down his rifle, threw his blanket round his shoulders and glided silently out into the night. Passing the cemetery, he came to where his brothers José and Manuel with their followers guarded the road by which the troops were forced to march to the attack. He told them to be ready for an assault at break of day, and he himself remained with the reserve. Just as day broke the forces of the

---

1 *Pinole* is a sort of flour made of ground maize, sugar, and cinnamon. It is very
  sustaining, as the writer happens to know.
2 *Tasajo* is jerked beef; the Biltong of the Boers

Government advanced behind a cloud of skirmishers composed of Pimas and of Ópatas. In spite of all their cunning and experience, Cruz and the men whom he had posted in the church tower and on the house-tops shot them like rabbits as they ran from tree to tree. Men dropped like flies, and if a villager fell wounded into the hands of the fierce Indians his fate was instant death. In one of their attacks they came upon the miserable "Saint" José Carranza, and shot him instantly. At last a body of the troops, led by the Pima Indians, gained a point from whence they could look down upon the town. Although night fell leaving the town untaken, yet from that moment it was seen that it was but a mere affair of time.

Mercado, in the camp, seated before the fire, had time to meditate upon the glories of the day. The losses on both sides had been severe, one company returning with but seven men, others without an officer, and dozens of men lay groaning on the ground. Throughout the night the wounded crawled into the camp, leaving long trails of blood upon the stones. Others sat pale and hungry round the fires, their heads tied up in blood-stained bandages. But even those were happy in comparison with the poor wretches who had had to be abandoned in the night. Crushed, shivering with cold, and at the same time burned with thirst, they lay like pheasants wounded in a wood, despairing, feverish, and with their nerves strained to the utmost, waiting the advent of the sierra wolves.

Mercado, who had read of glorious war, was horrified. Was this the trade Napoleon plied? Where was the honour and the fame to come in fighting miserable villagers, who had committed nothing worse than folly, and had refused to pay their taxes to the Government, which only knew of them as taxables, having performed no single function of a government except the sending of its tax collectors at due intervals.

But if the troops were in a miserable plight, what was the situation of Tomochic, full with wounded men, without a doctor, provisions scarce, and crowded all together in the three fortified *jacáls* and in the church? At daybreak thirty wounded soldiers and five officers were sent off to Guerrero under an escort, and from the summit of the dominating plateau the quick-firing gun began to play upon the church and batter at the town.

With the first light the Pimas and the Ópatas set off into the woods, and soon the rocks rang with their shots and war-whoops, as, under the thick pines, they massacred the wounded and then took their scalps.

All day the civilising Hotchkiss gun played on the church and town, and from behind the rocks the Indian scouts fired upon any one who dared to leave his shelter and to expose himself. About the valley, cows and sheep, frightened at seeing progress for the first time so near, strayed up and down almost too scared to eat. The Indians now and then shot one for food, the troops for sport and for the pleasure of destruction, so dear to men who go to carry Christianity into a heathen land.[1]

All the next day passed pleasantly enough, the troops watching their field-piece play upon the town. The doctor of the brigade, who was an amateur artilleryman himself, directed all the shots, and when they saw a piece of wall fall in a cloud of dust, he and the general opened a brandy bottle and drank the health of Don Porfirio Diaz, the liberator of his country and the presiding genius on her path towards progress, for by this time a train of mules had brought provisions to the camp. Thus did the people of Tomochic at the same time serve not only as an object lesson to the soldiers of what they in their capacity as men might look for from their Government if they should choose to have ideas of their own, but gave good sport to the officers and to the solitary scientific man, who in the face of all discomfort was by his shooting demonstrating that his election and his calling both were sure.

It soon became apparent that the people of the town were too much decimated to make more attacks, but still they stubbornly clung to the church and houses, firing occasionally, and sallying out at nights to get provisions from their fields. Water they had inside the town in wells, and in the maize-fields near the houses their miserable cattle strayed, and chickens cackled in the yards of the deserted huts. The general gave orders to send out and burn the crops and huts, and soldiers carrying petroleum cans set them on fire, and then returned beneath the burden of the wretched loot afforded by the place. Chickens and pigs and clothes, some old guitars and saddles, pictures of saints, and goat-skins were the treasures that they bore. This military operation took all day, and as the sun set on the mountain tops the splendid amphitheatre was lighted up by the flames issuing from the burning huts, and the blue smoke hung like a dirty rag against the background of the snow. Just before nightfall the besieging force saw a man let himself down from a housetop in the village and run towards the camp. They fired at him, as did the people people of the place, but he escaped, and waving a white handkerchief, came safely to the lines. He proved to be one of the prisoners taken a month ago. Cruz Chaves had proposed to him to take up arms against the Government, and he had done so, hoping to escape.

[1] If I should chance to have readers, they may remember the conduct of the European troops in China three years ago.

He brought the news that almost half of the defenders had been killed, that the Medranos who had acted as lieutenants under Cruz were dead, that Manuel Chaves and many more were badly wounded, and were being cared for by the women of the place.

The church was occupied (he said) by twenty men, and there the bulk of the non-combatants had taken refuge, and that some twenty men were still unwounded in the house of Cruz. Provisions too were short, and water they could only get at night. Cruz Chaves still kept up his spirits and went about encouraging the rest, comforting the women with his prayers and putting heart into the men by his example and contempt of death. The dead had all been buried secretly by night, so that no one should know exactly how many had keen killed.

The prisoner spoke of the fanaticism which animated all the men, and said the women seemed dumbfounded, not knowing why or wherefore they were called upon to die.

The news fell on the troops as rain falls on a dried-up field, comforting them for all that they had undergone.

Grouped round their fires, they sat and watched the burning houses pierce a hole into the overwhelming blackness of the night, and no one gave more thought to the poor people of the place than does a huntsman when a hare screams in her agony as she is torn to pieces by the pack.

Once more at daybreak the quick-firing gun took up its civilising toil, but all it did was to drill holes in the *adobé*, the calibre being far too small to bring the houses down.

Fatigue parties of soldiers were sent down, out of the range of the defenders of the church, to finish up the work of yesterday. Towards mid-day they returned laden with booty and triumphant. Inside the town the miserable people saw their crops destroyed, their houses burned, and all they held most dear destroyed, but made no sign, firing a shot at intervals when any of the spoilers came too near.

The general and the officers were all indignant at their stubbornness. It seemed like insolence, in men without a uniform, without an officer who had gone through a military school, and ignorant of tactics as they were, to keep in check a force three times as numerous as their own, all duly uniformed, and officered by men who had commissions stamped and signed by the chief magistrate of Mexico.

So must have felt our cavalry in the Transvaal when, from behind the rocks, a band of men looking like chimpanzees and dressed in rusty black stepped out and took their arms, bidding them strip, and leaving them only an eyeglass here and there to veil their nakedness.

Shame, patriotism, duty, or what not had spurred the general to declare that the town must be taken by assault. He might as well have waited until thirst and hunger did their work; but not unnaturally a soldier thinks his first duty is to fight, and in this case a red flag fluttering at the top of a tall pine stung him to fury, for nothing moves a reasonable man so much as a new flag.

Tamper but with a flag, change blue for green, add or suppress a cap of liberty[1] or star, adjoin a crown or an heraldic monster of some kind, and your most wise sedate philosopher sees red and longs to slay his fellows, so that the majesty of his own bunting may be vindicated.

Certain it was that something had to be undertaken, for there were telegraphs but two days off, and presidents like to have news about their arms when troops are in the field and when the national standard, flutters in the breeze.

Besides, it was but reasonable to try and take the rocky plateau on which stood the town, for if once taken, those in the church could not annoy the soldiers with their fire. So on a splendid morning in October, bright and clear, the sun upon the mountain tops glistening like crystal and the last smoke ascending from the smouldering houses mingling with the air, the bugle sounded the advance.

Dirty and ragged, shivering with the cold, the soldiers hurried down the hill, then coming to the final climb, rushed forward, receiving as they went a fire which was converged upon them both from the church and from the house where Chaves and his men were still entrenched. As they advanced, a cross fire took them in the flank, for Chaves had detached a party to fire behind the rocks, having the instinct of a frontier fighter in his blood, which in such situations makes a man who knows the ground worth twenty soldiers whose fighting has been done in colleges and by arithmetic.

Still they pushed upwards, eager to come to closer quarters, and once more the shouts of "Death to Lucifer!" "Long live the Power of God!" rang in their ears. Wild figures rushed from tree to tree, screaming like Indians, as the Tomochitecos sullenly fell back upon their town.

---

1 Students have often remarked the similarity of the cap of liberty to a nightcap, but have not been able to give any reason for the cause. It may be that the cap of liberty is symbolic of the fact that man is only free in bed.

Mercado marched beside his company, a rifle in his hand, which he fired now and then mechanically. His throat was dry, a taste of powder in his mouth, and all his uniform was smeared with blood. How, he could not explain, but still he stumbled upwards, tripping on the stones and sheltering himself behind the trees.

Soon they came on the bodies of the foe, and the fire slackened, but in front a boyish voice cried shrilly, "Long live the Power of God!" and at each cry a man fell dead beside Mercado as he ran. A soldier then cried out, "I see him; fire all at once," and aimed, but as he spoke a bullet pierced his skull and his brains spattered out over Mercado's boots.

Several men fired, but still the voice cried, "Death to the cropped heads!" "Live the Power of God!" It was the last cry that was heard, for as they ran they came upon the body of a boy not more than fourteen years of age, ill fed and ragged, with a bullet through his head, his eyes wide open, and with his rifle clenched between his hands.

His face was livid and his open mouth showed his white teeth, which seemed to smile at death, whilst a red foam oozed slowly from his lips.

The plateau gained, the soldiers threw themselves behind some rocks to rest, whilst some went round and gathered up the arms under a desultory fire from the church tower and from the house of Cruz, the only buildings which had remained with any one alive. But still the obnoxious and unconstitutional red flag waved from the pine tree, and orders came at any risk to tear it down.

A sergeant and some soldiers rushed out, crouching down almost to the ground to gain the tree, when from a hole behind a rock a gun was thrust, and the sergeant, staggering, fell dead without a sound.

The soldiers rushing on, shortening their rifles and firing as they ran, swarmed round the hole like bees. A captain joined them and was crying, "Stop, the man is wounded," when a gigantic head, the long grey hair flecked here and there with blood, appeared above the ground; a rifle followed, and, a shot echoing, the captain fell dead in an instant on the man he wished to save.

Then with a shout the soldiers dashed into the hole, using their bayonets as if they had been spades.

Miguel, who from a little distance off had seen his captain fall, drew near, and looking down into the hole saw that the mass of bloody broken limbs, grey hair, and entrails had been Bernardo, and stood stupefied, thinking that Julia now was free, but that she still was shut up starving in the town.

The soldiers, worn out with fatigue, lay for the most part round a little stream upon their stomachs, lapping the water as it passed, like dogs, and just as greedily. A sergeant counted the rifles, solemnly arranging them in rows, and like a splash of blood was laid upon a rock the torn red flag which had at last been torn down from the pine.

The plateau taken, nothing but death remained for the fanatical inhabitants grouped in the church and in the house of Cruz. But as the greater part of them were women and young children, the state of desperation of the men is easy to imagine, but to describe it only one of themselves could have essayed the task.

The troops advancing, burned the other portions of the town, so that at last only the house of Cruz and the church with its tower were standing, and from them at intervals came desultory shots.

The Hotchkiss gun, brought up to but a hundred yards, fired now and then, but did but little damage beyond raising clouds of dust and keeping the inhabitants fast prisoners in the church.

But whilst the villagers endured the pangs of hunger and of thirst, the troops had been refreshed after their efforts in the cause of patriotism by the arrival of a sutler bringing a load of demijohns of the rough spirit called sotol.[1]

Having lost so many men, the general now determined to burn out the people in the church, which, by the fact of his having taken several stone-built houses near it, had become attackable without much risk to life.

His plan was that the soldiers should gather a quantity of faggots and dry stalks of maize, and under cover of the quick-firing gun rush from the stone-built houses to the church porch, where they would be too near for the men posted in the tower to do much damage to them. As the church had a timber roof, the plan looked good, as if it once took fire the refugees would be obliged either to stay and be smoked out like bees, or trying to escape, be shot to the last man as soon as they came out.

A little river ran between the encampment and the church. This, as the soldiers passed, exposed them for a moment to a direct fire from the church, but having passed it they could shelter behind rocks. Thus making a diversion, their comrades rushing from the houses could set the church on fire. Excited by the spirit they had drunk,[1] the soldiers hurried on across the river, losing four or five men in the few seconds that it took to cross.

1 It is made from aloes, and is really less lethal than many kinds of whisky.

Once safe amongst the rocks, they made their way to the deserted houses, and there prepared their wood, petroleum, and faggots, then sallying out piled them in the church porch, the Hotchkiss gun and the picked party of the Pimas and the Ópatas fired on and killed all those who dared to show themselves upon the roof or tried to fire from any of the windows of the church.

Soon flames burst from the porch and a dense pall of smoke enveloped everything. But from the roof shouts of "Long live the Power of God!" "Long live the Blessed Virgin!" still were heard, and from the door three or four desperate men, their hair ablaze and firing as they ran, leaped out and burst a path to safety through the soldiers to the fields of maize. More would have followed, but the church door falling from out its hinges interposed a barrier of flame. As the church burned the troops advanced under the cover of the smoke and took position to attack the house in which Cruz Chaves and his men still sullenly held out. All stood and watched the church burn, horrified, knowing that it was full of women and of children who would all perish with the men. So thick became the smoke that nothing could be seen, only long lines of sparks shot out like fireflies in the dark.

Then for a moment came a shift of wind, and from their camp the soldiers saw a woman climb to the topmost of the burning tower and heard her shriek, "Long live the Power of God!" and jump down into the body of the blazing church. Next came a sound as of a powder factory blowing up, as the roof fell and after it the tower.

Then silence, and long columns of thick smoke, jewelled with sparks, shot up into the sky.

Nothing was left of what had been the little mountain town except the house of Cruz with its three tiers of loopholes and its red flag floating defiantly above the roof. Long tongues of fire still shot up from the church, and now and then beams fell with a loud crash which echoed through the valley, and now and then a dropping shot came from the still untaken house where Cruz held out, determined to give up his life and those of all his people to what he thought the greater glory of the Lord. The house was built so solidly that the quick-firing gun had no effect upon it. It was protected from a rush by barricades,

1 "La tropa estaba muy excitada por el sotol."

and its position was stronger far than had been that of the demolished church, as it commanded all the roads which led to it, standing upon a rocky eminence without a rock or tree for yards on every side.

The general judged that it would cost too dear to take it by assault, and with a soldier's eye he saw that the position had, by its very strength, defects which made its capture but a work of time.

Bare and exposed as the house stood, now that the others had been burned, it was impossible for those inside to get at water but by cover of the night.

So, certain of his prey, the general gave orders to his men to retire out of range, and, having posted sentinels, sat down patiently to wait. But as a measure of precaution, and being probably a man of scientific mind, he had the bodies of the dead defenders of the town dragged, by night, underneath the walls of the beleaguered house, hoping thereby to strike despair and terror or perchance to spread a plague amongst the people all closely packed together and without provisions in the place. Next day one of the prisoners Cruz had taken got away and crawled into the camp, but so reduced by hunger that it was several hours before he could give any information of what was passing in the doomed house upon the rocks. A little later, rising from a bush like an Apache Indian, right in the middle of the space, appeared a woman, who tottered towards the tents. She proved to be of about eighty years of age, bent, grey, and starving, and said that Cruz had let her go, and she had lain all night hidden behind the bush, fearing to get into the line of fire, as bullets passed above her head at intervals.

The general, either from a wish to spare his men or being touched when he thought of the state of things inside the house, where dead and dying, live men and children, all without food or medicine were huddled close, without a hope but of releasing death, prevailed upon the crone to go back with a message to the chief.

After a thousand vacillations she consented, and hobbled off carrying a letter from the general to Cruz. It called on him for unconditional surrender of the place on pain of being taken by assault and executed with all the other male defenders of the town.

The women and children he gave leave to come out to the camp, and promised them a pardon and security. In half an hour the old woman hobbled back, the soldiers crowding to look at her as if she was some strange sort of wild beast. Cruz had refused the terms, and sent to say that he and all the men preferred to die, and that he doubted if the women and children would be safe. Once more the messenger went back to assure him of the general's good faith. Then Cruz decided to let out the women and children, all except his own and several others who had elected to stay and perish with their relations and their friends.

The general was dumbfounded, being really touched or fearing what the newspapers would say. However, nothing remained to him but to go on to the end.

Then from the door of the doomed house issued a train of spectres dressed in rags, their faces livid and their legs so weak that they could scarcely totter through the stones. Torn petticoats and ragged shawls covered their misery; their eyes were downcast, and a low murmuring of sobs and groans came from their thirst-burned mouths.

The soldiers, who had crowded up to gaze, were stupefied: some crossed themselves, and others muttered, turning away to hide their tears. They opened out respectfully and made a way for the appalling troop of famine-stricken wretches silently to pass.

An old bowed, white-haired man came first, leaning upon the shoulder of a girl, thin and discoloured and with her head bound up in dirty bandages through which appeared a dark and bloody stain. After them came a crone whose face was bloody with an unbandaged wound upon her head. One woman walked erect, carrying a sobbing child, reduced by hunger, but still unsubdued and stoical.

A group of girls whose faces had been handsome before that famine set its mark upon them, wrapped up in gaily coloured tattered shawls and Indian blankets with large black and scarlet checks, staggered along holding each other's hands.

Then came a boy, about six years of age, with the blood dripping from his leg, who limped and sobbed a little as he walked. Next came the mass of misery, a wave of human jetsam which had almost lost humanity. Bent bodies, staring great black eyes, long ragged locks of hair, and dirty flesh showing blue and livid through their rags, they looked like faces in a nightmare; and last of all hobbled the crone who had been ambassadress, babbling and talking to herself, and stopping now and then to stoop and pick a flower or pluck some grass to nibble like a beast.

Miguel Mercado looked intently at the miserable band to see if Julia was amongst them, but, as he could not see her, it appeared that she was one of those who had remained to die with the last faithful few within the town. His task was made the harder as nearly all the women covered up their faces with rags or dirty handkerchiefs, not wishing to be seen in all their misery.

But little now remained to make the triumph of the law complete. From the last house no shots were fired, and not a sign of life appeared but the obnoxious flag still floating in the breeze. The cattle strayed through the deserted maize-fields, the chickens roosted in the trees, and pigs went in and out the houses and devoured the flesh of those who but a day or two ago had been their masters and now lay rotting in the sun. The general saw that the besieged must try to sally out by night to get provisions and draw water from the stream, so, having set his guards round about the watering places and in the fields, he sullenly retired into his tent. The moon rose bright and cold, for at that season of the year and at that altitude the nights were piercing, and the soldiers, wrapped in their greatcoats with blankets over all, were almost freezing at their posts.

All night at intervals the bugles sounded, echoing from post to post, carrying despair into the hearts of the besieged, or perhaps filling them with hope; for those who die for an idea, however foolish, commonly die cheerfully, thus taking their revenge upon the world. At midnight, after the moon had set and a profound and pitchy darkness reigned, the sentinels descried some phantom forms approach the river's edge. They fired at once, and the echoes of the hills indefinitely multiplied the sound, so that it seemed a hidden battle in the obscurity and terror of the night. The Pima Indians stood to arms at once, and gliding through the rocks and shrubs like snakes, found nothing at the river but some jars of water which the heroic martyrs of the "Great Power of God" had filled and hoped to have been able to take back into their fort. Their villainy having been checked, nothing of further note occurred that night, except that the women and the children who had been taken prisoners disturbed the soldiers' rest a little with their untimely lamentations and their coughs. Next day a band of soldiers crawling through the rocks were able to approach the barn where Cruz had all his prisoners, without being seen and fired upon, for the beleaguered Tomochitecos gave no sign of life.

Getting as far as possible beneath the loop-holes of the fort, they broke a way into the barn and led the prisoners out and back into the camp. They found that two of them had died of thirst. The rest included a lieutenant and some thirty men, all much reduced by hunger and by cold. During the whole time occupied in getting out the prisoners the fort had never fired a shot. But though they gave no sign of their activity, every one knew that they were ready and determined, and that to rush the place might cost the lives of many soldiers; and besides, a feeling of compassion, mixed with a real admiration of their bravery, had touched the general. All day he walked about before his quarters, not speaking, except now and then to ask the doctor how long he thought the besieged could hold out without water, and then towards evening sent another messenger to Cruz.

Amongst the Pima Indians was an old chief called Chabolé. One of the old time Indian hunters, he had traversed all the Sierra Madre of Chihuáhuá and Sonora more than a hundred times. In better days he had known Chaves well, and had with him taken up mules to sell upon the frontiers of the United States.

Calling him up, the general asked him, "Chabolé, would you dare take a message to Cruz Chaves in his house?" "Yes, general," he answered; "God bless me, why not?"

Then taking up a bottle of sotol, he left his rifle leaning against a wall and quietly stepped down into the path towards the stronghold which hitherto had been the road to certain death.

The soldiers watched him near the strong stockade, expecting at each instant to hear a shot and see him fall; but nothing happened, the door was opened, and he quietly disappeared into the house. In twenty minutes he returned unharmed, whistling an *habanera* softly as he walked. He came up to the general, saluted, and laconically said, "They will hold out till God reclaims their souls."

It seemed that on arriving at the palisade the men inside had shouted, "What is it that you want? Long live the Power of God!" He, without answering them, had called out, "Cruz, Cruz, do you hear? I am come to give you an embrace, a drink, and to ask you to surrender." "Come in," they cried. He went into the gate and found himself in darkness, and heard a voice say, "Shake hands, and let me have the drink." They shook hands in the dark, and Cruz, taking the bottle, drank a little, and then taking his old friend by the shoulders pushed him gently out, saying, "Go and tell them that we do not surrender but to God."

The evening set in with an icy wind, and about sunset one of the rescued prisoners was found to have fired upon the troops when in the power of Cruz. Without delay they took him to a fire and shot him, and his body then was cast into a bonfire which the general had been obliged to light to burn the slain, as the whole camp was rendered pestilential by the stench which was exhaled by the dead rotting bodies torn to pieces by the swine.

Justice thus done and duty vindicated, for it is known that a live traitor smells at least as bad as any traitor dead, the troops disposed themselves to pass the night with the best grace they could, as at the break of day the general had determined that the place was to be taken by assault. The odour of the burning bodies tainted the air; no sound was heard, but now and then beams of the smouldering church and bits of wall fell suddenly, and a thin penetrating rain wetted the sentinels and made them miserable as they passed slowly to and fro. It seemed as if in the drear sadness of the night that man had challenged his Creator and had wished to show Him that he too could make a hell.

At daybreak all the men assembled round great fires, stamping their feet and drying their wet clothes. At ten o'clock the soldiers, carrying faggots and dry straw, advanced to the attack. Once more the Hotchkiss gun, brought to short range, belched forth its bullets, and with a cheer the soldiers rushed the palisades.

For the last time the cry "Long live the Power of God!" came from the doomed Tomochitecos, and then three soldiers climbing on the roof broke through a hole with bayonets, and as an officer tore down the flag, they flung the lighted faggots and the straw into the body of the house. The men inside fired up the chimney once or twice, and then flames bursting from the windows, drove the soldiers to the ground. Their patriotic task was over, the majesty of law avenged, and the triumphant bugle, like the morning cock, crowed cheerfully over the scene of ruin and of death.

An officer on horseback galloped up hastily with orders from the general to save the women and to bring out the suffocating men and shoot them instantly.

Soldiers with litters, which might as well have been called biers, penetrated with difficulty into the horror of the burning house.

They came out carrying bundles of rags and human flesh, some living and some dead, out of what Heriberto Frias calls "that ambient of hell." Most of the living died as soon as they came out and breathed fresh air; others, half-dying, looked at their conquerors with glassy eyes, and some who just could stand menaced the soldiers with their scorched and wounded arms, and mumbled out their war-cry, setting out their faith in the fallacious Power of God, with their lips blistered and blackened by the flames.

All were as thin as skeletons, and on their bones hung bloody, powder-darkened rags.

Not one of them could walk more than a step or two, for, though some few had passed the horrors of the siege without a wound, hunger and thirst had brought them almost to death's door. The bodies which the soldiers brought out of the burning house were thrown at once into a bonfire, which blazed and spluttered and sent out greasy sparks. The seven survivors who were destined to be shot were laid face upwards in a doorway which the fire had spared. Amongst them was a woman, whose blackened and scorched hands still held a rifle bent and twisted with the heat.

Her breast was bare, and over it an empty bandolier was strapped. She was the wife of one of Cruz's brothers, and as they laid her down she murmured, "Long live the Power of God!" and died, her eyes remaining open and her jaw falling almost on her breast.

Beside her was laid Cruz, with an arm bound up in a blue bandage dripping blood, his right leg shattered by a rifle-ball.

Bareheaded as he lay, reduced by want and watching, his masses of black hair and jetty beard, with his pale face and air of resignation, made him a model from which a painter might have taken Christ.

The general, plagued again with goads of conscience or that humanity which often is the soldier's bane, shut himself in his tent and sent the doctor to represent him at the final scene.

When all was ready, the dying men were taken out into an open space.

Cruz asked to be placed next his brother, which was done.

One who could hardly speak begged Cruz to give him a scapulary which he wore about his neck, which all thought had magic powder in it which could restore a man to life. "Give it to him," said Cruz, and the man held it to his lips. Then a young officer with the firing-party drew up his men.

"Kneel," he called out in trembling tones; but none could do so except Cruz.

Advancing till their rifles about touched the dying men, the soldiers fired, and all fell dead but one, Cruz falling like a stone, shot through the heart, his great black eyes remaining open wide and fixed, as if he looked into eternity.

The last man, wounded horribly, was writhing on the ground when he received another bullet, struggled to his knees, and shouted, "Long live the Power of God!" and fell, a bundle of black, blood-stained rags, upon the ground.

Of the one hundred men of Tomochic fit to bear arms none had escaped, and of a thousand soldiers only four hundred now remained.

About a hundred women and some children had been spared, and the great cause of progress and humanity had gained a step. The troops remained a night encamped on what had been the plaza of the town, to rest and celebrate their victory.

Early next morning they set out, and looking back saw nothing standing of the doomed town but a few huts and the still smoking ruins of the church.

The Sierra Madre stood out blue and flecked with snow; the pine woods formed a black and threatening mass; and in the foreground, under a pile of wood, the bodies smouldered, whilst the swine, grunting in the ashes, tore the half-burned flesh of their dead owners, and a thick, nauseating smoke ascended up on high.

Progress

San José

The house stood on a little hill, on one side looking out upon a plain on which fed sheep, cattle, and mares, and flocks innumerable. Upon the other side, a wood of thorny trees, talas and ñandubays, seemed to wash up to it as waves wash on a rock. Nothing but cattle tracks led through the wood, and here and there a little muddy stream ran through it, fringed with pampas-grass. Parrots and parroquets flew shrieking in the branches of the trees, and built their long and hanging nests from a dead bough. Humming-birds fluttered round the flowers, hovering like butterflies as they sucked out the honey from their hearts. Deeper in the recesses of the thickets, carpinchos had their lairs, and now and then a band of half-wild horses fed in the open glades. A hum of insects filled the air, and tortoises like walking stones trailed themselves on the sandy soil, and fell, as it appeared, rather than walked into the stream. The river ran, a yellow flood, between the banks of trees. Snags now and then protruded from its depth, and camelotes[1] brought down by the floods were wreathed about them like gigantic eels. Herons and pink flamingoes sat and fished contemplatively, and on the gaunt dead branches of the willows vultures sat and nodded in the sun. An air of mystery and of danger brooded on the place, especially upon the "pass," to which tracks of unshod horses led, making one wonder who the riders were who passed so frequently.

On either side the "pass" the water deepened suddenly, and at the landing on the farther side the trail led through high banks on which tall feathery tacuaras grew. The sort of place it was that made a man take his reins short on coming from the shelter of the trees into the open sandy flat before the crossing, and feel for his revolver, whilst looking carefully to see if birds sat still and did not seem alarmed.

Upon the farther side, and gleaming whitely here and there through the dark trees, ran sandhills, giving an air as of the desert where the luxuriant vegetation ended and the sand began.

1 The camelote is a very thick-growing water-lily, which sometimes about chokes small streams. It no doubt has a scientific name which would cut it out of the writer's recollection if he looked it out and used it.

White and flat topped, battlemented, and with two towers to flank it, stood the house, built round a courtyard in which was set a well. Its massive gates, on either side of which was caged a jaguar, shut it off from the world. On the tiled floors of courtyard and of galleries the heavy spurs the gauchos wore just dangling off their heels clanked with a noise of fetters as men walked or lounged about the store, where the proprietor, master of the lives and destiny of a whole province, did not think any shame to sell his goods.

In South America, as in the East (and Scotland), trade does not vilify but on the contrary raises its votary, and people do not make distinctions between the man who sells a thousand pounds of coal and the small dealer who sells tea, gin, sardines, and the other products with which commerce blesses all the world. Outside the gates some straw-thatched houses held the general's guard and all their families. Their horses grazed upon the plain, and they, except when now and then they had to cut a throat by the command of the Supreme, were quietly pugnacious; that is to say, they fought among themselves, first blood for a quart of wine, to show their valour, or occasionally about their women, but they left the peaceful population to themselves, with the exception of now and then stealing a horse or two or carrying off a girl.

Their general ruled them with a rod of iron tempered with personal suavity, treating them half as children, half as savages, and they responded after the fashion of their kind, taking all leniency for weakness, and thinking power was given to a man by some wise providence which was beyond their ken.

The inside of the house was bare, with here and there some pieces of old Spanish furniture, great massive chairs and straight-backed sofas, seated with leather and studded with brass nails. A picture of the owner of the house, drawn by some tenth-rate painter, stared down from the wall. In it the subject sat upon his horse, which appeared stuffed with sawdust, dressed in a gorgeous uniform, and pointing with a Napoleonic air over a country in which grew flowers unknown in South America, springing up at the charger's feet and seeming in some places to sprout out from his legs, after the fashion of the blossoms of a Judas tree.

Wooden and oily as was the painting in its gaudy frame, it yet convinced one at first sight that it must be a likeness of the sitter; crude and horrible, but haunting like a picture in a dream. On a thin silver plate upon the frame the legend ran, "General Don Justo José de Urquiza, Napoleon del Sur."

Spanish-America has been so fertile in Napoleons (of the West and South), that no one was astonished at the title, but looked upon it as an aspiration towards perfection in the military art.

Set here and there on brackets and on French tables which, with chairs gilt and rickety, and looking as if they had been bought at the selling-up of a ruined courtesan of the Rue Notre Dame de Lorette, stood statuettes of General Bonaparte upon a camel at the Pyramids, of the First Consul, and of Napoleon at Austerlitz — in fact, of the whole gamut of the life of him who seems to be an ignis-fatuus to every general of the south. The gem of the whole palace (as it was called by the devout) was the great ballroom cased in looking-glass. The walls were panelled in enormous frames of looking-glass; the ceiling, broken up into squares in semi-Moorish style, was thickly coated here and there with gold. The chandelier, in which gilt strove with crystal for the mastery in vulgarity, was large enough for a cathedral, and the table-tops were glass. This marvel of artistic beauty, reminding one of those famed mansions built decidedly of hands in the Redyk at Antwerp, the general had built to please his daughter Manolita or Rosita, for I forget her name.

Such was the palace. Outside a Moorish-Spanish-looking house; inside a mixture of the house of a conquistador and a French brothel, and serving in itself as an apt illustration of the culture of the country under the general's rule.

All Entre Rios knew the place.

Throughout that grassy, undulating Mesopotamia, shading off into forests of hard-wooded, prickly trees where it confines with Corrientes, it was a word of fear.

Did not Don Justo de Urquiza live there, the gaucho general who at Pabon defeated Rosas, putting down Centralism, and at the same time raising up himself, after the fashion of all liberators since first their trade began? From his front door, or, to be accurate, from the *palenque*[1] where the horses all were tied, down to the town of Concepcion del Uruguay, for twenty miles ran a continuous avenue of cabbage-like ombús. Ostriches fed amongst the sheep, and stalked as tame as barn-door fowls close to his house, and, more surprising, fed in safety from the Ibicuy up to the Yucuri, no man disturbing them, although their feathers fetched at least three dollars for the pound. Deer were as common as were calves throughout the land. They scarcely raised their heads as Christians sailed

1 The *palenque* was a post, usually about six feet high, to tie horses to. It stood in front of every house.

across the plains upon their horses, or if they did, rose lazily, stamped once or twice, and snorting struck into a shambling trot which tempted the unwary gringo[1] to pursue them, an undertaking as unprofitable as that of chasing a coyoté in the sage-bush prairies of the north.

Carpinchos in the rivers were as tame as ducks. They lay and sunned themselves like swine, and waddling awkwardly plunged into the stream, wallowing like hippopotami with their broad backs awash. Biscachas on their mounds were as self-confident as the traditional British citizen in the seclusion of his house, or more so; for they feared no tax-collector, under the rule of peace to all the brute creation which Don Justo had decreed. Nothing was shy but the wild horses in the woods and deltas of the rivers, where they passed their lives as free as albatrosses.

Nothing was chased, shot, caught with bolas, snared, or annoyed, by order of the general; and all the gauchos knew his punishments. The first offence, a fine; the next, to be staked out between four posts with fresh hide ropes which the hot sun contracted; the third, deprived of horses, and obliged to march amongst the infantry; the fourth and last, death by the knife, for cartridges were dear, and knives and cutting throats a subject for a jest amongst a population to whom the sight of blood was constant from its youth.

For leagues on every side of San José horses and cattle had no other brand than that known as "La Marca Flor,"[2] the astronomic sign with which Don Justo marked his beasts. His flocks and herds stretched over plains and wandered through the woods, no man, however willing, ever daring to kill one; for spies were everywhere, and cover up the trail, no matter how he would, walking his horse for miles through streams, choosing the stoniest ground, or crossing and recrossing his own tracks till they became like rails at Clapham Junction, still there was some one cunning as himself to trace him to his rancho and say, as did the prophet in the Scriptures, "Thou art the thief."

The wielder of such arbitrary power was of a mean appearance, as have been other great ones of the earth. Short, stout, and grey he was, with bushy whiskers, his diaphragm imprisoned, as a general rule, in uniform, and bulging on his belt. He took the air in an old Spanish carriage hung on leather springs, which, swinging high and pitching like

---

1 "Gringo" equals foreigner. It was applied even to Englishmen.
2 It was in this wise ❧ After the general's death the writer has ridden many horses of
   the brand, though during his life it would have been a dangerous experiment to try.

a fishing-boat as the rough team of six half-broken horses, driven with long hide reins and guided by a boy who had a lasso fastened to his girth and hitched on to the hook upon the pole, jolted across the plains. Behind this equipage followed a guard composed of gauchos wilder than the horses that they rode, long haired, and with their naked feet stuffed into boots made from the skin stripped from the hind-leg of a horse. Their toes protruding grasped the stirrups like a vice, and from their heels dangled and jingled huge and rusty spurs, which clattered on the ground like fetters when they walked. Their arms were carbines, which for convenience they never cleaned, but bore them rusty, as befits a man not born to be the slave of anything. They loaded them up to the muzzle with anything that came to hand, and seldom fired them but on holy days, and then with much precaution and no little danger to themselves, and after shutting carefully both eyes. Their sabres usually they turned to daggers, or, if they did not, stuffed them in below the girth; for their chief weapons of offence were bolas, which they slung to a hair's-breadth, after the fashion of the Benjamites, and never missed their aim.

Most of their horses were half wild, and more than half, unbitted; but that did not disturb their riders, who rode them with their long hide reins buttoned into a thong tied round their jaw, and with a halter always in their hands, in case they suddenly stepped in a tuco-tuco[1], or crossed their legs and fell.

As the old coach rattled along the rutty track, crossing the muddy streams and bounding over holes, the escort galloped after it, as a shoal of porpoises accompanies a ship, crossing and wheeling round from side to side, throwing their hats upon the ground, and leaning down to pick them up again, all at full speed, and as if each one of them had half-a-dozen necks. They rolled their cigarettes and struck a light from flint and steel, all at a gallop, and on horses which, if you touched them accidentally, were almost sure to buck. The riders' hair and ponchos fluttered in the wind, and now and then they swung their whips, which hung from straps upon their wrists, in circles in the air. Occasionally they yelled, out of the joy of life, and galloping cursed their horses and their mothers if they stumbled on the ruts, treating them to the choicest epithets they knew, "as if they had been Christians," and winding up their litany of oaths upon a certain woman of ill-fame, who, after having borne a bastard to the Fiend, incontinently burst.

1 The "tuco-tuco" is a burrowing animal, and has, no doubt, his scientific name and address.

As the wild cavalcade swept past the solitary houses surrounded by their peach groves, and each with their ombú growing beside the well, such of the inhabitants as were about would gaze towards it and gravely murmuring, "There passes the Supreme," retire indoors, and pray that the Supreme would pass them by without a visit, which by experience they all knew meant expense.

He, wrapped in dignity, with all the windows of the coach drawn up to keep out dust, sat smoking stolidly, holding a cigarette between his fingers coloured bright orange at the tips with juice. If a mishap occurred, as it did now and then, in crossing rivers or the like, the general would emerge, and sitting in the shade of his own carriage, give orders to his myrmidons to light a fire. This they accomplished by collecting bones, dry grass, and thistle stalks; and then producing from the recesses of the coach a kettle, the general would send for water, heat it, and solemnly drink maté till the repairs were done. Before him, with the kettle in his hand, would stand a soldier, usually a black, who poured the water, settled the yerba in the ground, and saw that all was right by sucking up a little of the brew through the *bombilla* before he passed the beverage to his chief. He, seated on a bullock's skull or on a stone, talked and chaffed pleasantly, after the fashion of an Eastern potentate, with all his subjects, between whom and himself there was slight difference but the power of death, which power he wielded easily, and almost with an air of jocularity, which well became the place.

Sometimes, instead of driving in his coach, the general would set out with his rustic cavalry upon an ostrich hunt. High and disposedly he sat his horse, a black for choice, and hung with silver trappings, with its tail squared off above the fetlocks and its mane hogged half-way down, and cut in castles after the fashion of a box hedge in an Elizabethan garden, but leaving a long lock. His toes just touching his heavy stirrups with a crown beneath the feet, his legs encased in patent leather boots worked into patterns in the front with gaudy-coloured silk, his silver-mounted whip dangling from his right wrist, and in the hollow of the left hand his heavy silver reins, he looked the gaucho leader that he was, although he never had attained the arts of horsemanship of his great rival Rosas, who, it it said, could jump on a wild horse without a saddle or a bit and conquer him. But as he was, he looked the part, and every portion of the complicated gear the gaucho wears was in its place. His silver headstall with the throat-latch loose upon the throat, the bit with silver eagle swinging on a hinge beneath the lower jaw, the massive silver cups on either side the mouth, all glittered in the sun. His flat hide rope with which to stake his horse at night was plaited in an ingenious pattern round the neck, and on it hung his hobbles, made of raw hide and furnished with two buttons (for buckles were unknown upon those plains) and a thick silver ring.

His saddle, with its various saddle-cloths and its two pieces — one of hide and one of leather — placed between them and the tree, was broad and heavy, and at each end was mounted with thick plate. The girth, six inches broad, of whitest hide, had his own name and brand ("La Marca Flor") stitched into it with a hide-strip cut fine as packing-thread. Above the tree he had a goat's-hair cloth from Tucumán coloured dark blue, and upon that a piece of leather of the river-hog, edged with charol[1] kept in place by a white surcingle of half-tanned hide. His spurs, whose rowels you could scarcely span, dangled below his heels, and silver chains, which met above his instep in a lion's head, maintained them in their place. The culminating glory of the man and horse was in the breastplate, which was of silver scales, and in the middle of it shone an ounce of gold struck in Bolivia. His knife and sheath were silver beautifully worked, and on his saddle, just behind his thigh, on the off side, his lazo, plaited and carefully coiled, hung ready to his hand. His ostrich bolas, which he carried round his waist, were covered with a lizard's skin, and over his left arm he carried a fine poncho of vicuña wool, which fluttered as he rode.

Arrived at where the hunt was to begin (although it might have started at his house), the riders all spread out to form a fan, and cantering slowly forward, soon found in front of them a band of ostriches.

The general gave the word, and in an instant, without the shogging of the legs and wagging of the elbows which one associates with putting a horse into a gallop suddenly in hunting-fields at home, the horsemen all had sprung into full speed. With shouts, and with their greyhounds bounding in front of them, the outmost edges of the fan, which at the start had been a good half-mile apart, contracted, enclosing in a wedge the frightened birds. The bolas whistled through the air, the ranks were broken, and each man attached himself to a particular group of ostriches. Skimming across the high brown grass, their wings extended wide

---

1 *Charol* is patent leather, but it would not sound right to the writer to use the English word in describing a gaucho saddle. "Darse charol" is used in South America to express "putting on side."

to catch the wind, they fled. If they could get out clear and turn down wind, they generally escaped, for horses could not catch them but against the wind.

But the pursuers strained every nerve to cut them off, and now and then one fell, his legs entangled in the balls. If the man who had thrown had time, in passing he dismounted, and with a slash cut off the head; if not, he left the ostrich struggling on the ground, certain of being able to come back upon his trail and pick it up again. If by some accident he missed his mark, as he scoured past he stooped and picked the bolas from the ground, or, if he did not see them, threw down his hat or handkerchief to mark the place; then quickly he unfastened a spare pair from round his waist, or took them from beneath the sheepskin which he wore upon his saddle, and galloped onward, shouting, his hat blown back and kept in place below his chin by a silk cord, forming an aureole about his head. The general, after a perfunctory cast or two, usually sat upon his horse like an equestrian statue and surveyed the chase. On every side groups of wild horsemen and of frightened birds were disappearing on the low horizon of the plain. Nearer, some had dismounted, and after killing, skinned the ostriches, throwing their pelts like huge white fleeces on the ground. The greyhounds gorged themselves with flesh, and slowly men appeared upon the waves of the prairie, their horses bathed in sweat, some lame, but all with several ostrich skins upon their saddles, from which the blood dripped slowly on to the horses' flanks.

They gathered round the general, who sat smoking on his horse, unloosed their girths for a few minutes, and then striking into a canter which looked like clockwork, galloped the league or two of "camp" to San José.

There they received some bottles of Brazilian rum, and after having roasted several sheep or an ox in the hide, feasted like cannibals, all sitting round the fire. When night fell, women appeared mysteriously, as their first mother did in Eden, and, some one playing a guitar, the strings of which were mended up with strips of hide, they danced the "Gato," the "Cielito," and the "Pericon," whilst others sang wailing *jarábes* in the high falsetto voice which their progenitors had brought from Spain after inheriting it from Africa. Their dances were all slow, and danced almost without lifting their feet above the ground, and had much waving of their handkerchiefs, except a valse, which they danced nearly all the time unmoved, and with a rapt expression on their faces as if they were accomplishing an act of faith or a religious rite. The ball took place in a long shed called locally *galpon*, and was illuminated by bowls of mutton fat in which wicks floated, giving out a little light and a strong smell of grease.

The women sat all in a row waiting, as Scripture says, for any man to hire them. The men came in and out from beside the fire when they were tired of eating, danced solemnly, and then, treating their partners to a drink of gin, which they both drank out of the bottle's mouth, either resumed their places by the fire and fell to drinking maté or to discussing horses' brands, or stood in groups about the shed, addressing compliments to the dancers upon their prowess and their charms. Outside, the stillness of the plain was broken but by the bleating of the folded sheep or the shrill neigh of stallions fighting for their mares.

In the thick belt of trees which fringed the river for a league on either side, the fire-flies flitted, looking like sparks thrown off by the interior fire of nature, against the dark, metallic-looking leaves.

As night wore on, the blazing bones and wood gradually smouldered down into a glowing cake, throwing a bluish light upon the sleeping figures by the fire. Slowly all noises ceased, except the munching of the horses tied to their stake-ropes, then they too stood still hanging their heads and resting their hind legs alternately. The southern stars shone out, milder and with a greater luminosity than the sharp diamonds of the north, and in the moonlight the white, flat-topped house with towers and battlements stood out so sharply that it seemed made of cardboard and had an air of Eastern mystery. Towards dawn a thick white mist crept upwards from the river, and the dew falling lay like frost upon the sleepers, making them turn uneasily and draw instinctively their ponchos and their rugs over their heads, while horses shivered at their stake-ropes, and hunching up their backs, stood sulkily, with their heads bending to the ground like chickens in the snow.

So did life pass in San José, the general at home living more or less like an Eastern pasha, only with fewer wives, but just as great a power over the lives and property of those around, and on the rare occasions when he was called by business or by politics to Buenos Ayres being regarded as a sort of legendary hero whom boys were taught to reverence at school for his past services, or as a sort of pterodactyl come to trouble smaller animals. But as it often happens that a tyrant in the worst moments of his tyranny is safe through fear, so does it often come about that when he has repented him of bloodshed and lives a quiet life endeavouring to do as much good as he can, that politicians under the guise of patriotism, assassinate him to advance themselves, under the pretext of the welfare of mankind.

So it fell out in San José and with Don Justo, then grown old and fat, kindly but still tyrannical in a paternal way, as befits one who in his youth has been a man of blood.

The gauchos liked him, for he had been their leader, and his rule had not been bloody in comparison with many of the liberators and the patriots who abounded in the land. He might have gone down to his grave in peace, and been remembered as a kindly man according to his lights, had he not had a son.

In this respect he and the prophet Eli were alike. Not that the people of the province cared much about Cesario's doings with the ladies, but they objected, the virus of commercialism having befouled their blood, to his political economy. That is to say, he made himself unpopular by his exactions, and the opposition politicians used his sins to stir up animosity against the general, who probably, after the fashion of most rulers, thought himself beloved when, but at most, his subjects tolerated him.

One Lopez Jordan, a man who had seen service on the frontier, drew to himself some followers, and went about plundering and killing cattle, waving the national flag, and talking loudly of the rights of man. This of course means he thought his rights were not sufficient for his wants, and poor mankind as usual was the stalking-horse.

Most probably Urquiza, had he thought the matter serious enough, would have sent out and caught the leader of the bands and had his throat cut, or sewing him up in a green hide, have left him in the sun to perish miserably. But he, secure in his long years of quiet rule, let the thing go till Jordan had become a formidable foe. Then he prepared to gather men to take the field, but would not listen to the warnings which he received from time to time that he himself was in great danger of assassination, and that his guards were bribed. It is not probable the general had ever heard of Nemesis, except as one of the gods the heathen worshipped before we were baptized. But, be that as it may, the general was chiefly occupied in breeding fine-woolled sheep, crossing his cows with short-horn bulls, and in endeavouring to breed that *opus majus* of the gaucho breeder — a well-marked "Tuviano" horse, who should have all the colours — black, brown, and white — in equal blotches fairly disposed upon his back, and in listening to his life.

Seated one evening in his plate-glass ballroom, quite unattended but by a negro boy or two, and taking maté with his daughter, he heard a sound of spurs upon the courtyard tiles. A dog or two barked noisily, and the door handle of the monstrous ballroom turned. He called, received no answer, went to the door himself, opened it, and looking out, beheld the passage full of men. He spoke to them, asking the reason of their presence, and then one Luna, a tall, one-eyed negro, stepping forward said, as he drew his knife, "Death to all tyrants," and the rest crowded in. The general, who was quite unmoved, retreated slowly, and the murderers, hacking and cutting at him with their knives, pursued him round the room. Luna's first blow wounded him in the arm, and as he dodged about the meretricious glass-topped tables the blood dripped on the marble floor as, with a sword a negro boy had brought, he fought his way to where a sofa and some chairs formed a momentary defence.

Just as he reached it, his daughter, who had found a pistol, opened fire. Her first shot broke a looking-glass, and the next wounded a gaucho who was striking at her father with an axe. He turned without a word, thinking he was attacked behind, and as he turned Luna stooped forward and ran him through the back. He fell without a groan, and as his daughter fired again, killing a man and wounding Luna in the hand, the murderers rushing forward finished him as he lay motionless upon the gaudy sofa, his life-blood ebbing and his dull eyes turned to his daughter, who still stood at the door, her pistol in her hand.

So died Don Justo de Urquiza, last of the gaucho leaders; and one night, seated by a fire and smoking quietly beneath the southern stars, one of the murderers told me the story, and added that the sight of the dead man and the wild group of gauchos in the glass-fitted ballroom in the flaring light often came back to him, though he owed many lives, and by God's favour could, when obliged, despatch a Christian as easily as he could kill a sheep.

But, he remarked, though as a general rule it was not good to spare, for those you spared usually lived to make you rue your clemency, he still was glad that no one harmed the girl, "for by the life of Satan," as he thought, "her children would be men."

Progress

La Tapera

Men as they loped across the pampa on their horses, greeting each other from afar, as sailing ships speak at a distance, running down the trades, used to avoid the place. Round the remains of the deserted house, and all about the grass-grown mounds, which once had been *adobés*, but which the winter rains had melted back to mud, straggled remains of a deserted peach grove. Cattle and horses had rubbed the trees till they shone bright as a malacca cane, and sheep had left their wool in the rough fibres near the roots. A squat ombú, shaped like an umbrella, grew near the fallen-in well, and cast its shade at midday on a stray horse or cow, for people shunned the spot, knowing *las animas* at night made it their trysting-place. Thus, reasoning men, though not afraid, being aware their baptism would shield them from the attacks of ghosts or evil spirits, yet did not care to take the risk of riding through the peach monté of the Tapera, as the deserted house was called. For "squares" on every side of it stretched a gigantic warren of land-crabs, in which a horse sank to the shoulder without warning, and wags when heated at the pulperia with square-faced gin or caña used to say that the real reason of the ill fame which the place enjoyed was from the danger of its *cangrejál*.[1] But the same men, the fumes of caña or of gin evaporated, were no more anxious than the rest to ride up to the place, or give their horses water at the well, although no land-crab's hole had any terrors for them. No matter how or when their horses fell, they were all certain to come off upon their feet, holding their reins or halter in their hands.

Even at noonday, when the shade of the ombú spread gratefully over the cracked and gaping earth, and lizards flattening themselves against the stones drank in the sunbeams, reflecting gems of light from their prismatic backs, and when in the still air a hum of insects made the deserted rancheria appear to be Inhabited with midday ghosts, no one off-saddled by the well. At evening as the sun sank out of sight, dipping at once below the flat horizon, as it had been at sea, biscachas sat and

1 *Cangrejo* = crab; *cangrejal*, the place of the crabs.

chattered on their mounds, and teru-teros, flying low, uttered their wailing cry, men passing by settled their hats upon their heads, and whirling their rebenques in the air, passed like the Walkyrie, their ponchos fluttering in the wind. At night the armadillos emerging from their holes trotted about, looking as if they had survived from some old world in which they knew the pterodactyl and iguanodon. Then terror glued the hair of those who, passing in the offing of the grassy sea, imagined that the fire-flies flitting in the trees were spirits, whilst the harsh cry of the chajá re-echoed through the night as if some soul which had departed confessionless and lost bemoaned its fate. Yet, of itself, nothing in the Tapera spoke of anything but natural decay, and nothing made it different from any other house, deserted on the plains, either from natural causes or from Indians' attack.

By the slow, yellow, deep-sunk stream below it, pampa-grass and sarandí grew thickly, and from the muddy banks small landslips fell as the water lapped against them in the floods and tortoises now and again put up their heads, and when alarmed sank out of sight as if a stone had fallen into the pools. One pictured in one's mind the house peopled and cheerful, with its corral for horses and for cows, all made of ñandubay secured by thongs, each post seeming a knee from some wrecked vessel, and honeycombed by ants, which yet could not destroy its iron heart. The smell of folded sheep bleating at daybreak in the enclosure made of prickly bush entered the nostrils of the mind instinctively, and in the wiry grass tame horses fed, grouped round their bell-mare, whilst ostriches mingled familiarly with cows and stalked about close up to the corrals, as in the still clear air the tuco-tuco's cry rose up from underneath the ground.

Nothing spoke of a tragedy, as happens often when men travel to a spot where some king met his death, and find a tea-garden set up, with the slain despot's effigy used for advertisement. But no advertisement defiled the lonely place, and grasshoppers still twittered in the sun, and parroquets flew chattering through the trees, and over all the sun shone brassily, exaggerating all, till on the plain a distant rider loomed like a windmill, an ostrich seemed a tree, and birds upon the wing low down upon the edge of the horizon bulked large as bullocks, whilst the pale pampa deer at every spring covered a league of sight. Sometimes a traveller in the heated atmosphere discerned a lake, and, riding to it, found himself standing dryshod on the spot which he had seen with water lapping to the reedy edges of the pool. Cities arose and hung roof down-wards in the air, and castles (those of Trápalanda) formed in the sky, and trees upon the farther side of hills were visible, their roots growing in the sky, whilst their boughs floated like the arms of some great jelly-fish in a backwater on a beach. Now and again, and looking carefully on this side and on that, two gauchos, either looking for strayed horses or going to the neighbouring *esquina*, would meet upon the plain, and after greetings spoken from afar (for it is not a prudent thing to come up quickly to a man you do not know), rode up, and after asking with minuteness as to each other's health, got off their horses quietly as cats get off a wall, and fastening them to the long tufts of grass, sat down to ask the news and pass the time of day. Then, if they had no cards, and when a cigarette had been laboriously made by chopping up tobacco with a knife long as a sword, and paper cut from a sheet as large as the announcement of a bull-fight, and fire procured with care and oaths from flint and steel, the talk would surely turn on the deserted house.

"Strange how it should be so, but so it is, that God the Father has divided all men into Whites and Reds, whereas the animals are of one party, eh, Tio Chinche?"

"Well, Nõ [sic = Ño?= *mode of address]* Carancho," the other would reply, "the animals are animals, but why is it that you say this?"

"Ah yes — yes, si Señor, I recollect it well. Lopez Jordán was then our chief, and we had galloped all the province, from the Ibicuy right to the frontier by the Yucari, close to the Mocoretá, and into Corrientes, where men all speak the Guarani, a heathen speech scarce fitter for a Christian than is Neapolitan or English, or any of the idioms which the Gringos jabber in their beards. Jordán, as you remember, was a Red, and so was I . . . why . . . ah, yes, why, . . . because my father was one, and because a party of the Reds had taken me, and, as you know, once in the files, there is no pardon if a man deserts.

"Well, as I said, for months we wandered up and down, fighting and killing all the Whites we met, . . . the good times, eh?"

"Me pango dijo el chimango."

"Good times, yes, times for men. The cattle that we killed, and ate their beef cooked in its hide, the houses that we burned. . . . Women, . . . yes . . . but I have had my absolution . . . from a priest in Gualeguay, and did my penitence, walking on foot a month, beside the infantry, Canario *[sic=Carancho?]*. . . women, . . . why, brother, were you never in the wars?

"So, one day, after months of the work, months without ever drinking broth or taking maté, and with the vice quite contraband, for black tobacco was not to be had, we came up to this place. I rode a half-tamed horse, a black with a white nose and feet, son of a mother who could never have said, No; fitter, indeed, to be a perch for a wild bird than for the saddle of a Christian man. We came, I say, to where the walls of the Tapera stand. It was not a Tapera then, do you see; not a Tapera but an estancia, well stocked, fit for the Anchorenas, with sheep in the corrals and a manada of fat mares, all piebald, with colts fit for the saddle of a president.

"One we called Pancho Pajaro was in our ranks, a youth well favoured, and a rider fit to get on a wild colt and take it, to finish taming, to the moon. He galloped up, and said, 'This is my father's house,' and we who had hoped to plunder all the cattle and the sheep, for the estanciero was a White, were not best pleased, but still, as was our custom, were about to pass the house, as it was that belonging to the father of a comrade, and so was sacred; and besides the night was falling, and in war it is not prudent that you should camp close to a house, unless, of course, that it is burned. But as ill-luck, or good, would have it, for the thing turned out to our advantage, as we were wheeling into column, from the trees, a party of the accursed Whites broke cover, and charged upon us with a shout.

"I had no cartridges, and was obliged to rely upon 'white arms' entirely; and my horse without a mouth, and hot as if he had been nurtured on red pepper and dry wine of Spain, gave me but little chance. Crack went the guns, and lazos whistled, bolas hurtled through the air, and as God willed it, or His Blessed Mother chose, we routed them, and they fled through the trees, just as the night was coming on.

"Pancho, who rode on a cat-coloured horse, fat and well bitted, spurred out from the ranks, twisting the bolas round his hand, and launching them, threw and entangled the hind-legs of the last White, just as his horse emerged from the peach grove out upon the plain."

"Ah, Nō *[sic = Ňo?]* , that is the way . . . the bolas, eh! . . . the bolas, do not deny the shot as pistols do."

"That is so, Tio Chinche, and, as I said, the horse, being caught round its hind legs, soon faltered, and Pancho, riding like the wind, ranged up and drove his sword through the man's back, before that he had time to leave his saddle and seek the shelter of the trees. He fell without a groan, the blood staining a fine vicuña poncho, which I had hoped to buy from Pancho when the fight was done.

"He, getting off his horse, advanced and turned the body over with his foot."

"To cut his throat, eh, Nõ *[sic = Ño?]* Carancho?"

"Yes, and to cut out your tongue, thief of the sacrament, who stops a man upon his tale, as he who draws off his attention just as he swings his lazo in the air. . . . There was no need, for the man fell dead as Namuncurá, and the moon falling on his face showed Pancho that he had killed his brother, and from that time would be accursed of God.

"That is the story, gossip, and the reason that the house became deserted; for Pancho, wandering away, turned infidel, and lived with the wild Indians till his death, and his old father dying without sons, the rancho fell into decay. God in His mercy made all kinds of men, the Whites and Reds alike; He sets them up and down, as we do ninepins, and all life is a fandango."

"Yes, Nõ *[sic = Ño?]* Carancho, but all do not dance, eh?"

Then, slowly saddling up, they used to mount, and strike into a little trot until they came to a slow-running stream, where, after watering their horses, and exchanging salutations, they would separate and sink into the plain, as birds sink out of sight into the sky.

Progress

314

A Chihuahueño

No one, at first sight, would have taken Miguel Saenz for a man born on an Indian frontier, or for one who in his youth had handled arms.

Short, fat, and looking as if he had been cut by an unskilful workman out of walnut wood, he wore a faded black cloth jacket and the bed-ticking trousers which so many frontier Mexicans affect. A wide and steeple-crowned *poblano* hat, stained here and there with perspiration, and girt with a heavy, sausage-like band of silver tinsel, sat like a penthouse on his head and overshadowed the whole man. His occupation in fine weather was to stand against the wall of his *jacál* wrapped in an Indian blanket, and criticise adversely the horsemen of the village as they passed, whilst not neglecting to put in a word or two more favourable as to the charms of all the girls, and speculate on those their clothes veiled from the public gaze. His business was to play on the guitar, and sing to melancholy accompaniments in do minor, wailing *jarábes* treating of love disdained, of Indian battles, and of the prowess of celebrated horses, for he was *musico*, that is to say, by strength of wrist and perseverance, and with the natural advantage of being a little deaf, he had arrived at some proficiency in what he styled his art.

As he sat nursing his guitar, and with a bland yet cunning smile upon his pock-marked face, no one would think that he had been a frontier rider, and that still, though his abdomen overhung the pommel of his saddle, that, once upon his horse, he was fixed there as firmly as a knot upon a tree. He looked out on the world through his black, wrinkled, and Indian-looking eyes, tired with surveying miles of prairie for hostile "sign," and gazing out intently into the night against attacks by the Apaches, indulgently, being aware of all its frailties and his own. "Trust not a mule or a mulata wench," he would observe, or "If a woman is a harlot and gets nothing for it, she might as well remain respectable," with other adages of a like cynical and primitive philosophy formed half the staple of his talk. These he enunciated with so much unction and such gravity that they appeared to be not only the epitome of human wisdom, but the high-water mark of his own personal experience, which he retailed half humorously, half sadly, for the behoof and guidance of the listeners, and as a sort of vade mecum to mankind.

"Weapons are necessary," he used to say, "but no one knows exactly when; therefore, your knife should come out easily, and pistol locks be kept well oiled, for fear of novelty." "Never go up to a *jacál* where dogs are thin, for he who does not feed his dogs will starve his guest," he used to say, as with an air of having proved his statement by experience. "In entering chaparral, note if the birds sit quiet on the trees, for if they fly about, be sure some one has recently passed by, and on the frontier all are enemies till they have proved themselves as friends, and so of life." "Waste not your graces on a deaf man," and "amongst soldiers and with prostitutes all compliments are held excused," and "who shall say it is the post that is at fault if the blind man did not observe it in his path," were of the flowers of his rhetoric which he bestowed upon a listening world after a glass or two either of sweet Tequila or mezcal.

Born in Chihuáhuá and having migrated up and down the Rio Grande from the Pimeria to Matamoros, and wandered with the Indians in his youth in the Bolson de Mápimi and from Mojavé to the Rio Gila, fate had at last brought him up in a backwater of frontier life in San Antonio, Texas, where, in the quarter called after his native town, he sojourned, waiting the time when he should find himself in funds to return home and end his days in peace.

In the meantime, and because, as he himself averred, it was not good for man to live alone, he had taken to himself two wives, and induced peace between them by frequent beatings, till, as he said, they learned to love each other and live in charity and with the fear of God.

Outside his hut, built like a bird's nest, with canes and wood, and roofed with empty tins of kerosene, his saddled horse all day stood nodding in the sun, and when his master had occasion to repair in his capacity of *musico* to any merry-making, he mounted, getting to his seat as actively as in his youth, all in one motion, and taking his guitar from one of his attendant spouses, struck a slow lope, holding his instrument balanced on his thigh, and with the diapason sticking out after the fashion of a lance. "Don" Miguel Saenz — for, as he used to say, not only was the title his by right, but in Chihuáhuá the treatment (*el tratamiento*) was universal in the province — had, besides proverbs, much lore of Indian battles and of revolutions, which on occasion and with circumstance he would unpack.

Then as he sat immovable with his right hand stealing occasionally behind his back to assure himself that his revolver was in place, his dull unblinking eyes would suddenly become illuminated, and as he talked of battle, murder, rape, and sudden death, you saw the Indian blood assert itself and the inherited ferocity of centuries shine in his face, and then in spite of rusty black cloth coat, fat stomach, and ill-tuned guitar, that "Don" Miguel was not, as he would have expressed it, "one of those mules that a man can drive before him with the reins."

In early youth he had been taken up and forced into the ranks by some "pronouncing" general in Chihuáhuá, and his adventures in the revolutionary campaign, which led him up and down over the plateau of Anáhuac, furnished him with ample anecdote and opportunity for the indulging to the full of that quiet philosophic cynicism which is the characteristic of all those Mexicans who have a strain of Indian blood.

"Soldiers and harlots," he would say, "are much alike, each give their souls for money, and their love and hate are swift, and dangerous as a tiger's leap, therefore be friends with them as if you shortly might be enemies, and do not give your arm for them to twist, or they will break it in the socket, and then laugh. Have you not seen an Indian mother catch a rabbit or a bird, and give it to her children to torment? See how she shows them how to put out its eyes with thorns, and break its wings, in order that their hearts may become steel, and that their souls may suffer others' tortures and their own, without a tear."

War in Chihuáhuá and Sonora, before the advent of "Don Porfi" to the presidential throne, was not a kindergarten. No one surrendered who was not weary of his life, for if he did, the Indian mother's lessons usually made his death a boon to him. Marches were desperate in the keen air of the high plateau, and the infantry was lashed along behind the cavalry by officers with bare machetes in their hands. Those who fell out never fell in again, for, to encourage those who kept the ranks, they were incontinently shot, or if a foolish sentimentalism saved them for a time, their death was certain if a picket of the enemy came on them, even supposing that they did not die of thirst like baggage animals who sink beneath their packs.

With a cruel humorous twinkle in his eye Miguel would tell how, when the troops came to a water-hole, a guard was set to keep the over-driven infantry from drinking till they burst.

Once, as he said, when sitting on his horse, worn out and thirsty, certain men annoyed him overmuch by importuning him to be allowed to drink.

Troops, as he said, learn only by experience, so he determined to make experiment on some of them for the good guidance in the future of the rest. Beckoning up two or three, he let them drink, which they did heartily, lapping the icy water with their fevered tongues. In a few moments they were seized with violent pains, and in a little time lay down and "died like doves" quite quietly, so that in future no one bothered him when he sat tired on his horse guarding a well.

"Our Saviour gave His life for all, and I, Don Miguel Saenz, not being born a saviour, yet saved the life of many a good soldier merely by giving this example, that is in their own persons, for discipline is as the soul of military men, and if the body perish, let but the soul be saved and all is well."

And as he said it he would chuckle fatly, and the villainy of a fat man has something unnatural and bloodcurdling, and acts upon one, as the speech of Balaam's ass, which must have been more disconcerting to its rider than all the antics of a buck-jumper.

For foreigners in general he had the easy tolerance and contempt of all inhabitants of South and West America, reckoning them up as men who cannot ride, and therefore are not to be taken seriously. For North Americans, whom he termed "Los Gringos," his feelings were more mixed; the western and therefore riding section of them, in his eyes, were worth consideration when on their horses, but their rough manners and want of knowledge of the world — on foot — induced in him an attitude half pitiful and half contemptuous. The northerners, who throughout Texas are termed "men from the States," he looked on as a man convinced of witchcraft might look upon a wizard, half in alarm, mingled with loathing, and yet with admiration of his power and wickedness.

Spaniards he called "Los Gachupines," and probably had never seen one, but seemed to think them a sort of dragons roaming about, politically inclined, scheming by night and day to take away that liberty which so few Mexicans enjoy, but which each one of them imagines that his fathers shed their blood to consecrate. Speaking himself a harsh old-fashioned jargon of Castilian, plentifully garnished with Indian words, he yet had his own theories as to diction, holding that "Gachupines" whistled like the birds, that Germans cried, and that "Los Gringos" spoke as if attacked by syphilis.

"Los Indios bravos" sat like a nightmare on his mind, although in San Antonio, Texas, they were as rare as they would be in Liverpool; but having heard their war-cry in his youth, it had remained for ever in his ears, as men blown up in mines, in after years, are said never to lose a singing in their heads.

"The Indian," he said, "is such a kind of beast; you cannot kill him with a stick or stone." The animals being, as is well known to all philosophers, created solely with a view as to the easiest way a man can find of killing them. "The Indian dies hard, and when you have him wounded on the ground, do not approach at once, for no coyóte better can feign death. Therefore stand still and fire upon him as he lies, twice, thrice, or even four times, until you see no twitching of the limbs when the ball strikes him. Even then be cautious, and, having lit a cigarette, keeping your eyes upon the body all the time, advance with your gun cocked, and, on arriving at the carrion, drive your knife two or three times into the heart. Then he is dead and you can glorify the Lord and take his scalp." No self-respecting frontier man, Yanqui or Mexican, who did not in those days conform to the Indian custom, as far as scalping went; and though they spoke of Indians as "savages," or as *los barbaros* (according to their kind), themselves were to the full as great barbarians as any warrior of the Lipanes, Comanches, Coyoteros, or of the Mezcaleros, who dug for roots of wild mezcal along the shores of the Rio Gila or wandered in the deserts of the Mápimi. So that the listeners who heard the Chihuahueño's counsels of perfection as to Indian fight, were not surprised, but testified their admiration at his wit and his "hoss-sense" by a sententious *bueno* or "jess so," according to their nationality, for to all frontier men no Indian was ever good, till he was well filled up with rifle bullets. Still, in his heart of hearts, the ex-Indian fighter, now turned half pimp and half guitar player, rather admired the Indian though he feared him, in the same way that a fat white housekeeping shopkeeper in the East admires the Arab of the plains.

Both frontier Mexican and Eastern shopkeeper seem to see their vices and their virtues typified, and, in some measure, purified by the wild life led by their prototypes. So may a politician reading Machiavelli bring his hand down violently upon the book, and say, "This was a man indeed: to what heights might I rise if I could only frame my lies with such intelligence."

Thus would the Chihuahueño chuckle long when he read or heard of some successful Indian raid, so that it did not touch his native village, which he referred to always as *mi tierra*, looking upon it as the centre of the earth.

"Yes," he would say, "I see the thing and how it fell about. Likely enough the idiots saw a herd of horses feeding on the plain, and did not see the lumps upon their backs, which were the feet of Indians clinging to them. So they allowed them to approach, and then each horse turned a Centauro in a moment and they all were slain except the women, who would be carried off to work in the *tepeés*.[1] "

Books did not bulk too largely in the Chihuahueño's mind, though what he read became a portion of himself, never to be forgotten, and to be commentated on, as something which the whole world knew, just as it knew of sun and rain, of change of seasons, and the precession of the equinoxes.

The old romance called the *Twelve Peers of France* he had, bound in grey parchment, and lettered on the back by some one who preferred his own phonetic spelling of the names to the mere trifling of grammarians. It read, "Istoria de Carlo Mauno y los dose Pares." On Carlo Mauno would he often talk, saying he held him for the chief of emperors, being, as he was, a valiant man, and having killed most of the people that he met. A view of the Imperial function perhaps more suitable to the meridian of Baghdad than of Mexico.

"Alejandro el Mauno" with his horse Bucefálo came the next in his esteem, and from his story he would draw sage apothegms and rules for life, which gave him great consideration amongst such of his compeers as could not read, or, at the best, had learned laboriously to spell out a prayer in Latin pronounced like Spanish, and but little understood.

Riding, apparently, amongst the Greeks, held quite as high a place in public estimation as in Chihuáhuá, for it appeared a king owned Bucefálo, and, as there was no heir to the throne, put out a *bando*, offering the crown and his fair daughter's hand to the successful rider of his horse. All the *ginetes*[2] came from far and wide, each with his *quarta*[3] in his hand, his legs enclosed in *chaparreras*[4] and wearing silver spurs which made a noise as when a hailstorm falls upon a roof.

1 A *tepeé* is the tent of the Indians; it was usually made of skins.
2 Ginetes = horsemen.
3 Quarta = whip in Mexico.
4 *Chaparreras* are the long leather overalls used by ranchmen.

But "el caballo Bucefálo" bucked so hard that he despatched them all at the third jump, leaving them *mal parados* and with their "baptism half broken," causing them all to swear abominably, and making some of them in their disgust desert their faith and go and join the Turk.

Then appeared Alejandro, not yet El Mauno, but, as it soon was seen, with indications of his greatness, for he had armed himself for his attempt with a great bit, which weighed half an arroba, and his spurs were of the size of the tops of oil jars, all of solid plate. When Bucefálo saw his armament, he straight gave in, and Alejandro, mounting at a bound, raced him up to the king, and, stopping him, caused him to rear, so that he hung suspended for an instant over the very throne. This pleased his majesty, who at once took the bold rider to his heart, marrying him incontinently to the princess, who was wonderfully fair, and should have made him happy, but that the love of other women caused him to fall from grace, and lose eventually his kingdom and his life.

It fell in this wise. As it so chanced, the Grecian State happened to be at war with Persia, whose king was Dărĭo, and whose daughter (name unknown) was also passing fair. After the victory, in which both Bucefálo and El Mauno performed prodigies of valour, cutting down Moors as if they had been grass, and taking many scalps, it chanced that Alejandro in his tent, being athirst, called for the Persian princess to bring him one of those beverages ("uno de estos brebages") which those infidels affect. She, having put a potent poison in the cup, brought it to Alejandro, who straight drank, and instantly swelled out enormously and ultimately burst. "Thus do we see," the Chihuahueño said, "how that the love of women is a curse, and, reading history, you may light upon things that are useful to a man as guides in life."

His learning and his skill on the guitar, together with his fund of anecdote, made him a favourite in the society in which he moved, and his companions would lament that, though he had two wives, he yet was childless, and that no son would fill his place when he slept with those Chihuahueños whose souls are twanging their guitars in paradise. A shade of sadness sometimes obscured the twinkle in his eye, when he would say, "No, señor, children I have none, neither by Carmen nor Clemencia. No Christian boy will close my eyes when they have put the *baqueano*[1] in my hand."

---

1 *Baqueano* means a guide; hence the consecrated wafer is the great *baqueano*, as it leads to heaven.

Then pensively, and with an air as if his life had had its sweetness and its charm, he used to say, "I had a son once in my youth, born of an Indian woman, a Mojavé squaw, who should by now be grown to man's estate. *Barajo!* The little rogue, son of an Indian harlot, he must have taken many a Christian's scalp by this time if he has turned out such a devil as his dam."

From the Stoep

A southern settle, placed to face the sun, the stoep was built — into the wall which flanked the entrance gate. The seat was made of square red tiles, unglazed; the arms of masonry. The Spanish masons, who had done the work, had so contrived it that the sitters' feet just dangled off the ground, after the fashion in which children sat at church in an old Georgian pew. The aloe hedges over which waved canes, protected by a ditch half filled with mud, in which grew tamarisks that love the sea, pretended to keep out such public as there was, and gave a good example of the truth of the old proverb, which sets forth "that fear guards vineyards more than does the wall." The gate itself stood in a patch of sand. Before it countless feet, of men and asses passing continuously for ages, had worn deep ruts, which ran like little railways in and out between the stunted herbage and the palmettoes, in the sandy earth. Thus did the builders of the pyramids contrive their gardens, hedging them about with canes and mud banks, over which a calf might jump, content if they but had a gate, set up alone, against the wilderness. So do to-day the people of the furthest east build gates, up to the spot where stands the stoep, so close to Europe that the goatherd singing in the Anjera can almost frame his song to the accompaniment of the reed pipe his fellow plays in Spain. Springing up here and there, the sweet alyssum flecked the grass, and here and there ranunculi grew rank, whose golden cups turned brightest orange in the last glare of the declining sun. Cicalas twittered, frogs croaked musically, and on the beach the surf played dreamily, grinding and grating pebbles on the sand and rounding off their corners as imperceptibly as life rounds off the edges of the mind. As evening deepened, and the purple haze crept on the town and hill, flattening them out till they appeared to rise out of the water like a gigantic whale left high and dry by time, the passers-by, whose feet and those of generations of their kind had formed the patterned pathways in the grass, grew more fantastic, as their shadows on the sand lengthened and stretched out behind.

Parties of men armed with their spear-like brass-hooped guns danced past like fauns, their short brown cassocks swinging in the wind. Upright and lithe they walked, their strong brown legs glowing like burnished copper as they bounded on the sand. Now and then one of them would leap into the air, and flinging up his gun, catch it, and whirl it round his head, then fire it pointing to the ground, and loitering behind a minute, load, pouring the powder loosely without wadding into the stork-necked barrel, and with a bound or two, which left the impress of his naked toes on the hard sand, rejoin his fellow tribesmen as they returned towards their white-mosqued village on the hill. They crossed a shallow river and entered into the thick bush fringing the ramparts of the mouldering castle, built by the Portuguese, that overlooks the Moorish fort, in which the carronades marked with the crown and cypher of the third George of Merry England lie on the stucco platform, beside their mouldering carriages of maple wood. Then, for the day had been the feast of the Ashora in the town, a group of villagers, all armed, stood on a rock to meet them, and amidst firing they all passed into the brushwood and disappeared out of the ken of those who sat upon the stoep.

Then, as a current of light air, precursor of the sunset, rose, the fishing-boats, their sails goose-winged to catch the breeze, looking like nautiluses as the eye just caught their bulwarks and the masts appeared to rise out of the golden water, swept towards the harbour, and were absorbed in the white buildings of the town.

The sun sank lower, and a belt of trees, just on the point which forms the nose of the gigantic whale of land, stood out so clearly for a moment that it seemed that they had shot up from the earth full grown.

Now from the town across the river, laid almost bare by the retreating tide, and leaving flats of sand which looked like glass under the sunset's glow, the stream of country people coming from market ebbed towards the mountain villages, which lay almost invisible behind their cactus hedges in the scrub. Men on lean ponies, dressed in brown weeds like friars, their hoods drawn up, and packing-needles in their hands to goad their beasts with, passed in companies, in twos and threes and singly, all seated sideways or on their laden animals with their legs dangling upon either side the neck. Behind them women came in bands, dressed all in white, with towels on their heads, and round their naked legs brown gaiters kept in place with string. Some carried children on their backs, and some their purchases from town; but one and all chattered like parrots in a maize-field as they trotted through the sand. As night drew near the breeze fell lighter, and the boats which had been making towards the harbour seemed to lie motionless, and then stood in towards the shore, until they almost touched the surf, to catch the air which about evening rises in the bay. A glow of red and orange, turning to violet and to carmine, spread upon the sky and then broke into points, as if the northern lights, tired of the Arctic cold, had drifted down towards the straits. The dying sun just touched the white sails of the *Carmen Perez* as she lay swinging in the tide, and then grew fainter, leaving her ghostly, and her yellow hull almost invisible, whilst on her deck the Spanish sailor, making believe to keep an anchor watch, intoned a Malagueña so high and quavering that its trills sounded scarce human; and if the cadence, which, once grasped, stirs every fibre of the soul, had not been so well marked, one might have thought the ghost of some Morisco hovered in the air, raising lament for Loja, for Alhama, and the green valley with the rocky town which the Rey Chico lost.

The long procession from the town grew more strung out, and now and then some charcoal-burners passed, dusty and coal-smeared. They drove their asses with their empty baskets on their backs, plodding as patiently behind them as they had been one flesh, raising occasionally a shrill falsetto objurgation on the mothers of the humble beasts who, knowing that in all their race there never was a mother who went wrong, or refused milk to any of her foals, bowed their meek heads, resigned to all the folly of mankind, and shuffled on their little feet, scarce moving from the ground.

As darkness crept upon the town, the sand, the bay, the Roman galley docks, the wooded foot-hills, and the white sierras above Tétuan, blending them all into a purple mass, and binding them to Spain as if once more the straits were land, the lights shone out like fire-flies, and from Tarifa point an eye of fire streamed out upon the sea. Sailing-ships working through the straits looked like gigantic moths, and steamers left a trail of sparks amongst their smoke, as they passed ceaselessly between the silent coasts. Now the returning villagers had almost ceased to pass, and in the gloaming here and there white-sheeted women showed like milestones on the brush-covered hills.

The voices of the people going home still sounded in the distance in the increasing gloom, and then were stilled.

Up to the stoep hobbled a beggar, white-bearded and brown-clad, toothless, and looking like a friar by Zurbarán. He begged, pointing to heaven, in the name of God, then fell a-talking upon things in general, leaning on his stick, turned off without a word after the fashion of the country, and striking into a dog-trot, which any man of twenty might have envied for its springiness, was gone as he had come, his brown clothes blending with the gloom of the palmetto and lentiscus scrub, and his bare feet making as little noise as if a hare had passed along the track.

Then came two women running with an ass, which they beat on with oleander boughs. They passed so lightly with their eyes bent down upon the ground (not to appear to see the unbelievers on the stoep), that they might almost have been shadows or the reflections of the others who had passed before. When all had gone, out of the twilight trotted past a dog, brown as a jackal and as lean, his tail stiff curled above his back, his ears pricked forward, and his gait as regular as a machine, well oiled.

He made a wide detour and then returned back to the trail and melted out of sight just as the moon rose up above Meníwish, throwing its shadow on the sand, which it turned to a lake of light backed by great banks of shade. Then silence fell upon the night, broken but by the never-ending low complaint of the vexed surf upon the shore, making its moan to nature and the night, for all the misery the waves endure, torn by the winds and tossed.

Mariano Gonzalez

If it is true that only simple folk shall be the real inheritors of the earth, it may be said with equal truth that those who fail possess it presently. Whilst the world claims a man and he enjoys the esteem or hatred of his fellows, he can inherit nothing, or, at best, only inherit property, the true primeval curse.

The praise of men, the pettiness of greatness, and the attachment to the thousand nothings which ensure success, so cramp a man that he is left without the leisure to enjoy his life. Life only really is understood, either by simple men whose cares and joys are bounded by the parish where they live, or by those disillusioned folk who look out on the world as a cow looks out on a road, resting her head upon a gate. Your true Nirvana can only be attained by those who, in the sun, the tides, the phases of the moon, the miracle of buds and flowers, green leaf and then dry boughs again, find happiness, and pass their lives in thinking without bitterness on that which might have been. Occasionally on some lost island beach in the Pacific, in ranches on the plains, in hulks upon the Oil rivers, in seeming uncongenial places up and down the world, we come across them. Sometimes, indeed, amongst the busy haunts of men they live detached, aloof from all around them; but in every case their touchstone is the apparent failure of their lives.

That is, they must have had some quality which put them out of tune, made them too sharp or flat, not up to concert pitch; in fact, unfit for excellence in the pursuits their fellows prize, and rise to eminence by following, becoming county councillors, generals, and admirals of routine — eminent, worthy, and uninteresting — dying high in the respect of those who, born without appreciation, endue their heroes with their own qualities intensified. Something of pathos clings to those who, having left the world alone to run its maddening course, have thus become, as it were, moth-eaten gods in threadbare marriage garments. To be a god is to be quite detached from all around, or else so permeated with everything as to be part of it. So live the trees, the grass, the birds, and beasts, and, as a general rule, those men from whom alone one can expect something out of the common; something within themselves which far surpasses all accomplishment. A painter or a poet (all but the greatest) may excel and yet be common as a countess in Mayfair, or as a shop-girl in the Brompton Road; but the beach-coomber or the man left stranded by the waves of life may be a drunkard, possibly a thief, but it is hard for him to be a snob, for if he had been he must inevitably have drifted to success.

The world is to the snob; he easily outgoes the cad, the merchant, the philosopher, the artist, poet, or what not; for they, if they are really true, must show themselves such as they are, whilst the snob's art is to appear something that he is not.

In general, the storm-stayed prisoners of Fate pass all their time in waiting for a wind; but their peculiarity is that if, after their years of waiting, it should blow, fair towards the port which they have dreamed about, making it in their vision only an antechamber to the heaven of the Apocalypse, they would not set their sails. Pride may be keeps them back, or a dim feeling that they are happy where they are, or a vague fear of the continual roar of cabs, or something which they cannot formulate; in the same way a bird long prisoned in a cage fears to fly out, although the door is open wide and not a cat in sight to make him doubtful of the strength of his long-unaccustomed wings.

Such a one I knew, who, though at times he ventured out, always returned again and closed the door of his own cage.

An eddy of the misdirected stream of life had left Don Mariano high and dry in the Jews' quarter of Morocco City, where he lived with a Jewess, such household gods as had escaped the wanderings of forty years, and a small store of medicines, which had served when he was once a veterinary surgeon, and with which he "cured" the infidel, both to their satisfaction and his own.

Born at Morón, not far from Seville, his native accent, thick and lisping, and which cuts off, as his compatriots say, "the half of all the words, and eats the rest," had made it next to an impossibility for him to learn another tongue. Rumour, without whose aid we could not live, as she secures for us the romance of both our own and other people's lives, said that he once had been a Carlist colonel. This may have been the case — in fact, it must have been; for he was tall and well set up, and had the address and presence which the world gives to a colonel, but which nature, all unmindful of our hierarchies, as frequently bestows on a chiropodist. One thing was certain, that he had seen much world, and, as is not infrequent in such cases, having seen much, thought it was just as well to have seen all, and, by a process of hallucination which travellers so frequently endure, actually knew as much (or more) about the countries which he had not seen as about those which he had really visited. So, as he spoke a word or two of Guaraní and Quíchua, he thought he spoke Tagálo and Malay, and as there were no people in Marákesh who spoke either of them, no one was any wiser than himself. Withal a gentleman, so to speak, by the grace of God, and not by any effort of his own. Tall and grey-bearded, his courteous address and grave repose of manner contrasted strangely with his spluttering Andalusian speech, making it seem as if Don Quixote and his squire were really but one man, as happens often with his countrymen, with whom set manners often mask buffoonery.

In fact, all serious men lie under grave suspicion of their wit, for gravity is usually the mask of an interior nothingness, and on the long-faced formalist the onus lies of demonstrating that he is not so foolish as his appearance seems to indicate.

Don Mariano was no fool, although the wisdom of his speech, stuffed full with proverbs and containing worldly lore enough to have made the reputation of a bench of bishops, did not exactly tally with his practice, which showed him clearly as a man simple and childlike, and, though a rank blasphemer against every faith, one of those people whom his countrymen term "only fit for God."

His house stood in a dirty lane at the extremest end of the Jews' quarter, shut from the city by a massive gate, through which a stream of loaded asses and of mules passed ceaselessly as streams of bees pass laden to a hive. Dead cats and fowls and rotting offal made the stones slippery as ice, and buzzing myriads of flies hung in the air and settled on the sores of animals or round the eyelids of men sleeping in the sun.

Drivers of mules and camels shouted to their beasts; men passed bowed under burdens, and a rank smell of sweat mingled with odours of decaying fruit and spices hung like an atheistic incense in the air.

Jews in their box-like shops sold fly-blown biscuits and cheap calicoes, with sardines, children's toys and teapots, cheap little coffee cups and Spanish knives with wooden handles; or, sitting on a mat upon the floor, worked silver ornaments, all marked with cabalistic signs, or fashioned rings in which emeralds and rubies of enormous size were cheaply imitated in coloured glass backed with tinfoil, and with the silver visibly alloyed with lead till it looked dull as zinc. All wore long gabardines of blue and white striped cloth, confined about the waist with a frayed sash or greasy leather belt. Square Arab bags, worked in red worsted or in silk, in which they kept their money, handkerchiefs, and papers proving that each of them had the protection of the consul of some Power, dangled against their ribs. Their greasy side curls fell to the corners of their mouths, and their black skull-caps, blending with their hair, seemed to have grown out of some fountain of interior grease which joined them to the skin.

Many had scabby heads and bleary eyes; yet all looked clever, and not a few were men who at the call of business put on European clothes, and, jogging to the coast upon an ass, took ship to Europe and became for a brief season smart modern traders, and then, their business done, returned home to Marákesh, and, putting on their gabardines, haggled contentedly for coppers in the rank smell of the ancestral filth of the Melláh. Camels and asses blocked the way, and tribesmen from the Atlas, holding each other's hands, strolled up and down, timid and insolent at the same time, and looking furtively about like a wild animal just caught and put into a cage. Children with bare shaved heads and grave as senators looked out of doors, and from the windows Israel's daughters leaned, bawling to one another, as they combed their hair, across the narrow street. Right at the end stood Mariano's house, outside as tumble-down and ruinous as all the rest, but, the door passed, one entered into an atmosphere of cleanliness and rest, the like of which was not in the whole town.

Passing through the *saguan*, you went up stairs as steep as pyramids from one side of the patio, and reached a balcony, on to which all the rooms opened, after the Moorish style. Some carpeted divans with leather cushions, worked in concentric patterns, ran round the upper court.

In the chief room, over which the smoke of cigarettes hung like the incense in a temple, the owner sat — usually dressed in white, his naked feet thrust into Moorish slippers, and his frilled shirt as beautifully got up as if it had been washed in Seville or Madrid. About the room hung arms, rifles, and daggers from the Sáhara; "kief"-pipes and bags made by the Atlas mountaineers, and on a nail the spotless white burnouse with which "Dr. Don Mariano" concealed his European clothes when walking in the street. His medicines all set out in pots, in broken bottles, and in old cigar-boxes, ranged on a shelf or two, proclaimed his calling and election sure. These and his "library," consisting of some tattered novels by Galdós, and the *Whole Art of Veterinary Surgery*, by a Professor of the Science in Granada, with a small treatise on *The Use of Mercury And Other Simples*, by a B.A. of Salamanca, were his chief titles to be called Doctor, a status which procured him general esteem both in Marákesh and amongst the neighbouring tribesmen both of the hills and plains.

Well did he know the Arabs' constitution by long practice, their love of powerful medicines, and the necessity that anything he gave should act immediately and with sufficient force to kill an elephant. Seated in an old rocking-chair, the seat and back patched with black oil-cloth, he dealt his "simples" out with as much confidence and disregard of consequences as he had been the god whom he styled "Escolaprio," and whose bust in plaster he had seen, austere but fly-blown, as it frowned down from the top shelves of the apothecary's in his own native town in Spain.

Still, nothing serious ever happened to him, for if the patient died, his friends declared that Allah willed it so, and if he lived they gave the praise to God the Merciful and the Compassionate, from whom is victory and strength, ignoring usually both Mariano's intervention and his fee, although as sure as they were ill they sent for him, just as we do in the like case ourselves and with the same result.

Long contact with the Moors had brought about that curious attitude in which a man becomes so much a part and parcel of the folk with whom he lives that, though he frequently abuses them himself, he cannot tolerate a stranger even to criticise.

The doctor wore a white burnouse above his clothes when he rode out upon his pacing mule, and his white beard and stately carriage gave him the air as of an Arab sheikh, and nothing pleased him more than to be greeted as *tabíb*, a title which in his mind exceeded "doctor," either by virtue of its strangeness, or, perhaps, merely as a chintz exceeds mohair, or a Scotch Presbyterian exceeds the strictest Nonconformist of the south in pitch of snuffle and intensity of whine.

Often, a little money made, he would return to Spain, but the nostalgia of Morocco City always drew him back, although the European comforts of Morón could not have been excessive or its stress of life much greater than that of the decaying city which possessed his soul.

A Moor amongst the Spaniards, and a Spaniard with the Moors, he lived his life as many of his countrymen must have lived theirs in Moorish times in Spain.

But, in the same way that a wounded horse makes homewards, by roads instinctive, known to him alone, across the plains, to die in the green pastures where he gambolled as a foal, Don Mariano always looked to lay his bones in Spain; though had he died in his own country, his ghost would certainly have walked the Jammal-el-Fanar, lingered about the Kutubieh, or perhaps roamed about the palm wood which washes round Marákesh like a sea.

From the first time we met, when he was talking of the great and true, of bullfights, revolutions, horses, women, and of those things which interest men in every clime, seated with a strong woman of a travelling Spanish show, a Japanese, one "Tiki-riki," and some waifs and strays washed up upon the sands of life, we straight were friends.

Years, and occasional brief spells of intercourse and mutual gifts of books and native curiosities and the receipt of letters now and then in which he anxiously inquired after the health of all my family, though he had never seen a member of it, cemented friendship till it was understood I was to see him buried if it should chance that I was in Marákesh when he died.

It did not so fall out, and he lies lonely, far from Morón, under the walls of the great city of Yusuf-ibn-Tachfin, and I write this by way of epitaph, hoping the moss may gather tenderly on the unnoticed grave of the *tabíb*.

Faith

"I told you," said Hamed-el-Angeri, "of how once on a time all beasts could speak, and of how Allah, in his might, and for his glory, and no doubt for some wise cause, rendered them dumb, or at the least caused them to lose their Arabic. Now will I tell you of a legend of the Praised One who sleepeth in Medina, and whom alone, Allah has pardoned of all men."

He paused, and the hot sun streamed through the branches of the carob tree, under whose shade we sat upon a rug, during the hottest hours, and threw his shadow on the sandy soil, drawing him, long of limb, and lithe of pose, like John the Baptist revealed by Donatello in red clay.

Our horses hung their heads, and from the plain a mist of heat arose, dancing and shivering in the air, as the flame dances waveringly from a broken gas-pipe lighted by workmen in a street. Grasshoppers twittered, raising their pandean pipe of praise to Allah for his heat, and now and then a locust whirred across the sky, falling again into the hard dry grass, just as a flying-fish falls out of sight into the sea. "They say," Hamed again began, "that in Medina, or in Mecca, in the blessed days when God spake to his Prophet, and he composed his book, making his laws, and laying down his rules of conduct for men's lives, that many wondered that no nook or corner in all Paradise was set apart for those who bore us, or whose milk we sucked, when they had passed their prime."

Besides the Perfect Four, women there were who, with the light that Allah gave them, strove to be faithful, just, and loving, and to do their duty as it seemed to them, throughout their lives.

One there was, Rahma, a widow, and who had borne four stalwart sons, all slain in battle, and who, since their deaths, had kept herself in honour and repute, labouring all day with distaff and with loom.

Seated in a lost dúar in the hills, she marvelled much that the wise son of Ámina, he to whom the word of God had been vouchsafed, and who himself had owed his fortune to a woman, could be unjust. Long did she ponder in her hut beyond Medina, and at last resolved to take her ass, and set forth, even to Mecca, and there speak with God's messenger, and hear from him the why and wherefore of the case. She set her house in

333

order, leaving directions to the boy who watched her goats to tend them diligently, and then upon the lucky day of all the week, that Friday upon which the faithful all assemble to give praise, she took her way.

The people of the village thought her mad, as men in every age have always thought all those demented who have determined upon any course which has not entered into their own dull brains. Wrinkled and withered like a mummy, draped in her shroud-like haik, she sat upon her ass. A bag of dates, with one of barley, and a small waterskin her luggage, and in her heart that foolish, generous, undoubting Arab faith, powerful enough to move the most stupendous mountain chain of facts which weigh down European souls, she journeyed on.

Rising before the dawn, in the cold chill of desert nights, she fed her beast from her small store of corn, shivering and waiting for the sun to warm the world. Then, as the first faint flush of pink made palm trees look like ghosts and half revealed the mountain tops floating above a sea of mist, she turned towards the town, wherein he dwelt who denied paradise to all but girls, and prayed. Then, drawing out her bag of dates, she ate, with the content of those to whom both appetite and food are not perennial gifts.

As the day broke, and the fierce sun rose, as it seemed with his full power, the enemy of those who travel in those wilds, she clambered stiffly to her seat on her straw pillion, and with a suddra thorn urged on her ass to a fast stumbling walk, his feet seeming but scarce to leave the ground as he bent forward his meek head as if he bore the sins of all mankind upon his back.

The dew lay thickly on the scant mimosa scrub and camel-thorn, bringing out aromatic odours, and filling the interstices of spiders' webs as snow fills up the skeletons of leaves. The colocynths growing between the stones seemed frosted with the moisture of the dawn, and for a brief half-hour nature was cool, and the sun shone in vain. Then, as by magic, all the dew disappeared, and the fierce sunlight heated the stones, and turned the sand to fire.

Green lizards, with kaleidoscopic tints, squattered across the track, and hairy spiders waddled in and out the stones. Scorpions and centipedes revived, and prowled about like sharks or tigers looking for their prey, whilst beetles, rolling balls of camels' dung, strove to as little purpose as do men, who, struggling in the dung of business, pass their lives, like beetles, with their eyes fixed upon the ground.

As the sun gradually gained strength, the pilgrim drew her tattered haik about her face, and sat, a bundle of white rags, her head crouched on her breast and motionless, except the hand holding the reins, which half mechanically moved up and down, as she urged on the ass into a shuffling trot.

The hot hours caught her under a solitary palm tree, by a half-stagnant stream, in which great tortoises put up their heads, and then sank out of sight as noiselessly as they had risen, leaving a trail of bubbles on the slimy pool. Some red flamingoes lazily took flight, and then with outstretched wings descended further off, and stood expectant, patient as fishers, and wrapt in contemplation during the mysteries of their gentle craft.

Then the full silence of the desert noontide fell upon the scene, as the old woman, after having tied her ass's feet with a thin goat's-hair cord, sat down to rest. Long did she listen to her ass munching his scanty feed of corn, and then the cricket's chirp and the faint rustling of the lone palm-trees' *[sic]* leaves lulled her to sleep.

Slumbering, she dreamed of her past life — for dreams are but the shadow of the past, reflected on the mirror of the brain — and saw herself, a girl, watching her goats, happy to lie beneath a bush all day, eating her bread dipped in the brook at noon, and playing on a reed; then, evening come, driving her charges home, to sleep on the hard ground upon a sheepskin, in the corner of the tent. She saw herself a maiden, not wondering overmuch at the new view of life which age had brought, accepting in the same way as did her goats, that she too must come under the law of nature, and in pain bear sons. Next, marriage, with its brief feasting, and eternal round of grinding corn, broken alone by childbirth once a year, during the period of her youth. Then came the one brief day of joy since she kept goats a child upon the hills, the morning when she bore a son, one who would be a man, and ride, and fill his father's place upon the earth.

She saw her sons grow up, her husband die, and then her children follow him, herself once more alone, and keeping goats upon the hill, only brown, bent, and wrinkled, instead of round, upright, and rosy, as when she was a child. Still, with the resignation of her race, a resignation as of rocks to rain, she did not murmur, but took it all just as her goats bore all things, yielding their necks, almost, as it were, cheerfully, to her blunt knife, upon the rare occasions when she found herself constrained to kill one for her food.

Waking and dozing, she passed through the hottest hours when even palm trees drooped, and the tired earth appears to groan under the fury of the sun.

Then rising up refreshed, she led her ass to water at the stream, watching him drink amongst the stones, whitened with the salt scum, which in dry seasons floats upon all rivers in that land.

Mounting, she struck into the sandy deep-worn track which, fringed with feathery tamarisks, led out into the plain. Like a faint cloud on the horizon rose the white city where the Prophet dwelt, and as the ass shuffled along, travellers from many paths passed by, and the road grew plainer as she advanced upon her way.

Horsemen, seated high above their horses in their chair saddles, ambled along, their spears held sloping backwards or trailing in the dust. Meeting each other on the way, they whirled and charged, drawing up short when near and going through the evolutions of the "Jerid," and then with a brief "Peace," again becoming grave and silent, they ambled on, their straight sharp spurs pressed to their horses' sides.

Camels with bales of goods, covered with sheepskin or with striped cloth, swayed onward in long lines, their heads moving alternately about, as if they were engaged in some strange dance. Asses, with piles of brushwood covering them to their ears, slid past like animated haystacks, and men on foot veiled to the eyes, barefooted, with their slippers in their hands, or wearing sandals, tramped along the road. Pack-mules, with bundles of chopped straw packed hard in nets, or carrying loads of fresh-cut barley or of grass, passed by, their riders sitting sideways on the loads, or, running at their tails with one hand on their quarters, seemed to push on their beast, as with the curses, without which no mule will move, they whiled away the time. A fine red dust enveloped everything as in a sand storm, turning burnouses and haiks brown, and caking thickly on the sweaty faces of the men.

Nearing the city gates the crush grew thicker, till at last a constant stream of people blocked the way, jostling and pushing, but good-humouredly, after the way of those to whom time is the chiefest property they own.

Dark rose the crenellated walls, and the white gate made a strange blot of light in the surrounding brown of plain and roads and mud-built houses of the town.

Entering upon the cobbled causeway, she passed through the gate, and in a corner, squatting on the ground, saw the scribes writing, the spearmen lounging in the twisted passage with their spears stacked against the wall. Then the great rush of travellers bore her as on a wave into the precincts of the town.

She rode by heaps of rubbish, on which lay chickens and dead dogs, with scraps of leather, camels' bones, and all the jetsam of a hundred years, burned by the sun till they became innocuous, but yet sending out odours which are indeed the very perfumes of Araby the blest.

Huts made of canes, near which grew castor-oil plants, fringed the edge of the high dunghill of the town, and round it curs, lean, mangy, and as wild as jackals, slept with a bloodshot eye half open, ready to rush and bark at any one who ventured to infringe upon the limits of their sphere of influence.

She passed the sandy horse-market, where auctioneers, standing up in their stirrups with a switch between their teeth, circled and wheeled their horses as a seagull turns upon the wing, or, starting them full speed, stopped them with open mouth and foam-flecked bit, turned suddenly to statues, just at the feet of the impassive bystanders, who showed their admiration but by a guttaral "Wah," or gravely interjected "Allah," as they endeavoured to press home some lie, too gross to pass upon its merits, even in that bright atmosphere of truth which in all lands encompasses the horse.

A second gate she passed, in which more tribesmen lounged, their horses hobbled, and themselves stretched out on mats, and the tired pilgrim found herself in a long cobbled street, on which her ass skated and slipped about, being accustomed to the desert sands. In it the dyers plied their craft, their arms stained blue or red, as they plunged hanks of wool into their vats, from which a thick dark steam rose, filling the air with vapours as from a "solfatara," or such as rises from those islands in the west, known to those daring men "who ride that huge unwieldy beast, the sea, like fools, trembling upon its waves in hollow logs," and braving death upon that element which Allah has not given to his faithful to subdue. Smiths and artificers in brass and those who ply the bellows, sweating and keeping up a coil, unfit for council, but by whose labour and the wasting of whose frames cities are rendered stable, and states who cherish them set their foundations like wise builders on a rock, she passed.

Stopping, the pilgrim asked from a white-bearded man where in the city did the Prophet sit, and if the faithful, even the faithful such as she, had easy access to the person of the man whom God had chosen as his vicegerent upon earth.

Stroking his beard, the elder made reply: "Praise be to God, the One, our Lord Mohammed keeps no state. He sits within the mosque which we of Mecca call Masjida n'Nabi, with his companions, talking and teaching, and at times is silent, as his friends think, communing with the Lord. All can approach him, and if thou hast anything to ask, tether thine ass at the mosque door and go in boldly, and thou wilt be received."

The pilgrim gave "the Peace," and passed along in the dense crowd, in which camels and mules, with horses, negroes, tribesmen, sellers of sweetmeats, beggars, and water-carriers, all swelled the press.

Again she entered into streets, streets, and more streets. She threaded through bazaars where saddle-makers wrought, bending the camels' shoulder bones to form the trees, and stretching unshrunk mare's hide over all. Crouched in their booths, they sat like josses in a Chinese temple, sewing elaborate patterns, plaiting stirrup leathers, and cutting out long Arab reins which dangle almost to the ground. Before their booths stood wild-eyed Bedouins, their hair worn long and greased with mutton fat till it shone glossy as a raven's wing. They chaffered long for everything they bought. Spurs, reins, or saddle-cloths were all important to them, therefore they took each piece up separately, appraised it to its disadvantage, and often made pretence to go away calling down maledictions on the head of him who for his goods wished to be paid in life's blood of the poor. Yet they returned, and, after much expenditure of eloquence, bore off their purchase, as if they feared that robbers would deprive them of their prize, hiding it cautiously under the folds of their brown goat's-hair cloaks, or stowed in the recesses of their saddle-bags.

A smell of spices showed the tired wanderer that she approached the Kaiseria, wherein dwell those who deal in saffron, pepper, anise, and cummin, assafoetida, cloves, nutmegs, cinnamon, sugar, and all the merchandise which is brought over sea by ship to Yembo, and then conveyed to Mecca and Medina upon camels' backs.

Stopping an instant where a Jaui had his wares displayed, she bought an ounce of semsin, knowing Abdallah's son had three things specially in which he took delight, women, scents, and meat, but not knowing that of the first two, as his wife Ayesha said in years to come, he had his fill, but never of the third. The Kaiseria left behind, she felt her heart beat as she neared the mosque.

Simple it stood on a bare space of sand, all made of palm trees hewn foursquare, the walls of cane and of mud, the roof of palm leaves over the mihráb—, simple and only seven cubits high, and yet a fane in which the pæan to the God of Battles echoed so loudly that its last blast was heard in Aquitaine, in farthest Hind, Irac, in China, and by the marshy shores of the Lake Chad.

As she drew near the mosque not knowing (as a woman) how to pray, she yet continued muttering something which, whilst no doubt strengthening her soul, was to the full as acceptable to the One God as it were framed after the strictest canon of the Moslem law. Then, sliding to the ground, she tied her ass's feet with a palmetto cord, and taking in her hand her ounce of semsin as an offering, passed into the court.

Under the orange trees a marble fountain played, stained here and there with time, murmuring its never-ending prayer, gladdening the souls of men with its faint music, and serving as a drinking-place to countless birds, who, after drinking, washed, and then, flying back to the trees, chanted their praises to the giver of their lives.

A little while she lingered, and then, after the fashion of her race, which, desert born, cannot pass running water, even if they are being led to death, without a draught, she stopped and drank. Then, lifting up her eyes, she saw a group seated beneath a palm tree, and at once felt her eyes had been considered worthy to behold the man whom, of all men, his Maker in his life had pardoned and set His seal upon his shoulder as a memorial of His grace.

As she drew near she marked the Prophet, the Promised, the Blessed One, who in the middle of his friends sat silently as they discussed or prayed.

Of middle height he was and strongly made, his colour fair, his hair worn long and parted, neither exactly curling nor yet smooth, his beard well shaped and flecked with silver here and there, clipped close upon his upper lip; and about the whole man an air of neatness and of cleanliness. His dress was simple, for, hanging to the middle of his calf, appeared his under-shirt, and over it he wore, as it fell out upon that day, a fine striped mantle from the Yémen, which he wrapped round about him tightly after the fashion of a cloak. His shoes, which lay beside him, were of the fashion of the Hadhramút, with thongs and clouted, his staff lay near to them, and as he spoke, he beat with his left hand upon the right, and often smiled so that his teeth appeared as white as hailstones, new fallen on the grass after an April storm.

Advancing to the group, the pilgrim gave "the Peace," and then, tendering her offering, stood silent in the sight of all the company. Fear sealed her lips, and sweat ran down her cheeks as she gazed on the face of him to whom the Lord of Hosts had spoken, giving him power both to unloose and bind.

Gently he spoke, and lifting up his hand, said, "Mother, what is it you seek, and why this offering?"

Then courage came to her, and words which all the Arabs have at their command, and she poured forth her troubles, telling the prophet of her loneliness, her goats, her hut, of her lost husband and her sons all slain in battle, in the service of the Lord. She asked him why her sex was barred from Paradise, and if the prophet would exclude Ámina, she who bore him, from the regions of the blessed. With the direct and homely logic of her race, she pressed her claims.

Well did she set out woman's life, how she bore children in sore suffering, reared them in trouble and anxiety, moulded and formed their minds in childhood, as she had moulded and had formed their bodies in the womb.

When she had finished, she stood silent, anxiously waiting a reply, whilst on the faces of the fellowship there came a look as if they too remembered those who in tents and dúars on the plains had nurtured them, but no one spoke, for the respect they bore to him who, simply clad as they, was yet superior to all created men.

Long did he muse, no doubt remembering Kadíja, and how she clave to him in evil and in good report, when all men scoffed, and then opening his lips he gave his judgment on the pilgrim's statement of the case.

"Allah," he said, "has willed it that no old woman enter Paradise, therefore depart, and go in peace, and trouble not the prophet of the Lord."

Tears rose to Rahma's eyes, and she stood turned to stone, and through the company there ran a murmur of compassion for her suffering. Then stretching out his hand, Mohammed smiled and said, "Mother, Allah has willed it, as I declared to you, but as his power is infinite, at the last day, it may be he will make you young again, and you shall enter into the regions of the blessed, and sit beside the Perfect Ones, the four, who of all women have found favour in his sight."

He ceased, and opening the offered packet, took the semsin in his hand, and eagerly inhaled the scent, and Rahma, having thanked him, stooped down and kissed the fringes of his striped Yemen mantle, then straightening herself as she had been a girl, passed through the courtyard, mounted on her ass, and struck into the plain.

His Return

The goats'-hair tents, surrounded by their blue-grey hedge of piled-up camel thorn, stood in a semicircle, forming a little shoal in the vast ocean of green grass chequered with poppies, marigolds, and borage, which stretched on every side for miles until it joined the marshes of Zimoúr. Grass and more grass, and still more flowers, in which the little kids skipped joyously. Herbage in which the bursting cattle lay and chewed the cud; in which the mares and foals wandered and fed, raising their heads to answer the shrill neigh which now and then came from the stallions tied before the tents. A vast green plain in spring; in summer a brown waste, and in the winter a great slough of mud. A plain on which, from their first strange eruption into the history of the world, sprung from their dry stony steppes in the Hedjáz and Yémen, Arabs have wandered, fought, and fed their flocks, tilling the soil but fitfully, passing their lives in patriarchal fashion, and remembered after death but when their son's or grandson's horse stumbles upon their ragged headstones grouped about the whitewashed kouba of a saint. A world in which men pass their lives so close to nature, and in such communion with their flocks, that looking at it, the incomprehensible, mysterious story of the Old Testament becomes as plain as if we saw it acted out before our eyes.

In the square castle, with its crenellated walls, set in its frame of green-leaved apricot and peach trees, lives the scriptural "king." Time and the march of centuries (which have slipped passed [sic = past] unheeded by the dwellers in the tents) have changed him to a Moorish governor. In all essentials, in his proud, scornful eye, his lust for women and for power, in his injustice, or his perhaps still more unjust attempts at righteousness; his love of horses, and of a simple prehistoric pomp, he has remained unchanged. Save that he carries a long gun balancing on his saddle instead of holding in his hand a spear, when he rides out to watch the ploughmen work (the oxbird, white and Egyptian looking, following the plough) the difference is not great. The same white flowing clothes, in which even a negro looks majestic, the same bare sandalled or soft slippered feet; the turban or the string of camels' hair bound round the head; no matter if the Moorish kaid hides in a pocket of his caftan a cheap Waterbury watch, — the two are one.

Isaiah and the minor prophets, and he who wrote the immoral story of the Jewish harlot Esther, and of Hamán, her bold compeer, have set down for us the inward and perhaps spiritual graces owned by the wicked "king," and by the Moorish kaid. Mean in essentials, lavish in superfluities, after the fashion of the Eastern of all time; slow and sententious in their utterance, delivering a proverb as if it were something which they themselves had lived through, or at the least had met with and noted for the first time in set recorded speech, the kaid and king touch hands above the world of telegraphs and steam.

The "king" still lives, for ever set in the pages of the minor prophets, as a Roman emperor lives, carved in an amethyst; and the kaid, does not the harmless and perhaps unnecessary tourist still depict him for us in his primeval childish villainy — a villainy so elementary as to be almost virtue, when compared with that to which rises the flight of those whose lot is thrown in lands of school-boards and the advantages of modern life? Around them both the quiet pastoral life flowed and flows peacefully, and as unmoved by outside influences as is the image of a landscape mirrored in a lake.

To goats'-skin tents, to grassy plains, and the quiet life all undisturbed except by fears of the exactions of the kaid, which after all to him seemed quite as unavoidable as death, Bu'Horma's thoughts went back with longing from the confinement to the barracks, in a distant city in the service of his king. Long idle days he sat outside the palace gates, starving and dozing, whilst flies in thousands buzzed about his ears. Whole days he wandered in bazaars amongst the throngs of white-robed, noiseless-footed citizens. In the long tortuous kaiseria, gay with red sashes and embroidered bridles, and handkerchiefs from the far looms of the mysterious Manchester, where Christians (Allah in his might destroy them all!) labour by day and night, so that the faithful may have wherewithal to wipe off sweat, he loitered listlessly. Sometimes he sat and listened to the water bubbling in the rills of tiles which intersect the mosque, praying at intervals, sleeping for hours, a bundle of white rags upon the stones; then waking, prayed again, but with his thoughts still straying to the tents. Sometimes, upon his lord's behest, perched on a high red saddle, more or less dilapidated, and with his gun held upright, like a spear, or balancing across the saddle-bow, he trotted over plains, crossed rivers, and scaled mountains, enduring hardships and in peril of his life, to bring the news of the arrival of a new lot of bicycles for his liege lord in Fez. As he passed goats'-hair tent or reed-thatched hut upon the way, he spoiled the people to the utmost of his power, holding, as all the Arabs hold, that power is given by God into man's hand to use, and that authority is to be exercised, or it will shortly fall into contempt.

Although the dwellers in the tents were mere facsimiles of what he was himself before his fortune called him to the sword, he did not pity them, loving, as every Arab does, only his family, and holding all mankind an enemy if they are born a mile beyond his tent.

Once, and once only, did Bu'Horma during his service really enjoy and see the real old Arab life of blood and plunder, the love of which lies at the root of every Arab's heart. Once, and once only, but so acutely that it tinged his life to his last hours, unsettling him, and displacing in his heart at last, even his birth-love of the low black tents.

A kaid after, like Ahab, having run his course of blood, of tyranny, and lust, and being besides suspected of having concealed much wealth, the Sultan sent an expedition to his castle, to take and bring him back to Fez. In an evil hour the kaid, having waxed strong, essayed to kick, after the fashion of his scriptural prototype, Kaid Jeshurún. Mustering his guards, he placed them on the wall, setting his women, with turbans on their heads, between the *tapia* battlements to make a show of force. His money he threw down a well, and having poisoned several jars of oil and honey and some loaves of bread, had his best horses saddled in the courtyard, and waited, with a train of powder laid to his wives' and children's rooms, for the assault. He had not long to wait, for the emissaries of the court, though few in number, had, in the Moorish fashion, made themselves friends of members of the tribe the kaid oppressed. Upon their ragged horses, their tattered, sand-stained *haiks* streaming out in the wind, the tribesmen mustered, thick as vultures gather to the carcase of a camel left upon the road. Carrying their spear-like guns hooped round with brass, and with their single pointed spurs strapped on their naked ankles, and hanging loose below their heels, their bridle-hands held high on the near side, as they were steering boats, the tribesmen with their faces veiled in linen rags soon swarmed about the walls. Whirling about like gulls upon the wing, they wheeled their horses, firing as they turned, after the fashion of the Parthians or

Comanches, their bullets raising little puffs of dust from the mud walls, then pausing to reload, another troop advanced, and so the game might have gone on for ever, and no one much the worse, as they took care to keep well out of range, except just at the moment of attack. Inside the kásbah the kaid had little need to stimulate his bodyguard, for each man fought, not only with a halter almost dangling on his neck, but with the fear of torture in his mind. The women from the courtyard down below passed up the rifles, ready loaded, and the men on the walls fired till the guns grew hot, killing a horse or two, and now and then bringing a soldier to the ground, but as they fired the crowd of tribesmen always increased, so that the kaid and all his followers knew that their doom was sealed. Just about evening time, as the light failed, and cartridges within the fort were running short, tribesmen and soldiers, dashing to the door, forced it and entered with a rush. The kaid, drawing a box of cheap Algerian matches from an embroidered bag, lighted the train, which fizzled and went out. Then springing on his horse, with but three followers, he galloped through a gate which a black slave held ready for him, and in the failing light, amidst a fire of desultory shots, soon vanished in the dusk, his dead-white face and grey beard dyed with henna, peering back for a last look upon his home, as, his legs tucked against his horse's side, with voice, with spurs and bit, he urged him on across the plain.

The setting sun flushed the mud walls a brick-dust pink and blended all the crumbling towers and mouldering battlements into a Babylonian-looking mass as the wild horsemen and the red-clad soldiers poured into the fort. The doomed defenders were soon hacked to shreds under the knives of the fierce riders, and then the older men commenced the search for money, whilst the rest made for the apartments where the women were confined. Before the door two or three soldiers of the kaid fired a last volley, and almost before the smoke had cleared away were dead, their throats cut and their bellies ripped up by the long knives from Mequinéz which all the tribesmen wield. In the courtyard a donkey, struck by a bullet, slowly bled to death amongst the corpses of the kaid's men, who, naked and with their noses and their ears cut off, lay stiffly in the dust, their blood coagulating, and the flies already buzzing round their wounds. Inside the women's rooms shouting and cries were heard, and then the body of an old negress, dripping with blood, was hurled down from the roof into the yard, where it lay, indecent and grotesque, looking like dirty indiarubber in the sun, and all was still. Then, the first fury over, the women were shared out amongst the men. A tall thin Arab girl fell to Bu'Horma's share.

"Reeking she came to me," he said, "from the hot kisses of her ravishers. She looked at me, her eyes cast down, her veil in tatters, as the tears fell slowly down her cheeks. She looked at me, and at once there came into my soul that which I never felt. That night I spared her, sleeping by my horse, and in the morning she was sitting by me, and when I waked she rose and took my horse to water at the well."

For three days did the conquerors ransack the place for money, but found none; and in the meantime several of them died from eating of the poisoned honey and the oil.

Bu'Horma, "caught in the eyelids" of the Arab girl, dozed in the shade until at last the signal came to saddle up and ride. Long did the girl plead that she might go with him, but he, knowing the precariousness of Arab life, or perhaps fearing satiety, or because his horse was lame and could not carry double, turned a deaf ear, though, as he said, "Her prayers made me feel like a young lamb left motherless and which has not learned to graze." So taking five-and-twenty dollars, all his share of the sacked kásbah, from his bag, he put it in her hand, and rode away erect upon his horse, looking out steadfastly upon the plain.

Years passed away, and still the Sultan never gave the word which would enable poor Bu'Horma to return to his beloved tents. His beard grew thick upon his chin; by careful, well-considered theft he had acquired good clothes and arms, even a horse, and still he lingered lounging at the palace gates, or now and then was sent on expeditions against the mountain tribes.

At last the longed for, almost despaired of, order came, and he was free to go.

At daybreak, mounted on his horse, he passed the city gates. Perched on his high red saddle, gun in hand, and on his head the high-peaked fez just peeping from his turban, which marks the soldier of the mahksen, he kept upon his way. At times he ambled swiftly at the Eastern pace, which, whilst it bends the horse's legs into fantastic shapes, yet leaves the rider so unshaken in his seat that he can carry in his hand a jar of water, and not spill a drop; at others drawing to a walk, but always with a wary eye turned upon every side, he rode past dúar and past kásbah, never alighting from his horse till his day's march was done.

On the fifth evening he was near his home, and saw on every side of
him the well-remembered plains. Though years had passed, straight as a
pigeon homing through the air he ambled to the tents. All was unchanged,
the mares fed in the flowery grass; the colts played, whinnying, at their
heels; sheep bleated, and the camels strayed about, looking as if they had
survived from some anterior world: all was the same as it had been when
first he went to Fez.

Seated upon the ground, his back against the side wall of the tent,
his father sat, looking but little older save for his snowy beard, for time
seems to do nothing on an Arab of the plain, except to dry the tissues,
and make sinews harder than in youth. Gravely his father welcomed him
as he had only seen him yesterday, and then Bu'Horma, getting off his
horse, saw and embraced his mother, who raised the shrill Lu-Lu which
Arab women raise to show their joy. Brothers and sisters came and stared
at him with dry unsympathetic eyes, having grown up to man's estate
during his absence at the capital.

Night fell, and from the tent which served as mosque rang out the
call to prayer; cows lowed, and sheep and goats were driven to the fold;
and in the khaima Bu'Horma and his folk ate *baizar* drank *libben* from
a great wooden bowl which passed from hand to hand. Long did they
sit and talk, after the fashion of their race, of money and the scarcity
of bread, and of the price of eggs in Tangier, and if the Sultan soon
designed to take the field, gathering the taxes as he went in person, at the
sword's point, as Sultans all have done since first Mohammed drove his
camels on the road. Much did Bu'Horma tell of Fez, and of the wonders
of the town, its mosques, its houses seven storeys high, and of the tricks
of those who dwelt there, with much about the Jews, the Christians, and
much lore he did unfold of courts and policies, and things that he knew
nothing of, such as the ship our Lord the Sultan had just bought which
mounted in the air like *El Borák*, and in three days could go to Londrès
and come back again to Fez.

Then when the family lay down to sleep he wandered out, and looked
at the familiar stars, watching them rise above the distant hills, just
where they rose when he, a boy, kept sheep upon the plain. Long did he
ponder, thinking much upon the world, and of the girl who for three
days had held his heart after the sack of the kaid's kásbah in the south.

Opening his lungs, he sniffed up the night air, and smelt the well-
remembered smells, of cows, of sheep, of camels, with all the scents

which hang about an Arab dúar from the far Yémen to the Sáhara. All was familiar, and at the same time strange to him; something was wanting in the old life, to which he had longed for, for so many years, and as he stood a feeling grew on him that it was best for him to go. Then as he walked about his eye fell on his horse eating its barley greedily, upon a mat spread out upon the ground. He waited patiently till it had finished the last grain, and slowly saddled up; then, with a last look at the sleeping tents, he mounted silently, and settling his haik, touched his horse with the spur, and vanished noiselessly into the night, upon the road to Fez.

Progress

El Khattaia-Es-Salaa

"For you see," said Hamed-el-Angeri, "it was in the time when all the animals could speak."

He stood in the bright sun, his short brown cloak reaching but to his knees; a string of camels' hair was rolled about his head, and with the look of one who states a fact the whole world knows upon his face.

In the deserted orange-garden, with the trees all run to wood, its irrigation rills of white cement choked up and broken, and the few flowers run wild, great bushes of geraniums climbing into the pear and quince trees, and jasmine twining up the oranges and *azofaifas*, no sound of the great noisy, dusty Fez broke through. All was neglected; the myrtle bushes, some of them blown down, had rooted and formed arches in the ground. The green-tiled paths were thick with weeds, and broken up where mules and horses had been led to water at the tank. The tank itself was full of stagnant water, in which lived frogs and snakes. From the tall elm tree in the corner storks chattered and perhaps called to prayers, for though it may have been that all the birds and beasts could speak in Arabic upon a time, surely the semi-human stork (which with the porpoise shares the title of the "friend of man") still can talk, although he does not care to let us fathom his discourse.

So quiet the garden was, that when the lizards chased each other through the dead grass, the noise they made was as distinct (in its degree) as if a troop of cavalry had passed. A scent of mint and of decaying orange blossom filled the air; all was old-world and still; and the bare-footed, white-clothed people passed about amongst the trees, as they were shades of some old life, making one feel, in looking at them, as one feels in looking at some prediluvian footstep, stamped in the rock, which once was river mud.

"Yes," said the Angeri, "once Allah let all animals both speak and pray to him in Arabic, so that men, listening to them, could understand their speech." A dreadful time it must have been, if with their speech they also enjoyed reason, and could accuse us to our faces of all our crimes against their kind. Who that could contemplate their speech and not go mad, with thinking upon all that they might say? But as it happened, God having let them all speak (once upon a time), and as the God the Angeri knew was Allah, the merciful, compassionate, capricious, envious, the invisible, and therefore unapproachable, except by prayer, that smoke the human mind gives off under its fire of cares, the animals had all to pray, or else to lose their speech.

Whether the power of speech with the added obligation of incessant prayer was worth the trouble it entailed, we may well doubt; but so it was, and every beast, in those days, prayed five times a day. The lions and tigers, no doubt, begging the giver of their speech to send them antelopes and deer to prey upon, and they, in their turn, praying (as we do ourselves) for help in danger, and for deliverance from all the ills of battle, murder, and of sudden death. Five times a day they prayed, and prostrated themselves before the Lord. The doves and pigeons cooed their prayers (in Arabic) from every tree. The shy gazelles out on the plains stood by the water-holes, and at the stated times turned towards Mecca, and gave their thanks to Him who giveth victory, and blessed His Prophet's name. The asses bending underneath their loads, stood at the corners of the streets, whilst in the shade their drivers slept, and by their instinct finding out the Kiblah, all gave thanks. Camels upon their knees, in circles underneath the stars, in the blue-grey zaribas of dead thorns, when all was silent in the night, gurgled and bubbled out their praise, their pack-saddles looking like islands, as they lay outlined in the night.

All space was filled with a vague sound of insects humming as they prayed, and in the still clear air the hawks hung motionless when from the mosque towers rose the voice of the muezzín. Fishes in rivers and in seas, and in the little streams, just where the water forms a "linn," hung quivering, or else rising up to the surface looked towards Mecca, and adored their Lord. All nature prayed, and man, hearing their voices, prayed in unison, whilst Allah from his appointed place looked down approvingly, being content with all that he had done. What were the feelings of mankind, when they thus found themselves in actual touch with the souls of all the praying animals, Hamed-el-Angeri knew not. Most likely that he never gave the matter even a passing thought, not knowing that the power of speech is after all the only evidence of the possession of a soul, or, at the least, the only thing by which we, in our arrogance, lay claim to an essential difference from the other animals, whose life seems quite identical with that of man.

350

What reasons weighed with Allah to take back the gift of speech, even the Arabs cannot say. Whether it was that animals, puffed up with pride, claimed, as they well might claim, a place in Paradise for having strictly followed nature and Allah's law, it is not clear. Whether having lived according to their lights, they did not think it just that they should share in the Jehánnum to which both Christians and Mohammedans alike cleave with the utmost force of their believing souls, counting it only just that those who choose to live after the laws of reason in this world, should in a future state enjoy a limbo of their own, no man can tell.

But so it happened that the celestial firman on a day went forth, withdrawing from all animals but man, the power of speech. All beasts and insects, birds, fishes, and the creeping things, knew that if they wished to pray for the last time in the same tongue as man and to be comprehended, both by vertebrate and by invertebrate, according to their kind, in their petitions to the one God, the indivisible, the incomprehensible, the giver and the withdrawer of their common bond, they must assemble and give praise, before the mógreb of the appointed day.

Loud lamentations filled the world; from caves, and lairs, and holes, from tree-tops and from the innermost recesses of the woods, from woven habitations dangling on the thistles and the grass, from caverns in the ocean depths, from where upon the waves float miles of animalculæ, and from the air in which a million midges winged their way, passing their briefest lives in joy and praise, weeping and sounds of woe were heard upon the breeze. Each made his moan according to his kind, and, at the morning call to prayer, animals, insects, and the birds prayed fervently that Allah should not take away their speech. Shy wood-deer timidly peeped out, and moles stopped swimming in their dark, waveless sea, and, working to the surface of the ground, just raised their noses, and gave thanks to him who, from that evening, was about to strike them dumb. Timid and savage, winged, furred, and hairy, all the beasts in their degree sadly prepared to thank the giver and the taker of their link with man. Fish in the sea in shoals, rising above the waves in scaly millions, glorified the Lord. The whales and porpoises, wallowing like galleons in the swell, prayed as they rose to breathe, and flying fish, darting ablaze with topaz and with jacinth tints, reflected in the sun, as if a flight of crystal prisms had suddenly found life, all joined the general thanksgiving, as they skimmed lightly on the tops of waves, and disappeared like showers of diamonds in the spray. In the deep forests of Guiana wilds and on the Amazon, the sloths, clinging to greenhearts and to ceibas, shook off their torpor, and, opening their eyes, joined in the general chorus of their fellows lazily, but with conviction, as churchwardens half slumbering in church, thinking upon the mercies of the Lord, and of the ægis thrown round the villainy of man by the great power which, with a fellow-feeling for the great, has shielded them throughout the week, and hoping for protection in the week to come, awake just at the prayer for the High Court of Parliament, and vote their meed of praise. Out in the Sáhara, the ostriches, shyest of all living things, grouped round the water-holes, and, after having drunk their fill, turned towards farthest Mecca, bowed their willowy necks, and swelled the general chorus of the universal prayer. Then, spreading out their wings, scudded before the wind like ships, and disappeared into the wastes of sand. Far in the middle-mere of Patagonian and Pampean grass the rhea and huanaco, to-day most silent of all beasts, stood ranged in troops, and as the north-east wind blew rigging of white filaments between the grass stems, and on the tops of reeds, they looked across the sea of green in which they lived, then out upon the ocean and the sands of Africa, towards the Kiblah to which upon that day men and the animals all for the last time gazed and adored as one.

Then, satisfied that they had done all that lay in their power, wheeled and dashed off across the plains, snorting and stretching out their wings, passing like thunderbolts before the villages, where at their holes biscachas sat and poured out their hearts, whilst on the mounds grave little owls twisted their solemn heads towards the east, and prayed as solemnly as if they were ordained and duly made the Levites of the beasts.

The serpents and the snakes, who in their efforts to escape the primal curse, which has exposed them to the folly and malignancy of man, made greater use of speech than all the other animals combined, were strenuous in prayer, and reared their heads in ecstasy of praise.

So as the day wore on, the muezzins duly calling at the stated hours, all animals had prayed and given thanks.

Men at their mosques, and at the doors of saints' tombs, prayed in the usual way, almost as if their prayers conferred a favour upon Him to whom they were addressed, just as alms are a favour, not to the beggar, but to the man who gives, for does he not thus, at the same time, quiet the suppliant's cry, obtain the approbation of his kind, and lay up treasure in those realms where neither beggars whine, nor anything transpires to offend the nicer feelings of those souls who by their own exertions have attained to Paradise.

The day drew on, and the long shadows falling on the deep and lane-like streets, in which the white-clad people moved noiselessly about (like souls in limbo, or like fish in an aquarium, in a light cloud of dust), lit up the mosque towers in a glow of pink, and slanted through the orange trees, making kaleidoscopic patterns on tiled patio floors, showed that the sands were running through the glass, and that the time appointed by Allah, the capricious one, was drawing nigh.

A hush fell on the world and on the animals, a sort of shadow of the cross which, from that evening, all of them must bear, crept over them, making them melancholy, and yet resigned, with the sublimeness of their patience, which leaves man's faith, his reason, and the whole gamut of his moral qualities thousands of miles behind.

At last the hour of the mogréb drew near, and all our fellow-creatures for the last time prepared for evening prayer. Long did the cry ring out, rising and falling and prolonged almost beyond the force of human lungs. Far did it carry and resound, bringing with its long trills and quavers the decree of dumbness to the myriads of those who hitherto had, like ourselves, rejoiced to thank Allah in the same tongue as man. At last it ceased, and the cool evening chill fell on the heated world, bringing fresh life, and planting in each breast desire to thank Him who made day and night, bridled the sea, and set the stars to run for ever in their courses, made moon and sun give light, and caused the unceasing miracle of the seasons' round to glorify His name.

When from the almináres of the mosques which dot the world from China to the sands of far Shingiet, the last long-drawn-out "Allah Ackbar" had blended with the air, a mighty host of animals, each in their kind, and after their degree, stood forth for the last time to pray. Turning towards the city in the sands, they first stood silently, and gazed towards the east. Then, lifting up their heads, a roar as of the sea which breaks upon the outer islands of the Hebrides, filled the air, as they all testified to the one God, the Great, the Merciful, Compassionate, who giveth victory to those who call on Him, and to His Prophet, the careful camel-driver, he whom Kadijah loved, and of her said, "By Allah, she shall sit at my right hand in Paradise, for, when all men shot out their lips in scorn, she, only she, believed, and comforted."

They ceased, and, as the guttural Arabic died on their lips, the power of speech was gone. Tears stood on hairy lids, dropped from great limpid eyes, and fell on desert sand, were showered like rain-drops on Pampean grass, rendered the sea more salt, and splashed on house-roofs, as the dumb birds flew each to its sleeping-place.

But whilst the animal creation had for the last time registered its praise, one little lizard, sporting in the sun, had let the hours slip past. Running, back downwards, on the ceilings of the mosques, all day it chased the flies, basked in the heat, flattening itself against the white-washed walls, its feet expanding flat, like paddles, and its slim tail acting upon the air to steer it as it whisked through horseshoe arches, and shot out upon the vine leaves which grew up outside the holy place. Chasing its fellows in the sun, and catching flies, the sand ran through the glass, and, at the mogréb, when the last quavering "Allah" died away, only the lizard, in its joy of life, did not give thanks to God.

Despair fell on it, and its tiny grief shook its prismatic sides, whilst little tears stood in its beady eyes. Its tail hung quivering, and its head bowed miserably, as it stood silently and without power to glorify the Lord. Then, darting to the mosque, it flittered up the walls, its little feet showering down lime upon the worshippers. Just over the mihráb it stopped, and, as the faithful in the mosque below looked up at it, scratched "Allah Ackbar" with its claw upon the roof, and, scurrying back, was lost beneath the eaves.

"So," said the Angeri, "it saved itself from Allah's wrath, and showed its faith; and from that time we know it as *Khattaia-es-salaa*, that is, the prayer-scratcher; praise to His Holy name."

A Renegade

Memories of Aluch Ali and Dragút stir at the very word.

Mansur-el-Alj, who built the gate of Mequinéz, Don John of Austria, Hernando Perez de Pulgar (el de las Hazañas); the galleys in which the miserable captives rowed, Moslem or Christian, according as the blood-red banner of Algiers or as the lions and castles of the Catholic king flew from the jackstaff; all the wild sea life from Tarifa to the Dardanelles which filled so large a space in the chronicles of Spain and Italy, like coloured glass in a kaleidoscope, take shape and then dissolve into the mist of time at the mere mention of the name.

Cervantes as a prisoner, his struggles to escape, his sufferings, and the dictum of the Dey when he was ransomed, that he felt safer now the lame Spanish prisoner was gone; Rippérda, ex-Prime Minister of Spain, trampling upon his hat, changing his faith, and raised to be Prime Minister of El Mogréb, then settling down at Tétuán where his descendants long were known as "Oulad-el-Conde" (the count's sons); Dragút a prisoner in the Maltese galleys, chained to his oar and recognised by La Valette, the Grand Master who himself had been a slave, with the remark, "The chance of war, Señor Dragút," to which he answered, "Yes, and the change of fortune;" these and a thousand other true fairy tales of the long-passed time when the rovers of Sallee laid contributions on the trade of Europe, at their sweet will, are bound up with the name of renegade. The Mamelukes, the Janissaries, the Slavonian Guard of Abderahman caliph and ruler of the Andalus; men like Pellew, the prisoner of the ferocious Muley Ismail Sultan of Fez, he who could mount his horse, draw forth his scimitar and behead the slave who held the stirrup all in one motion — outcasts from Christendom, and prisoners of war who, like the Calabrian peasant Aluch Ali, saw no respite from their labour at the oar till they had changed their faith   all these were renegades.

Priests snatched from Spanish or Italian villages, often torn from the very altar in their vestments, knights, squires, and peasants, with noble ladies not a few in those wild times of "rugging" and of "reiving" in the inland sea, often denied their faith when hope of ransom or release had died, and turned Mohammedans. Not far from Mequinéz a village still exists in which the people all are descended from the captive Christians who denied their faith in days gone by. One is a Frenchman, another English, and a third Italian, whilst the chief magistrate, Mohamed-el-Gitani, is quite unconscious that his ancestors had journeyed from Multán, to make him kaid of Agurái.

To-day, the glories of the renegade are past, and usually either in Turkey, Tunis, Tripoli, or in Morocco he is a fugitive from justice in his own country, a man to whom all faiths are equal, so that they bring him bread, and worst of all he is looked down on and despised by his own brethren in the Lord. But notwithstanding that, there are some few who still forsake the most economically advanced of all the creeds, and turn to that which is, at least, a newer faith. In general they are Greeks, Italians, or Spaniards from the southern provinces of Spain, but now and then one of the self-elected chosen of the Anglo-Saxon race stamps on his hat and gravely, as befits his status in humanity, assumes the Tarboosh, yellow slippers, and contemplative life so dear to monotheists, but which we who still dally lovingly with polytheism, can never comprehend.

In a vast plain, and sheltered from the sun but by a tent, lying awake at night and scanning the familiar stars, or in the hottest hours watching the wind raise dust in columns (monuments of life) on the horizon, the conception of a not impossible one God, not caring overmuch for that which He has made, but to be appealed to when the flesh weakening, causes the spirit to repine, appeals at times to all who have lived either in deserts, pampas, or in any other of the vast open spaces of the earth, and more especially when the nights are fine. Seated upon the sand the rude astronomers or astrologers (for all is one) of old could not have set the starry heavens full of gods in the same way that dwellers amongst hills peopled their theologic world with hamadryads, nymphs, fauns, satyrs, and all those lighter incarnations of the Deity which only cloud the spectral palette of the human mind, where mists hang on the mountains, and which, in the keen searching light of desert life, would be as greatly out of place as if Mohammed should have filled his bible with the miracles on which our mysteries rest.

Conviction, coming neither from the east or west, but springing in the heart of man, as does a mango (from underneath a cloth) out of an orange or a lemon pip set by an Indian juggler in a pot, is the sole motive, as a general rule, which makes a renegade worth the attention of philosophers.

Si Abdul Wáhed, as he became after conversion, could not most certainly have appealed to any body of right-thinking men, that is, to men who have erected as a fetish, a God called duty, which they in theory adore, but which they leave in general to other men (giving up to their brethren that which they chiefly love themselves) to follow, as an example of conviction, in either of his faiths.

Stout and red-haired, his cheek-bones high, grey-eyed and freckled, Si Abdul Wáhed was a type of those inhabitants of the north of England who, having achieved the exterior graces, yet never attain to either the spiritual or the commercial virtues of the Scot.

Still less has the saving gift of humour, that humour which as far surpasses wit, as whisky beer, and which, rising superior to climate and the terrors of the Calvinistic faith, has made North Britons kindly in their hardness, and rendered them easier of endurance to foreigners in spite of all their angularities than the majestic and pure-blooded cis-Tweedian Celto-Saxon, fallen to their share.

A Scottish renegade, either in Turkey or North Africa, or in whatever land fortune has given him as his inheritance, would rise inevitably to be a Vizier, perhaps become a King. At the least he would produce a thousand reasons why he had changed his faith, and quarrel with you on each one of them, no matter if you agreed with him or took the other side. He would remain a Scot of Scots no matter how he changed his faith, his dress, his habits, or increased the number of his wives.

Talk to him but of Scotland, whilst he sat dressed as a Turk on a divan, and bit by bit his Oriental manner would fall from him, and, the tear standing in his eye, he would discourse upon the Trossachs, the Kyles of Bute, regret that Providence had not vouchsafed to him to see the railway to Fort William, and then, if you indulged him with a "crack" on "Glesca" and remarked that your great aunt sat under Dr. Chalmers, become your friend for life.

So that, look at the matter philosophically, it is an arguable point whether a Scotsman ever is a renegade, so deep into his being has bitten the affection for the life, the customs, mists, the mountains, and traditions of the land which he has taken such good care to leave.

Si Abdul Wáhed was a renegade of quite another sort, neither conviction nor necessity having impelled him to the momentous step.

As he appeared when seated sideways on a mule, with his feet dangling on its neck, and on each side of him a basket full of water-melons, whilst ambling from his garden into Tlemcen on a market-day, nothing revealed the curious mixture of philosopher and gipsy grafted upon a civil engineer that the man really was. The philosophic and the gipsy grafts were patent after the shortest of acquaintanceship, and the possession of an old theodolite, thought by the members of his new faith to be some species of quick-firing gun, was all the proof, beyond his word, of his once having been an engineer.

Although no citizen of Tlemcen, Christian, Turk, Moor, or Jew, had ever called his word in question, or impeached his strictest and Quixotic honesty down to the pettiest of the affairs of life, he did not seem the man to have taken levels, or measured fields, still less to have surveyed a railway, or in fact done anything but amble, sitting sideways on a mule, to sell his fruit in town.

No sudden access of disgust at the abominations of our modern state, no wish to lead a contemplative life, still less religious doubts or fervour, had induced the quondam engineer to change his faith, and turn a renegade.

Wandering one day in Seville, where he had lived a year or two, he knew not why, and where he learned the language of the place from gipsies, bull-fighters, and the grammarians of Triana, his eyes fell on a Moorish tile, covered with writing in the Cufic alphabet. Most men in his position would have looked, admired, and then passed on, or, if their curiosity had been aroused, have bought a book dealing with ancient Arab writing, have studied it for a short time and then forgotten it in the daily whirl of newspapers, of telegrams, and of the million things which intervene between us and our life. He who was fated to deny his faith and end his days a renegade under the title of Si Abdul Wáhed was of another sort.

He lost no time in poring over books, but taking ship at once came to Orán, and there joining a caravan, arrived at Tlemcen, and at once became a Moor. Speaking no word of Arabic at the time, his knowledge of the precepts of his faith could not have been extensive, but his resolve was fixed, and after circumcision, which he insisted on, and underwent with a blunt pair of nail-scissors, as was his pride and pleasure to relate, he married a young Arab girl, and, having bought a garden on the outskirts of the town, sat down to pass his life. Whether he learned the Cufic alphabet, or that of Mecca, or if indeed he learned to write the language of his faith, or read it, he never said, but he spoke Arabic abominably, and with the burr of Newcastle-on-Tyne.

He made no boast of his conversion, after the fashion of most renegades, nor ever said that he had found light, hope, or rest, or any of the things which converts generally find to salve their consciences. Knock-kneed and shuffling in his gait, his haik and caftan hung upon him as rags hang on a scarecrow, and his red beard and freckled face showed him a European half-a-mile away. His naked arms protruded from his cloak, fat, round, and hairy, and his splay feet looked monstrous in his slippers, whilst the whole man seemed ill at ease in the loose Arab clothes.

Conversion had not brought conviction with it, for he abused his co-religionists, calling them dirty Arab thieves, and when he dined with Europeans he took his glass of whisky, "just like a Christian," as he said, so that his entertainers wondered why it was that he had changed his faith.

What had impelled him to embrace a creed which he quite openly abused and laughed at, is difficult to say, and he himself never referred to it.

Perhaps the *tedium vitæ* born of the modern world worked in him, secretly prompting him to fly from newspapers, from quick communications with uninteresting lands, from snobbism, the dogmatism of the pseudo-scientist, the lies, conventions, and the immeasurable meannesses which we have deified, and to seek refuge under the orange trees in his walled garden in the suburb where, in his sanctuary, the patron saint of Tlemcen, Hasan-el-Andalousi, sleeps under his green-tiled dome.

All this may well have been, or none of it; but on the sandy track bordered on both sides by the orange gardens, on Fridays, mounted on his mule, Si Abdul Wáhed jogs on to the mosque, dismounts and leaves his slippers at the door, washes devoutly, goes through the form of prayer, then getting on his beast goes home again, forgetting or not caring for the West, so that the orange blossoms drop like rain upon his path as his mule plods slowly through the sand.

Progress

A Yorkshire Tragedy

It was an idle day, in every street men stood about and talked in whispers, or squatting on their heels as miners do, accustomed to a narrow seam, stared blankly, as they smoked their short clay pipes. A pall of coal-dust almost obscured the sky, and on the grass and leaves of trees, on slates and window panes, and on the tops of posts, it formed a sort of frost, but black and hideous as of a world decayed.

It clung to wires and made them furry as they were caterpillars, and upon hair and beards it stuck about the roots beyond the power of any soap to clean. Round eyelashes it lay like paint, making the eyes seem sunken and still giving them a brilliancy which looked unnatural.

The village where the miners lived was built of dark grey stone and in a series of long rows divided by partitions, each section with its water-butt, its low stone wall in front, and with a gate which as a general rule stood open, having lost the hinges, or was tied up with string.

The shops were little stores in which were sold grey flannel shirts and boots with wooden soles, cheap bacon and strong cheese, currants and Abernethy biscuits, sized calicoes and twist tobacco, with clay pipes, each with its perforated cap of tin kept in its place by a thin chain which dangled from the stem.

The streets were worn into black waves by heavy carts, and the thick mud, summer or winter, never seemed to dry. Children and whippets ran about the place: the former playing at old-fashioned games, as tig and hopscotch, long forgotten in the south; the latter walking about with dignity, as if aware of the consideration they enjoyed, but not presuming on it, for every child wore wooden clogs and used them with a skill only long practice gives.

Chapels and drink-shops elbowed each other in the town, and a small park in which grew stunted trees that sprang from earth that looked like scoria of a coalpit was chiefly used by lovers, who, seated on the benches with their arms round each other's necks and waists, hugged and caressed each other after the fashion of primeval man, before the public eye.

Such was the town — bleak, black, and desolate, a hive of eating- and of sleeping- boxes, brick-built and roofed with slates.

A dog-fight or a pigeon-flying match, a game of football or of knur and spell, a rabbit-coursing where the whippets tore the rabbits limb from limb, to the delight of all the crowd, more democratic in their love of blood than are their betters at a pheasant battue, were the amusements of the men.

The women stayed at home, working or gossiping across the low stone walls, and fed their children, of whom they had not quivers but whole arsenals well stocked, on Swiss canned milk, tinned meats, and biscuits, to save cookery — an art in which they were so little skilled that what they wasted would have kept two families in any other land.

Upon the Sabbath day they went to chapel, listening to sermons about hell, of which they heard so much that most of them could have drawn plans of it as accurate as Ordnance Surveys, done with such spirit and regard to truth that the proprietor of the domain might have been proud to hang them in his house.

A sordid class distinction, scarcely apparent at first sight, but yet intense, kept the sport-loving colliers and their employers separate; but yet bound to each other, as marriage binds together man and wife, for the protection of their children's property.

The poisonous air had blasted all the trees, which stood black, gaunt, and sere, leafless and lifeless as they had been the ghosts of forests long departed, in the times when fields were green and England merry, and when the sun shone clear without a pall of intervening smoke.

They stood like finger-posts upon the path to progress, pointing the way, but having perished on the road.

The only highway led into country as desolate as are the mountains of the moon. The gritty hay and oats, which ripened late, fought with the north-east wind, and struggled through the coal-dust in the search for sun, which shone but rarely and as if it were ashamed. Commerce and agriculture seemed to have been about to kiss and then had separated, having drawn back disgusted at each other's countenances.

In the drear fields sheep black as tapirs fed. Their wool could only have been used to make the broadcloth used at funerals. They seemed to feed on refuse, for all the fields were strewn with tins, old boots, and bottles, through which the blighted-looking grass vainly essayed to grow.

But though the aspect of the place was dull and cheerless, almost beyond the wont of northern villages, a silence brooded over it that crept into the soul.

The flag upon the pumping-engine of a new pit close to the railway station was fluttering in the air, showing that coal had recently been struck, but the great wheel was still; no clank of chains marked the descending cage, and on the elevated platform ran no train of trucks to be mechanically tipped over on the bing.

It was not "t'idle day," for generally when colliers "play" the "rows" resound to shouts, the dogs tug at their chains, and streams of men pass in and out the public-houses, smoking and talking, if not merrily, at least with that loud Saxon jollity which finds delight in noise.

In the drear town the blinds were all drawn down. Police and soldiers stood about the corners of the streets, and children played in a subdued and melancholy way at reading "T'Riot Act."

Men with their faces scarred with the blue marks that "burning" in the pit imprints on many of their class, lounged, dressed in black, in knots, and talked as dogs might talk after a beating or as slaves when ordered out to death. Their eyes were downcast, and they seemed afraid of something which they could not see, but felt, as children feel the horror of the darkness in a room. Yet through their fears and feeling of amazement mixed with awe, resentment pierced, suppressed but bitter, such as perhaps a horse feels towards his rider who, in his terror at a stumble on a stone, tugs at the bit and violently spurs.

"Government didn't oughter shoot men daawn like that," a scarred old miner muttered, and the rest, the silence broken, soon took up the tale. "Lads didn't rightly knaow what was afoot, when magistrate he come riding oop with t'soldiers and police, and started twittering something out, for all the world like chaffinch; said it was T'Riot Act, and then they fired and shot lad, that's t'bury oop at Oddfellows."

Then by degrees black-coated mourners, dressed in their Sunday clothes, some with the scarves of their society, for "t'corpse" had been "a brother," lounged into the street.

The children stopped their play, and at the gates of the mean houses hosts of women stood, each with a bit of black pinned on their sleeve and faces newly washed. Processions from the neighbouring villages slowly tramped up, and formed before the lodge.

The soldiers and police stared silently, and by degrees the crowd swelled imperceptibly till all the street was full.

Into the lodge the leading "brethren" streamed and seated stiffly, smoked, and in silence spat upon the floor. Their Sunday clothes gave off a smell of camphor, which, mixed with sweat and with the dubbin of their boots, pierced through the fumes of shag and negro-head. Nothing was said for a considerable time, whilst from the crowd outside a murmur rose — as from the cattle in a pen waiting for shipment, as the drovers twist their tails — half pitiful and half resentful; and as the "brethren" heard it, sitting in the smoke, a growl went round, and a man ventured a remark that "Lads could wreck the Riding if they had a mind."

No one responding, he gazed up at the roof and then spat noisily, puffed at his pipe, and swore beneath his breath, whilst his companions pretended that they had not heard, and smoked on silently.

A brother rising stiffly to his feet looked round the room, and after smoothing down his hair, hawked, cleared his throat, and putting his still burning pipe into his waistcoat pocket, called for volunteers to carry "the diseased oop to t'cemetery." When marshals had been duly chosen, not without wrangling, the crowd assembled in the street in which the man "shot by t'Government" had lived. The blinds were all drawn down, but at the gate of all the rows the people stood, and in the misty air the sound of bands converging from the collieries was heard. An ancient hearse drew up before the door, drawn by a chestnut horse, and as they stood and smoked expectant, their hats upon their heads and their black clothes hampering their limbs like fetters, the "brethren," looking at the horse, winked and remarked upon his four white feet, and then recalled the saying that in his case it were best "to return whoam withoot un', for he would never stan' no work."

When the last band had snorted through the street, and not an inch of standing-room was left, "the corpse's brother" went about with wine, followed by several of the dead man's children carrying cake on a Britannia metal dish.

Good manners plainly pointed out to all that they must first refuse, and then on being pressed yield, and break off a bit of cake and ask for "just a bit tastie o' t'wine." Then, on more pressing, resolutely take a good thick slab, and drain the goblet to the bottom till the feast was done, but all in silence and solemnity as the occasion called for, and as the eyes of all the lookers-on demanded should be done. Once more the hawking, red-faced miner stood to the front, and taking off his hat, asked that the minister should pray a bit. Standing upon a chair, the reverend lifted up his voice. Skating upon thin ice, he spoke of the "diseased," praised him and prayed for him, but warily, not wishing to offend the powers that be, but yet indignant at the manner of his death. Then as a melancholy sun shone out and fell on his thin hair, which hung upon the collar of his coat and gave him the appearance of a saint at second hand, he warmed, and launching forth, called on his God to pity and to save, and to provide for "these his children," and he pointed to two girls dressed shabbily in black, who, with a woman holding fast their hands, had been the family of our departed brother in the Lord.

Amens and muttered oaths gurgled up from the crowd, who shuffled with their feet, raising a black and penetrating dust.

The "bit o' prayer" despatched, the minister called for an 'ymn, leading it off himself in such a key that few could compass it. Still they all joined, and as the doggerel floated in the air, raised and prolonged by the rough voices, silently the police took off their helmets under pretence of mopping up their hair. The soldiers listened woodenly, and in the hearse the chestnut horse stamped heavily at flies.

The maimed rites over, the procession got in line, the driver of the hearse seated upon it sideways so as to be in touch with those who followed, and smoking as he drove. In the dark sunless air the tramping feet raised clouds of coal dust, and as men walked they coughed and spat upon the ground, talking in undertones on politics, religion, and the price of coal.

Arrived before "t'cemetery" gate, the hearse drew up, and four tall brothers taking out the "chest," bore it upon their shoulders to the grave. Four others lowered it, and the Levite, stepping forth, again took up his parable, speaking about the virtues of the dead, of faith, good works, and of the state of man, flowering to-day, to-morrow failing, and then cast out into the oven — a phrase which, though it might have terrified some men, was taken by his hearers as liturgic and received with groans.

Then he committed to the earth the dead man's body, certain, as he averred, both of the resurrection and the life to come, and on the coffin fell the gritty soil, as if it mocked him by its blackness and its uncompromising grime.

Last act of all, the grave was trodden in, the wooden shoes of those who dug it trampling it hard, as they walked to and fro upon the grass.

All was now over, and the brethren solemnly shook hands, the bands struck up a march, and through the fields the miners straggled homeward, not in procession but confusedly.

Progress

Beside the grave two or three mourners smoked a sympathising pipe, and by the hedge the chestnut hearse-horse, with the reins twisted round his feet, nibbled the growing grass, whilst in the fields the purblind pit ponies, the only real gainers by the strike, wandered listlessly about, as if they missed the whirring of the wheels and the familiar gloom.

MᶜKechnie v. Scaramanga

"Man, an awfu'-like thing yon law o' general average. Dod aye, I mind aince being the matter of a hundred pound oot by it."

He paused, and spat reflectively into what he, having traded in his youth to Portland Maine, St. John's, and Halifax, knew as a cuspidor. His whole appearance showed him at first sight a man who for the most part of his life had sailed out of Aberdeen or Peterhead.

His iron-grey hair was thin upon his head, and made a halo round his brick-dust face, on which the sun, the storm, and whisky of full fifty years had done their worst. His beard was stiff and bristly, and grew high upon his cheek, and underneath the chin, looked like the back of a wild boar or porcupine. His upper lip was shaved and blue, his teeth stained yellow with tobacco juice. Thick tufts of bristles overhung his eyes and sprang from out his ears, and his enormous hands, once muscular and hard with hauling upon ropes, although immense, were soft and flabby, though still freckled by the sun which tanned them in his youth. Upon his middle finger was tattooed a ring, and round his wrist a bracelet which he tried hard to hide by pulling down his cuff. Not that he was ashamed of it, or ever for an instant posed for anything but what he was, but, as he would explain, "Mistress MᶜKechnie thocht it didna' look genteel. A woman's clavers, aye ou aye; but then, ye see, Mistress MᶜK. raises a wild-like turley-wurley whiles, aboot a feck o' things that dinna matter, for I say when a man has got the siller that is the principal." And certainly he had the siller, for from a mere tin-kettle of a tramp, bought upon credit and in which the saying was if you should drop a marlin-spike it would go through her plates, he had attained to the possession of a fleet which peopled every sea.

But though good luck, which he referred to as the "act of Providence," had thus befriended him and seated him in his own private room in the great office, which he once likened to a liner's cabin, the highest praise in his vocabulary, he yet remained at heart the self-same pawky, pious, superstitious, and hard-fisted sailor man that he was when he first sailed in a whaler to the Arctic seas from Peterhead. His friends and his contemporaries knew him as Andrew Granite, whether because of his resemblance to the stone, his character, or simply from his birthplace, or from all combined, no one was sure. But from the Clyde to Timor-Laut, whenever any of his ships was spoken and ran up her number, a smile went round extending from the forecastle to the bridge, and some old shell-back was pretty safe *[Sp. seguro=safe]* to say, "One of old Andrew's coffins, damn them, a Granite liner; yes, by God; sink like a stone in some place some day, or run upon a shoal marked in no blooming chart; Andrew will grab the insurance money, and then go off to kirk."

Withal he was a genial, simple, whisky-drinking, pious, and not unkindly man, with all the low-class Scotsman's love for law and pride in never being over-reached, and with a gift of story-telling which a long life at sea had sharpened and improved.

His conversation ran on bottomry, on jettison, demurrage, barratry ("a grand word yon," he would explain), and barnacles. Much had he got to say about Restraint of Princes and the like, of berth notes, back freights, charter party, cessio clause, frustration of adventure, and as to whether frost and rats fell under act of God, or might be held as perils of the sea. Much did he like to dwell upon "diceesions o' the Coorts," quoting with unction Stamforth *v.* Wells, Hadley *v.* Baxendale, and Vogeman *v.* Parkenthorpe, with comments of his own upon the judges, with much about the lunar and the calendar in the vexed question of the "Charter" month, much of the usages of trades and ports, all which he held "redeeklous," deeming them part and parcel of a scheme against the Granite Line. An elder of the kirk "outby Bearsden," where, as he said, "he stopped," he yet believed that Providence was a malicious demon on the watch to do him damage, sending foul winds and snapping shafts of screws, blowing off heads of cylinders and heating brasses in an arbitrary way, as if the power referred to had nothing else to do but to watch him and his affairs through a celestial magnifying glass which he kept screwed into his eye after the fashion of a watchmaker when looking at a watch.

The house "outby" where Andrew Granite "stopped" was built of such well-hewn and finely pointed stone as to resemble plaster, so neat were all the joints, so sharp the edges, and though substantial, did not seem designed to live in, but rather as a model from some exhibition of what no house should be. Roofed with dark blue metallic-looking slates, it stood in its own carriage-sweep, which, laid with furnace slag in lieu of gravel, formed as it were a yellow ochre river flowing between the bulwarks of green grass which bounded it, and which, as the possessor said, were "trimmed square by the lifts and braces and ran down sheer into the tide." He used to add that "in a ship, ye ken, ye canna let minavellings lay aboot, an' for a gairdner ye couldna' get a better man nor steadier than an auld sailor, if ye can keep him frae the drink."

Laurels and rhododendrons, the latter "bonny heebrids," as the seafaring "gairdner" called them, stunted and withered by the wind, stood ranged beside the avenue in rows, each with its Latin nickname dangling from a wire upon a piece of tin, as if it was convicted of some crime against its fellows and was doing penance for its sins. Cast-iron hoops contrived to look like withies bordered the road; and to make all things sure, enamelled plates with the inscription "Parties are requested to keep off the grass" reminded people to be cautious how they walked. A battlemented lodge and wrought-iron gate with a huge gilt monogram upon the top stood sentinels at the edge of the domain. Clumps of young spruce trees were disposed at intervals to break the wind, which bent them over opposite the side it blew, and stripped them bare where they caught all the fury of the blast.

The inside of the villa was suitable to its exterior grace.

Plate-glass and varnished yellow pine gave it a sort of likeness to a ship. White fluffy mats lay on the floors, and on the walls were water-colours, so well finished and so smooth that they could easily have been mistaken for the best kind of chromo-lithographs.

Wax fruit and feather flowers, and humming-birds, looking distorted ghosts of their bright selves, were stuck about upon the mantelpieces, covered with glass shades. A banner-screen with a ship worked in crewels stood before the fire, which in a bright steel grate burned till the twelfth of May, and then until October was replaced by coloured paper shavings so contrived as to present the appearance of a waterfall. Mistress McKechnie, a large, high-coloured lady, dressed in black silk and girt about the neck with a gold chain from which a watch was hung which dangled loose or else was stuck into the waistband of her gown, sat in her "droring-room" in state. A large medallion of her lord, with a stout wisp of his stiff hair fashioned into a cable round the edge, was pinned upon her breast. It showed him at the age of thirty, grim and ill-favoured, and had been taken in the port that he called "Ryo" by an artist who he said had been "an awfu' clever chiel," and certainly should have been heard of in the world of art for his stout realism and adherence to the truth.

The owner of the house sat in his sanctum, which, like the cabin of a ship, had small round windows, and was adorned with books, bound in morocco bindings, which he never read, and with a coloured photograph of her he always called "Mistress M^cK." and stood in awe of; for she came of "weel-kenned folk," and had some tocher and a temper which was not always safe "to lippen to."

With cigars lighted, his friends about him and their glasses filled, Mr. McKechnie used to give full play to his imaginative mind on many subjects which had appealed to him during the course of his career — as law pleas about ships, soundings in various ports, the absence of all lights on certain coasts, the charms of ladies he had known about the world and his success with them, and other things of a like nature which he discussed more freely when certain that his wife had gone to bed. One tale led to another, but the tale that his friends all loved the best was one he never failed to tell after his second tumbler of stiff toddy, when, with his feet in carpet slippers worked in yellow beads, and with a fox's head in blue in high relief upon the instep, he would light a Trichinopoly cigar, and after, with the story-teller's instinct, having forced his friends to press him, take up his parable.

"Hae ye all got your glasses filled? Weel — aye — I am a sort o' temperate man masel', but speerits, ye ken, are a fair panawcea, that is when taken moderately." To such a proposition no self-respecting Scotsman has an objection, and they all used to fill, and, "paidlin' " with their ladles, inhale the fumes of the hot spirit, puff their cigars, and wait expectantly.

"Ye see, ma freens, law is a kittle sort o' gear, especially sea law, as mony o' ye ken I know fu' feel *[sic = weel?]*. But the maist awfu' thing is what they ca' yon general average — ay juist fair redeeklous. Ye ken what Mr. Scrutton says — he's an M.A. and LL.B. and has juist written the maist compendious work on contrack of affreightment as expressed in charter-parties — a pairfeck vawdy-mecum. Ane ye ca' Mackinnon helpit him, and between the twa they lay ye aff a'maist a'thing that can arise between a charterer and a shipowner upon the sea.

"Charter-party, sort o' dog Laytin, *carta partita* they ca't. In the auld days they juist wrote it in duplicate on a single sheet o' paper, and then divided it by indented edges, each part fitted to the other. That's hoo they got the name, indenture.

"A feck o' things ye'll find in Scrutton's book, ma freens, sort o' auncient like. Whiles when I havna' much to do I tak' it doon and lauch, man I lauch ower it till ma heid juist whummles like a sturdy sheep. Oo aye — ye're richt — I'm sort o' wandered.

"Weel aweel, I'll tell ye now about a wild-like tulzie I had aince with a lash o' Dawgos a' aboot yon cursed general average. Man, it was this wey, ye ken — whiles I juist wonder that a man like Scrutton — Mackinnon is na' blate either — does na' dae something to get the law changed. Na, na, ye could na' richtly look for it; it's the man's bread, ye ken. Aye, I'll heave roond, I'm subject to thae digressions; so was Sir Walter Scott and others I could mention. Ye mind aboot the seventy-twa, or it may be the seventy-five, freights were fairly high and shipowners were ettlin' to mak' some siller. Bad times we are havin' noo — yon cuttin' prices, I juist ca' it cuttin' throats — but in the seventy-five — that's it — I had a boat was gaein' oot to Smyrny wi' a feck o' cotton goods. Somehow or other she just snappit her screw shaft, and if she had na' just by a special providence come across a tramp out o' the Hartlepools she micht have wandered aboot yon islands just like Ulysses — him thae raise sic' a dirl aboot in Homer; for, ye ken, I ha'e a sort o' tincture o' the humanities.

"The tramp just gi'ed her a tow in to Saloneeky. Losh me, then there cam' the salvage racket, the maist infernal intrikit affair ye ever saw. A man juist has to go to the slauchter like a lamb, if aiver a ship makes fast a cable to any o' his boats. Scrutton has it textually, that unless the charter amounts to a demise — but I'll no deave ye wi' technicalities. Ye'll get it in Sepia *v.* Rogers, or Hubbertey *v.* Holts, and when ye hae it, mickle wiser may ye be.

"Fill up, men, it winna' hurt ye, and there's plenty mair . . . ah — yes, yon maitter o' the salvage was sort o' seekenin'."

"The worst thing, though, was that the freighters were a' upon me for demurrage. Sirs me, I was fair gyte, and I juist yokit on Scrutton (the vawdy-mecum, ye mind) as if it had been the Holy Scriptures. Ma heid fair dirled wi' Sangivetti *v.* Postlethwaite and a heap o' cases very much resembling mine. I thocht I had a bit issue anent the cesser clause, and awa' I went to my awgents in West George Street. I laid my case before them, and they lauch't at me — fair lauch't. They told me the point was clear that I stood liable. Man, I whiles think the very elements are a' against the shipowner. What wi' they cursed strikes drawin' awa' the trade, the employers' liabeelity, and the infernal intrikitness o' the law, a body hasna' got a chance.

"Ye'll mind, Geordie, when we went tae sea thegither, sax-and-forty years ago — it was maist a' wind jammers in thae days?"

The crony thus interpolated took his black oily Burmah cigar out of his mouth and grunted, "I mind weel. A man juist signed for his salt horse and his salt pork, nane o' your tin-bag then," and, after looking at the ceiling, spat into the fire.

"Aye, that's so, a sailor man was a richt felly then. Nane o' yer comin' aboard withoot an airticle o' kit except a knife and a pair o' sea-boots, and slingin' the latter doon the forepeak and fa'ing drunk upon them.

"Na, na, we a' had oor bit kists wi' plenty dunnage in them — and as for your employers' liabeelity — set them up — a sailor man juist took his ain life in his hand."

Geordie having grunted something about a long yarn and a rope-maker, Andra' came, as he said, back to his course, and once again took up his tale.

"I juist cabled oot orders to my awgent in Awthens to proceed to Saloneeky to arrange for chartering a vessel to tak' the stuff on to Smyrny; the body juist agreed wi' the captain o' a Greek schooner, ane they ca'ed Scaramangy, heard you ever sic' a name?

"His craft was ane o' they Levantyne-built bits o' things, awfu' gay wi' paint, a kind o' gin-palace afloat, ye ken the things, Geordie? She lookit weel, and my awgent cabled me that, wi' God's blessing, he hoped she would do the trip to Smyrny in aboot three days. I couldna' thole yon 'God's blessing' in the cablegram. A man has his ain releegious opinions — ye mind I'm an elder in the U.P. kirk outby Milngavie (ye canna' get the richt doctrine here in Bearsden, a mere puir imitation o' the Episcopawlians, a sort o' strivin' after being genteel, I ca' it); but business, ye see, is business. Besides, thae things are better understood, taken for read, as they ca' it up at Westminister.

"Yon blessing in the cablegram cost me a maitter o' some saxteen shillin' — the rates were awfu' high in thae times, ye mind. Saxteen shillin' just expended in a manner I ca' redeeklous, for the Almighty must ha' kent that I was putting up ma ain bit supplication when the cash was at stake.

"Yon Scaramangy had a wild-like crew on board; man, they Greeks dinna sail short-handed, I'se warrant them. Thirteen Dawgos forby himsel', and the bit schooner not above three hundred tons. Heard ye the like?

"I canna' bide a superstitious man, for I aye haud nae ane should stand between a man and Him; if a man wants Him, let him gang straucht, I say — through the Auld Book. Anyhow, Scaramangy had his Madoney — a

sort o' shrine, ye see — aft o' the mainmast, and a bit licht burnin' awa'
before it nicht an' day; an' awfu' waste o' can'le. Weel aweel — anither
Trichinopoly — ye'll na — aiblins anither tot. What! yer done? Geordie,
rax me the ginger snaps. Scaramangy — I didna' see him; but I hae seen
his like a thoosand times, maist-like dressed in longshore togs, wi' ane
o' thae Maneely straws, an' alpacy jacket, an' white canvas shoes — ye'll
mind the rig. Maist o' them has a watch-gaird on them like the cable o'
a battleship; ye canna' tell a gentleman nooadays, wi' everybody wearin'
their bloody Alberts. No a'thegither bad-like sailors are they Greeks; sort
o' conceity whiles the way they paint their bits o' schooners and their
barquentines; maist o' them yallow, wi' a bit pink streak, whiles a blue
ane, and sure to hae a figure-head, some o' they Greek goddesses. — No,
Geordie, Sapho was no' a goddess — she was a poetess, a queer-like ane
tae, just sent fair demented ower a felly they ca'ed — But I'm havering
— the humanities, ye ken, tak' an awfu' grip on a man.

"Scaramangy was most certain to hae had a wee bit curly Maltese dog
on board — I canna' bide them, rinnin' aboot yap, yappin' and filin' the
decks. Set them up; for ma ain pairt, I like a cat, or maybe a mongoose
— na, na, man, no a monkey — dirty brutes, the hale rick ma tick o'
them; seem to gae into a decline tae soon as ye pass the forties. Man, I
mind ane, I traded a coat and a bit Bible for him wi' a missionary in the
Cameroons. Puir brute, we had na' sighted the Rock of Lisbon, comin'
hame, afore he started hostin'. I had him in the cuddy, and ettled to
mak' him tak' some Scott's Emulsion. It would na' dae, and we had juist
to commit his bit body to the deep, the same as a Christian, just off the
Wolf Rock. I dinna' care to mind it. I lost my ain Johnny the same way.
Man, I felt it sae, I should hae liked to hae the wee devil stuff't, but his
mother said it would be heathenish.

"Nae doot o' it, yon Scaramangy would foul some other body's cable
when he lifted anchor, and find his throat halliards unrove — they're apt
to use them for a warp, ye ken, or some other kind o' deevilment; but,
anyhow, to sea he went in half a gale o' wind.

"There must hae been an awfu' haggersnash o' tongues, bad as the
Tower o' Babel, on board the *Aidonia*; that's what they ca'ed her — thae
Levantynes canna' dae a thing withoot a noise.

"Set o' curly-heided Dawgos, with their silver earrings and sashes
rowld round their hurdies — I canna' stan' a sailor man wi' a sash on
him, it looks sae theatrical.

"What happened only the Lord Himself and Scaramangy really ken. The Lord, for a' He kens, never lets on He hears, and Scaramangy was a naitural accomplished liar frae his birth.

"What he said was, that a pairfect hurricane burst on him, soon as he'd pit to sea. He couldna' get the topsails aff o' her, as nane o' his dodderin' deevils daur to gae aloft. So he juist watched them blow clean oot o' the bolt-ropes, and shortened the lave o' his sails the best he could — by a special interposeetion o' Providence he didna' lose ony o' his heidsails, though nae doots but he deserved tae.

"He says he and his cattle were in the awfu'ist peril that they ever experienced in their lives, the schooner almost on her beam ends, and the seas fair like to smother her.

"In the nick o' time, what think ye he did, man?

" 'Ran for some harbour,' 'lie to a bittie'; na, na, nae frichts o' him. He juist pit up a bit sipplication to his Madoney in the companion, and promised her (as if the painted bitch could hear him) that if she took him safe to Smyrny, that he would sacrifice something valuable as a sign o' gratitude. Heard ye the like o' that?

"God's truth, it mak's me mad to think aboot it — the folly o' the thing — and the gratuitous waste o' valuable property.

"Anyhow, he doddered in to Smyrny some gait or ither, and what d'ye think he done? He an' his men — aye, Geordie, nae doots he had the dawg along wi' them — went barefit oot to a shrine they had, and returned thanks to Him who stills the waves — that is, when He has a fancy tae.

"I dinna altogether disapprove o' that, for, prayer, ye ken, is usefu' whiles. Samuel pit up his sipplication to the Lord before he hewit yon Agag, and Joshua when he smote thae Canaanites, and even Paul — a gran' man Paul, sort o' pawky too — lifted a prayer when he was in juist sich a situation as was yon Scaramangy.

"Scaramangy and his Dawgos, when they had done their prayer, went aboard again, unbent their mainsail, and took it ashore and burnt it on the beach. Mad, ye say, Geordie — mad, aye, mad enough, but no on business matters.

"Ye can't think what they did then?

"They gaed awa' up to the British Consulate, and tabulated their claim, under the law o' general average, for the value o' the mainsail; for the deevils said, had they no made their vow, the Madoney wouldna' have interfeired, and the vessel would maist certainly hae been lost. No blate, yon Scaramangy — but mercy me, whatna' a conception o' natural laws he must have had! Fancy the Madoney expawtiating in the heavens, watching a storm like a fisherwife watching for her man when an easterly gale springs up, and no to be propeetiated without the promise o' an offerin'!

"After I got the cable, I fair sprang oot o' the hoose, and awa' to West George Street, to my awgents, and they tel't me Scaramangy was domiciled furth o' Scotland, and the case would have to be heard at Smyrny.

"It was juist held that whereas Captain Scaramangy, bein' in peril on the deep, and havin' done everything within his power and in the compass o' good seamanship to save his ship — ma God! — and being at the point o' daith, had recourse to prayer. Furthermore, the Coort bein' o' opinion that the vessel must have foondered had there not been an interposeetion o' a Higher Power, decides that Captain Scaramangy took the proper course, and that his prayer and his vow being both heard and considered favourably by the Madoney, that she thocht fit to save the vessel and the crew.

"Therefore, the Coort held that the vow was instrumental in the first degree, and that the jettison o' the mainsail — which of course wasna' a richt jettison at all — was necessary, and that the shippers were all bound to bear their due proportion o' the loss.

"Appeal — nae frichts o' me. It cost me, one way and another, mair than a hundred pound. Appeal — na, better to lose than to lose mair; that's a Greek proverb — at least I think so, and no a bad yin.

"Yer gauntin', men; weel, weel, good nicht to ye — Geordie, rax me doon Scrutton fae aff the top shelf — there's juist a pint or twa anent yon cursed general aiverage I should like to look at before I turn in for the nicht."

Progress

A Convert

From Bathurst to St. Paul's Loanda: right up and down the coast; in every bight; upon the Oil Rivers; down Congo way: in all the missionary stations, in which the trembling heathen had endured his ministrations; in factory and port: by all the traders and chance travellers, no one was more detested than the Reverend Archibald Macrae. All that is hard and self-assertive in the Scottish character, in him seemed to be multiplied a hundredfold. All that is kindly, old-world, and humorous: all that so often makes a Scot more easy to get on with than an Englishman, in the Reverend Archibald was quite left out. Dour and grey-headed, with a stubbly Newgate frill under his chin; dressed in black broadcloth, with a white helmet shadowing his dark red mottled face, a Bible and umbrella ever in his hand or tucked beneath his arm (he said himself he "aye liked oxtering aboot the Word o' God"), he stood confessed, fitted to bring a sword rather than peace to every one he met. Withal not a bad-hearted man, but tactless, disputatious, and as obstinate as a male mule. "I hae to preach the Worrd, baith in an' out o' season, and please the Lorrd I'll do so," was his constant saw.

From the earliest times, the tactless, honest, and aggressive missionary has been a thorn in the flesh of every one upon the coast of Africa. Consuls and traders, captains of men-of-war, all know and fear him, and most likely he has kept back the cause he labours for more than a hundred slave-raiders have done. They kill or enslave the body, but such as was the Reverend Archibald enslave and kill the soul. His station, far up a river which flowed sluggishly through woods of dark, metallic-foliaged trees, was called Hope House. Sent out from Norway all in sections, it had been set up just on the edge of a lagoon from which at evening a thick white vapour rose. A mangrove swamp reached almost to the door, the situation having been chosen by the Reverend Archibald himself to thwart the heads of his society, who not unnaturally wished it should be "located" in a more healthy spot. Painted a staring white, with bright green shutters, none of which fitted the windows they were supposed to shield, without a garden or a patch of cultivated ground, Hope House stood out a challenge to the heathen either to come at once beneath the yoke of the Reverend Archibald and to embrace his demonology, or to entrench themselves more strongly in their befetished faith.

The Reverend Archibald lived what is called a virtuous life — that is, he did not drink, did not sell gin or arms upon the sly, and round about the precincts of Hope House no snuff and butter coloured children played. Hard, upright, and self-righteous, he stalked about as if cut out of Peterhead grey granite: a Christian milestone set up on the heathen way, with the inscription "That road leads to Hell." This he himself was quite aware of, and used to say, "Ye see I hae the Worrd o' God, and if the heathen dinna come to listen to it, they will all burrn."

Still, disagreeable and wrong-headed as he was, the Reverend Archibald was in his way an honourable man. "Conviction," as he said a thousand times, "should follow reasonable airgument." He himself having from his earliest youth argued upon every subject in the heaven above, the earth beneath, and on the water which may or may not be under the earth, was well equipped for battle with the comparatively lightly armed fetish-worshipper of the West Coast of Africa.

Seated in his black horsehair-covered chair, before his table with its legs stuck into broken bottles filled with paraffin to keep off the white ants, and with his Bible covered in shiny cloth before him, the Reverend Archibald passed his spare time looking up texts wherewith to pulverise such of the infidel who in his neighbourhood had conscientiously resisted all his wiles and held by their old faith.

Often in reading over and again the minor prophets — so called, he would explain, "not on account of their less authenteecity, but simply because of the greater brevity of their prophecies" — his Scottish mind was struck with the similarity of the scheme of life of which they treated and that of those with whom he lived. "Yon Zephaniah — he was a gatherer of sycamore fruit, ye ken — would ha' done powerfu' work amongst the heathen on the coast," he would exclaim, as he shut up his Bible with a bang and sat down quietly to read *Bogatzky's Golden Treasury*, and smoke his pipe. His library was limited to the aforesaid *Golden Treasury* of damnatory texts, *Blair's Sermons*, and some books by Black, which he read doubtfully, perceiving well that they set out a picture of no life known to the world, but because the scenes were laid in what he called "N.B."

The frequent poring upon these treasures of the literary art, and ponderings upon the precepts of war to the knife with unbelievers, so faithfully set forth by the more ferocious writers in the Old Testament, together with his isolation from the world, had made him even narrower in mind than when he left his village in the East Neuk of Fife. His blunt outspokenness and bluff brutality of manner, on which he prided himself beyond measure, thinking, apparently, that those who save the soul must of necessity wound every feeling of the mind, had set a void between him and all the other Europeans on the coast.

The washed-out, gin-steeped white men of the Oil Rivers turned from him with an oath when he adjured them to become Good Templars; the traders from the interior, when they dropped down the river in their steam launches or canoes, all gave Hope House the widest of wide berths, after the experience of one who, going to his station with his young wife from Europe, was asked if he had "put away yon Fanti gurrl, that was yer sort o' concubine, ye ken." As for the natives who had come beneath his yoke, he treated them, as he thought, in a kindly way, after the fashion that in days gone by the clergy treated the laity in Scotland — that is, as people conquered by raiders from the Old Testament, making their lives a burden for the welfare of their souls. Still, being, as are most missionaries, possessed of medicines and goodwill to use them when his flock fell ill, he had some reputation amongst those who had no money to go out and pay a fetish doctor on the sly. Upon the spiritual side, he was not quite so far removed in sympathy from those to whom he ministered; his God was the mere counterpart of the negroes' devil, and both of them were to be conciliated in the same way, by sacrifice of what the worshipper held dear. But in his dealings with his flock the Reverend Archibald Macrae took no account of isothermal lines. For him, morality, not that he much insisted on it, holding that faith was more important, was a fixed quantity. The shifting and prismatic qualities of right and wrong, by him were seen identical, no matter if the spectrum used were that of Aberdeen or Ambrizette. Occasionally, therefore, he and his flock were at cross purposes, for to the flock it seemed an easy matter to give up their gods, but harder all at once to change the daily current of their lives.

Conviction, it is true, had followed upon reasonable, or at least upon reiterated "airgument"; but when the Reverend Archibald spoke of what he called "a nearer approximation to the moral code of the Old Book," his catechumens were apt to leave him and retire to the seclusion of the woods. Nothing contributed more to these backslidings than the vicinity of an unconverted chief known by the name of Monday Flatface, who had his "croom" five or six miles beyond Hope House, upon the river side. The chief lived his own life after the way his ancestors had lived before him, accepting gratefully from the Europeans their gin, their powder, and sized cotton cloths, but steadfastly rejecting all their contending faiths. All the exponents of the various sects had tried their hands on him without success. Priests from the neighbouring Portuese settlements had done their best, flaunting the novel charms of purgatory before the simple negro's eyes, who up till then had known but heaven and hell. The Church of England, backed by the stamp of its connection with the governing powers, had tried its fortune on the chief, holding out hints of Government protection, but without effect. The Nonconformists too had had their turn, and sought by singing hymns and preaching to let in light upon the opinionated old idolater, and had all been foiled. Lastly, the Reverend Macrae, who bore the banner of the Presbyterians, had attacked in force, bringing to bear the whole artillery of North British metaphysics, dangling before the chieftain visions of a future when his children, brought into the fold, should be in spiritual touch with Aberdeen, be fed on porridge, and on Sawbath while away the afternoon in learning paraphrases and wrestling with the Shorter Catechism.

All had been in vain, and Monday Flatface, while taking all that he could get in medicines, cotton cloths, Dutch clocks, and large red cotton parasols, was still a heathen, a polygamist, some said a cannibal upon the sly, and regularly got drunk on palm-tree wine instead of buying gin after the fashion of his brethren who had come into the fold. But above all the rest, the chief was hateful to the missionary in his character of humorist. Naturally, those who leave their country to propagate their individual faith are serious men, and the Reverend Archibald was no exception to the rule. Your serious man has from the beginning of the world added enormously to human misery. Wars, battles, murders, and the majority of sudden deaths are all his work. Crusades for holy sepulchres, with pilgrimages to saints' tombs, leagues and societies to prevent men living after the fashion they consider best, were all the handiwork of serious men. A dull, gold-dusted-over world it would have been by now, had not a wisely constituted all-seeing Providence, in general denied brains in sufficient ratio to energy, and allowed success invariably to wait on iteration. So when Chief Monday Flatface took the Reverend Archibald's exhortations to amend his present naughty life, forsake his fathers' gods, and straight dismiss the wives he had himself with care selected, choosing them fat but comely, and such as best anointed all their persons with palm oil, as a mere joke, the missionary's fury knew no bounds. Had he but tried to persecute, or stepped an atom beyond what the general sentiment of the European traders sanctioned, the way would have been plain. In the one case the dignity of persecution, hitherto withheld, would, like an aureole, have shone above his head, and in the other a complaint to the nearest British governor would have procured a gunboat to bombard the village of the chief. But nothing of the sort occurred, and the old chief persisted in still flourishing like a green mangrove tree, and stopping up his ears to all the arguments of the Reverend Archibald Macrae.

Often they met and talked the matter out in "Blackman English," eked out with Fanti and with Arabic, of which both polemists just knew sufficient to obscure their arguments upon their disagreeing faiths. Still, as not seldom happens in the case of well-matched enemies, a sort of odd respect, mingled with irritation, gradually grew up between the adversaries. Naturally, neither the chief nor yet the missionary advanced a step towards the conversion of the other infidel. Their simple, bloody creeds, softened in the one case by the increase of indifference which even in East Fife has modified the full relentlessness of the Mosaic dispensation, and on the other by the neighbourhood of European forts and factories, gave them a starting point in common on which they could agree. Each looked upon the other as a keen sportsman looks on some rare bird or beast which he hopes one day may fall before his gun, but which he wishes to escape from every other sportsman in the world except himself. Often the chief would ask the missionary to work a miracle to satisfy his doubts. Sorely the Reverend Archibald at times was tempted to display magnesium wire, or to develop photographs, in short to bag his game by pseudo-thaumaturgic art; but having the true sportsman's instinct, always refrained, entrenching himself safely behind his dictum that "conversion should ensue after a reasonable airgument." The chief, on his part, was quite ready to be baptized if he could see some evidence of the missionary's supernatural power; holding quite reasonably that "airgument" did not quite meet the case in questions of faith. Still he had promised that, if he should ever change his mind, none but the Reverend Archibald should admit him to the fold.

So on the rivers and the coast things jogged along in the accustomed way: steamers arrived and hung outside the bars, fleets of canoes came down from the remoter streams to trade, and in the open roadsteads lighters took the goods, and krooboys staggered through the surf, whilst objurgating Scottish clerks, note-book in hand, counted the barrels and the bales. The sun loomed through a continual mist, and sheets of rain caused a white vapour to enshroud the trees, whose leaves seemed to distil a damp which entered to the bones. The traders strove with whisky and with gin to fight off fever and to pass the time, till they could make sufficient money to go home and rear their villas near their native towns.

Years passed, and up and down the coast, at factories and garrisons, upon the hulks, and amongst travellers who, coming from the interior, stayed at Hope House, forced by necessity to ask for hospitality, a rumour made its way. Over their gin, or stretched out smoking in their hammocks during the long hot hours after the second breakfast, traders and merchant skippers, Scotch clerks, and the occasional globe-trotters who waited for steamers in the various ports to take them home to write their ponderous tomes upon the countries they had seen as a swallow sees the land he passes over in his winter hegira, all agreed that a great change had come upon the Reverend Macrae. Not that his outward man had altered, for his beard still bristled like a scrubbing-brush; his face, with years and long exposure to the sun, had turned the colour of "jerked" beef; his clothes still hung upon him as rags hang upon a scarecrow in the fields, and still he faithfully "oxtered aboot the word of God," although the book itself, originally given to him by his mother in East Fife, had grown more shiny and more greasy with the lapse of years. But certainly a change had come to the interior man. Occasionally, and almost as it were apologetically, he would quote texts from the New Testament, and in his steel-grey eye the gleam as of a gospel terrier was softened and subdued. Though he was still as ardent to convert the heathen as before, his methods were more human, and, to the amazement of every one upon the coast, he sometimes said, "Perhaps the patriarchs were whiles sort of a' rash in their bit methods wi' yon Canaanites."

The miserable converts saw the change with joy, and convert-like were quick to take advantage of it, and to revert by stealth to practices which, before, the Reverend Archibald would have instantly put down. They dared to appear on Sawbath at Hope House without the "stan' o' black" with which the Reverend Archibald had provided them. Only the women clung tenaciously to European dress, cherishing in special their red parasols; but holding them invariably turned from the sun, which beat upon their well-oiled faces, melting the palm oil, and causing it to drop upon their clothes.

Traders and brother missionaries came by degrees to drop into Hope House to smoke and talk, and to endeavour to find out the reason of the change. But, as the Reverend Archibald never spoke about himself, their curiosity might have been fruitless, had not a brother worker on his journey home asked for an explanation, saying that, as he thought, "the Lord himself often worked changes in the heart of man for providential ends." Dressed in pyjamas of grey flannel, his feet stuck into carpet slippers, and seated in a hammock which he kept swinging with his toes, the Reverend Archibald, after thrice spitting in contemplative fashion on the floor, and after having killed a mosquito on his forehead with a bang, looked round and started on his tale.

"Ye see," he said, "ma freends, as the Arabs say, we are a' in His hands. That which has been the pride of a man's life — in my case it was airgument — may prove at last to be a stumbling-block, for we are all as worrms in His hand. Airgument, airgument, a weel discussed and reasonable airgument, was aye ma pride. By it, I thoct to do a mighty worrk before the Lorrd. But He, nae doot for reasons of His ain, has made me see the error of my ways, that is, has shown me that there are things man's reason canna touch."

He paused and wiped the sweat from off his brow, spat thoughtfully, sighed once or twice, and having asked his friends if they would take Kops' ale or ginger beer, resumed his parable.

"Ye mind old Monday Flatface? Many's the crack on speeritual matters we have had, the chief and I, in days gone by. Sort o' teugh in opinions the chief, a weary body for a man to tackle, and one I hoped wi' the Lord's grace to bring into the fold. Aye, aye, ye needna' laugh, I ha'ena pit ma raddle on him, as ye a' know, yet. May be though, mon, ae keel-mark would do us baith. Weel, weel, the chief and I had bargained that if he got grace I should baptize him: a bonny burdie he would hae lookit at the font wi' his sax wives. Polygamy, ye ken, has its advantages, for I would have convertit a' the seven at once. One evening I was just got through wi' catechising some of the younger flock, when doon the river cam an awfu' rout o' drums, tom-toms, ye ken, and horns a' routing, and the chief's war-canoe tied up opposite the hoose. The chief came out, an' I was thinkin' of some text to greet him wi', airgument, ye ken . . . I think I tellt ye . . . when I saw at once that there was something wrong. He lookit awfu' gash, and wi'oot a worrd, he says 'Big wife she ill, think she go die, you pray piece for her, and if she live, you pour the water on my head.' I told him that was no the way at all we Christians did things, but I would come and see his wife and bring some medicine and try what I could do. A' the way up the river the drums went on, man, it fair deaved me, and when we reached the 'croom,' in a' my twenty years' experience of the coast, I ne'er saw sic a sight. Baith men and women were a' sounding horns, blowing their whistles, and shaking calabashes full of peas. The ground was red wi' blood, for the misguided creatures had sacrificed sheep, poultry, and calves: an awfu' waste o' bestial, ye ken, forby sae insanitary, and as ye say, not of the slightest use. At the chief's hut the wives and children made an awfu' din, roarin' and gashin' themselves wi' knives, just like the priests of Baal in the Old Testament. Right in the middle of the floor lay the 'big wife' insensible, and as I judged, in the last stage of a malignant fever. The chief, holdin' me by the airm, says, 'Save her, pray to your God for her, and if she lives I will believe.'

"Humanity, humanity, shame to me as a Christian, that I say it, but 'tis just the same, no matter if the skin is white or black. We a' just pray when we are wantin' ony thing, and when we've got it, dinna thank the granter o' the prayer.

"I pushit through the folk, and felt the woman's pulse, and syne, prisin' her mouth open a bit wi' a jack-knife, I gied her some quinine. Then I knelt doon and wrestled in prayer wi' a' ma heart, for the tears just rolled off the old chief's face. Sair I besought the Lord to show His power, if He thought fit to do so; but prayer, ye ken, is often answered indirectly, and as the night wore on the chief aye askit me, 'Will your God heed you?' and the woman aye got worse. An awful position for a minister of God to be placed in, as ye may understand. Syne Flatface roused himsel', and saying, 'I will call then on my God and sacrifice to him after the manner of my fathers,' stotted outside the house. The drums and whistles and the horns raised a maist deafening din, and in the hut the smell of perspiration and palm oil was sort o' seekenin'. After a spell o' prayer the chief came in, sweatin' and ashy grey, his hand bound up and carrying a finger which he had chappit off upon the altar of his gods. It garred me skunner when he laid it on the sick woman's breast, and once again I sunk upon my knees, prayin' the Lord to hear the heathen's prayer. Ye ken, mon, his faith in his false gods was just prodeegious, and I felt that a stanch Christian had been lost in the old man. Long did I wrastle, till aboot the dawn, but got nae answer, that is directly, and the woman aye got worse. Just as the day was breaking, and the false dawn appearing in the sky, the chief said, 'I will pray again, and once more sacrifice.' When he came in he stottered in his gait and laid another finger beside the other on his wife. Ma heart just yearned to him, and I yokit prayin' as if I had been askin' for my ain soul's grace, and syne our prayers were heard."

As he talked on, the night had worn away, the frogs ceased croaking, and the white tropic mist which comes before the dawn had drifted to the house and shrouded all the verandah in its ghostly folds. Long shivers of the tide crept up the river, oily and supernatural-looking, and little waves lapped on the muddy banks, making small landslips fall into the flood with an unearthly sound. The listeners shivered over their temperance drinks, and once again the Reverend Archibald began.

"Maist like she had the turn; it might have been the effect of the quinine, or of the prayers, or it may be the Lord had looked in approbation on the sacrifice. I canna say, but from that time the woman mended, and in a week was well. Ah . . . Flatface, weel no, he's still a heathen, though we are friends, and whiles I think his God and mine are no so far apart as I aince thocht."

He ceased, and from the woods and swamps rose the faint noises of the coming day, drops fell from the iron roof upon the planks of the verandah with a dull splashing sound; the listeners, shaking the missionary by the hand, dispersed, and he, looking out through the mist, was comforted by the confession of his weakness and the relation of his doubts.

Progress

The Laroch

The grass-grown-over "founds" and the grey crumbling dry-stone walls of what had been a house, stood in an island of bright, close-grown grass. About the walls sprang nettles and burdocks, and in the chinks mulleins stood out like torches, veritable hag-tapers to light the desolation of the scene. Herb robin, and wild pelargonium, with pink mallows, straggled about the ruined garden walls. A currant bush, all run to wood, with grozets and wild rasps, still strove against neglect. In the deserted long-kail patch, heather and bilberries had resumed their sway. Under the stunted ash, a broken quern and a corn-beetling stone, grown green with moss, spoke of a time of life and animation, simple and primitive, but fitting to the place. On every side the stone-strewn moor stretched to the waters of the loch, leaving a ridge of shingle on the edge. The hills were capped with mist that lifted rarely, and only in the summer evenings or in the winter frosts were clear and visible. Firs, remnants of the Caledonian forest, sprang from the rocky soil and stood out stark, retiring sentinels of the old world — the world in which they, the white cattle, the wild boar and wolf, were fellow-dwellers, and from which they lingered to remind one of the others who had disappeared. The birch trees rustled their laments, sadder than those of earthly chanters, or of the strains of a scarce-heard strathspey coming down through the glens with the west wind. The rowans on the little stony tumuli showed reddening berries, as they turned their silvery leaves towards Loch Shiel. All was sad, wild, and desolate, the soft warm rain drawing up from the ground a mist, which met the mist descending from the sky, and hung a curtain over the rocks, the strath, the loch, and everything, and glistened greyly on the wet leaves of trees. A leaden sky, seen vaguely through the rain, and broken to the west by "windows," seemed to shut out the narrow glen from all the world, confining it in plates of lead — lead in the skies, and in the waters of the loch.

Desolation reigned where once was life, and where along the loch smoke had ascended, curling to heaven humbly from the shielings thatched with reeds, with heather, and with whins, the thatch kept down with birchen poles fastened with stones, and on whose roofs the corydalis and the house-leek sprang from the flauchter feals. But now no acrid peat reek made the eyes water, or pervaded heart and soul, with the nostalgia of the North — that North ungrateful, hard, and whimsical, but lovable and leal, where man grows like the sapucaya nut, hard rinded, rough, and angular, but tender at the core. All, all were gone — gone to far Canada, or to the swamps and the pine-barrens of the Carolinas, to Georgia, to New Zealand; nothing but Prionsa Tearleach's monument, set like a lighthouse on the shores of a dead sea, the sea of failure, seemed to remind one that the pibroch once resounded through the glens. Heather and tormentil, with cotton-grass, that seemed to have preserved the feather of some bird extinct for ages, eye-bright and knapweed, hare-bells and golden rod, prunella, meadow-sweet, with the bog asphodel on the green springy turf near swamps, and foxgloves in the woods, all bloomed, and thought not on the departed children who had plucked them when the strath held men. It may be that the plants regretted the lost children's hands that gathered them, and were their only mourners, for thought must linger somewhere, if only amongst flowers.

In the old plough-marked ridges of the forsaken crofts the matted ragweed grew, to show the land had once been cultivated. Nature smiled through the middle mist, which shrouded loch and hill as in derision of the changes which mankind had suffered, and looked as tolerantly upon the tourists, water-proofed to the ears, as she had gazed upon the clansmen, who must have seemed as much a part of her as were the roe who peeped out timidly from the birch thickets to watch the steamboat puffing on the lake. Yet still about the laroch a hum of voices hung, or seemed to hang, to any one who listened with ears undeadened by the steam-hooter's bray — voices whose guttural accents seemed more attuned to the long swish of waves and moaning of the wind than those which, in their throaty tone, mingle with nothing but the jangle of a street. Voices there were that spoke of the dead past, when laughter echoed through the glens — the low-tuned laughter of a silent race. Voices that last had sounded in their grief and tears, as the rough roof-tree fell, or worse, was left intact, as the owners of the house turned for a last look at their shielings on the solitary strath.

An air of sadness and of failure, as if the very power which placed the ancient owners on the soil had not proved strong enough to keep them there, hung on the hills and brooded on the lake — a Celtic sadness, bred in the bone of an old race, which could not hope to strive with new surroundings, and which the stranger has supplanted, just as the Hanoverian rat drove out his British cousin and usurped his place. Land, sky, and loch spoke of the vanished people and their last enterprise — their first and last, when far Lochaber almost imposed a king on England; pushed on his fortunes, shed its blood for him, and when, beaten and desperate, he fled for life, sheltered him in the greyness of its mists. But in the soul-pervading, futile beauty which hung over all, the laroch gave as it were a keynote, as the tired, vapour-ridden sun at times blinked on it and shone upon its ruined walls. It seemed to speak of mournful happiness and of the humble joys of those who felt the storm, the sunshine, and the rain as their own trees and rocks had felt them, dumbly but cheerfully, and who, departing, had left no record of themselves but the poor rickle of grey stones, or the faint echo of their hearts heard in the notes of a lament quavering down through the glens and mingling with the south-east gale. The silence of an empty land, from which the people had been driven sore against their will, and had departed to make their fortunes, and to mourn their stony pastures to the third generation and the fourth, oppressed one, whilst the winds echoed through the corries as if seeking some one to talk with about days gone by.

On the peat hags the struggling sunbeams glinted, lighting them up for a brief moment, as the flaming chimney of an ironwork in a manufacturing town breaks through the vapour of the slums and lights the waters of some dank canal, giving an air as of an opening of the mouth of hell, black and unfathomable. The stunted willow and dwarf alder fringed the margin of the rushy streams, which gurgled in deep channels, forming small linns on which the white foam flecked the tawny peat water, or, breaking into little rapids, brattled amongst round pebbles, or again sank out of sight amongst the sedge of flags. Their tinkling music was unheard, except perhaps in ears which had grown blunted with the roar of cabs. Perchance it was remembered as a legend heard in childhood is remembered faintly in old age. Straggling across the hills, the footpaths, long disused, lay white amongst the heather, the stones retaining still a smoothness made by the feet of those who, in their deer-skin moccasins, had journeyed in the past from the lone laroch to other larochs, which once had all been homesteads dear to the dwellers in them, and to-day were silent and forgotten as the half-subterranean dwellings of the Picts.

Still the sweet-gale gave out its aromatic scent, the feathery bracken waved, the hills towered up into the sky, flecked here and there with snow, and nature seemed to call to the departed people, telling them to return and find their land unchanged. She called to ears long deaf, or rendered unresponsive in their new homes, for nothing broke the silence of the glens but the harsh cry of the wild geese, flying unseen amongst the middle region of the mist, calling on high the coronach of the departed and the dead.

Snow in Menteith

All the familiar landmarks were obliterated. The Grampians and the Campsies had taken on new shapes. Woods had turned into masses of raw cotton, and trees to pyramids of wool, with diamonds here and there stuck in the fleece. The trunks of beeches stood out black upon the lee, and on the weather side were coated thick with snow as hard as sugar on a cake. The boughs of firs and spruces swayed gently up and down under the weight of snow, which bent them towards the ground.

Birches were covered to their slenderest twigs with icicles. Only the larches, graceful and erect, were red, for on their feathery branches snow could find no resting-place. On the rough bark and knotted trunks of oak trees feathery humps bulged out, through which protruded shoots with sere brown leaves still clinging to them, and on them ruffled birds sat moping, twittering in the cold.

A new and silent world, born in a night, had come into existence, and over it brooded a hush, broken but by the cawing of the crows, which fabulated as they flew, perhaps upon the strangeness of the pervading white.

Even in Eden, in the days before man's fall and woman's motherhood, all was not purer than the fields and moors under their burden of the carpet formed of the myriad scintillating flakes.

But in the copses and the shaws of oak and birch a change had come, more wondrous even than the transformation of a piece of rough grey coral, as it sinks prismatic and transfigured by the waves, dropped gently from a boat upon the beach of a sunlit lagoon.

The trees, congealed and tense, stood silent, quivering and eager for the embrace of the keen frost, their boughs all clad first with a thistle-down of cold, and then towards the tips with diamonds fashioned to their shape through which the shadow of their bark just faintly gleamed, whilst, here and there, there sparkled facets rarer and brighter than the gems of the Apocalypse. A murmur born of stillness lost itself against the blackness of a clump of firs, and yet was all apparent and persisting, as if the spirit of the frost, looking out from the north, was murmuring a self-approving blessing on his work. The sharp air hung the breath in a grey cloud against the sky. Nature was silent, and a rabbit, loping through the bush, stirred the soft echoes of the frost-nipped weeds, leaving behind a trail which seemed gigantic, with its brown markings made by the impress of his furry feet melting the new-fallen snow. In the dark woodland burns the wreaths blocked all the streams, and in the silent pools, congealed and swept clean by the wind, the little trout loomed twice their natural size in the refracted light which penetrated through the ice. The roe-deer and the hares, and the great capercailzies, sending a shower of sparkling particles from the dark fir trees when they took their flight, seemed to have come into their own inheritance; and woodmen, plodding heavily, their axes thrust beneath their armpits, their hands deep buried in their pockets, looked like interlopers strayed from a pantomime into the transformation scene of frost. The wind amongst the sedges of the shallow pool in the sequestered clearing where the rabbit-eaten ash copse straggled close to the water's edge discoursed the only music of the spheres to which our ears are tuned, and whistled in the rowans, swinging their hanging spathes of bark against their boles for its accompaniment.

Out on the hummocks of the withered grass it caught the frosted bracken, twirling it round and round upon itself, and leaving at the roots a circle in the snow which seemed the footprint of some strange new northern animal, brought by the magic of the night from the far realms of frost.

And as the hills and woods had all become unrecognisable, the mantle of pure white spread on the earth formed a blank page on which nothing could stir without a record of its passage being writ at least as permanently as was the passage of its life.

Badgers, who had adventured out for food, left their strange, bear-like tracks in woods where no one had suspected that they lived. Roe, plunging through the crisp white snow, made a round hole marked at the bottom with their cloven feet, and leaving at the edge a faint red trace of blood.

The birds, in their degree, imprinted traces clear and distinct as those their ancestors have left in rocks from the time when the world was all a snowfield or all tropics, or all something different from what it is, as wise geologists, quarrelling with each other as they were theologians, write in ponderous tomes.

Even the field-mice, pattering along, left tiny trails like little railways as they journeyed from their warm nests to visit one another and interchange opinions on the strange new scene.

Round holly-trunks sat rabbits, mere brown balls of fur, eating the bark and scuffling to and fro, leaving well-beaten paths towards their burrows, at whose mouth some sat and washed their faces in the snow.

Across the frozen pond, upon whose surface lay a thin rime of frost, a fox had left his footsteps, frozen hard, mysterious as fresh Indian sign found by some solitary hunter on the head waters of the Rio Gila, and as ominous. Birds as they flew threw shadows deeper than at noonday on the sand, so deep they seemed to bite into the snow, as if it were determined that no living thing should pass above it and not leave its mark.

But as the desert is an open book to the Indian tracker, who remarks the passage of each living thing in the faint marks it leaves upon the grass, so did the snow reveal all secrets to the most inexperienced eye.

Even when it had cleared away, the grass remained black and downtrodden, and looked burned by every footstep that had passed.

But if it changed the woods to palaces of silver and of diamonds, the hills to Alpine ranges, and the fields to vast white chessboards, blotting out the roads, which it filled solid to the hedges, what a change it wrought upon the moss! The Flanders Moss that once had been a sea became an ocean, for as the peat-hags and the heather turned to waves, and as the sun lit up their tips with pink, they seemed to roll as if they wished once more to wash the skirts of the low foothills of the carse. Foaming and billowing along, they turned the brown peat moss, set with its bushes of bog myrtle and lean, wiry-growing heather, into an Arctic sea — a waste of desolation, brilliant and desolate, and upon which the sun reflected with a violet tinge. As the waves seemed to surge around the stunted pines and birches, all looked dead, extinct, and as remote from man as when the Roman legions camping on the edge of the great moss constructed their lone camp, last outpost of the world on this side of the Thule of the frowning Grampians to the north. As night fell slowly on the drear expanse of white, Ben Lomond, catching the last reflection of the setting sun, turned to a cone of fire, and at its foot the pine woods of Drummore stood out intense and dark as if cut out of blackened cardboard, and by degrees the hills and woods melted away into a vapoury mist.

Then from the bosom of the moss came a hoarse croaking, as a heron, rising slowly into the keen night air, after his day of unproductive fishing by the black frozen pools of the slow Forth, flapped heavily away.

Pollybaglan

Alone it stood, outside the world, remote and desolate, washed by a sea of heather, just where the sluggish Forth, meandering slowly like a stream of oil through Flanders Moss, had formed a grassy link, but not of those which, as the saying went, were worth a knight's fee in the north.

In times gone by, the moss, which in most places marches with the Forth, leaving a narrow ribbon of green turf, had been drained off and floated down the stream, exposing in its place some acres of stiff clay and a dull, whitish scaur. In these the steading stood like some lacustrine dwelling on the river's edge, shut from the world by moss. Moss, moss, and still more moss, which rose piled like a snow-wreath to the west, and south, and east, whilst on the north the high clay bank sank steep into the flood.

The drumly water flowed between banks of peat, through which at intervals a whitish clay peeped out, like strata in a mine. Slowly it flowed in many windings towards the sea, cutting the Flanders Moss across, receiving as it went the streams which gurgled deep below the surface of the ground, forming canyons in miniature, and issuing out to join the river through a dense growth of bulrushes, rank-growing coltsfoot, and low alder bushes. The deep black pools, on which the foam brought by the current slowly whirled round and round before it took its course down stream, were menacing in their intensity of gloom. Rarely the sun fell right upon them, and when it did its light never appeared to pierce the water, which seemed to turn it back again, as if the bottom held some mystery down in its amber depths. Perhaps in ages past some Celtic fishers, paddling their coracles, had chosen out the place to build their cottary, remote from all mankind and inaccessible. But having chosen, with the instinct of their race, they gave a name to it which, strange and incoherent to the Saxon ear, to them was typical of the chief feature of the place. Stream of the ragweed it was dubbed by the rude settlers, perhaps when all Moss Flanders [sic = *Flanders Moss?*] was a forest, stretching to the sea. And still the ragweed grew luxuriantly in the stiff soil, commemorating the keen eyes of the first settlers, although the meaning of the name had been long lost and twisted by the Anglo-Saxon tongue past recognition by the Celt.

The road, which wound about in the white clayey soil between the banks of moss which shut out the horizon, was laid on faggots, and in places drew so near the river's bank that a cart's body passing seemed to overhang the stream. Such as it was, this track was the sole link with the unquiet world which had its being on the far side of the great moss. But that the quiet of the mossland farm should not too easily be broken by swift contact with mankind, the path ran up and down to every house upon the moss, making strange zigzags and parabolas, till it emerged at last on the high road. Carts in the winter time sunk to their axles, whilst in summer horses' feet stuck in the cracks formed in the sun-baked earth.

But though the road was bad, to make communication still more difficult, at intervals rough farm gates barred the way. Hung loosely, and secured by rusty back-band chains of carts, or formed of barked and crooked oak poles stuck into horseshoes in a ragged post, they either forced you to dismount and pull laboriously each bar from its confining horseshoe, or tempted you to open them on horseback, when their schauchling hinges and bad balance usually drove them on your horse's hocks as you essayed to pass.

When all the obstacles were overcome and you had reached your goal and slithered through the clay which formed the fields between the river and the moss, the world seemed leagues away. That is, the ancient world in which men plough and reap and sow, watching the weather as a fisherman watches the shaking of his sail, possessed one, and real things resumed their sway, whilst agiotage and politics, with arts and sciences, fell to their proper value in the great scheme of life. The scanty crop of oats, growing, like rice, in water which seemed to lie eternally in the depressions of the clay, although the dwellers in the farm averred that it "seeped bonnily awa' at the back en'," became as all-important as the Stock Exchange. The meagre turnips and potatoes, drooping and blackening with disease, between whose furrows persicaria and fumitory grew, moved one's compassion, and excited admiration for the men who, in the fight with Nature, wrung a livelihood from such unfruitful soil. Fences there naturally were none, but piles of brushwood fastened with rusty wire to crooked posts did duty for them, whilst broken ploughs and carts which had seen weary service on the clayey roads, stood in the gaps and did as well as gates.

Some scattered drain-pipes lying in the fields looked like the relics of a battlefield of agriculture, in which the forces of the modern world had been defeated in the contest with the moss.

But road and drain-pipes, thatched farm-house and broken fences, the stunted crop and wind-hacked ash tree growing by the farm, were but the outward signs, whilst the interior significance lay in the billowing moss, the sluggish river, and in the background of the lumpy hills, which from the steading seemed to rise sheer from the heathy sea.

Vaguely the steading and the cultivated land stood out for progress; the broken carts and twisted ploughs seemed to stretch out their hands to Charing Cross; but moss and mountain, river flowing deep, the equisetum growing on its banks, and the sweet-gale, its leaves all wet with mist, reminded one that the forgotten past still lived in spite of us.

Deep in the soughing of the wind, waving the heath with furrows and shaking out its dry brown seeds on the black soil, came the sighs of a race whose joys were tinged with melancholy, and in the mists which crept along the faces of the hills its spirit seemed to brood, making the dwellers in the land appear as out of place as a poor Indian, dressed in a torn frock coat and with an eagle's feather stuck in a hard felt hat, looks in a frontier town.

The tussocks of the heather were not made for boots to tread upon, nor the few acres of poor soil, redeemed at many times their worth fee-simple, to be sown in a fourfold rotation, or to have top dressing and bone manure shot from an agricultural machine upon their clay. A pair of Highland garrons ought to have scratched the surface of the ground, yoked to some pristine plough by ropes which cut into their chests, or harrowed with a thorn bush, and the broken implements which lay about but seemed to accentuate the undying presence of an older world. But as the place in which a man is set to live always proves stronger than his race or creed, the dweller in the farm, though not a Highlander, had put on all the exterior and not a few of the interior graces of the Celt.

Tall and shock-headed, and freckled on the red patches of the skin which a rough crop of beard and whiskers left exposed, his eyes looked out upon the world as if he had a sort of second sight begot of whisky and of loneliness. His monstrous hands hung almost to his knees, which in their turn stuck forward in the way a horse's hock sticks back; but for all that he crossed the moss as lightly as a mountain hare springs through the snow before a collie dog. Although his feet, encased in heavy boots,

looked more adapted for the muddy roads which wound through his
domain than for the heather, he seemed to have become, during his
lifelong sojourn in the place, as light of foot as any clansman on whose
feet in the old times the dun deer's hide was tied to form a moccasin.
The country people said that he was "awfu' soople for his years," which
may have been some five-and-forty, or, on the other hand, threescore, for
nothing told his age, and that he was a "lightsome traveller" — not that
his travels ever carried him more than ten miles from Pollybaglan; but
then with us to travel is to walk. Withal a swimmer, an unusual thing
amongst the older generation in Menteith.

"Ye ken, man laird, whiles I just dive richt to the bottom o' a linn,
and set doon there; ye'd think it was the inside o' the Fairy Hill. Trooties,
ye ken, and saumon, and they awfu' pike, a' comin' round ye, and they
bits o' water weeds, wagging aboot like lairch trees in the blast. I mind
ae time I stoppit doon nigh aboot half an hour. Maybe no just sae much,
ye ken, but time gaes awfu' quick when ye're at the bottom o' a linn."

These talents and his skill in walking on the moss, together with his
love of broken carts for gates, did not perhaps go far towards making
him an agriculturist such as a landlord loves; but looking back into the
past, although his rent was often in arrear, he laid up, so to speak, and
quite unconsciously, a real treasure for his laird, which, though moth
may corrupt, no thief would waste his time by breaking through to steal,
as it lies gathering dust on the top shelf of some one's library.

And as the older life had entered into the body of the Lowland
"bodach," making him seem a Highlander in all but speech, so had it
filled the air of the oasis in the peaty moss, that the dry reeds upon the
river-banks were turned to chanters, and gave out their laments for the
forgotten namers of the land.

Well did they call it by the name Menteith, "the district of the moss,"
for moss invaded the whole strath, filling the space which once had
been a sea with waves of heather and bog asphodel. Stretching from
Meiklewood, it kissed the Clach-nan-Lung. Lapping the edges of the
hills upon the north and south shores of the heathy sea, it put a peaty
bridle on the Forth, and from its depths at evening and at morn rose a
white vapour which transformed it into a misty archipelago, upon whose
waves the lonely steading rode, like the enchanted islands which old
mariners descried, only to lose again into the fog at the first shift of
wind. Birch trees and firs reflected on the mirage of the mist floated like

parachutes, and heath and sky were joined together by the vapoury pall which brooded on the moss, billowing and boiling as if some cauldron in the bowels of the earth was belching forth its steam. Fences were blotted out, roads disappeared, and from the moss strange noises rose, as Forth lapped sullenly up against the bank where Pollybaglan stood.

Progress

400

A Traveller

He stood, a square, grey figure in the hall, and, looking upward at the pictures of my grim-visaged ancestors in their full-bottomed wigs, said, "Bonny scenery, aye, bonny scenery." The criticism was as novel as it was unexpected, and was the introduction to a bickering friendship which extended over years.

His greasy cap and crisp grey hair which melted into one another, hodden grey clothes, and greenish flannel shirt, but with one touch of colour in his bright red cheeks, like apples tinged with frost, made him look like the stone which, in the district where he lived, was known as the "auld carlin wi' the bratty plaid."

"Laird, I hae travel't it, yes, fack as death, richt through frae up aboot Balfron."

A man may make the circuit of the world in as short space of time as it seems good to him, and yet not earn the title of a "soople traveller," for "travelling" means to walk. Thus we refer to pedlars by the name of "travelling merchants," and tramps as "gaein' aboot" or "travelling bodies," saving thereby their pride and ours, and not contributing to wear out shoe-leather any the faster by the mere application of the word. But, still, in using it we usually extend our pity to the traveller, who is a sort of a survival of the times when all men rode, if only on West Highland ponies schauchling through the mud. Used by a poor man, it generally infers that he is going to ask a favour, or by a tenant to his landlord, that the times are bad.

"Laird, I just travel't it. Thank ye, nae soddy, laird," and as he spoke he drained a good half-tumbler of raw whisky to the dregs, in such a quiet, sober, and God-fearing way, it seemed an act of prayer.

Of all the tenant farmers it has been my luck to meet and chaffer with, none could exceed the traveller in making a poor mouth. Seasons were always backward, markets bad, and sheep had foot-rot or the fluke, the "tatties" were diseased — "Man, laird! I felt the smell of yon field out by Gartchurachan whenever I cam forward to the trough-stone, ye ken, fornent the Hosh."

The act of God was instant at his farm, tirling the slates or hashing up the rhones, leaving the sarking bare, so that the snaw bree seepit thro' upon the stirks. "I just tak' shame to pit horse in yon rickle o' a stable, and a' the grips are fair dune in the byre. Laird, I just biggit a' the steadin', that is, I drave the stanes and drainit a' the land to ye. Siccan a farm for tile! man, I hae pit in more than ten thousand since last back en', and still she's wet, wet as Loch Lomond. I'm just tellin' ye, ye'll maybe hae to tak' it back and try it yersel', for I am just beat wi' it. . . . What? tak' it off my hands at Martinmas! Na, na, I'll fecht awa' in it, though I'll hae to hae a wee reduction, or maybe a substantial ane, just to encourage me to carry on my agricultural operations. Aye, dod aye, I'm sayin' it."

His farm was grey and square, with the house planted down upon the road, leaving an angle which ran out from the farmyard, planted with cabbages and with some flowers which wrestled with the wind. No tree grew near the place, which, high and desolate, stood solitary, exposed to the full fury of the south-west wind. An air of neatness without homeliness pervaded everything. Carts with their shafts upright stood under sheds, and on a rope, stretched from the stable to the byre, hung braxy sheep, their bodies black and shrunken, their skins, new flayed and pink, fluttering about like kites.

But if the roadside farm was dreary in itself, a mere corrál of coarse grey stones topped by blue slates, the distant hills atoned for all shortcomings in the foreground of the view.

From the high moorland platform where Tombreak seemed to be stuck down like a child's house of bricks, the Grampians rose, making a semicircle to the north and west. Lumpy, and looking like misshapen vegetables, monstrous and brown, their chain was broken here and there by peaks, and here and there by mountain burns which glistened on their sides as streaks of foam gleam white upon a horse's flanks. Ben Ledi and Schehallion to the east, with Stuc-a-Chroin, Ben Voirlich, Ben A'an, and Ben Venue; nearer Ben Dearg and Craigmore, and to the west Ben Lomond rising solitary, a vast blue cone about whose top floated a vapoury cloud, as if the soul of the volcano long extinct hovered about its once accustomed haunts, stood sentinels, frowning down on the mossy strath, set with its lumpy hillocks grown with stubbly oak, and on the still blue lake with the grey priory and the castled isle. Far to the north snow-capped Ben More, with its twin paps, peeped out between the shoulders of the bolder hills, showing its beauties timidly, and at the faintest shift of wind retreating back into the mist — that veil which shrouds the Highlands in its mystery, shutting them off for ever from the south.

Below the farm straggled the village of Balfron, a long grey ribbon in the mist. Nearer it showed a Scottish toun all bare of flowers, but cosy in its clartiness, in which barefooted children ran about and played at "bools," wiping their noses on their coat sleeves, or went to school wearing their boots uneasily, as ponies from the far-off islands of the north hobble along in the first dignity of shoes.

Above the toun with its ancestral trysting-tree clamped round with iron hoops, its antiquated toll-house, now turned sweet-shop, and in whose windows fly-blown toffy and flat-looking ginger beer winked at the passer-by, who knew, perhaps, that there was liquor more alluring to be had inside — the Campsies rose, a wall of green, broken but by the Corrie of Balglas. Their grassy sides and look of pastoral quiet made a sharp contrast with the Highland hills, only ten miles away. The two hill ranges were as far apart as is a northern shepherd, wrapped in his plaid and "sheltering awee" behind a rock whilst his dog slumbers at his feet, his coat all wet with mist, and a gull-followed southland ploughman labouring at his craft.

Upon the plateau, with the hills to the north and south, the wind raged ceaselessly, and many a weary mile upon the moors after his sheep my tenant must have "travelled" before his face took on the dark red polish which, staring out from his grey aureole of hair and Newgate frill, looked like a red bottle in a chemist's window when you passed him in the gloaming on the road. Long contact and familiarity with sheep had given him something of the grace of a West Highland wether, which he resembled somewhat in his mind; for, in a land in which most men are cautious, not delivering their souls without due hedging, manward and Godward, as befits a Scot, he stood out easily the first. Prudence in his case almost amounted to a mania, so that in any case a bargain must have been a torture to him; for if he lost, he naturally cursed God and man, and if he gained by it, bewailed himself for having lost the chance of getting better terms. No word he spoke without a qualifying clause. Thus the best harvest ever known to man, to him was "no that bad," and a fine Clydesdale horse "a bonny beast, but no well feathered on the pastern joints."

No Ayrshire cow but was "a wee thing heich abune the tail," which dictum he would modify, and, sighing, say, "but we are a' that," and thus humanity and all the race of cows were either justified or stood arraigned, according to your taste.

As was to be expected from a man so gifted for success amongst the men with whom he lived, he was "well doing," that is, he had amassed some little money, chiefly by "travellin' " about to cattle markets and picking up cheap beasts. In fact, he was an instance of the Scots proverb, that "the gangin' foot aye picks up something, if it is but a thorn." No one who saw him walin' his way across the moors leading his collie by a piece of common string, with his long hazel shepherd's crook thrust through his arms behind his back, making him look like a trussed fowl, or driving home some of his purchases through a mist upon the muddy roads, could ever think of him and death as having anything in common that should one day make them friends. So like the stubbly oaks he looked, which grew in the Park Wood upon his farm, and which themselves had braved a thousand tempests and a hundred pollardings, that he seemed likely to endure as long as they. But your cursed cold or heart disease, or his neglect in taking whisky at set hours, or something which no doctor can foresee, proved his undoing, and he departed "travellin' " to a tryst, his collie following at his heels, and his long shepherd's staff in hand, willing and eager for the coming deal.

Tough, knarred, and kindly, with his apple cheeks and his thick fell of crisp grey hair, his hodden clothes and cheery smile, no matter whether he had got the best of his opponent in a bargain or the worst, he took away with him some of my life and the kind memories of the whole countryside aboot Balfron.

Ben Lomond and Ben Ledi still look down upon the carse; in the Park Wood the twisted oaklings rustle in the breeze, and by Tombreak the wind sweeps ceaselessly.

"Andra" is gone, his collie dog perchance comes to another whistle, and his roan Iceland pony mare maybe ekes out her life in a fish-hawker's cart; but her lost owner, I would like to think, there in the spheres, is "travellin'," if only "goin' aboot," for it may well be that they hold no trysts where he dwells now; but still I know that it is ill to stay "the gangin' foot" after a lifetime of the road.

A Vestal

At first sight you could tell her nationality: faded and worn, her hair an iron grey, although not striking looking, yet there was something indefinable that spoke of Spain.

She walked as women walk who, in the plaza of their native town, have been accustomed since their youth to a cross-fire of eyes and compliments or quodlibets from all the passers-by. Although not educated — that is to say, in school-board learning, which enables those who possess it to tell at once the latitude of Guaymas, or on what parallel of longitude the Island of Lord Howe is situate — she yet had plenty of that homely knowledge of the world called the "brown science" in the Spains. Somehow you saw at first sight that she must be religious, and yet divined the portals of her heaven would be opened wide, not to saints only, but to all those who knocked.

For years she had worn the same kind of black clothes, and hat, which, though not fashionable, still retained an air of self-respect. Though her position was not brilliant, she yet remained a human being, without apologising for her continued presence upon earth. In fact, had she been asked to set forth her philosophy of life, it is most likely that she would have thought (all in humility and faith) that she performed as clear a function as a queen or beggar-woman, both of whom she probably in her own mind respected, as being creatures of the Lord, to whom, either as Christian or citizen, she gave her mite.

All the ridiculous watering-place in which she lived looked on her with respect, but tempered with contempt. They knew her story, simple and yet pathetic, and being sentimental, as uncultured people, be they rich or poor, are sure to be, they were twice moved — once by the pathos, and again amazed by the extreme simplicity of what had moved them. So may a ploughman sitting at a play exclaim contemptuously, "Do you call this acting? Why, the man speaks just like a friend of mine who lives in the West country, down to Megavisey."

The Vestal, for so she had been named by a passing journalist (the people of the place could never find out why), lived on the third floor of a great hotel, in which at certain seasons of the year, just as the planets have their stated movements, Russians and Spaniards and then Englishmen succeeded one another — all dressed in London, all rich, and all and each of them speaking indifferent French, learned in the brothels and the restaurants of Paris, with fluency, and just sufficient accent to betray their origin. Thus may St. Paul, whilst in the provinces, have made himself respected when he said he was a Roman citizen; but the hall-porter in the Roman house probably smiled a little at his "thalve," and knew him for a Jew.

But though the vestal lived, slept, ate, and had her being generally, in the hotel, she was not of it, and had as slight connection with the sojourners as has a passenger with members of the crew, even upon a voyage round the Horn westward in a wind-jammer. Her rooms — for she had two — were furnished, as is usual in a French hotel, in a bastard style of Louis the Sixteenth. A nymph upon a rock of Parian marble piped to three sheep as large as donkeys, and to her crook was hung the dial of the clock. The chairs were covered with cheap Lyons silk, the colour so contrived as to look faded, and with their legs twisted and curled after the fashion of the old-world barley-sugar sold in a Scottish shop. The doors were large and double, and the brass on them lacquered to appear like bronze; they left a draught when shut, quite strong enough to work an air-motor, and faced the windows opening to the floor, admitting the Atlantic breezes as continuously as a well-bratticed mine admits the air. The parquet floor was slippery, and here and there pieces were loose, which gave in walking an impression of a pebbly beach or road new metalled, over which no roller had been passed. Rugs were laid on it here and there, which slithered as you walked, and overhead was hung a monstrous chandelier, which in the original had perhaps held candles, then passed to gas, and finally had been brought up to date with china tapers in which an electric light was introduced with the illuminating power of an old tallow dip.

Nothing less homelike or less comfortable could well be found than was the "salon" of the apartment where the Vestal lived.

Her bedroom, furnished without the least pretence, did not look out upon the sea, and in it usually she sat upon a rocking-chair doing interminable needlework, mantles of virgins and petticoats for saints. Stuck on a nail was a small holy-water stoup from Lourdes, and on the head-rail of the bed a rosary of black and silver beads was hung. Long use had made the beads as smooth as glass, the filigree Maria was polished bright as wire by constant slipping through her hands. A Spanish picture of a Christ hung at the bed head, with a palm passed through the cords which held it. Bad though the painting was, it yet was dignified, though dark and gloomy, and carrying out the proverb "To a bad Christ much blood," but yet no doubt brought up the scene at Golgotha before her eyes as clearly, as if Velasquez with his brush dipped in life had painted it.

These properties, and the vases of wax fruit kept from the assaults of time and flies by round glass shades, were all her property, except a parrot in a cage, and two large boxes of papery leather, designed to fall to pieces easily under the railway porters' hands, in which she kept her clothes.

Antediluvian looking, and wiser than mankind, the parrot sat as if it tolerated life, with a half-kind contempt. Cribbed and confined within its cage, it yet contrived to keep a superhuman dignity, accepting nuts or sugar as a god accepts the adoration of his worshippers, or as a clergyman reckons up imperturbably the halfpence and small silver in the offertory, not feeling in the least elated by the sum, but taking it as something due to his position, and which confers some merit on the bestower of the gift.

Dearly the Vestal loved him, but, in a measure, all her love was wasted, for she, knowing but little French, lavished all her affection in the Spanish tongue upon the cynic bird, who listened attentively, put down his head for her to scratch, and then, whistling a bar or two of a fore-bitter, condemned, in English, both his own and other people's eyes to regions where members of all religions upon earth mutually send each other to be purged of their contempt.

This was the interior of the Vestal, simple and melancholy, and not such as at first sight might be supposed to bring about content, but yet she passed her life without complaint in the performance of the duties by which she gained her name.

Ten or twelve years ago, said the hotel-keeper, a Spanish gentleman had appeared at his hotel. With him he brought a woman of about thirty years of age, quiet and well-looking, who appeared to be half mistress and half nurse. This was corroborated by the weather-wizened women, older than the rocks, known euphemistically as flower-girls, who, as they stood about in wind and rain, pretending it was summer, and pestering the passers-by with faded violets and damped-off carnations, had known the couple when they first arrived. The gentleman, they said, "was all a nobleman," for he had shown his quarterings and his nobility of soul by buying violets largely and ignoring change. The lady they were not so sure about, for though she took the violets, carrying them, so said the ancient flower-maidens, as a bear might take a musket in its paw, she yet appeared to think the expense unwarranted, and even now and then remarked in broken French that the flowers were faded, which naturally had never been the case.

The scandal-loving watering-place — watched over by the stucco virgin on the rock on which the wind and surf roar ceaselessly, which kings in exile make their refuge, and where once an empress had her palace, and in which today perhaps more lunatics have built their follies than in any other place on earth — was scandalised.

Little enough it cared for ordinary vice. Countesses of Mourzouk and Mogador, Princesses of Mohacs and Pondicherry at times abounded; Bella Chiquitas and Panderos fairly swarmed, and people, as they passed in carriages, talked of their diamonds and their furs, and of the time when they were washerwomen. But theirs was vice the people understood, knowing the princesses and countesses were of the ordinary kinds who spring up like some sort of hot-house flowers reared in a bed of gold, flourish and blossom for a season, and then sink back to dung. But the old Spaniard and his mistress were another kind of folk. A rich man with a mistress who neither tossed his money in the sea, gambled or drank, or made himself and her remarkable in any way, set every tongue awag. Their very presence was an insult to the place. Ladies who copied demi-mondaines' clothes, learned all their patter, and sung all their songs, were justly scandalised, and refused to sit in the same dining-room with the unconscious pair. Mothers, outwearied with the task of hawking round their daughters to be sold, were shocked to think that in the same hotel a woman lived who flouted openly the rules of the trade union of their sex, and yet aspired to be considered human and deserve respect.

Had not the aged sinner been a man of wealth, the protest of an English rural dean would have been listened to, and the offending pair incontinently thrust out into the street. But money has its privileges, and even rural deans, unless, of course, they are prepared to pay in cash for their opinions, have little weight against a man who settles promptly all his bills on the first day of every week. So, barring now and then some few remarks in which the name of Rahab figured prominently, the frequenters of the hotel who came from England were content, after their national fashion, not being able to deal adequately with this sporadic branch of a great social evil, to which one would have thought the streets of London had accustomed them, to make believe that the abomination set up stark before their eyes really did not exist. Thus did they save their faces and their consciences, for, having with their hearts protested, they had the satisfaction of assuming that their protest was successful, and that the stumbling-block had disappeared.

As for the Russians and the Spaniards, they being mostly of the class of the gold-plated Philistine, were inwardly amused, and thought the Vestal's lover was a fool for having taken to his purse a woman who did not do his judgment credit with the world. But, quite oblivious of the scandal that they gave, the Vestal and her lover unconcernedly pursued their lives.

No one knew whence they came, except that they were Spaniards; for they formed no friendships and had few acquaintances, although they did not shrink at all from such society as came into their way. Early each morning, in sunshine or in rain, they went to mass, the Vestal dressed devoutly in black clothes, and on her head a thick lace shawl after the manner of the more old-fashioned of her country-women. There she would kneel upon a chair and fall into that ecstasy of prayer which seems so easy to so many Spaniards, and which may be brought about by faith, or yet again come from a mind not occupied with other things, in the same way as those easily influenced by mesmerism often are quite uneducated, for faith and education are sworn enemies.

The *ite missa est* pronounced, she would rise stiffly from her chair, mutter a prayer or two, shake out her petticoats, bow reverently towards the altar, and walk down the aisle — not in the way of Protestants who tread the mansion of their God as it were paved with eggs, but boldly, and with an air of being upon good and yet respectful terms with the tripartite deity, who in His turn was bound to treat her with consideration, remembering that it was He who had created her and that she was a daughter of the Church.

Having received the holy water from her friend's yellow hand, the pair would walk along the cliffs, passing beneath the tunnels which the inhabitants aver were made by action of the waves, but which appear to an unprejudiced observer to be the work of a municipality anxious and willing to assist unheedful Nature in her task. Breakfast, and a brief siesta, with a drive amongst the pine woods, and their day was done.

At nightfall, in the seclusion of their dreary jimcrack rooms, they played at tric-trac or bezique, or wrestled with the unilingual parrot, vainly endeavouring to teach him to discourse in Spanish, but without success. Thus did the uneventful day of these bold sinners against God and man glide past without event, year in, year out, and day by day, until at last tongues tired of wagging, and the watering-place accepted them as harmless, having got fresh subjects to discourse about, and even feeling proud of its own charity and comprehension of the Christian faith. Nothing disturbed the even tenor of their days but an occasional trip to Spain, from which they both returned mildly elated with a gentle patriotism, but secretly rejoiced to find themselves once more in France and comfort, where doors turn on their hinges, windows shut closely, dinners are good, and trains leave stations at a seasonable hour. There seemed no reason but the laws of nature why their quiet idyll should not have lasted as a lichen lives upon a rock, growing still closer and still greyer as the consuming years pass over it.

But, though the Vestal did not see it, it was plain that the more desperate sinner of the two was wearing fast away, to where all goodness and all wickedness become identical, in the obliterating waves of time.

His well-cut London clothes, which, as to every Spaniard, were his pride, hung loose pon him, and his sharp-toed and shiny boots wrinkled like autumn pease-cods hanging dry upon their stalk. Doctors he held in execration, saying they only served to kill sound people, but he took patent medicines for a time, with regularity. He dropped them, and by slow degrees his cigarette, which had been all his life his *vicio*, and without which he would have seemed almost indecent had he appeared in public, and as it were undressed.

Long did he linger, getting feebler by degrees, and always tended by the Vestal with the dog-like faithfulness which distinguishes the women of her race.

Priests sat with him, and he confessed, no doubt, his weakness (for men of his sort rarely attain the dignity of sin), and made his peace with Heaven and with man. Masses innumerable were said for his recovery, and the poor Vestal must have wearied Heaven with her entreaties; but even Heaven is impotent in cases of the sort, though prayer, no doubt, is useful to the man who prays.

The end came gently, and he set out on his journey in the old Spanish fashion, with a priest praying at the bedside, the candles lit, and the poor Vestal trying to hold him back by grasping fast his hand.

When he was decently laid out, looking transparent and the colour of a vellum-covered book, the Vestal passed the time between the preparations for the funeral, sitting beside the bed and looking stonily at his dead face, pressing his hand between her hands and praying silently, raising her head occasionally as the grey parrot bit the wires of his cage and whistled his sea-songs.

The funeral and the arrival of the dead man's brother and relations from Madrid, and the ensuing days of misery, passed in a dream; but the next morning early, after mass, mechanically she wandered to the cemetery, taking some flowers in her hand, and sat down by the grave. She spoke to no one, asked for nothing, and when the brother of the dead man asked her where she would like to live, answered, without a moment's hesitation, "Here!" He thanked her for her care of his dead brother, and said the family were grateful to her, and that they would allow her money sufficient to remain in comfort at the hotel where she had lived so long. She said that she expected nothing less from the relations of the man who for so long had cared for her, thanking them all minutely, and by name, after the Spanish fashion, and saying that she would not forget them in her prayers.

When all had gone, she went back to her rooms, put all in order, and mechanically took up her life just as before, for still the dead man was the object of her care. Her day was just as full, or just as empty, as it was before. The morning's mass, in which she prayed for her dead lover's soul with all the fervency of entire belief, was followed by the walk along the cliffs, in which she thought of him with the true believer's certain hope of seeing him again some day just as he was on earth — a state of mind happy or miserable according as one's faith or one's imagination gets the upper hand, for the two qualities are deadly enemies and seldom live together in one breast.

Punctually every afternoon at three o'clock, a cab, paid for most scrupulously by the relations of the dead man in Madrid, takes her up to the cemetery. There, with a bunch of flowers in her hand (held like a musket by a dancing bear), she treads the shell-strewn alleys to the grave with the same confident yet humble step and air with which she trod the aisles as she walked down from mass. Before the grave she stands a little and weeps silently, and, kneeling, places the flowers upon the turf above the head. Then, drying up her tears, she walks down to the cab and drives to the hotel, to shut herself up with her few belongings and unilingual parrot for the night.

The Vestal still pursues her daily task, although ten years have passed since her first visit to the cemetery. Rarely she speaks to any one, but yet seems happy in the contemplation of her grief; and when, some day, her task is over and her parrot sold, perhaps to a seafaring man who may appreciate his forecastle humour and his chanties, 'tis ten to one that the good people of the watering-place in which she lives will wonder why it was that passing journalist endowed her with her name.

A cross with the words "Here lies Don Fulano" and the R.I. P., last irony of an unquiet world, marks where her friend awaits her and the possibly fallacious trumpet's call; but his relations in Madrid, although consenting to her prayer to lie beside him, have tempered kindness with discretion and refused to let her name be sculptured on the cross. But thou, St. Anthony (I hope), before whose shrine she prays and in whose offering-box she drops a coin each morning, mass over, when the acolytes, pinching and pushing one another, have all left the church, wilt hear her prayer, saint who healest hearts, by granting their desires. Surely it is not much to ask from one who has perchance learned charity amongst the choirs celestial, to let the word "Ines" be added to the cross, for, after all, "Fulano" but means So-and-So.

Appendix

Cunninghame Graham's Use of the Scots Language

In reading the stories and sketches of Robert Cunninghame Graham, it is impossible to ignore for long the fact that he is a very Scottish writer. References to the Scots and Scotland abound, even in the stories most firmly located in remote parts of the world. Amid the events and characters and evocations of his beloved South America and Spain, a Scottish phrase or word, a memory of Scotland, will frequently surface and make a link across the seas.

Yet Graham's habitual narrative and descriptive discourse is a highly educated, even erudite, Standard English mode of expression, flavoured richly with Spanish vocabulary and the cultural framework of the Hispanic world. There are only a handful of stories in which Graham makes extended use of the Scots language for a narrative purpose. This is not surprising, given Graham's social background as a member of the Anglicised Scottish aristocracy, his extended residence in England and abroad, and his involvement in public and cultural affairs beyond Scotland. It is, rather, remarkable that a man whose normal mode of expression was not Scots should have had the confidence and fluency to tackle a colloquial Scots idiom as the main vehicle for any of his fictions. Therefore, it is of interest to examine a number of such stories to identify how well Graham uses Lowland Scots and what purposes it may be serving for him that English could not achieve.

There is a group of such stories and sketches that would repay some examination conveniently clustered in the three collections that he published between 1900 and 1905, *Thirteen Stories*, *Success* and *Progress* (collected here in *Living with Ghosts*, Volume Two of the Collected Stories). In *Thirteen Stories*, there is "A Pakeha". In *Success*, there are two stories, "Beattock for Moffat" and "A Fisherman". In *Progress*, there are "McKechnie v. Scaramanga", "A Convert", "The Laroch", "Snow in Menteith", "Pollybaglan" and "A Traveller". The uses of Scots that these stories exemplify are very varied and show how Graham selects and controls his language to suit the intentions of stories with widely varying settings and characters.

Before looking at the stories individually, it is worth considering where Graham found inspiration and models for his Scots writing. The most obvious source is the natural talk in Scots which Graham heard all around him when he was living in his native district of Menteith and trying to run the family estate of Gartmore. Dealing with neighbours and tenants, with tradesmen and shopkeepers, in the village streets, at market and on local social occasions, Graham was living in a Scots-speaking environment from which he drew the currency for his characters' natural discourse. Even after Gartmore had to be sold and Graham moved to a smaller house at Ardoch, this local speech, in Menteith and more generally the West of Scotland, continued to fuel his writing for the rest of his life. Another important source, the model for how his Scots language would look on the page, was literary, the writing of Scots both of his own day and of a previous generation. In the later Victorian period and in the Edwardian age, the Scottish popular and local press regularly published stories, sketches and verse in Scots, a practice that Scottish newspapers have in more recent times largely given up.* Every week, Graham would have read in his local and Glasgow newspapers examples of contemporary colloquial expression that provided useful models for him to follow in his own sketches. Added to these, of course, were the powerful examples of the great Scottish literary figures, whose work Graham knew well, notably Sir Walter Scott, John Galt, James Hogg and Robert Louis Stevenson, and the lesser lights of the Scottish 'Kailyard' movement, whom Graham scorned for their sentimentality in his writings about Scotland, but whose linguistic example he could not totally ignore.

In the story, "A Pakeha", Graham describes a meeting upon the country road on a typical Scottish wet day between his narrator, an English-spoken 'Graham' figure addressed as 'laird', who says very little except to prompt his Scots character, an elderly neighbour, Mr Campbell. Graham signals that one of his concerns in the story is to be Scots language by referring to Scotland in the second sentence as "the land *dove il dolce Dorico risuona*" (i.e., the land where the sweet Doric resounds). The sketch is basically a monologue (with a brief introduction in standard English) almost totally composed of Campbell's reminiscences (in well-imagined and convincingly represented Scots speech) of early days in colonial New Zealand. Graham makes Campbell an engaging and likeable character, who maintains a nearness and intimacy with the 'laird' and with the reader through the regular use of familiar Scots interjections: "*Aye, laird*', *'ou aye', 'Losh me', 'Dam't', 'ye ken'*, etc. He also uses many characteristic Scots idioms (*forbye a wee bit jaunt, it'll maybe tak' up, a wheen captins, no fashed wi', I dinna care to mind it*, etc.) and distinctive Scots vocabulary items (*clachan, darg, biggit, threap, gleg, hettled, blate, sweir*, etc), which suggest a speaker rooted in the traditional rural part of Scotland. There is also a consistent attempt to suggest a Scots speaker by the use of non-standard pronunciations of words like *seekenin', pairfect, gaen', conseederation, weemen, vendeecated, sax* and *Australlia*; and a mangled formulation, *filanthrofist*, which is clearly a form derived from a written rather than an oral source. In the same way, Graham's use of the dubious longstanding publisher's device of apostrophes to suggest (wrongly) that a Scots form is a contracted form of an English original (awfu' for awful) indicates he is following the established literary conventions of written Scots from the eighteenth to the mid-twentieth centuries. Thus, "A Pakeha" demonstrates that Graham is quite at ease in rendering the speech habits and patterns of a Lowland Scot reared in a traditional rural environment.

The same can be said for the justly-praised story, "Beattock for Moffat", which is basically an English narrative interspersed with Scots (and a little Cockney) dialogue. There are three characters, two brothers from rural Dumfriesshire, one of them very near death, accompanied by his London wife. The exchanges in Scots between the two men are well handled by Graham, although he seems less sure with the Cockney discourse of the woman, who speaks less frequently. There is the same use of Scots idioms (*we'll gie ye a braw hurl, birlin' at the claret, no nigh hand, ye mind, aye used, yon wee bit mound, a feck of things, a richt guid fecht*, etc.) and Scots vocabulary items (*gash, braw, heughin', shilpit, stour, kirk, tatties, dour, thrawn, breer*, etc.) There is also the secondary layer of distinctive pronunciations (*meenister, illeeterate, pairadise*). Set as they are within the framework of a vividly described railway journey through Britain from London to the Scottish Borders, the snatches of dialogue are convincing representations of familiar Scots characters talking about their shared local experience.

The story, "A Fisherman", employs a narrative method intermediate between the two stories considered above. The English narrative which describes the progress of a voyage by steamer through the Firth of Clyde to Greenock is broken by two substantial monologues and a final comment, spoken by a retired fisherman dressed in a shabby formal suit and carrying a potted geranium. His method of talking about his life is reminiscent of "A Pakeha", and the same linguistic techniques are employed. There is a rich use of Scots idioms and vocabulary (*doited, rickle, corbie, wersh, haar, bannock, splores, clarty, kyloes, kists o' whistles, flauchter feals*, etc.), with the addition of a number of Scots phrases inserted into the English discourse (*heids and thraws, stan' o' black, a goin' aboot body, a guid conceit*, etc.). In addition, there are the renderings of Scots pronunciations of familiar words (*eddicated, leddie, sipplication, gerawnium, habeetuated, speerits*, etc.) one or two of which, however, may not ring true as everyday Scots to a reader of a later generation.

These three stories clearly show Graham in command of his Scots material and sources. He is perhaps less convincing in the two stories, "McKechnie v. Scaramanga" and "A Convert". The trouble may spring from the fact that his speakers are further away from the traditional Scots speech with its wealth of idiom and vocabulary. Captain McKechnie and the Reverend Archibald Macrae are men of more education, a wider experience of the world and of dealing with non-Scottish speakers. In their vocations, they make less use of the core of Scots language, and apart from a few items, their Scots is thinner in texture, mostly an accent with characteristic pronunciations and variants on familiar standard English words. Perhaps Graham does not make the best choice in making "McKechnie v. Scaramanga" an extended monologue (after a necessary introduction in English). The account by McKechnie of an episode at sea involving the loss of a ship and its cargo, and the legal ramifications connected with it, does not have the vividness and interest of the earlier stories and gives Graham less scope to present a colourful character with a rich distinctive voice. There are Scots idioms and vocabulary (*weel-kenned, clever chiel, kittle sort, clavers, turley-wurley, minavellings, haggersnash, tulzie*, etc.), Yet perhaps there is a sense of Graham straining for effect rather than finding a natural expression, and when we come across a possible excess of awkward pronunciations (*diceesions, redeeklous, heebrids, panawcea, Saloneeky, awgents, airtickle, Madoney*, etc.), there may be a sense that Graham is ill at ease with his character and the language.

"A Convert" concerns the attempt by a Scottish missionary, the Reverend Archibald Macrae, to convert a West African chief, Monday Flatface, to the true Presbyterian faith. The narrative is mainly in a third-person Standard English, with occasional brief Scots colloquial quotations from Macrae. As already mentioned, Macrae does not come across as a very broad Scots speaker. It is only in the latter part of the story as the events move to a climax and resolution that Macrae's voice takes over the narrative and describes how he has to face a crisis of conscience, recognising that his God was ultimately no more powerful than that of Flatface and that his attempted conversion was a failure. Macrae's language is effectively colloquial Scots, without so many specifically Scots words and idioms as in McKechnie's speech in the previous story. Graham is definitely more relaxed in his writing, feeling less obligation to load the monologue with Scotticisms.

Two descriptive sketches, "The Laroch" and "Snow in Menteith", show another aspect of Graham's use of Scots. These are not narrative pieces and have no characters to voice their thoughts. The 'voice' throughout both is that of Graham, creating natural descriptions of features of a Scottish landscape. The *laroch* of the first sketch is a site of abandoned and ruined buildings, crofts in Lochaber deserted by the Highlanders who had once lived there, forced to emigrate to new lands overseas after the destruction of their clan society. In the course of the sketch, Graham uses several Scots and Gaelic words, and also words referring to that society, naturally in context (*founds, grozets, loch, strathspey, rowans, shielings, reek, pibroch, clansmen, rickle, corries, linns, brattled, coronach*) without specially picking them out for notice. The result is that they give an underlying tone to the writing which is directly attuned to a Scottish reader. By contrast, "Snow in Menteith", describing winter in the area near his family house of Gartmore, contains virtually no specifically Scottish words. Only the mention of *shaws, rowans* and *peat-hags*, and a few place-names, indicate that the setting is in Scotland. Clearly Graham is angling this sketch towards a non-Scottish readership.

It remains only to comment on the two stories, "Pollybaglan" and "A Traveller", where the use of Scots is divided between the use of Scots words in a Standard English descriptive context and the quotation of colloquial community comment and character self-expression. "Pollybaglan", a description of a run-down farm on Graham's own estate, contains embedded Scots vocabulary (*scaur, steading, drumly, schauchling, soughing, garrons, bodach*), and local comments (*seeped bonnily awa' at the back en', awfu' soople for his years, a lightsome traveller*), but the most striking piece of Scots is the brief account by Pollybaglan's tenant farmer of his delight in swimming underwater among the *trooties* and *saumon* and *they bits o' water weeds*. "A Traveller" is richer by far in these uses of Scots: the tenant-farmer described here is a restless man, the *auld carlin wi' the bratty plaid, a soople traveller*, a *gaein' aboot bodie* with the *gangin' foot*. His speech is broad, drawn from the rural environment, in a manner reminiscent of "A Pakeha" and "Beattock for Moffat", and Graham's brief evocation of this memorable character shows that he is at his most comfortable with the Scots language when it has emerged directly from his regular dealings with the people of his beloved Menteith.

Graham published other stories using Scots in other collections, both earlier and later, but the group considered here probably illustrate most clearly the variety of treatment that he employed and the varying degrees of success that he achieved.

* This topic is fully discussed in a valuable survey of the Scottish Press, *Popular Literature in Victorian Scotland: language, fiction and the press*, by William Donaldson, Aberdeen University Press, 1986. A wide range of examples of prose writing in Scots from the pages of Scottish newspapers are to be found in a companion volume, *The Language of the People: Scots Prose from the Victorian Revival*, William Donaldson, Aberdeen University Press, 1989.

(AMcG)

Index to the Stories in Volume 2

Lightning Source UK Ltd.
Milton Keynes UK
UKOW050022100912

198683UK00001B/15/P

9 781849 211017